COLD TRACE

"**Masterful, refined and compelling.** A thought-provoking narrative handling complex themes with sensitivity and depth."
— *Literary Titan*

"**Suspenseful, gripping, and disturbing!** Engages the heart with the same fervour it engages the mind."
— *BookViral Reviews*

"**Heart-racing and captivating!** Remarkably penetrating and humane; a winding literary mystery series."
— *The Prairies Book Review*

"**A tense, exciting thriller.** A compelling entry to the Nick Severs series that's sure to delight new and old fans alike."
— *Entrada Reviews*

Winner: Gold Award – Literary Titan

Winner: Golden Quill – BookViral

D.V. CHERNOV

COLD TRACE

NICK SEVERS MYSTERIES

BOOK 2

heathen

HEATHEN PRESS, LLC

heathenpress.com

Copyright © 2024 by D.V. Chernov

All rights reserved. No part of this book may be reproduced in any manner whatsoever without written permission except in the case of brief quotations embodied in critical articles and reviews.

ISBN 979-8-9863298-5-7

First Printing, 2024

This is a work of fiction. Unless otherwise indicated, all the names, characters, businesses, places, events and incidents in this book are either the product of the author's imagination or used in a fictitious manner. Any resemblance to actual persons, living or dead, or actual events is entirely coincidental.

COLD TRACE

0

Tuesday was Leo's last day on earth. But he did not know this yet.

Leo was actually not his real name. His real name was Nikolai Smolnikov, but nobody who knew him knew that. His mother had died years ago, and he never knew his father, and so, to everyone who knew him now, he was Leo. He lived in Minsk, Belarus, but his mother told him that he was conceived in Lviv, Ukraine. Lviv was the city of the Lion. Lion = Leo. This was a detail no one else would know about him. It was a meaningful detail, and this meaning was known only to him. This is the way hackers liked things. And this is what Leo was—a hacker, and a damn good one at that.

That day he woke up late. When he opened his eyes, he saw bright, colorful glimmers dancing on his eyelashes. This meant that the morning sun had already climbed above the rooftops on the other side of the street and was now casting fiery rainbows through the ice that had built up on the outside of his window. He wanted to stay in the warmth of his bed for just a bit longer, but he had a lot to do today, and falling back asleep was a risk he could not take. He threw off the covers and walked across the cold floor to the thermostat to turn up the heat, and then to the kitchen to turn on the coffee maker. He pulled on his jeans and his hoodie and pushed his bare feet into his boots and left his apartment to get fresh croissants from the bakery on the corner. When he returned, chewing on a croissant, he climbed the steps to his apartment and saw Max at his door.

Max was not supposed to be here. *Or was he?* For an instant, Leo considered if he had possibly forgotten that Max was stopping by today. *Had he?* Leo climbed a couple more steps to his door and suddenly felt uneasy.

"Hi-i-i, Max," he said, swallowing down the croissant, and the words came out shaky and uncertain.

But Max did not say anything. He pulled out a gun and put the end of the barrel right into Leo's face. Leo smelled the sour scent of steel and spent gunpowder. He opened his mouth, thinking desperately of something to say, but Max shook his head and sighed. And then he pulled the trigger. And that was the last thing Leo ever saw.

1

Green chili breakfast burritos from Millie's Café on Summit Street were the best. The tried-and-true ingredients—bacon, potatoes, eggs, and, of course, green chilies—could have been had at any of dozens of restaurants and cafes around Denver, but Millie's breakfast burritos truly stood in a class above, and Nick was convinced that this was thanks to the final ingredient, listed in the menu simply as *cheese*. But this was no regular American cheese, Nick knew. When he pressed Millie on the subject, she said *cheddar*, but Nick saw the mischievous sparkle in her eye. Nick was not born yesterday. Sure, there could have been some good old Wisconsin sharp in these weighty wraps, but there was no hiding the fact that it had been "classied up" with the presence of a more refined, pedigreed European cousin. *Fancy cheese.*

"Is it Gruyère?" Nick interrogated Millie, who was determined to keep mum on the subject, and who turned her back to Nick, presumably busying herself with the old coffee machine. "Camembert?" Nick read off the next Google result for "*European cheeses*" from his phone. "Boursin? Neufchâtel?" He named off a few other fancy options, fully aware that he was probably not pronouncing them right, as he had zero working knowledge of the conversational French. He regretted his decision to opt for Spanish in both high school and college. This was definitely not a Spanish cheese.

Millie did not crack. Millie's husband, Frank, grinned at Nick from the kitchen. "Give it up, Nick," he rumbled. "It's an old family recipe." His big, tattooed arm deposited a large brown paper bag in the kitchen window. "Three burritos to go."

Nick picked up the heavy bag. "It's Gruyère, isn't it?" He was now convinced. He heard a subdued squeak out of Millie, who still did not turn around, but was obviously wiping her eyes with her sleeve.

"I knew it." Nick smiled and walked out.

Outside, the sunny February morning blinded him with the shine of fresh snow. After last night's blizzard, everything sparkled like fiery diamonds under the bright sunlight—from the sidewalks and street signs to the rooftops and the piney foothills behind them. Nick's boots crunched through the crisp powder down the sidewalk to his police Chevy Tahoe. He placed the bag of Millie's burritos on the floor behind the driver's seat and was about to climb behind the wheel when he heard a sound universally familiar to anyone who has ever lived in a cold climate—an anemic mechanical squeal followed by a series of clicks.

The distress call was emitted by the 1987 Dodge Ramcharger parked two spaces over. Nick knew that the vehicle in question was in fact a 1987 Dodge Ramcharger because it belonged to none other than Pine Lake Police Department's own auxiliary police officer—the town's feisty seventy-two-year-old librarian known to everyone simply as Ruth. The starter squealed again, failing to catch, even as the silver Ram's head on the hood defiantly charged on forward despite the vehicle not going anywhere.

Nick waved to the wispy cloud of blue hair floating barely above the steering wheel of the half-ton truck. "Wanna pop the hood, Ruth?"

Ruth smiled and waved back. She was wearing mittens and Christmas-red knitted earmuffs. Her head disappeared from view, and Nick heard the mechanical pull of the cable and the clunk of a releasing latch. He propped open the hood and peered inside the cavernous engine compartment. Boy, there was a lot of room under the hoods of these old cars! One could practically climb in and sit on the ledge of the fender, and still have room to work on the innards of this beast. He heard a couple of faint squeaks as Ruth cranked down the low-tech window.

"I think it's your battery," Nick said, examining the white, flaky oxidation growing thick on both lead terminals of the black plastic block. He looked at Ruth. "The cold snap may have done it in."

The wispy blue puff with red earmuffs shook emphatically. "Roy Junior just replaced it last year."

In moments like this, Nick felt as if he were managing a retirement community in which everyone refused to retire. Roy *Junior* was 65 and the owner of Roy's Garage, the sole service station in Pine Lake, opened after the war by his father, Roy *Senior*. It was no town secret that Junior's memory was not what it used to be, and he probably should have hired some help years ago, but on account of his being childless, and his professed lack of qualified help anywhere from Denver to Santa Fe, and his own plain stubbornness, he refused to. Given all these facts, it was impossible to surmise whether Roy Junior had actually replaced her battery last year, and if he did, whether it was with the right one. Despite all this, Nick knew that any suggestion that Ruth take her business to Service Street in Castle Rock would be ignored. Although only twenty miles away, Castle Rock could have been on the moon, as far as she was concerned.

Ruth was reliably stubborn. After a year of having her as an auxiliary police officer, Nick had come to appreciate her consistency. Unfortunately, the same reliability was not a virtue shared by her daily transport. She should have sold the old carburetor-wheezing beast years ago, but a sentimental attachment made this an impossible proposition. The truck used to belong to her late husband, and she had made it absolutely clear that this was the last vehicle she would ever drive on this earth, and that if she could be buried in it, this would be just fine with her.

The matter of the battery was pointless to argue. Nick lowered the hood. Ruth glared at him defiantly from behind the steering wheel, with her hands on the ready at the ten and two o'clock positions. Nick knew she was sitting on top of an old couch pillow, which gave her the height necessary to glare at him right now over the long hood. He entertained the thought of a hole large enough . . . He sighed.

"I can try to jump-start you," he said, but the radio on his belt crackled with static, and Patty's voice chirped in:

"Nick, you there? Come in, Nick."

Ray must have been hungry. Nick unclipped the radio from his belt and pushed the talk button. "I have the burritos. I just need to give Ruth a jump."

"Oh, it's not that, hon," Patty chirped back through the tiny speaker. "State troopers found a body on Elk Road at the 285 overpass."

Nick straightened up and looked down snow-dusted Summit Street toward the station, where Patty was currently sitting at the front desk. "Would you notify the County Coroner's Office for me?" he asked.

"I already did. They are sending an ME. Probably Brenda."

"OK, I'm on my way," Nick said. He turned back to Ruth. "Want me to call Roy Junior for you?"

She shook her head again. "I'll call him. You go on."

Nick nodded. Despite her respectable age, Ruth was anything but a damsel in distress, and Nick could tell when a rescue was not needed. Besides, Millie and Frank were just two doors down if she did end up needing help, and Ray was at the station just down the street. Nick knocked on the Ramcharger's cold hood, went to his Tahoe, and started it up.

Nick knew the spot in question. Elk Road was at the northern outskirts of his jurisdiction, where the concrete overpass of US Route 285 rumbled with traffic overhead, with two lanes snaking through the mountains southwest-bound toward Bailey and two more northeast-bound toward Conifer.

Under different circumstances, a drive down the winding, two-lane Elk Road on a sunny winter day would have been an idyllic western Americana treat with the snow-caked, bluish-green pine ridges scrolling serenely on the left, and the dark, icy rapids of Wisp Creek rushing through the rocky, twisty bed on the right. This was a scenery to savor, but not today. As Nick drove with the lights of his truck silently flashing, he thought about what awaited him. Patty had no additional details, so pretty much anything was fair game. Whatever the circumstances, this would be his second dead body since he had started at Pine Lake barely a year ago. Before that, it had been over two years since the department had to investigate a death. And before that—four years. Nick was setting some kind of a record for this town, and it was not one he cared to set.

When the overpass came into view, Nick saw the lights of the State Patrol's Dodge Durango parked on the shoulder at the base of the 285 onramp. In front of it sat the Jefferson County Coroner's truck. Nick pulled up level with the Durango and recognized Trooper Juan Diaz in the driver's seat. Juan's District 1 route frequently took him through Nick's neck of the woods. Juan nodded to Nick, pointed to the phone next to his ear and held out his index finger, indicating he would be right with Nick.

Nick nodded and parked on the opposite shoulder, leaving his lights on. He could see the body from here—a snowy human shape sitting up against the concrete base of the overpass, blending in with the pristine whiteness surrounding him. As Nick approached, he could already see one thing wrong with this picture—the body looked too thin for the weather, with no padding of a winter coat.

Up close, Nick could tell that it was a young man—maybe a boy—wearing what looked like a denim jacket with a hood, jeans, and Converse shoes. He also had on a beanie hat under the hood, with white wires of headphones emerging from under the beanie and disappearing into his jacket. The body was dusted with a layer of snow, making for an eerie arctic figure with snowdrifts around the boy's splayed legs and arms. The chest area of the jacket had been disturbed—probably by Juan looking for an ID.

Who are you? Nick thought. *Did you live around here?* Other than the three police trucks, there were no other vehicles parked in sight, and no footprints besides Nick's own and the ones leading toward the coroner's and State Patrol trucks. Overhead, forty or so feet above, morning traffic on the concrete decking of the bridge was turning into a steady stream. *Where did you come from?*

Nick took photos. The morning sun was yet to reach inside the concrete cavern under the bridge. Here, in the cold shade, he could see his own breath. The snow covering the body did not sparkle like fiery diamonds here—it was flat and white, and the tiny ice crystals covering the boy's face reflected only the bluish hue of his skin and lips. *Cyanosis*—Nick thought—a possible indication of hypothermia.

Footsteps crunched through the snow behind him. "Hey, there, Nick."

Nick turned around. "Hey, Juan." He shook the young trooper's hand. "How are Maria and the kids?"

Juan smiled, pleased that Nick remembered his wife's name. "Doing good, thanks for asking. Ernesto is turning two next month, so we are trying to figure out if we want to get day care so Maria can go back to work, or if she stays home with the kids."

"Well, what does *she* want?" Nick asked.

Juan laughed. "My friend, that depends on the day of the week."

Nick smiled.

"Did you find any ID on this one?" He nodded to the body.

"Tyler Wilcox, aged twenty-six, from Cleveland, Ohio. No wallet, but these were in his jacket." Juan handed him a plastic evidence bag with an Ohio driver's license, a worn-out twenty-dollar bill, some change, and a dog-eared, lint-caked yellow sticky note with something scribbled on it in pencil.

"Any abandoned vehicles up there?" Nick pointed up to Route 285 overhead.

Juan shook his head. "The nearest is fourteen miles away down by Indian Hills, and it's not registered to the victim."

How did you get here, Tyler? Colorado saw its fair share of hitchhikers—mostly starry-eyed kids from the Midwest making their way west to California. But they usually followed Interstate 70—a straight shot to LA. US Route 285 did not lead west. It hooked south through Colorado and into New Mexico.

"No backpack or anything?" Nick asked.

"Nope. Just a phone and the headphones. No sign of foul play. I'd say last night's weather got him. It got down to negative six degrees here, negative twenty with wind chill."

Nick nodded. The medical examiner would still need to give Tyler a once-over, but so far hypothermia looked to be the most likely culprit. It was sixty degrees at noon yesterday, before the sky went gray, and the wind blew in a surprise blizzard. That's mountain weather for you. Sometimes it even got the better of the locals.

Nick leaned in toward the side of the young man's head. He took out a pen and slipped it under the knitted edge of the beanie hat. It was stuck to the ear. "Does that look like blood to you?" Nick said. "Can this happen with hypothermia?"

Before Juan could respond, the door of the Jefferson County coroner's truck slammed shut, and Brenda's chunky winter boots crunched toward them. "Well," she said, pulling on her winter gloves, "you're not gonna like this. Tyler Wilcox is a father of two. His wife is a paralegal, and he is an orthodontist with a successful practice in Avon, Ohio."

Nick smiled. "That's great investigative work, Brenda. Should I be worried about my job?" He liked Brenda. She worked his first homicide last year. Given his current track record, this collaboration was beginning to look like a regular thing.

The pale-blue columbines of her eyes fixed on him, but the fine wrinkles in her face did not deepen into a smile. "No, hon, I just talked to him."

It wasn't like Brenda to speak metaphorically. "*Talked?* The dead *talk* to you?" Saying this out loud made Nick feel like he was on the set of a made-for-TV police drama.

Juan chuckled. "Did he say why he wore the wrong coat?"

"No. He is alive and well in Ohio, having lunch with his wife at the Red Lobster."

Nick stared at Brenda and then at his frosty imposter. "Then who is this?"

She shrugged. "Not Tyler Wilcox." Her deadpan pragmatism was unassailable.

Nick held up the evidence bag in his hand and examined the crumpled yellow sticky note through the plastic. "What about this note? Looks like maybe an address . . .? *347 Henderson A—* something . . . maybe *avenue*?"

"Already checked," Juan said. "No Henderson Avenue or street in the Denver area."

"We'll run fingerprints and dental against any open missing person cases," Brenda said. "Are you done with him? Can we go ahead and take him?"

Nick nodded. *Who the hell are you, buddy?* he thought. *And what were you doing with a stolen identity on my road?*

2

"Identity theft?" Claire asked. She set her wineglass down on the stone ledge of the firepit and used a wrought iron poker to persuade a half-burned log back into the blazing embers.

Nick had built the four-and-some-foot-wide firepit on one sunny weekend last December, clearing the snow from the old concrete patio below their deck and assembling the pavers he got from The Home Depot—the tan trapezoidal ones and the brick-colored rectangular ones—into a circle of three drystacked tiers. For such a quick and cheap DIY project, it turned out looking really nice, and he and Claire had since spent quite a few nights sitting with their patio chairs pushed up to the warm rocks, watching the dancing flames and talking. And this was the best and most unexpected benefit of this project: that they would just sit and talk, sometimes for hours, about anything and everything, from the news to their jobs, and dreams, and plans. This had become their weekly tradition, of sorts. After everything that happened last fall, they needed it. Nick needed it. Their relationship needed it. It brought them closer. It rebuilt trust. It made them stronger. Nick appreciated it. He was pretty sure Claire did, too.

"Yep," he said, taking a sip of his Bulleit bourbon and brushing a flake of glowing ash from her sleeve.

He knew identity fraud was rampant, but this was his first brush with it as part of an investigation. The body of the man now awaiting autopsy in the coroner's cooler in Golden was not who the ID in his wallet said he was. This fact made Nick indignant. Dead or not, using a stolen identity made this man a criminal. And now Nick as well as the Jefferson County Coroner's Office and possibly the Regional Crime Lab personnel would have to spend their time on solving this lowlife's death. Hopefully, with this John Doe—this *Not Tyler Wilcox*—being a criminal, his fingerprints would match up to a criminal record in the system, and at least identifying him would be easy.

"I wonder where he was going. Or where he was coming from," Claire said.

Nick shrugged. "Whatever it was, I am sure he was up to no good. People with good intentions don't hide behind false identities." He instantly regretted saying this.

"I did," she said without showing offense.

"You . . . were different. You didn't steal it from someone else."

"You'd say anything to defend me." *True.* "Maybe he had good reasons, too."

"You changed your name *legally*."

"Maybe he didn't have a choice."

"Why are you defending him?" Nick smiled, feeling slightly irked by this blatant disregard for legitimacy.

She shrugged. "I am not. I am just saying you don't really know anything about him or his reasons."

Nick tilted his head, considering. "Using another person's identity is stealing. Honest people know it. As do the dishonest ones."

She took another sip of her red, watching the dancing flames. "Identity is such an odd concept. We are given one when we are born. We have no choice in it, but we are expected to keep it for the rest of our lives. That seems so arbitrary. That arbitrary label stays the same while we don't—we grow, we change our appearance, we change our jobs. We even shed our old skin cells and grow new ones. After a few years, what is there left of the original you? And yet, here you are—*Nick Severs*. But who *is* Nick Severs? A cop? A teacher? A little boy with a skinned knee?" She looked at Nick through her half-empty glass.

"Yes. All of the above. Every day." He smiled, drawing an unspoken truce to this little difference of opinion. All philosophies aside, identity was just about the most black-and-white concept in investigations. There was nothing relative about it. The identity of the deceased was the single thread that led to everything else. It was intrinsically connected to their circles of family, friends, and enemies (not all mutually exclusive, by the way), and the places they had been to—jobs, gyms, gas stations, grocery stores. And there—somewhere between the people and the places—were the clues and the motives. But she was right, of course—Nick was not the same person he was even ten years ago. And she was not, either.

The log popped in the fire, and Nick watched a burst of sparks fly up into the evening sky against the darkening silhouette of the mountains. Out here, in the wilderness, identity was not always a given. In a city, crimes came with more facts: identities, fresh evidence, eyewitnesses, video surveillance. Not here. The mountains stripped away much of that. Denver was situated adjacent to millions of acres of wilderness and had 31 million visitors last year alone. It was safe to assume some never left. Things tended to just vanish in the wilderness. People vanished in the wilderness. Sometimes on their own, and sometimes at someone else's hand. All those miles after miles of gorges, ravines, and abandoned mine shafts as far as the eye could see made for a million ideal places to make a body disappear. And even if it was ever found, after months or even years of exposure to the elements, it was usually without identity and, thanks to the wildlife, missing a lot of pieces. The Jefferson County sheriff's website had dozens of cold cases posted—some missing, some found without identity, many going back decades.

This nameless joker who had stolen the identity of a Cleveland dentist, despite all his craftiness, had ended up a mere statistic. Maybe there was karma in this life after all. Nick smirked. In this day and age, there should really be an eleventh commandment added: *Don't covet another man's life.*

3

On Monday morning, Nick went for a run in the woods. Even during the winter months, he tried to get outside at least once every week. There was some perverse satisfaction in forcing himself out of the warm bed and into the frosty, murky world while the rest of the town was still sleeping.

Warmer temperatures over the weekend had melted most of the snow around town, but here, in the woods, there were still large patches of it under the pines, glowing like ghostly silver in the twilight. Nick tried to focus on his breathing—the measured gulps of icy mountain air that made his lungs burn—and not the effort of his feet pushing him forward on the knotty, sometimes slippery incline. These usually weren't long runs—about a mile to the Echo Rock, which was overhanging the lake, and then another mile back—but somewhere in those almost two miles, he usually found a way to make sense of this world. Maybe it was the left-right rhythm of his feet that re-grounded his mind. Or maybe it was the diffused predawn light, in which there were no lines between light and shadow, that made him see things more clearly. Whatever it was, Nick savored it, because the magic was always short lived: by the end of his run, the sun would be up, the world around him would be awake, and the light and dark would no longer bleed into each other.

Claire was not home yet from the night shift at the hospital, and although sometimes Nick could delay leaving for work just long enough for them to exchange a kiss in the doorway, today he had the John Doe death hanging on his mind, and he was eager to get to the station and hopefully get Brenda's autopsy report and close this case before the day ended.

He skipped breakfast but made himself a nice big travel mug of coffee to go. The Gaggia Classic espresso machine was one of the few luxuries in Nick's life, and as far as he was concerned, it had earned every penny he had spent on it with its mastery and reliability in the single task he had entrusted to it—making a good cup of coffee.

At quarter to eight, Nick climbed into his police Tahoe with his coffee in hand, and immediately his nose was assaulted by an offensive odor. Nick had always kept a clean cruiser, and the only thought off the top of his head was that perhaps some unfortunate woodland creature had sought shelter in the warm engine compartment and had subsequently died there. He took another cautious sniff and identified in the pungent bouquet the noxious notes of excessive flatulence and overripe cheese, which snapped his memory into focus. He cursed to himself, reached behind the driver's seat, and retrieved the large brown bag with what used to be three of Millie's green chili breakfast burritos. He had completely forgotten about them after talking with Ruth about her dead Ramcharger and then responding to the call about the John Doe. The bag drove around with him all day Thursday and Friday and then sat in his locked Tahoe over the weekend in his driveway.

Nick removed the offending article to the trash can in the garage and then drove to the station with his windows down and his heater on high.

That's when Brenda called him.

"Hey!" He picked up the call.

"Are you in a wind tunnel?" she asked, without returning his greeting.

He grimaced and rolled up the windows.

"Ah, that's better," she confirmed.

Not for him. "So, how did the John Doe autopsy go? Do you have the cause of death?"

"It's complicated," she said.

"I don't think that's one of the choices on the death certificate," he offered deadpan.

Brenda never laughed at his jokes. Deadpan or otherwise. Maybe she thought his jokes stank like the four-day-old breakfast burritos. She normally acknowledged them with only a small, silent pause, as if waiting for the air to clear, and then moved on. "I found Wischnewsky spots on his gastric mucosa," she proceeded to say.

"English, please, Doc," Nick appealed.

"Small, dark lesions in the stomach lining. These are often present in hypothermic deaths."

"So . . . that's exposure. Right? Natural causes?"

"Most likely. *But*—"

She emphasized the *but*. Nick did not like *buts*. *Buts* heralded complications.

"—I did find something else," she introduced the complication.

"What?"

"The victim also had considerable intracranial hemorrhage."

"Bleeding in his brain?"

"Skull."

"Got it. How *considerable*?"

"Enough to warrant a closer look."

"Could this not have happened as a result of a hypothermic death?"

"I don't know yet. I'll have to consult with a neurologist."

"But does it even matter? You just said you found the Wischnewsky spots." It felt good to use a newly learned scientific term in a sentence. "That means a hypothermic death. Right?"

"I said they are often *present* in hypothermic deaths, but the mechanism by which they occur is not well understood. They do show up in about half of lethal hypothermia cases, but we can't say they are a definitive indication of a hypothermic death."

"Why not?" This seemed like a pretty basic case of cause and effect, but Nick must have been missing something.

"Because they may just as well occur in people who experience hypothermia but don't die from it. We just never open them up and examine their stomach lining." She paused. Maybe this was her deadpan medical examiner joke? "In the absence of any other suspicious indicators, the presence of Wischnewsky spots during autopsy usually indicates a hypothermic death."

"So . . . intracranial hemorrhage would be considered a suspicious indicator?"

"It *could* be. Or not."

"Right . . . you need to consult with a neurologist." Nick pondered the twist. "Anything else remarkable?"

"A number of scars and small burns on his body. Quite a few."

"From what?"

"Don't know. But I do know something else."

"What?"

"I had the Regional Crime Lab run his DNA through CODIS."

"And?"

"And they got a match in the Missing Persons Index."

Nick straightened in the driver's seat. "Missing Persons? So, you know who he is?!"

"Ben Harris, aged twenty-three. Missing since 2001."

"2001? He must have been—" Nick attempted mental math.

Brenda solved it: "—two years old when he was reported missing from his home in Walsenburg."

"Walsenburg? As in Colorado? Down south?"

"Yep. Looks like his mother still resides at the same address."

"Let me guess—347 Henderson Avenue?"

"Yes. Want me to call her and have her come up?"

Nick considered it for a moment. A child missing for over twenty years was found dead with his home address in his pocket. Nick had so many questions, he was not even sure where to start. "No. I'd better pay a visit." News like this was best told in person. And if Ben had this address in his pocket when he died, it was best to see it in person, too.

Føur

Claire liked the night shifts. Some nurses didn't. *Most* didn't. A couple of nurses she knew had been trying to get off the nights for years. It wasn't easy to do. Even if she wanted to, she did not have seniority at Children's Hospital yet, so even thinking about this was a moot point. Still, she knew Nick wished she would work days. She understood why. Working opposite shifts made life difficult. She had to leave home at six thirty at night, right after dinner, and she did not come home till seven thirty or eight or even later in the morning—often missing Nick, as he had already left for the station. And in the evening, it was hard to leave him right after dinner, instead of snuggling up on the couch with a glass of wine. But the night shifts were only for a few days in a row, and then she would have several days off. Those in-between days when she did not have to work were always awkward—she would try to sync with Nick's schedule, but would never get her sleep schedule right, leaving her fuzzy-headed through the waking hours. This back-and-forth was hard, but it would last only for four weeks, after which she would get rotated to day shifts for the next four weeks. And then the cycle would repeat.

Still, she liked working nights. The hours after midnight belonged to a unique breed of people who populated a parallel universe most of *the living*—as they called the day-shifters—did not get to see. It was like a dark reflection of the world on the other side of the sunrise. Security guards, warehouse workers, cops, firefighters, and EMTs all went to work when most of the world around them went to bed. Night shifts weren't for everyone. Some people could barely survive here and couldn't wait to get out. Others thrived. She was the latter.

She liked that hospital night shifts were a lot different from the days. Things tended to be calmer, quieter. The administrative offices were dark. The lights in the main corridors were dimmed. The doors of the patient rooms were left open for easy monitoring, but the lights inside were turned off, leaving only the fuzzy glow of the medical-equipment LEDs to illuminate the little sleeping patients. The only bright lights on their floor were at the nurses' station, from where Claire and another nurse would command the hibernating ward, like from a captain's bridge of a spaceship traveling through darkness.

Tonight's shift was running smoothly. Of the twelve beds in their ward, only eight were occupied, and Claire and Tasha—tonight's other nurse—tag-teamed the 2100 (9 p.m.) meds and helped the kiddos change and get ready for bed. There had been no new admissions today, and at this point in the night, everyone was peacefully asleep, and Claire was finally able to make some progress in updating care plans and entering assessments into the charts. When she heard footsteps approaching down the hall, she tore away from the patient record on the computer screen, stretched in the swivel chair, and glanced at the clock—five minutes to one in the morning. She recognized the approaching gait even before its owner cleared the hallway corner. Ed—the night shift respiratory therapist. Ed's lanky figure sailed forward at his usual brisk pace, making the stethoscope around his neck swing from side to side with each step.

"Hey, Claire, hey, Tasha." He beamed at them. "Have you guys done rounds yet?"

"An hour ago," Claire replied. "But number six is about due for the IV antibiotic."

She looked at Tasha, who had just torn open a small packet of saltines from the break room.

"What? Don't judge me, bitch." Tasha gave her a sideways glare. "I didn't have time for breakfast." She fished out a saltine from the packet with her impeccably manicured nails. Claire wondered how she kept them from chipping with all the glove changes and hand washes. Claire had pretty much given up on nail polish on her work nights.

"I'll take the next one," Tasha mumbled, munching on the cracker.

"You better." Claire gave Tasha's chair a playful kick, and Tasha giggled.

"I'll walk with you," Claire said to Ed, grabbing her stethoscope and popping the wheel lock on the meds cart.

"How is Emma doing in school?" she asked, steering the cart into the hallway. Ed had been keeping her up to date on the school trials of his sixth-grader daughter.

He shook his head "You'd think it would get easier in the second semester. But I tell you, Claire, it's something every day. It's the other girls, or the boys, or the teachers—she finds something new to tick her off every day." He sighed. "Does it ever get better?"

"Nope." She shook her head. "Not with girls."

Ed leaned over the nine-year-old girl sleeping on her side in room 3. "Mia?" he said and touched the girl's shoulder. "Mia, honey, it's Doctor Keller. I just need to listen to your lungs, OK?"

"OK," the girl sighed and turned onto her back, rubbing her eyes and sleepily inspecting the visitors.

Mia had been admitted four days ago with a severe asthma attack that caused a pneumothorax—a small hole in her lung, probably because she strained so hard to breathe but couldn't. She spent two nights in the ICU and was then transferred to Claire's ward to recover. By Claire's own assessments, Mia was doing well, but Ed was the specialist.

He was so good with kids. Claire wondered whether it was harder or easier to do this job when you had your own children. On the one hand, it probably made it easier to relate to the kids here. But on the other, you got to see every parent's nightmares coming true. Every day. Working here made you realize just how vulnerable kids were. How fragile.

She and Nick had discussed the subject of having children once before. But this was just in passing, and this was *before* last fall. Before he knew she was fixing to bring about his untimely ruin and possibly demise. He had brought it up. At that time, he seemed open to the idea of having kids. She was honest and said she did not know. That was true then, and she still did not know now. They had not talked about kids since then. When you tell the man you love that you've been lying to him since the first day you met him, the subject of having children is not something that naturally follows. Maybe one day. Right now, she and Nick were doing good as they were. She felt them getting closer, reconnecting. Baby steps. This wasn't something she was in a hurry to figure out. Could she see herself as a mother? Possibly. A little girl (naturally, a girl) that would be just like herself—serious, intelligent, strong willed. But the commitment scared her. She could see how tempting it could be for women to pour themselves into motherhood—it provided an instant, singular purpose. It gave you someone who needed you and loved you back unconditionally—at least through the few early years. And it also offered a chance to do right everything that went wrong in her own childhood.

But all those reasons seemed selfish. Bringing another person into this world was a weighty decision and commitment. This world was a cruel, grimy place. She had seen it. This *gift* of life, as it was often called—how many times had she herself wished she had never been born. Why would she want to risk having another person—her own child—going through what she went through? Or through what these kids were going through?

Ed straightened up. "That's beautiful, Mia. Your lungs sound really, really good. How are you feeling? Are you breathing well?"

Mia nodded, her tired eyes fighting to stay open.

"OK, you go back to sleep. I will see you tomorrow," Ed said.

Maybe *this* was enough for Claire. She liked working with kids here. Liked protecting them, restoring them back to health. She liked this ward because here, they did not lose kids. Kids got better here. Usually. But that wasn't always the case in the ER and the ICU. This, here, she could do. Fixing someone else's kids felt right for her. Bringing her own into this world did not. Not yet, at least.

"How is Nick?" Ed asked, walking with Claire to room 6. "Still chasing the bad guys?"

"Every day." Nick was Nick. Sometimes she wondered how someone could be so steady all the time.

She made it back to the nurses' station at twenty past one. It was time for a break. She reached into her purse to check her personal phone. She had two missed calls and a voice message. She recognized the area code—*573—Cape Girardeau*. She did not recognize the number. She clicked the voicemail.

"Hello, this is nurse Julia Perkins at Saint Francis Medical Center. Your number is listed as the emergency contact for Rebecca Daniels. Please call me back as soon as possible at—."

But Claire had already hung up and swiped to her call log and hit redial on the red missed call.

5

The Walsenburg exit was a dusty stagecoach stop 160 miles south of Denver on Interstate 25. More south than Pueblo. So far south, it was practically in New Mexico. Nick pulled into a Phillips 66 station to refuel and get a coffee. He parked at the pump and watched a gust of wind kick up a cloud of dirt in the vacant lot across the street. The land was flat and treeless here. Here, nature was not trying to impress. This wasn't Denver with its rolling foothills and the shiny city skyline at the base of the jagged Continental Divide. This also wasn't Colorado Springs, with its lush pine valley in the shadow of the majestic, snow-capped steeple of Pikes Peak. Here, as far as the eye could see, was a high-plains desert mesa spotted with tufts of yellow-brown prairie grass, gray sagebrush, and patches of snow. In the west, far in the hazy distance, the pale blue teeth of the Sangre De Cristo mountains rose toward the pale sky. This was the precipice of the great American Southwest, and it had its own kind of rugged and desolate beauty.

Nick pumped the fuel, watching semitrucks thundering past on I-25. He thought about Ben, who disappeared from his family's life here over twenty years ago. The proximity of the interstate seemed ominous now. This wasn't a low-trafficked country road. This highway was part of a major shipping route reaching from Mexico to Canada and crossing a half dozen other major US interstates along the way. If Ben had been taken from here, he could have easily been hundreds of miles and several states away within just a couple of hours. Nick watched the trucks speeding past, some pulling one trailer, some two. So many trucks. It seemed at least a couple of them passed by every minute. Had to be hundreds each day. So much cargo. Some of it could have been illicit. Even right now, passing right in front of Nick's eyes. How would anyone know?

The click of the fuel pump brought Nick out of his contemplation. He got a coffee and continued on the access road toward downtown.

He had heard of Walsenburg before. Read about it. A long time ago. When he was a boy in St. Joseph, Missouri, north of Kansas City. Their house was just off Mitchell Avenue, a few blocks away from the historic home of the infamous outlaw Jesse James. It was a small white house that was made into a museum, where visitors could pay a couple of bucks to see the very room where Jesse was shot in the back of the head by his fellow gang member Robert Ford. Ford was twenty; Jesse James was thirty-four. Both were local Missouri boys. The gang was planning to ride south that day to rob a bank in Platte City. But Ford decided the governor's bounty on James' head was a better deal. *Nick had seen the room—the old wallpaper, the bullet hole, and all. By the time Nick saw it, the bullet hole was covered with a small glass frame, to protect it from people taking pieces.* After collecting the bounty, Ford was surprised by the public backlash. He was branded a coward, and someone even tried to kill him in Kansas City. He left the Midwest and set off for Colorado, settling in Walsenburg and opening a few saloons and gambling houses just in time for the silver rush in nearby Creede. In 1892, when Ford was thirty, a man named Edward O'Kelley walked into Ford's saloon in Creede with a shotgun and killed Ford. O'Kelley never gave a motive for the murder, but he was a Missouri boy, too—from Harrisonville, just south of Kansas City, so a few theories existed as to when and how he may have crossed paths with Ford or James before that fateful day in Creede. O'Kelley was sentenced to life in prison but was released nine years later thanks to a petition that garnered over seven thousand signatures pleading for his release, as he was considered a hero for killing Ford. *Only in America.* Ironically, O'Kelley probably would have lived longer had he stayed in prison, because he was killed two years later in a shootout with police in Oklahoma City.

For some undecided reason, Nick liked this story. There was circularity to it—a satisfying balance of sorts. It seemed like a story that should have some profound moral, but he was still not sure what it was. He just knew that it somehow perfectly encapsulated the ambition and the futility of both the American outlaw and of Nick's own chosen profession.

If being a onetime home to the man who had assassinated one of America's most famous outlaws was Walsenburg's claim to fame, that fame had passed some time ago, along with its fortune. It was once a town of coal-mining prosperity, but when the mines started closing after World War II, the prosperity went with them. Taking a turn from Walsen Avenue down the side street toward the address in his GPS, Nick saw the telltale signs of urban decline. Despite the occasional bright storefront, a freshly painted façade, or an impeccably maintained front yard here and there, one could not miss the peeling paint, cracking concrete, overgrown lots, and shuttered commercial properties around every corner. They all spelled out the same fact—that the recession here started long before the COVID recession, the 2007 recession, the 2001 recession, and even the 1991 recession. The recession here was systemic. Nick had seen neighborhoods like this in Denver and Kansas City—continuing their decline just blocks away from prosperous districts. He knew that in places like these, the only business that was doing well was addiction. Alcohol, meth, crack, heroin. Nick was certain the opioid pharma train had also stopped here more than once—those companies knew their target markets well. Sure, drugs existed everywhere. But in places such as this—desperate places—drugs really took hold. Here, drugs were not recreational. Here, they had become a way of surviving life itself.

The address was a small, one-story bungalow with a wooden porch and a rusted-out swing set in the front yard. The off-white paint was peeling in some places and had yellow stains in others. The wood of the porch was gray, dry, and cracked. Nick rang the doorbell.

Edie Harris was a slight woman in her sixties with a face carved in wrinkles deeper than her years. Age always revealed itself more in poorer areas, where people lived harder lives. Here, they lacked the disposable income to spend on the pursuit of eternal youth. People here did not have the luxury to worry about Botox, or fancy creams and makeup. Here, skin was just skin—dry and cracked, like the wood of the porch. Like the earth of the high-desert mesa on which this town was built.

"Where?" This was the first shaky word she said after he told her they had found Ben.

He conveyed to her the circumstances of Ben's reappearance. Her eyes glazed, and her spirit seemed to leave her body for a few breaths. She steadied herself in the entryway, but she did not cry. Maybe because she had cried out all of her tears over the twenty years Ben had been missing. Or maybe because she forced herself not to. People who lived harder lives tended to be more stoic. She led him into the living room, where Nick sat on a blanket-draped couch. It was a small living room with worn-out carpet and an old, tube-style TV. But despite being an old, shabby house, on a shabby street, and in a shabby town, this home was clean and neat inside. It was evident to Nick that Edie took pride in her home.

She brought him a small, framed photo, and sat down next to him on the couch. "We had four boys. Here is Ben," she pointed.

It was an old home photo—poor quality and lighting, but Nick could make out the serious gaze of a toddler staring into the camera from the arms of an older boy of maybe six or seven years of age. Two more small boys were wrestling on the floor next to a blurry Christmas tree. Nick looked at the room he was sitting in—it was the same one as in the photo. Maybe even the same couch.

"Josh there, the oldest, was almost eight. He is now a mechanic in Pueblo. Has a wife and two kids. Zach and John were six—they are twins. They are in Galveston now, working for an oil company. Ben was two and a half. This was the last Christmas they were all together."

Nick nodded. "How did it happen?"

Her gaze drifted to the window, where Nick could see the rusted swing and the edge of her driveway. "It was March 9, 2001, in the morning," she said. "The school bus just picked up his older brothers—" She stopped suddenly and put her hand to her mouth. Nick saw tears welling in her eyes.

"It's OK," he said, reassuringly. "Take your time." He took out his notebook and wrote down the initial details, giving her time to compose herself and feeling terrible about making her relive that day.

She cleared her throat. "I had a shift at the convenience store that morning, so I was going to drop Ben off at my friend's house. She had a little one too, and she watched Ben for me a few days out of the week. I started the car to warm it up and then took Ben out and put him in his car seat. I forgot my lunch in the kitchen, so I went back into the house to get it. When I went back outside, he was gone. I was only away for a few minutes. I called the police right away. They came. Then the FBI came later that day. But they could not find him. He was gone."

Nick nodded. "Ben had your address written down on a piece of paper when we found him." He took out his phone and showed her a picture of the yellow sticky note. "Do you have any idea how he could have located you?"

Her chin trembled and tears ran down her cheeks. "H-he w-was c-coming home?" She stuttered through the words. Nick looked around for a box of tissues but did not find one. He was about to ask Edie, but she had already pulled one of the square pillows from the couch and buried her face in it, sobbing quietly, squeezing it tightly into her. She looked even smaller now, rolled into this sobbing ball.

"I am sorry," Nick said. "I can imagine this is very hard for you. Is Ben's father around? Maybe I can talk with him?"

She raised her head and shook it, wiping her tears with her sleeve. "He passed some ten years ago. Drank himself into the grave."

Nick nodded. He had heard that child disappearances were hard on the families and that many relationships did not survive it.

Edie was still clutching her tear-stained pillow and staring vacantly into space, probably lost in her memories of that day. Looking at her, Nick reached the conclusion that she had probably had enough for one day. He stood up.

"Ben's body is at the Jefferson County Coroner's Office in Golden. We have to conduct a full autopsy, since his death was unattended. It will probably be a few more days before you can transfer him back here for a funeral."

She nodded silently with tears in her eyes. Nick felt powerless to say or do anything that would make this any easier for this grieving woman. He said he was sorry for her loss and left her his card, telling her to call him if he could be of any assistance. Any at all.

He drove back in the deepening dusk, thinking about Ben Harris. It was a story worthy of a Greek tragedy: a boy kidnapped at an early age, finally finding his way home after twenty years, only to die a few hours away from his mother's doorstep. How could fate be so cruel?

Where had he been for almost twenty-one years? Someone took him out of Edie's car that morning. But why? Nick had heard of cases in which a couple would kidnap a baby because they could not have their own. Why else would anyone want to kidnap a toddler? The feedings, the crying, the diapers . . . it would have to be someone who wanted all that. Someone stole

Ben. Someone other than his parents raised him. It's no wonder he ended up with a fake ID. Claire was right—reasons did make a difference. In Nick's mind, Ben was no longer the clear-cut criminal Nick had initially assumed him to be. Ben was the victim of a kidnapping all those years ago and of who knows what else since then. There were still so many unanswered questions about what had happened to this boy. But the abduction was not Nick's case to solve. It did not happen in Nick's jurisdiction. His investigation concerned only Ben's death, and the outcome of this investigation was now firmly in the hands of the county's medical examiner, and likely a foregone conclusion at this point. Regardless of what may have happened to Ben Harris prior to last Wednesday, his cause of death was most likely exposure to Colorado's harsh elements.

Nick thought about Edie Harris crying into that pillow, having lost again the son she had already lost once twenty years ago. Nick's investigation into Ben's death would bring no closure to her. No answers. Who would? So much has changed in these two decades. Walsenburg no longer had its own police department, and the Huerfano County Sheriff's Office was now providing law enforcement. Would they have the time and the resources to dedicate to a twenty-year-old cold case inherited from Walsenburg PD? Maybe, and maybe not. But Nick could. He could at least read the original investigation report. Maybe he could help in some way. Maybe then Edie would get some answers about Ben's fate.

The sun had now set, and Nick was driving through the desert in the darkness, interrupted only by the headlights of the occasional oncoming traffic. He stopped in Colorado Springs for a late dinner. It was almost 1:30 a.m. when he pulled into the driveway of their house. His phone rang. It was Claire. She would not have usually called this late, but she knew he had to make a road trip and was having a late night.

"Are you still driving?" she asked.

"Just got home. How is your shift going?"

She was silent for a moment. "My mom died," she said quietly. "She had a stroke."

$!x

Claire watched the landscape change beneath the wing of the airplane. First from the piney foothills of the Front Range to the flat, barren highlands of eastern Colorado, then to the boundless, snow-covered prairies of Kansas, and finally to the thick, leafless winter forests of Missouri. Flying east from Colorado was like traveling back in time. These rolling hills of Missouri were her childhood. Her young adulthood. Icy and bare in the winter. Lush, green, and suffocatingly thick and humid in the summer. This was the place she used to call home. When she was Katie Daniels.

This was *before*. Before the rape. Before she became Claire Arden. And before she met Roses. The place she was going now was the place where Katie's story had begun and ended. This was a place to which Claire had never really intended to return. But now another story had come to an end here—her mother's—and Claire had to surrender to this place once more.

Mother. This simple word was a twisted knot of memories and emotions left behind in the haste of Claire's escape, like luggage left behind on the Titanic. Now, as Claire's plane inched closer to her birth town on the map, she was mortified to find these feelings were still there, somehow still just as raw as they were all those years ago. She had trapped them here unresolved, because she had never intended to come back. Now they were waiting for her, pacing back and forth in this cage she had put them, waiting to devour her. But she had to proceed.

Mother was not safe. *Mother* was a double-edged word, with only a razor-thin line separating the dizzyingly intense extremes. Love and guilt. Empathy and wrath. *Mother* was a volatile equilibrium, and most days, Claire did not know which end she would get. Most days, Claire did not know which she herself felt stronger—her desire to run away or her craving for her mother's approval. Even now, Claire caught herself inspecting her own life through her mother's eyes: *A job and a boyfriend. But no kids? Sure, that's great when you are in your twenties, but you are not in your twenties, are you? Maybe things would have been different if you had stayed out of those college parties. Maybe you should have gone to the Christian college, like I told you? Maybe you shouldn't have gone to college at all.*

Tears welled up in her eyes, but she swallowed them down. These words hurt, because these were all the things she herself had thought at one point or another. How was it that after all these years, the little girl inside her still wanted something from her mother? There was a fear deep in her core that *Mother was right*, and Claire for years had done everything in her power to resist surrendering to it. She ran as far from it as she could. No, she did not need anything from this woman. This midwestern secretarial school graduate who had lived and died in the same small town she was born in. What did she know about being Claire? She and Claire were nothing alike.

Claire was thankful that Nick came with her. She didn't expect him to, especially with this new case he was working, but he insisted and told her he had to wait for the Coroner's Office to do their thing, anyway. Having him along helped. It was like having solid ground always within reach any time she felt like she was about to drown in the past. She looked at him in the seat next to her. He was reading the spy-novel paperback he had picked up at the airport. The small seat-back TV screen in front of him was tuned to the flight map channel, and every now and then, Nick's gaze would break away from the page and fix on the tiny silver airplane barely moving over the green terrain. It was as if he was keeping an eye on things, making sure they were still making progress toward their destination.

He noticed her examining him, smiled, and leaned in for a kiss. He switched the book to his left hand and put his right in her lap, interlocking his fingers with hers. She gave his hand a squeeze. It was a good fit. The right fit, even though it was so much larger than hers. She loved feeling his hand in hers. She loved *him*. She was happy, despite what her mother may have thought or said. What she and Nick had *was* good. Sure, she wanted more from life than just this. Someday, maybe soon, she would need something more to fulfill her than just work and Nick. But for now, this was a good start. The rest would come in time.

The plane was flying lower now, and outside her round window, she could see the individual cars, houses, trees, and even people on the ground, as if she were leaning over a miniature town, watching their lives from above. The plane dipped its wing and transitioned into a gentle banking curve, and the miniature landscape began scrolling faster in her window, until the broad, glimmering ribbon of the river entered her view. Claire made out the familiar metallic horseshoe of the St. Louis arch on the western bank. They were getting ready to land.

7

They rented a small silver Ford SUV in St. Louis. According to the navigation app, Cape Girardeau was two hours south down Interstate 55. Claire drove—mostly silently, occasionally breaking her thousand-yard forward gaze to jab her finger into the Seek button of the dashboard stereo whenever the growing static would begin drowning out the music, letting them know they were about to lose another station. Within the first half hour, the radio cornucopia of St. Louis had dwindled to a handful of choices—top forty, classic rock, and gospel. Nick offered to connect her phone to the Ford's stereo via Bluetooth, but she shook her head:

"It's fine."

Nick let it be. It had been less than twenty-four hours since her mother had passed away. They were going to be the first family to arrive in town. Claire's uncle, Alex—her mother's younger brother—was flying in from Florida later the same day.

Nick watched Claire covertly out of the corner of his eye while she was driving. She was calm on the surface, but he could tell there was agitation quietly building inside her. He got it. Coming back years later to a childhood home was a mixed bag of feelings. He tried to picture her as a teenager, driving down these same roads, jabbing her finger into the Seek button with the same distracted impatience.

Claire never talked much about her mother. Granted, for the first year of his and Claire's relationship, she had told him that both of her parents were dead. But even after he found out the truth, the details she had shared about her mother were slim. From what he had gathered, Claire and her mother did not really have a relationship to speak of. And Nick himself had no room to talk—his own relationship with his parents had been reduced to brief civil text messages for birthdays and major holidays.

Was this unique to his and Claire's generation? It was as if some tether between parents and children got severed at some point, leaving only the disappointed expectations as a means to relate to one other. In Nick's case, this tether broke not in a single catastrophic rupture but rather through the gradual stressing and straining of the bond between them. He did not blame his parents. They did the best they could. As did Nick. He found his own way in life after all, didn't he? There was nothing he needed from his parents now. No apology, no approval, and no validation. They were all their own grown-up people now.

Claire jabbed her finger into the radio. The digital dial scrolled through the frequencies like a spinning reel in a slot machine, and David Bowie's "Ashes to Ashes" came crackling through the speakers. Claire did not react, her eyes remaining fixed on the winding tapestry of the rural Missouri highway up ahead. Nick wondered if her brain even registered the songs right now, or just reacted to the staticky vacuum of white noise.

He let Bowie's lyrics soak in and studied the landscape. On the other side of the windshield was a bright and cold February day. Despite the cold, the snow cover had receded as they ventured deeper into Missouri's south. Here, snow clung in thin patches to the north faces of bluffs and gullies, leaving the rest of the land bare—yellow-brown crop fields and leafless woods thick with wiry underbrush.

Nick opened the GPS app on his phone. The blue dot of their car pulsed like a heartbeat, creeping down I-55 toward the small circle labeled *Cape Girardeau*. According to the GPS, they were eighteen minutes out. As if to confirm this fact, industry began to appear in the landscape. The first sign was a cloud of white smoke or steam pouring from a ventilation stack of some industrial structure in the distance. The closer they got, the more substantial it looked.

"What's that?" Nick nodded to the structure.

Claire glanced. "The cement plant."

The cement plant was followed by more industrial sites with mounds of rock and gravel, piles of timber, pallets of cinder block, and stockpiles of other building materials behind chain-link fences. A semitruck loaded with sections of large-diameter pipe was driving down an access road along the interstate, raising a trail of dust behind it. So far, Cape Girardeau reminded Nick of many other midsize midwestern cities—part rural, part agricultural, and part industrial. Perhaps more industrial than most.

Cape Girardeau was also a river city. Nick first saw the blue snaking curve of the river on the map, but it wasn't until Claire exited the interstate and got closer to downtown that he caught glimpses of the Mississippi glimmering behind the buildings. Yet downtown, the river was not visible, replaced instead with the view of a gray concrete wall towering some twenty feet above the street. A flood wall. Having grown up in Missouri, Nick knew the devastation floods could bring to low-lying lands. The same mighty river that brought water to the crops and livestock throughout America's heartland could also wash away entire towns. Nature defined this place, despite everything mankind did to make it their own. Just as Denver would always be defined by the Rocky Mountains looming to the west, Cape Girardeau would always be defined by the mighty Mississippi to its east, made no less prominent and perhaps only more ominous by the presence of the wall.

Claire pulled into the parking lot of St. Francis Hospital. She kept her hands on the steering wheel, staring at the glassy wall of windows in front of them.

"Ready to go in?" Nick asked.

She shook her head.

"Want to go somewhere else?"

She nodded and put the car in reverse. "Let's go to the house," she said, and her tone indicated she was not excited about either option.

She took Missouri 74 west, away from downtown. The office buildings, hotels, and shops soon vanished from view, and Nick was treated to more views of industrial plants, excavating equipment, and storage silos before the landscape turned hillier and more rural, the roadside woods thickened, and paved intersections disappeared, replaced with gravel driveways and country roads. After a couple of miles, Claire slowed down and turned onto one of these gravel roads, which was missing a street sign. The first house on the right was a small one-story ranch. Claire took the driveway cautiously, letting the car dip gently in and out of the potholes.

She pulled up to the front porch and parked. Nick wondered if she would want to sit for a while, but she turned off the engine and got out of the car. He followed. The cold, fresh air felt good after the drive. The house sat on a wooded lot with the requisite patch of lawn in the front. Even for February, the lawn looked worn out and thin. They walked up the three brick steps.

"Is it unlocked?" Claire asked.

Nick pulled the handle of the screen door, and it opened with a squeak of the spring. He tried the lever of the front door; it was locked.

Claire dislodged a loose brick in the porch step and picked up a brassy key.

"Huh," she said, evidently surprised to actually find the key there.

The house was clean and neat inside. Minimal knickknacks, unlike at *his* parents' house, the last time he saw it. A round-faced wooden clock with gold Roman numerals tick-tocked on the wall in the living room, oblivious of the fact that its services were no longer needed. An upright piano in the hallway between the living room and the kitchen had a thin layer of dust on it. *About a week's worth,* Nick thought. A few framed photos hung in the hallway. One was a studio portrait of smiling Claire with curly brown hair and a blue background—probably from high school. The next one was a black-and-white photo of a group of people taken on the lawn in front of the house. Based on their clothes and the thickness of the lawn, it looked like summer or early fall. Probably family. Nick leaned in, inspecting the faces.

"Your mom worked at the lumber mill, right?" he asked, settling on an attractive young woman in her twenties with light curly hair, standing on the right side of the group with her hands on the shoulders of a little girl in front of her.

"Yep. Just down the road from here."

"What did she do?"

"Oh, just office crap. Reports, memos, invoices. Got coffee for the fat white VPs. I don't know. I never asked much."

Rebecca Daniels looked happy, Nick thought. A happy, thriving woman outside her house, surrounded by family. He examined the balding man in a short-sleeved button-down shirt next to her.

"And your dad . . . *stepdad?*" he corrected himself.

"Dry docks. Overhauling the barges."

Claire walked off somewhere down the corridor, and Nick followed. The house was small. He counted three bedrooms and one bathroom. Claire went into the room on the left at the end of the hallway. It was a small bedroom with light blue walls and half-peeled kids' stickers next to the headboard. There was a medium-size window above the bed, and in the window was the tapestry of the river stretching from edge to edge. From the distance, the water seemed to be standing still. A towboat was slowly pushing a string of two barges up the river. From here, Nick could even see the other shore. Illinois. The state line was somewhere out there, halfway across the wide, watery expanse of the Mississippi.

Behind him, Claire opened the bifold closet doors and rummaged through the boxes and clothes on the shelf above the hangers. In the window, another daisy chain of barges emerged from around the bend, and slowly crept downstream across the window. Nick found the view relaxing. The barges moved sleepily, silently, at half speed.

"Nice view," Nick said. "Was this your room?"

She glanced at the window. "Yep," she said. "And all I saw every day were those damn barges. And at night, I'd hear the trains rumbling. Growing up here, it felt like everything here was just passing through."

She closed the closet doors, empty-handed.

"Can I help you look for something?" Nick asked.

"No. It's nothing. Let me just check the basement."

They backtracked toward the kitchen and then went down the steep, narrow stairway. Claire clicked the light switch. There were no surprises down here—a water heater, a furnace, cobwebs in the overhead joists, and the moldy smell of an old, damp basement. She pulled the string to turn on another lightbulb and illuminated a corner of shelves with boxes, more boxes on the floor, an old desk with chairs on top, a crate of old, empty milk bottles, an old cooler, a tin Craftsman toolbox, and a stack of old newspapers and magazines. Claire squeezed through the barricade of antiques to the shelves and began pulling down boxes and rummaging through their contents. Nick dusted off the corner of the magazine at the very top of the pile—it was dated November 1997. He was about to flip open the cover when something else caught his eye. Next to an old floor lamp and a set of well-singed fireplace tools, a decorative handle gleamed at him with a red spark.

He swiped away the cobwebs and pulled out what looked like a cavalry saber with a scabbard and a handle shaped like a falcon's head with ruby-colored stones for the eyes.

"What's this?" he asked.

Claire turned around, and a half smile crossed her lips. "Great-grandpa's sword."

"Your great-grandpa had a sword?"

"Well, *great*-great-grandpa, I guess. My mom's great-grandpa."

Nick inspected the artifact. It could have been the dim light combined with the patina, the dust, and the cobwebs, but holding it in his hands, he felt certain this piece had a history and was not just a cheap reproduction. He pulled out the blade a few inches from scabbard. The metal was dull but clean and free of rust. This was an odd saber, unlike any he had seen before. The blade had an unusually shallow curve, and there was no guard of any sort on the handle. It looked very different from the American Civil War cavalry sabers he had seen, or even from the ceremonial swords of the marines.

"Why did your great-great-grandpa have a sword?"

"I don't really know. It's always been in the family. All my boyfriends wanted to play with it. You can have it."

"What? No. I couldn't. Sounds like it's a family heirloom."

"Yeah. *My* family's. If you don't take it, it will just end up in an estate sale."

Nick swallowed and allowed himself to be convinced. He liked unique things, and he liked history, and this was definitely unique and had history written all over it—the way it looked, the way it felt, and the way it smelled—the sweet-sour aroma of old leather, steel, and brass. Sure, it could have been a fake, but he had a strong feeling it wasn't. He tucked it under his arm and had to restrain a grin. For one, he was looking forward to investigating the provenance of this weapon. And he also relished the fact that all of Claire's boyfriends wanted to play with it, but she gave it to him.

Claire finally emerged from the stacks and shelves with a small shoebox in her hands.

"What's in that?" Nick asked.

She bit her lip thoughtfully and shook the box lightly from side to side. It rustled. "Katie Daniels." She looked at him. "I don't want to stay here tonight. Do you mind if we get a hotel?"

"Of course," he said. "Hotel it is."

He used his phone to find and book a Marriott a couple of blocks from the hospital—not too far, but not too close, either. While they were driving there, Claire's uncle Alex called. He had landed in St. Louis and just got a car and was now driving to Cape Girardeau. Nick had never met Uncle Alex, but he had already come to appreciate him. Since receiving the news of Rebecca's death, Uncle Alex had done a commendable job of communicating with Claire regularly. Detecting Claire's growing inner turmoil as they descended deeper into her past, Nick knew she would need all the reinforcements she could get. He could tell that Uncle Alex's regular check-ins provided some additional degree of certainty and comfort for Claire. Nick looked forward to finally meeting the man.

They checked in, and Claire freshened up a bit before they headed to the hospital, where her mother's body was being held at the morgue. This was the first time Nick had entered a morgue for a nonwork-related reason. He waited in the small waiting room while Claire went in. The last time death touched his personal life was so long ago—in college, when his friend Marc killed himself. Nick did not have to see Marc in the morgue, but when he saw him later, in the casket at the funeral, he remembered thinking that it was not really Marc in that casket—*no longer* Marc. The dead always felt different.

Claire came out five or ten minutes later. The blurred mascara lines told him she had been crying, but she was not crying now.

She sat on the seat next to him and leaned into his side and put her head on his shoulder. He put his arm around her and kissed her head.

"The woman had everything already prearranged," she said. "She wanted to be cremated. She even already had the funeral home picked out and paid for. They are coming to get her tomorrow."

Nick squeezed her into his side. "Want to go get dinner and a drink?"

"Yes!" she said with exhausted relief.

They found a steak house across the street from the hotel. The food was good, but more importantly, the atmosphere was just what they needed after the day they had had. The dimly lit interior. Dark wood paneling. Overstuffed booth cushions and soft music. This place soothed their senses. Drinks were good here, too.

Sipping on her double rum and Diet Coke, Claire looked on absently as the afternoon traffic thickened in the street outside the big, tinted windows. This was the business part of Cape— strip malls, chain restaurants, chain hotels, and chain gas stations. A rush hour of people and traffic. But inside the restaurant, they were insulated from the world. At least for now. Nick studied the profile of Claire's face. She looked exhausted and sleep deprived.

"How are you doing?" he asked, taking a swig of his Bulleit and ginger ale.

"I'm OK." She kept her gaze on the cars. "Just tired."

He took her hand in his.

"She was only fifty-four," she said, still watching the endless flow of traffic. "That's still so young."

He nodded. "What's your favorite memory of her?"

She was silent for a bit. "There is this old cemetery on the north side of town. From before the Civil War. We went there every now and then to visit the grave of my great-grandmother."

"The one whose name you took on?"

She nodded. "I don't know how old I am in this memory. Maybe three or four. I just remember walking with my mom among the gravestones. It was summer, and she was wearing a flowered dress, and the air was hot, and I was feeling the sun on my skin. I was holding her hand, and her dress rustled next to me, and the grass was so green, and the trees so big."

Her lips scrunched into a small smile that looked like a harbinger of tears.

"What do you like about this memory?" he asked.

She thought about it. "Holding her hand," she finally said. "When I think about it now, I know that that hand belonged to a girl barely in her twenties, but to me at the time it felt so safe. She was my *mom*. To me as a child, she was as infinitely significant as the rest of the universe put together." She looked at Nick. "I don't know if that makes any sense."

"It does."

Claire's phone buzzed on the table, and she moved her eyes to check the screen.

"It's Uncle Alex. He says he is twenty minutes out."

Nick looked at his watch. "You want to just have him meet us here?"

"Yeah, let me text him." She picked up her phone.

Nick was tired, and the bourbon was making him feel mellow. Outside, the night was setting in, and the windows had turned into dark mirrors. Claire put down the phone and looked at him.

"There is something I have to tell you about Uncle Alex."

Nick looked at her. "He's gay, right? I figured as much when you said he lived with his partner."

"No. I mean yes, but that's not it. There is something else. I really hope this will not be an issue between you two, but I don't want to keep secrets from you, either."

This preamble was slightly disconcerting, but he nodded for her to continue.

"Alex was in a political activist group when he was young," she said.

Nick sighed with relief. "Why would you think I'd have a problem with this? I myself may not picket and carry signs, but

I have nothing against other people being passionate about politics."

"They bombed the US Capitol in 1983."

3!ght

This turn necessitated a refill of Nick's bourbon. When the waiter came, Claire nodded when he asked whether she would also like a refill of her Captain and diet.

Nick hid his emotions well, but Claire could read his face. He was uneasy with this new bit of information. She had expected as much.

"Is he a fugitive?" he asked.

She shook her head. "He did twenty-three years in a federal prison."

Nick looked slightly relieved. She knew he did not have much faith in the correctional aspect of the American correctional system, but even he would not deny that twenty-three years was a helluva long time to think about things. She *knew* Uncle Alex would never go back.

"You are not going to ask why they did it?" she asked.

He took a sip of his bourbon and tilted his head, considering. "I thought about it, but then decided it did not matter. When people choose to break the law and endanger lives, I don't think their reasons should make a difference."

Nick could be such a Boy Scout sometimes. *Of course* reasons mattered. Reasons mattered a lot. What else justified actions?

He must have sensed her indignation. "Look, I get it," he said. "They were probably what—in their early twenties?"

"Yes."

"So—just kids, really. They probably felt like the system was rigged and unjust. The '80s were not exactly peachy. The economy . . . the politics. We had recently lost the Vietnam War, and now there was what . . . Nicaragua, El Salvador, Grenada, Iran-Contra. Lots of young people felt like they had no power. Not just in the US, but around the world. So, I understand. I don't condone it, but I understand."

She nodded. "He told me that after the US invaded Grenada, he felt that inaction was tantamount to complicity. But he never intended to harm anyone. Their group started out with peaceful protests and picketing. After a few years, when nothing in the world changed, some members of the group quit and went back to their lives, others wanted to stay the course, and others decided that *direct* action was needed. They formed a militant splinter group and went underground. Alex was with that group. They decided to target federal buildings in order to draw attention to their cause. They called it *bloodless terrorism*, because before setting off the bomb, they would call in a bomb threat, to ensure the site was evacuated. No one died in their bombings, but eventually, they did spill blood. To finance their activities, the group would rob federally insured banks and armored trucks. During one robbery, a guard was killed in the shootout. This splintered my uncle's group. Some viewed this as justifiable collateral damage, and even began discussing assassinating government officials. Others, including Alex, were not willing to cross that line. He left the group because of this, but by then, the FBI was already closing in on them. He was already on their list. Everybody got arrested."

She could tell Nick was listening attentively to her story. Claire's uncle had been a taboo topic in her family—a shameful secret—and this had always irritated her. In fact, Nick was now the only person in the world she had ever told the whole truth.

He gave her a soft nod when she finished, and was silent for a long moment. "It sounds like your uncle had convictions and was willing to fight for them," he finally said. "And he also had principles and a line he was not willing to cross. I respect that.

I'm sorry he had to pay such a high price to learn where that line was."

She felt tears coming on again. She wiped the corners of her eyes.

"Is this why you said he has been distant from your family?" Nick asked.

She shook her head. "It started even before then. Coming of age gay in Missouri in the seventies was not exactly safe or good for him. Our family was not good for him. He and my mother grew up in a very strict Southern Baptist household. I don't know much about his childhood, but I know he had to leave before finishing high school. He ended up on the East Coast, and that's where he fell in with this activist organization. This was all before me. When I was born, he was already in prison. I did not even know I had an uncle until I was in high school and found a letter in the mail from a federal prison in Kentucky. I confronted my mother, and she told me the whole story. And I wrote to him. I wanted to understand. He wrote back, and we started to correspond. He'd write to me every week on Tuesdays. He said our correspondence made his weeks go by faster. His letters were intelligent. So philosophical and pragmatic at the same time. He read a lot of books in prison. Sometimes I would read the same ones and we would talk about them. He was released in the summer before my first year in college. He stayed with my mother for a few months and then moved to Florida and settled there. But we stayed in touch. When I moved back home after the rape, he called me every week, and we would just talk. Sometimes for hours. He was the only person I could really talk to back then."

"Why did you guys stop talking?" Nick asked.

He was right—it had been a long time since she and Uncle Alex had really talked. Too long. "Just . . . life happened, I guess."

He nodded, and then his eyes fixed over her shoulder, toward the front of the restaurant.

"Is that him?" he asked.

Claire turned around.

* * *

Nick wasn't sure what to expect from Claire's uncle now. The image he had in his head about this man had now been turned upside down with this new bit of information about his past. In Nick's experience, the past was anything but. People carried their past with them. It left a mark on their faces and on their souls. But, looking at the wiry, tanned man with short, bleached hair and a white goatee standing at the hostess' desk, Nick did not see an obvious mark of someone who had served twenty-three years in a federal prison. He did not see the mark of someone who had been convicted of domestic terrorism. Instead, he saw a very white, very toothy grin.

"Holy moly! Is this my Katie-Kat?" Uncle Alex wrapped his arms around Claire, and they held each other in the embrace, neither one clearly wanting to let go.

When they finally separated, Claire's uncle focused his attention on Nick. "Alex," he said simply, extending his hand and flashing his bright smile again. And when Nick shook his hand, he too got pulled in for a hearty hug. "It's *so* good to finally meet you, Nick. I've heard such good things about you."

Uncle Alex exuded comfort and ease. His hug felt sincere and familiar, without trying too hard. This was not at all what Nick expected from an ex-con. Uncle Alex was a man who had aged well and who dressed with a clear sense of intentional style. His tan chinos, his cognac-brown leather boots with white soles, and his untucked indigo-blue shirt that looked like silk were all just a notch too extravagant for this provincial Missouri town, yet he made it all work with the same effortlessness as everything else about his appearance and demeanor.

The three of them settled back into the booth—Claire next to Nick, and Alex across from them. Nick got the waiter's attention and Alex ordered a glass of red wine Nick had never heard of. Claire's hand found Nick's under the table, and she interlocked her fingers with his. Nick gave her hand a squeeze.

"So, how was the drive?" Nick asked.

"Uneventful," Alex beamed. "But you know, I realized this was the first time I've ever made this drive myself. Last time I came here, my driver's license was expired, and I had to take the Greyhound bus. Driving yourself is a completely different experience. You have to really stay committed to your destination." He shrugged in a manner that resembled a small shiver. "I can't say I've missed this place."

The waiter brought the wine, and Alex took a sip and settled comfortably in the overstuffed cushions, smiling at them both.

"But I have really missed this one," he said to Nick and nodded to Claire. "It's been so long since I've seen her in person."

Claire smiled tiredly.

"You know," Alex said. "The most vivid memory I have of Claire was the summer before she went to college. It was late at night, and hot, and I could not sleep, so I went outside. So, here I am, smoking a cigarette on the porch, admiring the river in the moonlight, and then the window of her bedroom slides open, and out she climbs, sneaking out to party with her friends on Marquette Island. She saw me and froze for an instant, but then she put her finger to her lips, and even by the light of the moon, I could see her eyes laughing. And then she just disappeared into the night."

He took another sip of his wine and smiled. "She's always been fearless. Going for whatever it was that she wanted. I was so proud of her for going to college. First one in the family."

Nick felt Claire's hand clench in his. He looked at her and knew—this story had brushed an old wound. On any other day, this wouldn't have fazed her, but after the last couple of days, her emotional resilience was worn thin. She gave them a small smile and stood up. "Sorry, I'll be back," she said and headed toward the restroom.

Nick followed her with his gaze, trying to gauge the level of her distress.

"Damn it!" Alex grumbled under his breath. "I didn't even think about it. Here she is back in Cape-town, probably flooded with all the old shit and trauma, and there I go, bringing up college! . . . *And* I called her Katie!" He shook his head. He looked at Nick. "How has she been, being back here?"

Nick shrugged. "Fine, considering. I think it's just everything together. And she hasn't slept much in the last couple of days."

Alex nodded and took a sip of his wine.

"What was her relationship with her mother like?" Nick asked. He had guessed it wasn't great, but Claire did not seem to be in a good space to talk about it there.

Alex sighed. "It was complicated. Rebecca had her own demons. Our father was an abusive drunk. He . . . hurt her. She never confirmed it to me, but I remember *knowing* when it happened. I could tell something happened. She was different ever since. She would never talk about it. She took it on as her own burden to keep it secret and to overcome each day. That stoicism gave her strength, but it also prevented her from giving Claire empathy when she needed it. Because if she acknowledged Claire's trauma, she would have had to acknowledge her own as well. And Claire did not react to her rape the same way Rebecca reacted to her own. Claire was utterly destroyed to her very core. I did not find out until much later. I was busy settling in Florida and was not in contact much. It wasn't till that Christmas when I came back to visit that I found out. I could tell something happened as soon as I saw her. Katie was just a specter of who she used to be. I asked Rebecca, but she brushed it off. So, I talked to Katie, and she told me everything. She also told me she wanted to change her name."

"And what did you say?"

"I told her go for it. I told her there were many times in my life I wanted to change mine and start over."

Nick nodded. On the other side of the bar, Claire emerged from the restroom.

"So, Claire told me you are a cop? A detective?" Alex asked, smoothly changing the subject.

"Yep. And a reformed English teacher."

"No kidding?" Alex grinned. "I had a crush on my English teacher in high school. He was a good dresser."

"I don't think I've ever been accused of that," Nick said. "Thankfully, I have Claire now, to keep me from committing serious fashion crimes."

Claire slipped into the booth next to him, and her hand found his and gave it a reassuring squeeze.

"Hmm," she said, picking up her glass. "I would not say you were totally helpless before you met me, but then again, you did pick a job that came with a uniform."

"You got me there." Nick laughed and took a drink.

"So, Nick. You are from Missouri as well? Kansas City?" Alex asked.

"Yes. I grew up in St. Joseph, just north of KC. My mother worked for the university there, and my father for a factory. And you live in Florida?"

"Yes, in Clearwater."

"What do you do in Clearwater?" Nick asked.

"My husband and I own a restaurant."

"Oh, that's great! What kind of food?"

"Cuban with American influences. My husband brings the Cuban side, in case you were wondering," Alex grinned. "You two will have to come visit."

"Absolutely," Nick said. "And what's your husband's name?"

"Santiago."

"I do love Santi," Claire said, looking into the bottom of her glass. "And I've only ever met him over the phone."

"Sometimes I think you love him more than me," Alex teased.

"Definitely," she smirked. She leaned back in the booth, raised her arms to stretch, and closed her eyes.

"Tired?" Nick asked.

She nodded.

"Ready to go get some sleep?"

She nodded again and opened her eyes. "Do you want to meet for breakfast tomorrow?" she asked her uncle. "We have a lot to figure out."

"Let's make it lunch, and no—we don't. Not right away, at least. Rebecca wanted to be cremated, so there is no rush to do the service. We can plan for something later in the year, maybe during the summer, when more people are able to attend. We can work out the details when you guys are back in Denver. How does that feel?"

"That feels . . . good," she said. "Thank you."

They all stood up, and Uncle Alex gave Claire another tight hug. "You guys go get some rest. We will chat more tomorrow."

He hugged Nick next.

"You can stay at the house, if you want," Claire said. "Nick and I got a hotel."

"I'll think about it," her uncle said. "You two have a good night. I love you."

9

The waves of the Black Sea lapped languidly against the dock in the night. Anatoli felt the breath of the sea on his face. The sea smelled of frost tonight, carried down into these temperate latitudes from the snow-capped peaks of the Caucasus Mountains in the east. No moon. No stars. No boat lights at sea. Just the eternal sloshing of the waves, rolling ashore one after another, after another. Sea-foam fizzed in the sand after each wave. Out there, away from the shore, the sea and the night were one. A dark horizon, breathing, growing closer toward Anatoli, closer to absorbing him into its void. He was at peace with that. He was at peace with the darkness.

The only visible lights were in the west—the distant glow of Odesa. There, miles away, beneath the bright towers of hotels and casinos, the city buzzed with tourists, traffic, and nightlife. Anatoli liked Odesa. He even owned a club there—Argo—but there were times he just wanted to be here, away from the noise, and the crowds. Alone with the measured breathing of the sea.

The Yacht Club Chaika was a small but upscale private marina with fewer than twenty boat slips. It was *exclusive*, as the brochure said, in that exact word, but spelled out in Slavic letters: *эксклюсив*, as businesses in eastern Europe and Russia often did to make themselves sound more trendy and more Western, even when there were perfectly adequate Slavic words available. Because anything *Western* was naturally always better? Anatoli detested this practice. It felt lazy, and cheap, and fake, like a counterfeit Gucci badge on a two-dollar Chinese bag.

What started in the early nineties after the Iron Curtain fell was still a widespread practice, despite Anatoli's fading hopes over the years. Directness was becoming a lost art. In all his fifty-two years of life, Anatoli had never felt compelled to cover up who or what he was. He was proud of it, and he did not need foreign words to describe it.

Despite the distasteful marketing, Anatoli liked this marina. It was located in proximity to his Odesa house, which sat in the *exclusive* hills east of the city. It was also the perfect place to dock his own eighty-eight-foot *Riva*, giving him easy access to the international waters without much scrutiny.

Anatoli was born in Belarus, but for as long as he could remember, his family visited the Black Sea for summer vacations. Sometimes they came to Odesa, sometimes a bit farther east, to Crimea, and sometimes all the way to Sochi. This was so long ago, and yet, the sea he was watching now had not changed at all. The only difference was that back then, this shore belonged to the Soviet Union. How the times had changed.

He had thought about that change quite a few times over the years. Did anyone see it coming? Did anyone have any idea that the world as they knew it was about to suddenly come to an end? That the mighty Soviet Union would just fall apart like some rickety Gypsy wagon?

These weren't idle musings. This wasn't even nostalgia—not at all. This was basic survival. Anatoli always tried to learn from the past. In this life, it paid to be informed and prepared. If one was informed and prepared, one had an advantage over everybody who was not, which was most people. His uncle Bogdan taught him that.

The past always made for an interesting study, in part because the past kept on changing. The past today was not what it used to be when Anatoli was young. If history was written by the victors, only half of the past made it into history books. That seemed only fair, in the grand scheme of things, but it certainly made it difficult for one to learn from the past if one did not have all the information.

Certain parts of the past were still as true today as they were when he was a child, like the fact that Anatoli's grandfather fought the Nazis. Belarus fell to the Nazis in the first months of the war, and it remained under German occupation for three years. In that period, Belarus had two million casualties, and the city of Minsk, where Anatoli now had offices, was carpet-bombed by the Germans until only rubble remained. In 1944, the Soviet Fifth Army under General Krylov liberated Belarus, and the Fifth kept pushing the Germans back west until all the prewar Soviet territory was liberated. A simple story of cause and effect. Of wanton aggression, heroic resistance, and righteous victory. But what Anatoli did not learn till much later was that two years before the Nazis invaded the Soviet Union, Stalin had signed a treaty with Hitler to carve up Poland and much of eastern Europe. Soviet tanks had rolled into Poland from the east just two weeks after the Germans invaded it from the west. Anatoli never read about that in school. No one had told him that. Probably because it did not make for a simple story. But the full story certainly made for a more valuable lesson.

But Anatoli did not learn the full story till much later. When the doe-eyed, ten-year-old Anatoli knelt down to kiss the Soviet flag and earnestly recite the oath of allegiance as he joined the ranks of the Pioneers—the Communist Party's youth organization—no one told him that the fat cats from the Party's top echelons in Moscow and even in Minsk had already betrayed the very principles he was swearing to defend. No one had told him that the great Soviet experiment of redistribution of wealth had already failed massively, and that within a decade, the whole world would know. All this Anatoli had to learn for himself later. And the lesson was simple. Regardless of the political or religious inclinations, people were just people, and they would do their best to accumulate security and wealth by any means possible. The best history lesson Anatoli ever learned was that, despite all the history textbooks, history was not black and white, but all sorts of shades of gray, and that everyone—even the victors—*especially* the victors—had shameful secrets they kept out of the books. Everyone—the pope, the president, and everyone in between. End of the history lesson.

When the Soviet Union fell apart, most of its three hundred million citizens were not prepared. They had lived for seventy years without understanding the concept of a free-market economy. They had never experienced the marvelous equilibrium of supply and demand. They had lazily come to depend on the state to provide them with everything—healthcare, education, housing, jobs. They had never even had to choose between two brands of toilet paper. They were unprepared for what came next. They were already behind. Already at a disadvantage, before the first cracks even began to appear.

But some were prepared. Who? For one, the Party fat cats in Moscow, Minsk, and every other station of government power, who had already found ways to profit from their positions. And the criminal organizations who had never really disappeared under Soviet rule. And also, Anatoli's uncle Bogdan.

Uncle Bogdan learned his lesson in the war. Not the righteous *Great Patriotic War* in which Anatoli's grandfather fought the Germans. But the other war—in Afghanistan. The Soviets had come to Afghanistan to support their ally—the DRA—and what was supposed to be a quick military show of force had turned into an ugly, drawn-out affair when the US and Pakistan decided to back the mujahideen insurgents. Some had since called it *the shameful war*. Some had called it the Soviet equivalent of America's Vietnam. But what one called it did not matter. In the end, history books showed that after ten years, the undefeated Soviet Union had failed to subdue a nation of illiterate goat herders. But that was not the lesson Anatoli's uncle Bogdan learned. The lesson he learned was not a historical one, and not even an ideological one. The lesson he learned was in economics, and one that opened the doors to his future business success. The lesson was that things had value, and the value they had often depended on who wanted them and how quickly. And the beauty of this lesson was that it did not matter at all what these things were or who were the people that wanted them. The only thing that mattered was that at the end of the deal, you got something more valuable to you than what you gave away. A prolonged stalemate war created the perfect conditions to produce a true free-market economy. There was plenty of demand and supply all around. In a free-market economy, things could easily become other, more valuable things. Uncle Bogdan discovered that crates of Soviet AKs could become burlap bags filled with Afghani opium poppy, and when those bags got to his former schoolmate's farm in Dushanbe, they could in turn become morphine, codeine, shirka, kuknar, and a few other choice drugs destined for the veins of Mother Russia.

That was in 1984. So, yes, when the Soviet Union collapsed in '91, Uncle Bogdan was ready. He already had a respectable drug supply chain under his command. He made so much money, he had connections in the government. He even paid to send Anatoli to study in New York. But that wasn't everything. Uncle Bogdan was a visionary. He diversified his business interests. Sex trafficking was not a whole lot different from drug trafficking. It was all about moving things to people willing to pay for them. When the Beatles sang about the Moscow and Ukraine girls in "Back in the U.S.S.R.," they could have as well been singing a commercial for Bogdan Azarev. By the late eighties, he was trafficking Soviet girls throughout western Europe and beginning to expand into the US and Canada. That's when he brought in Anatoli. When the Soviet Union imploded and the recession hit, the floodgates opened, and Bogdan was once again in the right place at the right time.

There were so many pretty, dumb girls who just wanted to be models and actresses in America. He and Anatoli could be really picky about the stock they sent to New York.

A car pulled into the empty marina parking lot behind him. Anatoli heard the door shut and the familiar click-clock of high heels approaching—Elena.

She put her hand on his shoulder and kissed him on his scruffy cheek.

"You are sad, Tol'ja?" She used the endearing shorthand of his full name, as his mother did when he was a boy. "Is that why you wanted to meet here and not at the Argo?"

Anatoli liked Elena. He still remembered, as if it were yesterday, watching one of Uncle Bogdan's men beating her in a basement in Prague in 1987 after she was first moved there from Moscow. She was one of the smart ones, and the smart ones had trouble accepting their new reality. The best ones you had to break in, his uncle told him. He was right, of course. Years later, she became a top recruiter for Azarev, and later ran the porn-production facility in Gdansk back when DVDs were a thing. Now she managed Anatoli's western US territory.

"We had an incident in Salt Lake City," he said, choosing to ignore her question and affection.

"What . . . ?! An *incident* . . . ?" She checked her phone. "But I—"

"—haven't heard anything about it? I know. Max came straight to me. The root of the problem turned out to be in Minsk, and I have already taken care of it. All you need to know is that the security protocols will be changing."

"Changing how?"

He could tell she did not like waiting and not knowing. She was smart. Adaptable. Still pretty even at her age. Even though this incident happened in her region, he did not hold her accountable. The real issue was in Anatoli's own company. This one incident could have turned out much worse, had Anatoli not been prepared. Informed and prepared.

"You did not do anything wrong," he said and touched her hand. "Max will contact you to go over the details."

10

Since Uncle Alex had insisted that he could take care of any immediate needs in Cape Girardeau, Nick and Claire decided to fly back to Denver a day early. Nick could tell Claire was ready to be done with this unplanned trip down memory lane. On the way out of town, they stopped at a post office. Nick ran in while Claire waited in the car. He chose to ship home her great-great-grandpa's sword rather than having to deal with TSA agents at the airport. He contemplated what to put down for insurance value and settled on $500. This may have been too much, but he figured that even if the sword turned out to be a replica, the sentimental value to Claire was worth at least that.

On the flight home, Claire slept for almost the entire two and a half hours. Nick tried to read his book, but his thoughts inevitably turned back to the case of Ben Harris, which was waiting for him at the station. In a period of just a few days, Nick witnessed Edie Harris go through losing her son for the second time, and Claire losing her mother. He could not do much for their grief, but he was hoping he could at least provide some answers for Edie Harris. He looked forward to wrapping up Ben's death investigation and digging into the file on his disappearance.

Once back in Colorado, Nick realized how much he had missed seeing those jagged Rocky Mountains on the horizon. Unlike in the endless rolling plains of the Midwest, here Nick could always tell direction based on the skyline. Now, being back among the snow-dusted piney slopes of the Front Range, wheeling through a tight, inclined curve on Route 285 under the bright, sunny Colorado sky, Nick felt like he could breathe better.

He dropped Claire off at the house and told her he'd be back in a bit—he wanted to stop by the station. By the time he pulled into the station's gravel parking lot, it was already late in the afternoon. There was only one other vehicle in the lot—the chief's Chevy Tahoe. Ray must have already sent Patty home for the day. Nick parked his Tahoe next to the chief's and went in, crunching through the carpet of pine needles and gravel.

If Ray had been taking one of his afternoon naps, the cowbell on the entrance door most certainly woke him up and put him on alert.

"Welcome back, Severs," he croaked from his office and cleared his throat.

"It's good to be back," Nick responded. "Let me grab some coffee," he added, spotting the promising green glow of the On button of the coffee machine. He circled behind Patty's vacant front-desk station and filled a cap half-full of dark, still-hot brew and went in to see the chief.

Ray's weathered Stetson hat hung on the coat hook by the door, ready for action. The old cowboy himself was reclining in his high-back office chair, resting the heels of his equally weathered square-toed Ariat boots on the corner of his desk. Ray's own coffee mug was in front of him.

"How were your travels?" Ray asked.

"Smooth," Nick said, settling into a chair. "Long day today, but smooth."

"How is Claire?"

Nick sighed audibly.

Ray nodded in understanding. "Tell 'er I'm real sorry for her loss, again, would you?"

Nick nodded.

"Was she close to her mom?"

"Not really. But . . . it's complicated, I suppose."

"It usually is, between kids and parents."

In the window behind Ray, Nick saw the familiar emerald-green reflection of the Solitaire game on his computer screen—one of only a few apps on his computer Ray had mastered to enviable proficiency. It helped him keep his mind sharp, he said.

"Did I miss anything?" Nick asked.

"It snowed yesterday. And there was a twelve-car pileup on 285 south of Bailey. Nobody got hurt, but it took them about an hour to reopen."

Nick nodded.

"Any news on your John Doe?" Ray asked in turn.

"We got an ID—a *real* ID. Ben Harris. Turns out he went missing as a kid from Walsenburg in 2001."

Ray whistled. "2001? No kidding? Good work."

Nick shrugged. "That was all Brenda. I can't take any credit. Now I just have to figure out what happened to him."

"Which time?"

Nick shook his head. "I know . . . as if getting kidnapped at the age of two is not enough."

"Do you have the cause of death?"

"Exposure, most likely. But Brenda is still working on it."

Ray nodded and took a sip from his coffee mug.

"Have you ever had a child-abduction case?" Nick asked.

Ray's knotted, calloused fingers traced the contour of his silver mustache. "Abbi White. September 10, 1979. Eight years old. Got off the school bus and never made it to her front door."

"Did you find her?"

Ray shook his head, and his eyes focused miles behind Nick. "With old age, I've found ways to make peace with most of my regrets. But I've never forgiven myself for not solving that case. The girl just vanished. The parents were devastated. We talked with everyone—neighbors, teachers, classmates, the mailman—no one had seen anything. We never even found a body. For all these years, I've found it really hard to look her parents in the eye. Her mother, Diane, died a few years back, never knowing what happened to her daughter. This will be one big regret I will take with me when I retire."

Ray turned silent, suddenly looking very vulnerable in the face of this memory.

"What do you think happened?" Nick asked.

Ray shrugged. "Anything and everything. Warren was the chief back then. He suspected a transient. Neighbors reported seeing an unfamiliar station wagon with a long-haired man at the wheel. We had Highway Patrol looking for her from Provo, Utah, to Colby, Kansas. Nothing. The case is still open. I have the file."

"Do *you* think it was a transient?"

"It could have been. As much as anything else, I suppose. We even looked at a satanic cult out of Colorado Springs. The late Betty Mills was convinced it was Satan worshippers that took Abbi. Chief Warren even sent me to Denver to a seminar on satanic cults. There was this guy named James McCarthy, and he had a whole organization—I think it was called The Sanctuary, or something like that. They ran programs for churches and law enforcement. They even took out ads in the local papers with tips on how to spot the Satanists and save your children."

For a case that went back over forty years, Ray's memory was impressively sharp. Perhaps the solitaire was working.

"Is this McCarthy guy still around?" Nick said with subtle sarcasm. "I still have some training hours to fill."

Ray smirked and shook his head; he knew when Nick was joking. "These were different times, Nick. We were taught to focus on "stranger danger"—to look for a degenerate outsider creeping around the playgrounds. Nowadays, first focus is always on parents and family friends."

Nick nodded. "So, did you look into *her* family?"

"Just the basics. The father had an alibi. The mother . . . well, she was *the mother*. Again—different times. I knew them both from church. They seemed genuinely devastated, to me, at least. But I was a rookie cop. I guess I could have missed things."

"Did Chief Warren bring in the bureau?"

"He sure did. The CBI came out and assisted with canvassing and the interviews. But after a week, they had to leave. There was nothing else they could do—we had no body, no evidence, no real witnesses."

"You said you still have the case file? Do you mind if I take a look?"

Ray perked up. "You want to?"

"Yeah." This cold case intrigued him. Even if he could not add anything to it, in the very least, reading through the investigation of Abbi's disappearance could give him some ideas for Ben's.

"OK, then." Ray did not have to go to the storage room for this one. He opened the deep drawer of his desk and pulled out a file. He did not have to look for it—he knew exactly where it was.

"I've kept it close, to always be top of mind. I've revisited it now and then, but no new leads have panned out."

Nick took the file and got a refill of coffee on the way to his office.

The file on Abbi White's disappearance was thicker than he expected, given that there was no body, no crime scene, and no autopsy. Opening it up, Nick realized that Ray had clearly done his footwork on this one. And then some. There was a handful of reports and also countless transcripts of interviews. There were also newspaper clippings, including a few on a satanic cult ring in Colorado Springs—*Ray had not been kidding*. There were also a dozen or so photographs—of the driveway and the rural street intersection from various angles, and a few of the house, and one photo of Abbi. It was an old studio photo, like for a yearbook. It was printed on the old, thick photo paper, but it was not yellowed—just turned to pale ivory, protected inside the folder in Ray's file cabinet for all those many years.

Nick arranged the photos on the desk and read the file from cover to cover. That took him less than thirty minutes. Then he just sat there, thinking, and looking at the photos.

There seemed to be nothing at all in this case to latch on to. The school bus dropped Abbi off at the end of her driveway around 2:45 in the afternoon, according to the statements from the bus driver and several classmates. Her mother realized Abbi was still not home at around 3:00. Somewhere inside those fifteen minutes, Abbi vanished without a trace.

Her father was at work. Several people confirmed that, according to Ray's interviews. Her mother was at home doing some cleaning and tending to Abbi's two younger siblings. Neighbors were sparse, and none of them saw anything unusual except for one report of an unknown station wagon and a long-haired man driving it. The vehicle and the driver were never identified. The school staff were interviewed but did not report seeing anything or anyone suspicious at or around the school on that day. The satanic cult, although a hot topic at the time according to the clippings from the Colorado Springs *Gazette*, turned out be a dead end when the police raided its worship center but discovered no evidence of child abductions or sacrifices, or any illegal activity, for that matter.

Nick sat with the documents in front of him for a while, reading and rereading the reports, letting the pieces and the people find their places in his mind. After 1980, the only new information added to the file was a 1992 DNA analysis Ray requested using a few of Abbi's hairs from her home. The lab was not able to obtain a sufficient sample. All trails went cold. If Ben Harris' disappearance in 2001 seemed hopelessly old, the disappearance of Abbi White stretched twenty more years further into the past. Someone took her, just as someone took Ben, all those years later.

At least Nick had Ben's body to work with.

Nick checked his watch—already after five. He could have still tried Brenda but decided to wait till tomorrow. He filed the papers and the photos back into the folder and locked it in his desk. The case of Abbi White needed to sit in his head overnight and percolate. Tomorrow, once he had a chance to chat with Brenda, he would take a look at it again.

11

"Ben Harris did not die of exposure," Brenda said.

It took a moment for her words to truly sink in. Nick knew something was afoot when she asked him to come up to the county office in Golden, but he was not ready for such a complete reversal of his hypothesis. From across the desk, Nick saw her lips move and heard the words, but his brain did not immediately register them, having been preoccupied all morning with the cold case of Abbi White waiting for him at the station.

"What . . . ? What did he die from, then?" Nick finally responded.

"After examining the decedent's brain and consulting with a neurologist, we both agreed that the victim died as a result of a traumatic brain injury."

"But . . . traumatic brain injury would mean physical trauma, right? Was he hit in the head?"

"Not exactly." She opened a folder and pulled out a handful of printed MRI scans. "See these dark spots in the back of the brain? These are microhemorrhages, and as you can see, there are quite a few of them. This is not the type of damage we would see in cases of blunt force trauma to the head. Where we do see these is in cases of blast injury. The damage to the eardrums is also consistent with a blast injury."

Nick studied the scattering of small, black, irregular-shaped spots that peppered the brain scan like a blast of buckshot. "A blast injury? Like an explosion?"

She nodded. "We do usually see these in soldiers and miners as a result of an explosion, but it also could have been anything capable of generating an extreme sound wave."

"And you are sure this is what killed him?"

"The neurologist said he has never seen anyone survive such extensive brain damage. He said it was most definitely lethal. In light of this, I can't rule his death accidental. Not at this point, at least. I am going to indicate the manner of death on the death certificate as 'Pending Investigation.' Unless you have a good reason for me not to?" She looked at him.

Nick shook his head. "Makes sense," he said. There would now most definitely be an investigation into Ben Harris' death. Brenda had done her part. Now it was Nick's turn to do his.

"Does he have any other signs of being in an explosion?"

"No. The victim had no other evidence of trauma anywhere else on the body."

Hmm. Nick stared at the bookcase behind Brenda's desk. It was stuffed with thick books and stacks of journals and files. Much like Nick's was when he was a teacher. Brenda was a scientist. Nick respected that. She followed evidence and logic. Just like him.

"And you are positive there is no chance hypothermia could have caused this?" he asked, hoping against all hope.

"Positive. Hypothermia may have accelerated the bleeding in his brain, but with this extent of brain injury, it did not make much difference."

"What about a health condition? An aneurysm?"

She shook her head. Nick reached for his notebook, his mind already having put away the case of Abbi White and now beginning to establish its bearings and points of reference in the death of the young Ben Harris.

"Do you have the time of death?" he asked.

"I'd say between 7 and 10 p.m. on Wednesday, February 2."

He jotted that down.

"What are you thinking?" Brenda asked.

"Well, first thing, I am going to look at the traffic cams on 285 —maybe they captured something." He sat silently for a moment, contemplating. "Wait—the other day you said you also found scars on him?"

"I did." She pulled out more photographs from the folder. "But they are all old. The back has parallel scar patterns as if from being flogged. He has small, shallow cuts and what looks like cigarette burns on the front of his torso and on his arms. All are anywhere from a few years to ten or more years old. Also, the humerus in his left arm was broken in childhood, probably between the ages of eight and twelve."

Nick looked at the photos "Can I see him?" he asked.

Brenda looked at her watch. "Yeah, but he is getting picked up at noon for transport to the funeral home in Walsenburg."

She led him around the corner from her office and down the corridor to the familiar double doors that separated the realm of the living with their carpeted floors, painted walls, office plants, and cushy furniture from the realm of the dead, which one could easily identify by its natural abundance of white ceramic tile and cold, clinical stainless steel.

They crossed to the back of the autopsy suite, and Brenda used her badge to unlock the door to the cold-storage room. There, she walked to the stainless-steel cooler unit, opened chamber number 8, and slid out the tray.

"Let me know if you need him turned over," she said.

Nick approached. As Brenda said, the scars were old and white. Some, like the three-inch-long straight cut on his chest, had healed rough and were perfectly visible under the bright lights. Others, like the line of round cigarette burns on his arm, were worn smooth and were barely noticeable except up close. There were many of them. Easily over a dozen just on the side closest to Nick. Ben's body told a story, and it was not a good one.

The young man's face was white, but with an unusual tinge of gray. Perhaps this was an effect of hypothermia. It was the color of melting snow. The face was also puffier and smoother than other bodies he had seen, almost as if it were not an actual face but a death mask. Nick tried to imagine Ben alive. His personality. What did he look like when he was talking? Laughing? Usually, he felt something. Some trace of the victim still attached to the body. But here, there was nothing. Something truly terrible had happened to this boy. Something that had detached his spirit from his body many years before he died. Nick felt this case beginning to really bother him. As much as he had hoped for this death to be accidental, this seemed unlikely now, given that everything else in this young man's life had been so intentional—someone had kidnapped him, and someone had tortured him for years.

He cleared his throat. "He looks like he lived through hell."

Brenda nodded. "Breaks your heart to think of the things someone did to him. What kind of monsters do this to children?"

Nick looked at Ben's face again. Pale and smooth, with flakes of blood still inside his ears.

"Did you say you found the FBI case number when you ID'd him in CODIS?" he asked.

"Yes. Want me to send it to you?"

"Yes, please." *It wouldn't hurt to get things rolling on multiple fronts while he looked into the traffic-cam footage. Maybe something from his disappearance would connect.* "And you already sent his belongings to the lab?"

"Yes. There wasn't much, but it's all at the RCL now."

Nick hoped against all odds that the smart techs at Jefferson County's Regional Crime Lab would be able to pull something useful off this kid's stuff, even though it had been handled by who knows how many people since Ben's body was found.

12

Reviewing the traffic cameras did not take long. The two closest ones to Elk Road were half a mile north, in Shaffers Crossing at the intersection of US 285 with County Road 83: one facing northbound and the other south. Nick watched the sped-up flow of traffic on both feeds from five to seven thirty for February 2, but did not see anyone walking along the highway during that time period. Shortly after seven, the storm moved in, and the camera feeds filled with snowy white noise. Nick stared at the whiteout on the screen, wondering if Ben was somewhere in it. There was a gas station in Shaffers Crossing. Did Ben catch a ride there, and then try to hitchhike farther just as the storm moved in?

It could be worthwhile to check out that gas station, talk with the clerk, and take a look at their surveillance footage for the day. Nick called the county and requested a forensic artist to put together a headshot based on Ben's autopsy photos. Nick could also show it around at the gas stations in Conifer and Bailey.

He then filed an affidavit for a search warrant to request a cell-tower dump—a list of all phone numbers that pinged the cell towers from Bailey to Conifer that day. Once he got the warrant, it would take another couple of days before he would get the data and would be able to check whether Ben's phone was on the list, and which towers it pinged.

So far, the events of February 2 had continued to be a mystery. Nick still knew nothing about the movements of the victim on that day, never mind the explosion that supposedly killed him.

What could have caused the explosion that killed Ben without mangling his body? Colorado was mining country, so that was the most obvious possibility to explore. Nick had also heard of decades-old munitions recently being unearthed on the grounds of the former Camp George West Artillery Range near Golden, but that was over thirty miles away from where Ben was found. He asked Ray whether he was aware of any active blasting in or near Pine Lake, or whether there had ever been any munitions found or other odd explosions in the area. Ray scratched his strong cowboy chin for a moment and concluded that he "reckoned he hadn't heard of any." Nick called the Mountain Precinct of the Jefferson County Sheriff's Office and asked the same question about the surrounding area under their jurisdiction. He received the same answer but in different words. He next called Park County Sheriff's Office substation in Bailey and got the same result.

What else could have caused the blast that killed Ben? He checked the CO-DOT bulletins, but currently no rock scaling or blasting maintenance work was being done on any of the Colorado highways including US 285. At this point he knew he was grasping at straws, but he nevertheless called Buckley Air Force Base in Aurora, and then Peterson Air Force Base in Colorado Springs and even the Air Force Academy in Colorado Springs—all three said they had no jets or other activity in the 285 corridor that day. As far as anyone was concerned, nothing exploded near US Route 285 and Elk Road that day.

Having exhausted all possibilities known to him, Nick decided to give it a rest until tomorrow, when Jason would be in. Pine Lake PD's auxiliary police Officer Jason Birch was a full-time mining engineer and Nick's go-to resource for any questions related to mines, engineering, and conspiracy theories. Nick never asked about conspiracy theories.

Nick checked his email. The FBI missing person brief from Brenda was waiting for him in his inbox. The agent in charge of the FBI investigation was Tim Beck from the Denver field office. Nick dialed the number for the Denver office, but evidently Agent Beck had transferred to the Albuquerque office some years back. Nick called the Albuquerque number he was given, and had instant success:

"Special Agent Beck," a deep baritone said on the other end of the line.

Nick cleared his throat. "Yes, this is Detective Nick Severs from Pine Lake, Colorado PD. I am following up on one of your old missing person cases. 2001. Ben Harris—"

"Yeah, I remember that case," Beck cut in without sounding impatient. "A little boy . . . two or three years of age?"

"Yes." Nick was impressed that this guy remembered a random case from twenty years ago. "Do you remember any of the details?"

Agent Beck sighed. "There weren't many. The kid just vanished off the face of the earth. No evidence. No trace. Maybe if it happened nowadays, we could have done better. But this was before the CARD teams."

"CARD teams?"

"The FBI's Child Abduction Rapid Deployment teams. There are several around the country now. Each one has a dozen or so specialists ready to deploy and work the case the instant it comes in. But back then—it was just me. I was twenty-five, and hardly a specialist in anything." He went silent for a moment, maybe reminiscing. "Why the interest?"

"We found Ben last week."

"What?! Where?" Beck got excited.

"Under an overpass off US 285. He was deceased and had a fake ID on him."

"Oh, God." Beck fell into silence.

Nick tried to add a silver lining. "If it weren't for the DNA samples you collected back then, we would not have identified him."

"How did he die?"

"We are still trying to figure that out. It's not clear-cut. But I wanted to talk with you in case there could be some relevant connection between his disappearance and death. I am not at all an expert on child abductions. Is it common for the missing children to resurface as adults?"

"No. That's extremely rare. In fact, this is the first time in all of my cases, and I've done a hundred and twenty-seven. If we don't find them right away, sometimes we find a body. Usually, we find nothing at all."

"Did you have any suspects in Ben's disappearance?"

"We looked into several, but no luck." Beck took a deep sigh. "Want me to send you the file? You can take a look with a fresh set of eyes."

This was not much, but it was something. And that was more than what Nick had at the moment. He said yes and felt the weight of this case pulling him deeper into the past, as if Ben's spirit itself had a grasp on him, taking him to the dark core of his mystery.

* * *

When Nick got home, Claire was not in the kitchen. Normally, she would have been making coffee right now, and getting ready for her night shift. That's when Nick remembered that today was her day off. The first of four in a row, which she would spend futilely trying to sync to his sleeping schedule, and that meant tossing and turning through half the night and keeping Nick awake. That would continue until it was time for her to go back to work and back to her nocturnal routine. Despite this, Nick was excited that they would get to spend the evenings and the nights together for the next few days. He was even more excited that they were getting closer to March, when she would go back to day shifts and things could be sane again.

"It's me," he yelled, going into their bedroom. Claire had just gotten out of the shower and was standing in front of the mirror, wrapped in her bath towel and brushing her wet hair, which cascaded like a dark waterfall down her neck and then over her pale shoulder and to the front. She watched him in the mirror as he approached and wrapped his arms around her.

"How was work?" she asked.

He loved the line of her neck, the way it transitioned so gracefully into her shoulder. There were small droplets of water still on her skin—a few on the slope of her shoulder, and some more leading down the hollow between the smooth arc of her shoulder blade and the subtle ridges of her spine.

"Better now," he said and slowly kissed the drops on her naked shoulder. He kissed the base of her neck, and then, softly, higher, near her ear, inhaling the scent of her shampoo or conditioner, or whatever it was she used to make her hair smell so bewitchingly good. She closed her eyes, and pressed her body into him, and felt the curve of her spine and every inch of her yearning to be close.

He traced the front of her extended neck with his fingertips. She was so breathtakingly beautiful. Her neck, her collarbone, her breasts, now barely covered by the slipping towel.

"Well, hello there," she smiled, and her hand reached behind her to touch him. She turned around, letting her towel fall to the floor. He felt the warmth of her body as she stretched out on her tiptoes and kissed him, and then pushed him toward their bed.

13

Nick woke up to the sound of wind outside. The wind wailed at the windows and sheared at the house walls, making them creak and strain against its brute, blunt force. This was going to be one of those days the likes of which the inhabitants of the Front Range got treated to several times each year: crystal clear, sunny, and with the wind blowing and gusting relentlessly from sunrise into the late hours, billowing in waves that swept over the mountains and across the high plains, shutting down ski lifts, overturning semitrucks, and ejecting unsecured trampolines from people's yards.

Nick called this wind *the Great Wind* because it was. Because it humbled Nick with the colossal scale of the continental atmospheric forces that worked like titans right above his head, moving massive volumes of air, hour after hour, from Wyoming to Colorado and farther on down, hundreds and hundreds of miles along the jagged, snow-capped spine of the Continental Divide. The *Great Wind* ruled over this rugged landscape, returning every now and then to reassert its dominance and to remind humankind of the power and the scale of nature.

And this wasn't an idle reminder. Out here, wind was one of the elements that could hurt you. A surprise gust of wind could push you off a narrow mountain trail into a fatal fall, as it did with the young guy hiking Quandary Peak last summer. Or it could turn a warm spring day into a blizzard in a matter of minutes, trapping you above the tree line without proper gear, as it did the couple from Texas who died of hypothermia on

Longs Peak. Or it could just plain drive you insane, as it did the early European settlers of the barren, featureless western prairies, where the relentless howl of the wind racing across the open plains drove them to what they called *prairie madness*.

This was the way it had always been. Long before Nick set foot here. Long before Ben Harris or Abbi White. Before the US Army reached these lands during the westward expansion, and before the Mexican and the French armies, and before the Spanish conquistadors, and even before the Pueblo, the Apache, the Comanche, the Arapaho, the Cheyenne, and other nations that fought the foreign invaders on this land. Maybe even before the Rocky Mountains themselves were here.

Claire was still asleep, having exhausted herself by keeping Nick awake through most of the night. Nick got ready for work, made enough coffee for two insulated tumbler mugs, took one of them to Claire's bedside table, kissed her goodbye, and walked out the front door at 7:30 a.m.

When he stepped outside, he could *feel* the wind. It was a sustained but manageable horizontal force that made him lean into it in order to keep his balance. And then he heard the gust coming. It started as a low howl in the distance. Nick looked at the nearby ridge and could see a wave forming in the sea of pines. It was rolling in his direction, kicking up clouds of snow that billowed like whitecaps in the squall. He heard it begin to whistle in the needles of the nearby pines as they began to bend and sway with the gust moving through them. Nick hurried to his Tahoe, feeling the icy breath on the back of his neck, and chased by the roar growing louder behind him. The gust shoved him toward the truck, and he struggled to open the driver's door, which had to be pried open like the clenched jaws of an alligator. He finally managed to squeeze inside without losing grip of his coffee, and the door slammed shut behind him. The gust battered the side of the Tahoe, making its hefty bulk rock on the heavy-duty suspension springs. As if celebrating the success of driving Man back into his shelter, the lodgepole pines in Nick's own yard caught the wind with their fluffy, long-needled green paws and danced triumphantly, in solidarity with millions of their conifer sisters throughout these mountains. Traitors.

Nick sat there for a moment, enjoying the comfort of this sun-warmed shell made of steel and glass as the *Great Wind* wailed outside. Finally, he started the engine, took a gulp of his hot coffee, and headed to the station.

Special Agent Beck came through, and Nick found the FBI file pertaining to Ben's disappearance already in his email. The attachment was a single, very large PDF file containing 142 pages in total, and it appeared to have been scanned in no particular order. Nick scrolled through the pages. There were dozens and dozens of documents here, including the initial incident reports—both from Walsenburg PD and the FBI, photos, interview transcripts, forensic reports and notes. This was going to take a while. Nick preferred to start from the beginning, so he scrolled around to find the very first document, which was the transcript of the 911 call.

Dispatcher: *Nine one one, what is your emergency?*

Caller: [unintelligible]

Dispatcher: *Ma'am? Can you hear me?*

Caller: *My boy is gone!*

Dispatcher: *Did something happen to your son?*

Caller: *Yes* [unintelligible]. *He is gone! Someone took him. You must hurry!*

Nick could picture Edie Harris, hysterical, on the other end of the line. He could imagine the distress and powerlessness she must have been feeling in those first moments of Ben's disappearance. Despair pulled at Nick's own heartstrings. He swallowed down the lump in his throat and scrolled down to keep reading. But then he scrolled back up and studied the detail that had unconsciously caught his eye. Perplexed, he pulled out his notepad and flipped to the notes he took when he visited Edie. He looked back at the transcript. *That's odd,* he thought. He hurriedly scrolled to the statement Edie gave to Walsenburg PD and read the first few lines. *Very odd.* He pulled up the statement she gave to the FBI and read the first few lines.

"SHIT!" Nick said out loud. "Shit, shit, shit," he repeated, jumping out of his chair and grabbing his keys.

"I'm going to Walsenburg," he shouted to Patty and Ray, not waiting for a response. By the time the front door of the station closed behind him, he was already starting up the engine of his Tahoe.

* * *

"You lied," he said to Edie Harris when she opened the door.

She retreated half a step back but did not deny it. Her thin, chapped lips trembled, and her eyes focused on something just to the side of Nick's face.

"You placed the 911 call at 12:55 that afternoon. I read the transcript of your call. You told Walsenburg PD that Ben went missing around 12:50. You also told the FBI the same. But you told me Ben was taken in the morning when you were leaving for your early shift. There is no way you could have forgotten this detail about the day your child was abducted. How do you explain this?"

Tears sprang from her eyes, but she stood still, and they just ran down her cheeks and gathered at the end of her chin. But Nick felt no sympathy for her.

"I'll tell you how *I* can explain it," he continued, firmly. "I think it's been twenty-one years, and you forgot how to tell this lie."

She turned around, leaving the front door open, and he followed her into the living room. Nick noted that inside the house now smelled of cigarette smoke; it did not the first time he came here.

"Your lie had obstructed the investigation into your son's disappearance. Why would you do that?"

She pulled a tissue from the box on the coffee table and slumped into a chair in the living room, burying her face in her hands. Nick heard a muffled wail.

The box of tissues wasn't here the first time Nick came. Neither was the pack of Marlboro Lights, a Bic lighter, and a small china bowl full of ashes and cigarette butts.

Nick took a deep breath and sat down on the couch. "Edie," he said in a softer tone. "What really happened to Ben that day?"

She sniveled and raised her eyes to the window, staring vacantly at the cars passing just beyond the rusted swing set.

"What really happened, Edie?" Nick repeated. "Did Ben disappear in the morning? Tell me the truth. You owe this much to Ben."

Her eyes moved from the window to the worn carpet at her feet. She took a breath that sounded like a sob.

"My husband worked for the railroad. Till there was an accident and he lost his leg." Her voice was shaky and raspier than before. "The railroad gave him an early pension and a good payout for the accident. With that money, we could've been fine. But he drank it away at the bar around the corner until there was no money left and not much of him left, either. I had four kids, all under the age of eight, and nothing to feed them. I had a job at the truck stop, but they couldn't give me enough hours to support my kids and my invalid, alcoholic husband."

She closed her eyes. "One day, a girl I worked with told me about this adoption agency. They paid money for children. She said wealthy families who could not have their own would pay money. It wasn't legal, but she said it was better for the kids. They didn't get stuck in the system. They went straight to good homes. They could have a good life. A better life. And the parents got paid. A win-win for everyone, she said, including the kids."

Nick felt a chill creep up the base of his neck. He really was not liking this turn of the story. But he did not say anything.

He just watched Edie closely, trying to decide whether she was lying again.

Her bottom lip trembled, and more tears sprang from her eyes. She dabbed her eyes with the tissue she held crumpled in her hand.

She looked Nick in the eye for the first time since she opened the front door and shook her head, as if pleading. "I could not work more and raise the kids at the same time. I could barely keep them fed as it was. The way we were headed, we would've lost the house and ended up homeless. And then what? Social services would've took *all* my children from me. Do you know what it's like—"

"—You . . . *sold* your son?" Nick interrupted her stream of rationalization.

She averted her gaze back to the window and nodded several times, sniffling. "I gave him cold medicine in the morning so he would go to sleep. Then I took him to the truck stop. I was told to park in the back, where the trucks turned around. A woman came in a black car. She had a baby car seat in the back. She gave me five hundred dollars, and I kissed him on his head and put him in her car seat. He was asleep, and that's the last time I saw him."

She burst into tears again.

Nick got out his notepad. "What time was that?"

"8 a.m."

"How did you contact her?"

"I didn't. The girl at work told me where to go and when."

"Did this woman give you her name when you met her? A number to call if you wanted to talk to Ben?"

She shook her head. "She said it did not work like that. She said I had to stay out of his life. That's how his new parents wanted it."

"And you just gave away your child to someone you did not know?"

"I know you think I'm heartless, but we were broke back then. We *really* needed the money. Even with food stamps, it wasn't enough. This was the best thing I could do for *him* and for my other boys. He could have a better life than we did."

Nick was trying his best not to judge her.

"Did this woman say anything else?"

"She told me what to say to the police. And she told me not to call the police for at least four hours, to make sure Ben was safely on his way to his new family."

Nick wrote all this down. "Did Ben ever contact you after this?"

She shook her head.

"Did this woman tell you where this family was? Were they in Colorado?"

She shook her head again. "She couldn't tell me. She said the adopted parents did not want me to show up in his life and complicate things for him."

Nick nodded. "Do you have any idea why Ben would have been in the Denver area when he died?"

She shook her head again and reached for another tissue.

He thought about telling her about the terrible scars on Ben's skin and the broken bones in his body, but seeing her sobbing into the tissue, he could not bring himself to be so cruel. He would tell her later, once he actually figured out a few things.

"Edie," he said and paused till she looked at him. "You did the right thing telling me this. I need you to do one more thing for me. For Ben. I need you to go to the county sheriff's office and tell them what you told me. You need to make an official statement, so we can find out what happened to Ben. Can you do this for Ben?"

She nodded.

14

Trapped. Hopeless. Desperate. These were all things Edie was probably feeling in 2001, waking every day to her part-time job, four little kids, and a disabled, alcoholic husband. Driving back to Pine Lake, Nick tried to put himself in her shoes. What options would he have? Get a second job? But who would have watched and raised her children, then? Go to night school to learn a trade? That took money and time, again. Give up her children legally by putting them into the system? He felt a bitter sorrow for this woman. What path forward did she have? What escape? It would have been so easy for her to turn to drugs; Nick had seen this plenty of times in his line of work. He may have seen it, but he had never *been* in the place she was in. It wasn't Nick's place or his job to judge her now. Or to defend her. Edie was in a terrible situation, and someone was there to take advantage of her. Someone told her she would be giving Ben a better life, and she was so eager to believe it. She made a terrible choice. She raised three boys by herself. And the price for that was Ben.

When Nick walked through the door of the station, Ray hollered from his office:

"Hey, Severs! You got evidence back from the RCL. I signed for you. Hope you don't mind."

No, Nick did not mind. He had been awaiting the forensics report on Ben's possessions.

Jason was in today. Nick saw his lifted Dodge Ram pickup truck in the parking lot, and now he saw Jason himself—his robust, broad-shouldered frame in a Carhartt jacket behind the front counter, squeezed into a side chair next to Patty. Nick topped off his coffee mug and patted Jason on the shoulder: "Hey, stop by when you are finished here. I want to pick your brain about something."

In Nick's office, there was a large brown paper bag on his desk. It had the word Evidence printed on its side, followed by the identifying case information and the chain-of-custody signatures. Next to it was an office manila envelope with the lab report.

Nick paused before opening the report, like a gambler considering the odds before placing his bet. He really needed something that would help make some sense out of this case. *Any* part of this case. Any useful evidence. Any lead, however weak. Yet, he was to be disappointed. The RCL did not find anything suspicious on the victim's belongings. There were no fingerprints other than his own. There were no traces of DNA in any form other than Ben's own blood on his headphones. And the phone that was found on the victim was a prepaid burner, with location services disabled, and no saved contacts or call history.

Nick opened the evidence bag. It had Ben's clothing and a plastic bag with his personal items. Nick spread out Ben's scant earthly belongings on his desk and examined them one by one—the wallet, the fake ID, the cell phone, and the headphones. None of these things individually or in combination shed any light on what caused his death. For that matter, these things told Nick nothing at all about their owner—not where he lived, and not the circle of people who knew him. Nick had a body and a name, but no victimology to speak of—there was nothing he could say about this victim except that he had been sold for adoption twenty-one years ago and then reappeared dead two weeks ago. Both events were shrouded in mystery.

Nick picked up Ben's phone—a plain black Motorola with a plastic back. It was a cheap feeling, lightweight slab, compared with the premium, glossy Samsungs and iPhones many people liked to flash around. Out of all of Ben's possessions, this phone was Nick's only possible breadcrumb to follow—if he could find where it was purchased and activated, he could possibly find video footage of Ben when he bought it. Between this and the cell-tower dumps, he could determine where Ben was going or where he was coming from.

There was a knock on Nick's door, and when he looked up, he saw Jason towering in the door frame with his big stainless-steel coffee tumbler in his hand and a bright grin on his face.

"You need me?" His voice thundered.

"Yep! Come, sit. I need your expertise."

"Shoot," Jason replied and folded his robust frame into Nick's side chair.

"Do you know of any mining operations by Elk Road off 285?"

Jason stared into the ceiling. "There is the Pine Junction Pit, but it's a couple of miles west, almost in Park County. Nothing closer."

"Do they do much blasting there?"

He shook his head. "No, it's surface only. They do sand and gravel."

Nick chewed his bottom lip.

"Why?" Jason asked.

"The coroner's office says our victim died from a blast injury, which caused fatal brain trauma."

"Hmm. A blast injury . . . in that area?" Jason scratched the back of his neck. "I just don't know what it could have been. Have you checked with Park County?"

"Yep. And Jefferson. I even checked with the air force—nothing. Are there any . . . geological events that could have caused this?"

Jason's mouth formed a pensive pucker. "Hmm. I mean, there *are* fault lines in this area, but I've never heard of an earthquake producing a sonic blast like this. Not to mention, we would have noticed an earthquake." He thought about it. "One thing to consider is gas emission. Given all the old mining tunnels in the area, it's not unusual for a concentrated mass of gas to escape. If it ignited . . . was he burned?"

Nick shook his head.

"When was this, again?"

"Two weeks ago. On the second."

"Hmm. This does not make any sense. Maybe the body was moved after the fact?"

"The medical examiner seems confident he died at that location. This kid was even wearing headphones. How loud would this blast have to be to do this much damage with the headphones in his ears?"

Jason looked at Nick. "He was wearing headphones?"

"Yeah. These." Nick slid the plastic bag with the bloody earbuds toward Jason.

Jason picked up the bag and examined the contents. "Well now, this does add an interesting possibility."

Nick raised an eyebrow. "You mean my mother was right and listening to Linkin Park too loud could have damaged my brain?"

"Ha! No. But have you heard of sonic weapons?"

"Umm. Like sound cannons that the riot police use?"

"Exactly."

"Are you serious? You think he was killed by sound? From these little things? How?"

Jason passed the evidence back to Nick. "I don't know. But if the police sound cannons can deter people from several blocks away, these little earbuds were only a few millimeters away from his brain. Someone could have messed with them, to make them lethal."

Nick scrutinized the headphones closely. They looked pretty normal, except for the few dried spots of blood on the white plastic. "OK, say someone did tamper with these. Why wouldn't the victim just take them out, if a sound was hurting him?"

Jason shrugged. "I have no idea *how* it's possible. I am just telling you it's not *im*-possible. Remember the Havana syndrome?"

Nick nodded.

"All those diplomats in Cuba were exposed to something, and they all had brain-related symptoms—ringing in their ears, headache, blurred vision, dizziness. Some had permanent brain damage. And there are still no answers, but many people suspect it was a sonic weapon of some sort. My point is there is still a lot we don't know about how basic environmental factors can affect humans."

Nick nodded, mulling over Jason's hypothesis. This seemed way out there, even for Jason, but it wasn't as if Nick had better theories to pursue at the moment.

"So, you think a digital forensics lab would be able to tell?"

Jason nodded. "Sounds like a good place to start. In the very least, they could open up those headphones and take a look."

15

On Saturday morning, the offices of OstTech Advisers Ltd. in downtown Kyiv were empty. The usual gaggle of techie, latte-sipping twenty-somethings who inhabited these cubicles and meeting rooms on the weekdays were nowhere to be seen—probably still sleeping at home, or gaming, or whatever else young urban people did on Saturday mornings these days—Anatoli really had no idea. He owned OstTech through a six-layer corporate structure involving four international trust companies, which made his connection to it more or less impossible for anyone to untangle. As far as the outside world was concerned, OstTech Advisers was a legitimate IT firm with legitimate customers. But the part of OstTech visible to the outside world was only the part Anatoli wanted them to see. Right here, in these same offices, a small group of trusted employees worked behind restricted access doors on what the rest of the OstTech staffers believed to be a highly sensitive customer account with very strict data-security requirements. This was not far from the truth. Regular OstTech employees would have been surprised to find that they already knew the customer in question. It was Azarev Enterprises—a legitimate international firm with several legitimate lines of business. It was no secret that OstTech was the primary provider of IT services to Azarev Enterprises. Anatoli had designed it to be that way. But what was a secret, however, was that the small team behind those closed doors supported Azarev's extensive and highly profitable illicit digital operations.

And they were not alone. At another OstTech office in Minsk, another team worked on active measures: hacking, ransomware, and malware. They were his private digital army. And Oleg was his general.

Anatoli liked Oleg. Oleg was his inside man at OstTech. He was the only one here who knew that Anatoli owned the damned place. Oleg knew the shadow side of Anatoli's business like the back of his hand, and he had helped it thrive under the radar of the authorities for almost a decade now. Anatoli trusted him. Oleg was as good with computers as Max was with physical violence. And Max was probably the only person who made Oleg uneasy.

In the panoramic windows of the conference room, the rosy February morning was blooming into a bright, crisp winter day. Twelve floors below, traffic was trickling down the Riverfront Boulevard, next to the serene, snowy banks of Dnipro. A thin, translucent crust of ice covered the deep, black waters. This view was worth the rent on this office.

Anatoli looked at Oleg. "OK, show me."

Oleg nodded and clacked a few keys on his laptop. "So, I've been working on a little side project, and I think it is pretty close to prime time." The large projection screen on the wall lit up, and a web page appeared.

Anatoli looked at the screen—it was an Instagram conversation between someone named Kyle30898 and Hanna. "What is this?"

"Just read," Oleg smirked.

Anatoli got his glasses out of his jacket pocket.

Hanna
I just dont want to go to school anymore . . .

Kyle30898
Is it cause of those bitches?

Hanna
yeah

Kyle30898
don't listen to those sluts
your beautiful

Hanna
you dont mean it

Kyle30898
yes I do
that pic you sent me was fucking hot

Hanna
[blushing emoji]

Kyle30898
I wish I could take you away from all those assholes
and your idiot parents
wish I could just hold you

Anatoli put his glasses on the table. "This looks like a textbook grooming chat. Is this Kyle one of ours?"

"Not exactly." Oleg's lips stretched into a grin. "There is no Kyle."

"What do you mean?"

"Kyle is a bot account controlled by generative AI. One of twenty such bots I set up for this experiment."

"AI? Why?"

"How many Lolis do you have being groomed right now?"

"Globally?"

Oleg nodded.

"I don't know . . . maybe a couple hundred."

"And how many will you be able to use out of these couple hundred?"

"Maybe two dozen."

"Why so few?"

Anatoli shrugged. "You know why. It takes time. The groomer has to identify the right target on social media, connect with them, build trust, and persuade them to meet. It can take months. A lot can happen in that time. It's not an exact science, as they say."

"Right, so, you have a business cycle that takes months and has maybe a ten percent success rate."

Anatoli laughed. "When you put it like that, it sounds pretty lousy."

"Because it is, but it does not have to be."

"With this AI thing?"

"You got it! Your groomers can only go through so many profiles each day, because they have other things to do. But the AI algorithm can be continuously scanning *all* social media sites and cataloging potential targets by gender, age, race, attractiveness, body type. It can follow a target across their TikTok, Instagram, Snapchat, Facebook, or other accounts, and it can assign success markers based on the things they say and like, the neighborhood they live in, social class of their parents, and more. And for any targets that meet threshold success markers, it can then use generative AI to initiate grooming. Which is what you see here."

"So, this *Hanna* is real?"

"Yes. She is fourteen and lives in Bristol. The algorithm estimates success rate with her to be at around eighty-five percent based on the prior grooming chats I fed to the AI to teach it. And that's the beauty of AI—the more we run this model, the more it can learn from the process, and this will improve its efficiency *and* effectiveness. And the best part, the algorithm can do this all day, every day, and everywhere—in any country and in any language. And when the target is ready to meet, the AI can alert your groomer in the area, and he can take over. And the rest . . . you know."

The rest was easy, Anatoli thought. The groomer would meet the girl a few times, building a caring relationship, getting her to trust him more, and further separating her from the other people in her life. He'd be the cool older boy with his own apartment. There would be drugs, alcohol. He'd be caring and romantic—a regular prince charming. Then he would rape her. Brutally. To get the point across. To break her mentally and then begin reconditioning. She'd learn he was the only one who cared about her. That to everyone else she was trash. He would continue supplying her with alcohol and drugs. And she would come back. And the next time, someone else would rape her. And afterward, he would give her money. And she would keep coming back. And that was that. It worked every time. *Easy.*

It was that first part—before the first meeting—that was the bottleneck to scaling. Oleg was a fucking genius, but Anatoli would never tell him this to his face—his hacker ego was already too much to manage. If this AI gizmo worked, they could have a ready supply of teens and preteens just waiting to be put into circulation. This would mean being able to grow and expand into new cities much faster. Oleg did not know this, but this new higher capacity was coming at just the right time.

"Can it work on boys?" Anatoli asked.

Oleg laughed. "Yeah . . . sure it can."

"OK. What do you need to get this going?"

"I need to run the algorithm through a full cycle. I can keep going with Bristol, or let me know if there is another city you want, and I will have the algorithm find and groom new candidates."

"Bristol is fine. Add a couple of boys and let me know when they are ready. I will have Jerome put someone on them."

"You got it, boss." Oleg shut the lid of his laptop.

16

"Oh, hell," Beck grumbled on the other end of the phone line when Nick told him about Edie's confession. "I have to say, I am not terribly surprised. Something had always bothered me about the mother in this case."

"Like what?"

"Just her behavior, afterward. It was a little . . . atypical. She was distraught when we were there for the initial investigation. But then, as months went by, she never reached out. Most parents would call regularly to check on the progress and heck, even express frustration if there were no results, but not her. I'd call her every now and then with updates, but she herself stopped calling. I knew she had a disabled husband and three other kids, and they were poor, so I assumed that was just it. But still, it never sat right with me."

"Did you ever suspect her?"

"We always scrutinize the parents. I thought maybe the father was somehow involved. Sometimes, where there are alcoholics, there is violence. Kids can get hurt. Killed. So, we looked. We looked hard. But nothing came of it. We found nothing that contradicted her story of what happened."

"Have you ever heard of kids sold for adoption?" Nick asked.

"Unfortunately, yes. There was another case a few months after Ben was taken. A little boy was abducted in Tulsa. Trevor. A friend of mine was assigned to that case. The mother was inconsistent about the details, so he pressed her, and she confessed she sold her boy to an adoption agency. She said very similar things—they told her what to say, what to do, to ensure the investigation would not go anywhere."

"Did your friend find this kid?"

"No."

"What about this adoption agency?"

"No. Not exactly." Beck went silent.

"What do you mean?"

"There was no adoption agency. Based on the description the mother gave, we connected that case to another ongoing investigation."

"What other investigation? Into what?"

"An international child-trafficking ring."

Nick felt his stomach turn. "Trafficking? You are saying Ben's mother sold him to child traffickers?"

"I am afraid that's the most likely scenario, given the information she gave you."

Nick stared at his computer screen, where a photo of little Ben, cropped from the same photo Edie showed him, stared back at him with those serious eyes from a page of the FBI file. As hard as it was to imagine this being possible, the story of Ben Harris just took a darker turn. Up until this point, there was room for less terrible possibilities. There was even room for Edie's reality, in which Ben was adopted by some wealthy childless couple. But life was not a Hallmark movie. Far from it.

"Did you ever uncover this ring?" he asked Beck.

"Based on the description we got from Trevor's mother, we were tracking a couple—a man and a woman with connections to eastern Europe. We knew they operated between Dallas, Oklahoma City, and Phoenix. There could have been other cities we did not know about. We had a sting operation in the works, but then 9/11 happened, and most of our resources got reassigned. When we finally managed to regroup in late 2001, the trail had gone cold. We suspected they used false identities to flee the country. And that was that."

"I don't get the whole adoption agency act. If they just wanted the children, why not just kidnap them? Why pay the parents money?"

"To have the parents on their side. To have them subvert the investigation. If the parents delayed reporting their child missing, or if they gave false evidence, this gave the traffickers more time to get clear from the area. They could take the child quietly and smuggle them more easily. Paying the parents for adoption ensured the parents had a vested interest in making the investigation fail. And why wouldn't they, if they believed they were sending their child to a better life?"

"Right." This scenario certainly fit Edie's situation. "OK, so, these traffickers . . . what do you think they did with Ben?"

"To them, a child is just a product, just like several kilos of coke or a box of counterfeit Gucci handbags. Their job is to move the product—either further down the supply chain or to the buyer. There are people who specialize in this. Whole organizations. We are not talking about one or two kids a month. Over three thousand children went missing around the world last year. There is a global market. There is a constant demand."

"What type of a demand?"

"Well, depends on the country they are sold into. A small percentage may actually be sold through shady adoption agencies, usually into the developed countries. In the developing countries, children are usually sold for labor. Farms, factories, fisheries—whatever the local industry. In some places like the Middle East and south Asia, they may be sold into domestic servitude. In Africa, it could be for mining or even private military. But pretty much universally, in any country including the US, stolen children often end up in sex trafficking."

"Sex trafficking?!"

"Yes—child prostitution."

"But Ben . . . he was only two."

Beck sighed. "I wish I had something better to tell you, Detective Severs, but there are real monsters living among us, with an appetite for that kind of thing. I can tell you this—I've seen photos and videos I wish I never had. I've seen what happens to these kids. These cases get under your skin."

Nick wasn't always an optimist, but right now, his reality refused to accept the possibility that Ben's mother had unwittingly handed him over to child sex traffickers. This was too terrible a twist of fate to consider. But he still had to explore this dark alley. If this was where things were leading, he had to follow

"OK, and then what happens? How do the traffickers pimp out the kids? On the dark web?"

"Sometimes. But usually what we find on the dark web is child porn. The actual trafficking usually happens on the regular internet—what we call *Clearnet*."

"Really? Why? Wouldn't the dark web provide more protection for the traffickers?"

"It would, but using the dark web requires a certain degree of technical savvy. Most of the traffickers' customers would not know the first thing about how to use it. But Facebook, Snapchat, Craigslist—everyone knows these, so that's what they use. Sometimes they list in the personals. Other times they list under services like housekeeping or massage. They will use fake photos to make the listings look legitimate but will use coded words. Like *roses* or *candy* means money. *Loli* means *Lolita*—an underage girl. *Body rubs* means—well, you get it."

"*Lolita* . . . like from Nabokov's novel?"

"Correct."

"So, if we know how they are doing this, can't we crack down on this? With today's technology?"

"We can and we do. Technology can help law enforcement, but on the flipside, it also makes just about every aspect of a trafficker's life easier—easier to recruit victims, easier to find customers, easier to get paid, and easier to cover their tracks. By the time we crack down on one site or app, they figure out how to use another. A few years back, we took down this site called Backpage.com. It was a notorious classifieds site for sex trade, including underage. Within weeks, copycat sites started popping up. It's a never-ending cycle. And it's not just in the US—it's a global issue. And the web just makes it all very easily accessible."

"Hmm," Nick said and wrote down *Backpage.com*. "And then what happens, after a pedophile finds an ad they are interested in? Does it work like any other prostitution deal?"

"Pretty much. They contact the number or social media account, which is managed by the pimp, and meet them somewhere—hotels, motels, massage parlors. Every big city has deals like this going down every day. Not as many as adult prostitution, but still plenty. These people will even travel to other cities for sex with minors. We call it sex tourism. Some even travel abroad."

"*Sex* tourism?"

"Yes. People will travel to places with more supply or lower risk. Some countries make it a lot easier to find and pay for sex with minors. Southeast Asia, South America, and eastern Europe are all common destinations for this purpose. Now, with the pandemic, travel has slowed down for a couple of years, but web streaming has been driving demand even higher. We are finding more and more live child pornography streaming services. And with the web, such operations can be all over the globe without having to physically move the kids across borders or state lines. But . . . all this did not exist when Ben was kidnapped. The internet was just getting started." Beck was silent for a moment. "Have you had any luck with the cause of death?"

"Well, there is progress, but not a lot of answers yet. The medical examiner confirmed that Ben died of a brain trauma, but we still don't know what caused it. I need to find a good digital forensics lab to analyze his phone."

"Hmm. I tell you what. The FBI has an RCFL—a Regional Computer Forensics Laboratory in Denver. Let me make a call. They should be able to help you with that phone. Electronics is all they do."

"Yeah!" Nick was ready for a lucky break. "That would be great. And hey, would you mind sending me anything you have on that trafficking ring? Maybe it will help jog the mother's memory."

Nick hung up and sat in his darkening office. The sun had already dipped below the jagged mountains a while ago, but his office lights were not on, and the only light came from his computer screen glowing softly, illuminating Nick's desk, but not quite reaching into the murky corners of his office.

The possibility that Ben may have been sexually trafficked as a child loomed darkly over this case, despite Nick's strongest desire for it not to be true. What else besides years of abuse could have left all those scars on the young man's body? How easily had he been snatched from normal life and disappeared into this sickening underworld. A few hours were all it took to change the course of his life forever. The few hours that Edie waited before notifying the authorities.

What kind of monsters made it their business to traffic children? This was Nick's first brush with this insidious industry. According to Beck, it thrived just beneath a thin veneer in "civilized" society, hidden behind innocuous coded words and messages on websites Nick himself had been to. Until now, Nick had a perfectly simple view on the online world. There was the "normal" internet—or Clearnet, as Beck had called it—filled with company websites and social media platforms that consisted mostly of people's selfies, babies, and kittens. And then there was the *dark* web, where, naturally, all the illegal stuff lived—drugs, sex, murder for hire. Of course, from time to time, the evil crept up into Clearnet. A mass shooter's live stream, a hateful rant, revenge porn. But these ugly things did not survive in the sunlight. The custodians of

Clearnet always acted fast to remove them, and everything went back to normal again.

This neat equilibrium of the internet versions of heaven and hell seemed like a natural order of things to Nick, and the two sides seemed as easy to tell apart as the difference between a neighborhood Applebee's family restaurant and a seedy biker bar in the bottoms of the city.

Until now.

He looked at the note he made while talking with Beck. *How thin was the veneer?* He opened his internet browser and typed in "Backpage.com." A page appeared with a half dozen US law enforcement shields across the top, ranging from the FBI to the Postal Service. The message below the shields stated that this site had been seized by the US Department of Justice.

Nick typed "backpage alternatives" into the search bar. Google brought back over one and a half million results. Nick clicked the first one, promisingly named Bedpage.com—it was a classifieds site that looked like Craigslist, with a list of states and cities on the home page. He clicked Denver and was deposited on a full page of category links that looked pretty much like any other classifieds—from furniture for sale to real estate, cars, boats, electronics, and fashion. Everything here was as expected. Except it wasn't. Nick clicked a few categories and was taken to empty pages. No one was selling cars here. There was nothing under Power Tools. Nothing in Men's Shoes. Out of over a hundred categories listed on the page, the only listings he could find were under Spa and Massage. When Nick clicked this category, he was taken aback by the explosion of colorful emojis decorating a full page of links. Like bright children's stickers, there were hearts, stars, lips, and rainbows, and flowers from roses to orchids, and cherries and peaches and lollipops, all intermingled with words that promised "new girls," "hot and young," "big breasts," "soft touch," "curvy body," "full service." Nick couldn't believe his eyes. He never expected this to be so obvious. With apprehension, he clicked one of the emoji-stickered links and was taken to a listing that featured photos of young, half-nude Asian women and advertised the services provided including body rubs, erotic massage, tongue, and even happy endings. "New girls every week," the ad claimed. He clicked another ad—more variations on the same theme. He clicked a few more.

Suggestive photos. Suggestive language. There was no doubt these ads were promoting prostitution services. When he was a beat cop in Kansas City, Nick had dealt with plenty of prostitutes and pimps. Prostitution was an open secret in every city in the country—everyone knew it was illegal, and everyone knew it was happening. But Nick had never seen it advertised so openly. And the girls all looked so young. Not quite children, but still young. Could they have been underage? It was hard to tell. Some of the photos appeared to be computer generated, which made those ads even more suspicious—who were the real girls behind these ads? How old were they, really? There were several dozen listings for Denver. Could a few of them be for children? Nick scrolled through the long page of colorfully stickered listings. How could someone tell? What was the code? Did the rainbow emoji mean something? The lollipops? The flowers?

Nick checked Colorado Springs—there were dozens of listings there, too. And more for Fort Collins, Pueblo, Boulder, and Grand Junction. Some listed addresses of massage spas, some gave phone numbers, some Telegram accounts. Ads were being added every day. Even *today*. *New girls every week*. Where did these *new girls* come from every week? Where did they go the next week? Nick clicked a few more listings, searching for any clues. More suggestive photos. More faces. More colorful emojis. Nick felt sickened. How could this exist here, on the same Clearnet as Facebook with its kittens and babies? With one simple Google search, Nick had found himself face to face with the grimy underworld of escort services, and he knew he had only scratched the surface. This was just *one* site. If this was right here in the open, what else was out there, hidden with just a little bit more care from the unintended eyes?

17

Nick tried his best to be good. This was Claire's weekend off, and he made every effort to resist checking his work email. Until 5:42 on Saturday afternoon, when his self-discipline caved in. Claire was in the kitchen, chopping potatoes and onions, and Nick had just lit the charcoal grill for the steaks. Returning from the patio with the lighter in his pocket and bourbon in his hand, he made an impulsive detour through their living room, where he quickly pulled out his work computer from the bag and powered it on. Surely enough—there was an email from Beck with two attachments. Nick double-clicked the first one without hesitation.

This was the case file of Trevor Simeka, age four, who was reported missing on June 17, 2001, from his home in Tulsa, Oklahoma. First was the initial missing person report, followed with a signed affidavit from the mother, Maureen Simeka, in which she admitted to placing Trevor in private adoption through an unknown woman who paid her five hundred dollars. There were many more pages in the file, but Nick did not have time to read them all now. He double-clicked the second attachment.

This was the file on the suspected child traffickers—Victor and Irina Talenko, a couple from Phoenix, Arizona, who were at that time aged thirty-two and thirty, respectively. Victor was a salesman for a gearbox manufacturer and traveled extensively through the Southwest and the Midwest, visiting various manufacturing and production plants. Irina was a medical transcriptionist working from home. Both were naturalized American citizens since 1999, having emigrated from Belarus in January 1992. Nick opened the internet browser and googled Belarus. It was an eastern European country west of Russia and north of Ukraine. The file contained several scanned photos—the naturalization headshots and then a series of surveillance shots showing a couple getting out of a station wagon at a gas station. Nick decided that in the naturalization photos, they both definitely looked eastern European. Victor had a round face and light brown hair. Irina had a sharp chin and dark eyes. Neither of them was smiling, but perhaps they were told not to.

"What'cha reading, there?" Claire's voice over his shoulder startled him, and he almost spilled his bourbon. She was standing behind the couch with a wineglass in her hand.

"Jeez, Claire," he laughed. "How are you so sneaky?"

"I am not," she said, smiling and taking a sip of her wine. "I called you. Twice. But you didn't answer, so I came looking for you."

"Sorry," he said. "I just wanted to take a look at this new information my FBI guy sent me."

"Who are these people?" she asked, leaning in for a closer look.

"Victor and Irina Talenko—our suspected child traffickers."

"You think they took that kid from Walsenburg? . . . *Ben*?"

He nodded. "They were key suspects in another abduction in Tulsa a few months after Ben. The FBI thought they were responsible for a whole string of kidnappings."

"Did they get caught?"

"No. They just disappeared. Probably used false identities to leave the country."

"Why do you think they were responsible for Ben's kidnapping?"

"It looks like their MO—to fake an adoption."

She nodded. "Are you going to look for them?"

"I'm going to give it a try. It *has* been over twenty years."

"Want me to look into it?" she said casually.

He watched her for a second, trying to determine if she was joking. She held a great poker face. "*You*, as in you and Roses?" he finally said. "Hacking? No thanks. I appreciate the intention, but I need to keep this investigation on the legal side. Especially with the FBI now looking over my shoulder."

She gave him a slight *I don't care* shrug and took another sip. "Is the grill ready for the steaks?"

He looked at the grill on the other side of the sliding patio door; the lighter-fluid blaze had pretty much died down. "Yep," he said and closed the laptop.

3!ght33n

Claire got home from her night shift just as Nick was leaving for the day. They kissed *hello* and *goodbye*, said their *I love yous*, and then he went off to work while she showered and crawled into bed, where his side was still warm.

She set her alarm for noon. She could have slept longer, but she was going to be off for the next two days, and she wanted to get onto Nick's schedule, to maximize their time together. When the alarm went off, she lay there for a while, listening to its insistent ring and fighting the desire to reset it for another hour. She finally turned it off and lay in bed for a few more minutes, getting her fuzzy brain focused on the day ahead. Eventually, she forced herself up, put on a T-shirt, and went to the kitchen to make coffee. With a hot mug in her hands, she settled on the couch in the living room. She did not turn on the TV, leaving its big rectangle black, like a dark mirror reflecting her even darker silhouette on the couch, backlit by the daylight in the window behind her. The house was quiet, and the street was quiet. She took a sip of coffee and sat still, soaking in this moment of midday suburban zen. The mail truck pulled up outside, and she distinctly heard the metal snap of their mailbox door open and then close. She liked being home during the daytime. There was something peaceful about this time of the day. With kids at school, and most of the adults at work, their street grew deserted—interrupted only by the occasional delivery truck or a contractor van. Sometimes, ten or more minutes could go by without anything happening. It was as if time itself had slowed down.

But there was also something eerie about this time. With most of the residents gone, this place felt postapocalyptic. Or post-society. The quiet created a vacuum of visible activity, but Claire knew this was a deceptive quiet. There were still people around, in some of the houses, behind the closed doors. Just as the graveyard shift was a peculiar subculture outside the flow of mainstream society, so were the *daytime people*. They existed everywhere. Here, on Claire's street, and on thousands of other quiet, suburban streets around Denver. When most residents of this world left their homes for work or school every weekday, the daytime people did not. They watched TV—maybe Netflix or maybe the actual *daytime* TV, with its endless reruns of sitcoms and game shows. They went to the stores during the day—not the busy weeknights and weekends, like the rest of the population. Because Claire worked the graveyard shift, and got to come home in the morning, she probably witnessed the existence of the daytime people more than the average mainstream nine-to-fiver did.

She knew some of them on her street—some were retired, some worked from home, answering emails and getting on back-to-back Zoom calls. Some were taking care of their preschool kids. And some were probably up to no good. Claire's mother used to tell her that "nothing decent ever happened after sunset" and used to ground Claire for sneaking out at night. But Claire thought that much, if not most, evil happened in between sunrise and sunset, right under her mother's God's eye. It only made sense—those were the hours most people were awake, so naturally, that's when most evil took place. Somewhere, behind one of those closed doors, someone was having an affair. Someone was committing a burglary. Someone was committing a murder. Or abducting a child. Or selling their child to traffickers.

Ever since Nick told her about the case he was working on, Claire's thoughts kept returning to it. Those two poor boys—sold by their mothers within months of each other. She recalled the photo she had seen in her US history class in college—black and white, from a newspaper, showing four little kids sitting on the stoop of their house with their mother standing behind them, hiding her face from the camera, and a cardboard sign in the yard: "4 Children for Sale—Inquire Within." This was in the late forties, if she remembered correctly, in Chicago. The teacher told them those kids had in fact been sold into different adopted families. Some of those sold kids could still be alive today. She thought of the little patients recovering from injuries and surgeries in her hospital ward. Most would recover completely and go on to live normal lives. It was comforting to know that modern medical science could fix them. But what about children sold by their parents? Trafficked? Was there anything that would ever fix the emotional trauma and scars? Did they have any chance of living a normal life again?

If the boys from Nick's case had been sold to the same trafficking ring, maybe they met each other. There couldn't have been more than one child-trafficking ring in that area, or could there? She googled "child trafficking" on her phone and read a couple of articles, absorbing data from various agencies and the horrifying investigative reports. Until now, she had only a sketchy understanding of child trafficking. Of course, the recent Jeffrey Epstein trial was a wake-up call for many, pushing the issue into the light, but even though she knew that the Epstein scandal was only the tip of a larger iceberg, she really had no idea how big this issue was. If anything, the Epstein scandal, with its focus on the luxury lifestyle and the involvement of politicians and even royalty, made this appear less *common*. As if it were no more than depravity at the whim of the mega-rich. But the reality of child trafficking was not limited to luxury apartments in New York and Paris, or private jets, or opulent Caribbean island estates. The reality was that a baby could be easily bought for as little as $400 in Southeast Asia. The reality was that fair-skinned boys cost more, and darker-skinned girls cost less. The reality was that there were whole networks of doctors, government officials, and illegal adoption agencies throughout the world that continuously supplied thousands and thousands of children to be sold for forced labor and sex. The reality was that in the US, one in seven reported missing children was to end up in the sex trade. The reality was that the number was likely higher, because most reported missing children were never found. The reality was that in Thailand, child traffickers would intentionally maim and cripple the kids they bought so they could make more money begging in the streets.

Claire stopped reading and threw her phone down on the couch. This world disgusted her. It was an ugly, cruel place. What kind of unspeakably horrible lives did the two boys in Nick's case live after being sold? With one of them now dead, was there any hope the other one was still alive?

What Claire wanted to do now more than anything was to open her laptop. She wanted to get her hands on those FBI files and start following the breadcrumbs—names, government records, phone carrier databases. She wanted to dig into this case and find these traffickers. Nick said they had vanished, but no one ever vanished completely. Claire knew where to start looking, and if she needed more help, she could reach out to Roses.

Roses. Claire took a deep breath and exhaled slowly, with control. This voice she was now hearing in her head, this fevered pitch was not *Claire* thinking—this was *Kat*, her hacker alter ego who until a few months ago ruled over much of Claire's life. But not anymore. Claire had banished Kat because Kat had gotten out of control and had almost wrecked the unsuspecting Nick's life. And Claire loved Nick. Claire did not want Nick's life wrecked. And sure, there was once a time when Claire needed Kat, because Claire was broken, and becoming a hacker named Kat helped her regain power and control in this life. But power and control were addictive. Claire had to stop before she had gone too far. Kat had to go. Claire did not need Kat now. Kat was just a device that helped her transition from Katie to Claire. Now Kat, and Roses, and the rest of that in-between life had been shut out of Claire's universe.

There was no Katie now. There was no Kat. There was only Claire now. That simple but powerful act of changing her name had really helped her heal. Claire had not been raped. Claire had not been a hacker. Claire was a nurse, and her boyfriend was a cop. They were just a normal couple who went to their friends' parties and contemplated having kids and talked with each other about such things as work, household appliances, and vacation plans. Claire was acclimating to this new life. Assimilating. She wanted to. What else was there for her? When she looked back at her past life, she felt like she had been a dandelion seed carried by the wind from one place to the next, until she landed in this one. With Nick. He was her grounding force. She trusted him, perhaps more than she trusted herself at times. The only other person she trusted this much was Roses. But Roses *was* the wind. And Claire was very aware that if she weren't careful, the wind could sweep her away again. Away from Nick. Away from this life. And she did not want that. Kat had to remain banished. And the laptop had to remain shut.

Her phone buzzed with an incoming call. She turned it over to see the number. Uncle Alex.

"Hey," she answered.

"Shoot! Did I wake you? I did not check the time before I called."

"No. I was just . . . thinking."

"That sounds serious! How are you doing?"

"Good." She smiled into the phone, even though he could not see it. "*All* good. Are you and Santi still going on vacation? When is it . . . in two weeks?"

She heard him sigh. "No. We decided we could not leave the restaurant for a whole week."

"Again?! You guys are workaholics. You are going to burn out and kill the business and possibly each other."

He chuckled. "No, no. We will go later in the year. Santi just really wanted to get this spring menu figured out. Besides—we live in Florida. It's like a vacation every day."

"I don't believe you," she said.

He laughed. "OK, you are right. It's not. But hey, the reason I called . . . for your mom's funeral, what do you think about waiting till her birthday in June and doing like a celebration-of-life party?"

She gave it consideration. "I actually really like that. I think it has a nice balance to it."

"Good. I can make another trip back in April or May and clean up the house a bit—we can do the party there."

"That would be nice. Let me know when you are coming out—I'll come and help."

"Perfect! We can talk about what you want to do with the place, then."

"Yep," she agreed, mechanically. Honestly, since coming back from Cape Girardeau, she had avoided thinking about this topic. Even being there, seeing her mother for the last time and holding her hand for the last time and for the first time in so many years—even all that did not induce a profound shift in Claire. Not right there and then, at least. But as she thought about it now, she was struck by the realization that there were actually now two reasons for her avoiding this subject. The first one she was well familiar with. It was old muscle memory by now. When Claire returned home to her mother after the rape, she left again several months later, feeling unheard and unhealed. Although her mother gave her what sympathy she was capable of, it came with a generous helping of shame and guilt. Sure, their relationship had been complicated for some time even before the rape, but at that point, Claire could not take it anymore. And so, she left, and for all these years, she had let her mother be the keeper of the past. And Claire found strength in that. Her mother and the past she held had become the opposite of Claire's true north—had become the point she was moving forward *from*. And now, with her mother gone, the past, too, seemed to have been released, becoming more distant and fainter with each day. This was a strange, lighter feeling. But it was also disorienting. Without that something to run away from, how was she to know the right way to go?

She now realized this was the second reason she was avoiding thinking about her mother and her past in Cape Girardeau. She had a career and a life she and Nick were trying to build. A *normal* life. A year ago, this would have all seemed like a fantasy. A year ago, she did not even want this. She had a different purpose then. Did she have a purpose now? What was it?

"Can I ask you something personal?" she said into her phone.

"Of course," her uncle replied without hesitation.

"How did you . . . start over after being away for so long? Was it hard?"

He chuckled on the other end. "Yeah. It absolutely was, even though I had twenty-three years to do nothing else but think about it. After all those years, there wasn't much left of my old self. Over time, my prior life got reduced to only a memory in the rearview mirror. I walked out a middle-aged man with no concept of who I really was."

"So, how did you know who you were supposed to be?"

"In prison, each breath I took was not my own—it was a payment of penance. When I got out, I wondered how many more breaths I had left in this life. I know, it may sound melodramatic, but that's the truth. Each breath of freedom I took was like a pact. A transaction with the universe—what would I give back? If I dropped dead tomorrow, would anybody say my life made a difference?"

"So, what did you decide?"

"I probably could have made some loftier goals, but I decided to start simple and only do those things that made me feel good about myself."

"And do you? . . . Still feel good about yourself?"

"It can be a daily test, but it works."

They were both silent for a moment.

"What's troubling you?" he finally asked.

"Nothing . . . just the whole thing with Mom. Closure of things, I suppose."

"You wanna talk about it?"

"Maybe later," she said.

She hung up with her uncle, and the screen of her phone returned to the child-trafficking article she had been reading before. The eyes of a small, dirty boy were looking up at her from one of the streets somewhere in Southeast Asia.

There was no denying that being Kat used to make Claire feel good. For the most part, it also made her feel good about herself. It wasn't all about power and control. It was also about justice, and about getting to those who believed they were beyond the reach of justice. Claire had no doubt Nick had the best intentions when it came to solving this case, but how far would he get? What if these traffickers were still in business? If they were, from everything Claire read today, they would be online. They would be using web streaming and private chat rooms and dark-web servers, but also, they would be on Clearnet—on social networks, personals, and porn sites. *Online* was Kat's world.

Perhaps she could let Kat out, just a little bit? What was the harm in having Kat just take a look? She knew Nick was trying his best, but he was getting nowhere. Kat could really sink her nails into this case and drag out something useful. Something Nick could use. And this would also make Claire feel good. Something to get her out of the doldrums of the endless treadmill of work and sleep. Something to give her something else to define her life besides her mother's death.

And ultimately, this wasn't *about* Claire—this was about the two stolen boys and the child-trafficking syndicate that was probably still in operation. She had a chance to do some good here. To help bring about justice. How could this be wrong?

She looked at the side of her laptop buried under a stack of magazines on the coffee table. The metal edge gleamed like a knife. Her blood quickened. Without hesitation, she reached over, grabbed her laptop, and opened it.

First, she had to get the files from Nick's work laptop. Nick was at the station, but it did not matter. Even if his laptop was at home, he had a pretty strong password protecting it. She knew this because she herself taught Nick how to create a very strong password. It would have taken her some time to brute-force crack it. But she did not need to. She knew there was an unpatched Remote Desktop Protocol vulnerability on his laptop, and so she used the hidden admin account she had set up a long time ago to log into his laptop while he was logged into it at work. Easy-peasy.

As she looked around his files, she had to chuckle to herself. Nick's penchant for organization was almost to a fault, and in his neatly organized file directory, it took her no time at all to find the reports. In the same directory she also noticed a spreadsheet titled P@$$words, and she had to frown to herself—she would need to talk to Nick about getting a proper password manager app. She copied the Talenko case file to her own laptop and also grabbed the FBI's Ben Harris disappearance report just in case.

She then deleted the RDP session logs—not that Nick would know to check the logs, but it was a habit, and Kat's old habits died hard—and then logged out of Nick's laptop. She took a breath. Possibly the first since she had opened her laptop a few minutes ago. Here she was—on the couch in the living room, with her MacBook open and two fresh folders of confidential information at her fingertips. It was just like the old days. She smiled.

19

The tower-dump request came through in the early afternoon. Nick held his breath as he downloaded the data spreadsheet and searched the logs for Ben's number. There was one hit—in Shaffers Crossing, at 6:17 p.m. on Wednesday, February 2. There were no pings recorded in Conifer or Bailey. Ben must have kept his phone turned off until he got to Shaffers Crossing. Still, this was something—the first trace of Ben prior to his body being found. Nick could request another data dump from towers north of Conifer, but first it was worth a shot to do some old-school canvassing. He printed out the headshot of Ben he got from the county forensic artist and headed to Shaffers Crossing, planning to start with the small two-pump gas station at the country store there.

The clerk at the country store worked on February 2 but did not recall seeing anyone who looked like Ben. Nick reviewed the security-camera footage for that late afternoon and early evening but did not find anyone matching Ben, either. He drove to Conifer and talked with the clerk at the Sinclair gas station, but got the same result. He was sitting in the parking lot of the Sinclair, looking for more places to try, when he received a call from the FBI's Rocky Mountain Regional Computer Forensics Laboratory telling him that his evidence was ready for pickup.

* * *

The RCFL was located in a corporate park in Centennial—an upscale suburb south of Denver with broad streets and mature trees. Nick liked mature trees. He felt sorry for the families who were buying newly built houses in some of the growing subdivisions in Highlands Ranch, Castle Rock, and Aurora. New builds did not get tall, leafy aspens and alders or the towering green cones of spruces and firs. New builds got twigs barely ten feet tall held in place with a couple of posts and baling wire. Nick wondered if these families knew it would take ten years or more for those twigs to actually become grown trees.

In the RCFL reception area, Nick was met by Kelsey Simms, a brunette in her late twenties, with gray slacks and blue blouse peeking out from under her white lab coat.

"It's nice to meet you, Agent Simms," Nick shook her hand.

"It's actually *Examiner* Simms," she smiled, and gave Nick a business card that identified her as a senior forensic examiner.

"Let's go look at your phone," she said and scanned her badge at the door, letting Nick into a large room with a half-dozen workbenches, each connected to the drop ceiling with twisted umbilicals of data and power cables. Some of the workbenches had computer monitors and keyboards on them. Others held various scientific-looking electronic boxes with switches, dials, screens, and wires. Nick had no idea what any of them were.

Examiner Simms scanned her badge again at the evidence locker and took out a plastic tub containing Ben's phone and the headphones.

"It's a peculiar thing," she said, setting the tub on the workbench. She took out the plastic bag containing the headphones and put it in front of Nick. "Were you already aware that these headphones had been damaged beyond the working condition?" she asked.

Nick shook his head, taking a closer look at the white earbuds through the clear plastic. They looked intact enough to him. Almost new, in fact, save for a few dried specks of Ben's blood on the hard white plastic of the earpieces.

"The damage is actually inside," she said. "Let me show you." She put on a pair of latex examination gloves with the efficiency of a medical professional. She then slid the headphones from the bag onto the surface of the workbench and pulled down the long, articulating arm of the magnifier light. "Do you know much about how speakers work?"

Nick waved his hand about. "Just the basics. I know there is a cone and a round magnet. The magnet makes the cone go back and forth, pushing air."

"Exactly. And it's the same in these tiny headphones, but everything is just a lot smaller." She turned on the magnifying light and used a metal dentist's pick to pry off the plastic cap from one of the headphones—the one with the letter *R* embossed on it. Inside was a small gray disk soldered to two tiny wires.

"This is your cone," she said, pointing at the gray circle with the pick. "But the interesting part is in the back." She pried the tiny speaker out of the plastic enclosure and turned it over, still attached to the two wires. "I've done some microsurgery here," she said, "to get to the innards, but you can see—here is the circular magnet, and here is the part of the cone that moves inside the magnet, called the voice coil."

Nick leaned closer to the magnifier, watching as she pointed out the microscopic components.

"Now, normally, the voice coil should look like nice shiny copper wire wrapped around that cylinder." She turned the magnifying lamp closer to Nick. "What you see here is very much not normal."

Nick followed the line of her metal pick to the small cylinder at the back of the cone. He could still make out the numerous loops of wire wound around it, but the wire was not shiny or copper in color. It looked dark brown, almost black, with a burned, bubbled-up, uneven surface.

"What would cause this type of damage?" he asked.

"Heat," she said without hesitation. "The dark bubbled stuff you see is the glue that normally holds the loops of wire in place. The fact that this glue liquefied and burned like this means the voice coil was subjected to abnormally high heat."

"And what could cause such abnormally high heat? The rest of the headphones don't look melted."

She nodded. "This means the heat was caused by what's called over-excursion—the voice coil moving too far outside the magnetic ring, causing a magnetic short circuit, which generates heat. If this continues for a prolonged duration, the voice coil will be damaged in the manner we see here."

As Nick's high school science teacher used to say, it was important to ask *why* at least three times before one could get to the root cause of things. Sometimes it took more than three. Nick had a strong suspicion Senior Forensic Examiner Simms was taking him on a journey to discover the root cause.

"And *why* would the voice coil experience such prolonged over-excursion?" he asked.

"Only one reason—an ultralow frequency from a high-power source."

"*Ultra-low?* So . . . loud bass?" Nick did his best to translate the scientific-sounding root cause into street speak.

She smiled. "In essence. But not just any bass. The frequency in this case was so low, it was actually in the infrasound range."

"Infrasound?"

"Yes. Humans can generally hear sound in the frequency range between 20 to 20,000 hertz. Anything below 20 hertz is called *infrasound*, and it is not audible to humans. However, even though humans can't *hear* infrasound, it can still affect them. This is because of something called *resonant frequencies*. Are you familiar with the term?"

Nick shook his head.

"Basically, all objects—living or not—have a natural frequency at which they vibrate. Imagine a child swinging on a swing. The child going back and forth is a frequency. If we push the swing in rhythm with the child swinging, we can make the child go higher and higher—basically amplifying their frequency. That's what a resonant frequency is—it matches the natural vibration of the object and therefore amplifies it. At high enough levels, resonant frequency can actually damage or break the object. Think of the classic cartoon scenario where an opera singer shatters a wineglass with her voice. This has actually been proven possible. It takes a very powerful singer, but if she can sustain a volume of around 105 decibels for a few seconds and just happens to match the resonant frequency of the glass, the glass will shatter. And humans are not immune to resonant frequencies, either. We are very complex objects with many parts and organs that have different densities and compositions and therefore different resonant frequencies. For example, it is known that the human eye has a resonant frequency of around 19 hertz, which is just below the audible limit. When exposed to this frequency, people report blurred vision or seeing artifacts in their peripheral vision. This has been used to explain some of the haunted locations by paranormal researchers, who claimed that something like an old boiler in the basement or damaged ventilation fan can create the vibrations causing people to see *ghosts*." She added air quotes around the last word. "And this is at just below the audible frequency. When we go lower in frequency and higher in power, things turn ugly very quickly. At around 15 hertz, people experience disorientation, nausea, anxiety, and trouble communicating. At around 8 hertz, they struggle breathing. It's generally believed that at around 7 hertz, high-powered infrasound will cause vibration of internal organs so severe as to produce tissue damage, bleeding, cardiac arrhythmia, and seizures."

"—And brain trauma?"

"I don't see why not. But there hasn't been much research published on this topic, for obvious ethical reasons. The harmful effects of infrasound were first discovered by a French scientist, Vladimir Gavreau, in the '50s. This was in the middle of the Cold War, and there have been some reports of both the Soviet Union and the West conducting military research in this area, but none of it has been made public. Published civilian research has focused on identifying environmental safety thresholds for infrasound in applications like heavy machinery, spaceflight, wind farms, and urban planning. But this does not mean there are no military applications. Do you remember the mysterious diplomat illnesses at the US embassy in Cuba a few years ago?"

Nick had come to expect that Jason's overeducated brain generated a fair amount of conspiracy theories, but he was not used to them being confirmed by an accredited scientific professional. "Yes. The Havana syndrome?"

She nodded. "One theory was that the diplomats were exposed to an infrasonic weapon of some sort. Their symptoms were consistent with this."

"But none of them died from it, right?"

"No, but they were exposed to a source far away, through building walls. Not headphones on their head."

"So, you really think this victim was killed by a sound he could not hear?"

She nodded. "Given the injuries he sustained, this is the most likely cause."

"But why would this happen? With all the millions, maybe billions of phones and headphones out there in the world, has this ever happened before?"

She shook her head. "No. Because phones have safety limiters built into them to cap the sound level at about 70-80 decibels. Anything louder than that is considered unsafe for human hearing. But"—she reached into the evidence bin and took out Ben's cell phone—"this particular phone was tampered with to deliver almost twice that much power."

"Tampered with? How?"

"This phone has malware on it that I've never seen before. It's very simple—it does only two things. It bypasses the volume limiter of the phone and also modulates any audible sound down to 6 hertz infrasound."

"So . . . this was definitely not some sort of a freak malfunction? Someone did this intentionally? To kill?"

"To do grave harm, at the very least. But this was definitely intentional. And very clever. Imagine you put on your headphones and press Play on your phone, but don't hear anything. What would you do?"

"Turn up the volume." Nick felt the hairs on the back of his neck stand up.

"Exactly. And by the time you realize something is wrong and you are not feeling too well, you are already having a seizure and can't do anything about it. Your victim suffered terribly, without really knowing what was happening to him."

In Nick's head, the puzzle board on which he had been carefully piecing together the picture of Ben's death just got kicked into the air, and Nick felt as if he himself went flying with all those pieces, with that sickly pull of gravity coming about at full swing. Ben's death was a murder. A premeditated murder. A sophisticated and sadistic murder that counted on the victim himself to power on the murder weapon and turn it up. Somehow, this seemed worse than someone just walking up to Ben and pulling the trigger. Maybe because Nick himself had been on the receiving end of everyday technology being turned into a weapon. He knew just how thin the line between those two states was.

"But if someone wanted to harm this person, why go to these lengths? There are many other, less . . . complex ways to hurt someone. Do you think the killer is making some sort of a statement?"

She thought about it for a moment. "I don't think so. Actually, this is just about the simplest way to kill someone. Think about it: no need to hire and send a hit man. No plane tickets, no rental cars, no security cameras. No need to worry about the cops matching the bullet to the gun. You don't even need to know where in the world your target is. All you need is their phone number. This malware can be loaded onto the phone remotely using common hacking tools. This could have been done over Bluetooth or Wi-Fi, or even cellular data. And then, the next time the victim plugs in the headphones, the malware will do its job. It's like a 'fire and forget' missile. And there is no physical evidence of the attacker left at the scene."

"And what about digital evidence? Any chance you can tell where this malware came from?"

She shook her head. "There is no indication in the program itself or the log files. I can tell only that it was installed on the device on February 1."

Nick mulled over this information. The pieces seemed to fit, but it all still sounded like science fiction. "And you are confident these tiny earbuds caused lethal brain trauma?"

"Well, it's not exactly like finding a bullet that can be matched to a gun. And we also don't have any recorded precedent of lethal use of infrasound. Still, between the damage to the headphones and the malware on the phone, this setup certainly seems up to the task. Generally, one would need some pretty large equipment to cause this much harm from a distance. But everything changes when using headphones. Headphones are perfect for delivering a sonic attack because they sit so close to the eardrums. And this type of headphones—earbuds—sit inside the actual ear canal, only about a half inch away from the eardrum. Earbuds also create a tighter seal than other types of headphones. This significantly intensifies the impact of the sound on the eardrum and the brain. And with two such high-powered sources of infrasound in one's ears pointing at the brain, you get the added resonance of the sound bouncing and amplifying from the inner dome of the skull. This further intensifies the effect on the brain."

Senior Forensic Examiner Simms was clearly no stranger to delivering expert testimony in court. This theory sounded not just plausible, but absolutely probable when she explained it.

"Who would be able to pull off something like this? What level of expertise would be required?" Nick asked.

"To deploy it? Not much—just some moderate hacking skills. But the underlying research and testing that went into creating it—that's a lot more sophisticated. I would not be surprised if this research was sponsored by a nation-state. This is the kind of stuff intelligence agencies dream up."

"Like who? China? Russia?"

She shrugged. "Or Israel or even us. Of course, that does not mean they are the ones who actually used it in this particular case. The technology could have been stolen and sold on the black market. This happens quite often."

She placed the headphones back in the evidence bag and handed it to Nick. He looked at the tiny murder weapons and tried to think of any reasonable scenario in which a long-missing kid with a fake ID in his pocket would attract this kind of attention.

20

Ben from Walsenburg, Trevor from Tulsa, and Abbi from right here in Pine Lake. Driving back from the RCFL, Nick wondered how he in a matter of just a couple of weeks had become the custodian of three missing kids' files. The three cases were connected by a perceptible thread of hopelessness. Hopeless because Abbi had been missing for more than forty-three years. Hopeless because Trevor had been for twenty-one. And hopeless because Ben was dead, and even though Nick had Ben's body and murder weapon, he still had not a single suspect. He needed to think.

He could have gone straight to the station, but his house was on the way, and at the house was his Gaggia espresso machine. The Gaggia packed more caffeine into a single liquid ounce than the generic drip at the station did into a whole cup, and right now, he needed all the help he could get. Pulling into the driveway, Nick saw a long, narrow UPS box at the front door. He walked to the front porch to examine the package and was startled for an instant when he saw his own handwriting on the manifest. But then he recalled what this was—the saber he and Claire shipped home from Cape Girardeau. He tore open the box and pulled the sword from the bubble-wrap cocoon protecting it. Under the bright Colorado sun, the fancy scrollwork and beading details on the scabbard and on the hilt seemed to lift up toward him, sharply defined. He was not an expert on antiques, but to him this looked like exquisite craftsmanship done one piece at a time—not the soft-edged, die-cast print of an assembly-line-produced replica. The rich patina of the brass pommel glowed warmly, and the ruby eye in the falcon's head gleamed like red fire. The initials *H. M.* were embossed near the eye. Nick pulled off the scabbard and examined the blade. The steel was clean with no rust, and adorned with only a myriad of fine scratches, a handful of gouges, and a few small chips on the cutting edge. There was no doubt in Nick's mind that this saber had been used for its intended purpose.

Nick was no stranger to carrying a weapon—he had one at his side every day, but the tactical matte black of his half-plastic Springfield XD-M 9mm just did not have the same feel as the ornate cold steel of this blade. Holding this sword took him back to the adventure novels of his youth—Dumas, Stevenson, London. The stories of swashbuckling heroism. There was an air of romanticism about this weapon. It looked and smelled of foreign lands and bygone times. It was made for swashbuckling. The XD-M 9 was not. Whose hands had gripped this weapon? How long ago? Whose blood had it spilled? When he had time, he would look into this. Maybe Ray knew a historical-weapons expert around these parts. When he had time . . .

He stuck the saber under his arm and went inside. The house was empty—Claire was probably at the gym in Castle Rock. He ground some fresh coffee beans and watched the Gaggia confidently extrude a steady stream of golden-brown brew into his cup, while his thoughts returned to the case. He would need to request another data dump from cell towers from Conifer all the way north to Morrison, in hopes he could catch another ping from Ben's phone. But beyond that, and with no victimology to speak of, there was nothing else left to pull on at this end of the case—it was a murder with no clues and no witnesses. The other end of Ben's case—his disappearance as a child—also did not look promising. Nick had shown Edie Harris the photos of Victor and Irina Talenko from the FBI file, but she could not confidently identify Irina as the woman who picked up Ben. It *could* have been Irina. Or not.

Nick snapped the lid onto his travel coffee mug and drove to the station. *It could have been Irina.* Nick desperately wanted it to be Irina. Even though Victor and Irina had vanished into thin air twenty years ago, and Trevor's case was just as cold as Ben's, at least in Trevor's case there was something Nick could dig into and try to trace—people, vehicles, places. In Ben's case there was nothing.

At the station, Patty was holding down the fort alone.

"Where's Ray?" Nick asked, surprised not to find the old chief with his boots kicked up on the desk, prepping for a discreet afternoon nap.

"Up at Curtis Mill. John called in a theft of some ranch equipment."

Nick nodded. No wonder he did not get the call on his radio. The old-timers in these parts did not dial 911—they called Ray directly, and Ray always picked up.

In his office, Nick powered on his computer and then took Abbi White's case file from his drawer and put it on his desk. He knew he wasn't going to get to it today, but he needed it there as motivation to keep pushing to solve Ben's case. And as a reminder that time was not on his side.

He opened the FBI file on the Talenkos and began combing through it for any possible links to Ben. The possibility of their involvement in Ben's disappearance was predicated on the assumption that they were involved in Trevor's disappearance first. Unfortunately, that assumption was not reassuringly strong. The Talenkos had no priors and were model citizens, as far as the federal government was concerned. The only reason they were on the FBI's radar at all was due to the fact that they had a passing encounter with a subsequently convicted child trafficker who was under surveillance in Santa Fe in 2000, but nothing else ever came of it. At least not until Trevor's mother, Maureen, gave her description of the woman who picked up

Trevor. When Maureen was shown several dozen photos of possible suspects, she picked out two she thought most resembled the woman she met. The first suspect turned out to be already in the custody of Albuquerque PD and was ruled out. The second suspect was Irina Talenko. Maureen did indicate that the hair color and style did not match, but Irina could have been wearing a wig.

Victor and Irina had their permanent residence listed in Phoenix at the time, but it appeared they spent a lot of time away from home, as Victor traveled for work, and Irina could do her work remotely. If Victor's travels took him as far as Oklahoma City and Dallas, then Santa Fe and Walsenburg were easily within his reach.

Still, during all the time while the FBI was watching the Talenkos, they had not ventured north to Colorado. But then again, they had not really done anything suspicious in those couple of weeks they were under surveillance. And then 9/11 happened, and surveillance had to stop. When Beck was finally able to have surveillance reinstated in November, the Talenkos had vanished. Could their disappearance have been a coincidence? Certainly. But in the context of the investigation, it was highly suspicious and likely incriminating.

The fact that Victor traveled for work offered a possibility that if he had been anywhere in the vicinity of Walsenburg in March, his employer would have had a record of this. Nick googled the name of the gearbox company Victor had worked for and discovered that it had been acquired by a larger industrial firm in 2015. He called the number on the Contact Us page and asked to be transferred to the HR department, where he talked with a nice young man who explained that, unfortunately, at the time of the acquisition, all old records that were past their retention period were not migrated into the company's new system but were destroyed, which, according to him, was a common practice.

Undaunted, Nick returned to the Talenkos' file and trudged on until he came across the FBI application for a wiretap. The wiretap was never activated because the Talenkos disappeared, and their phone account had been canceled. But what caught Nick's attention was the fact that the FBI file had the cell phone numbers for both Victor and Irina, and those numbers were still active in March, when Ben was taken. Granted, this all happened in 2001, before GPS transmitters were built into everything, but that did not matter—cell phones back then worked more or less the way they worked today. If Irina was the woman who picked up Ben from his mother on March 9, 2001, then her cell phone should have pinged off a cell tower in Walsenburg.

But confirming this quickly proved to be difficult. When Nick went to request a cell-tower dump from AT&T, he found out that AT&T retained dump files for a period of seven years, which meant he could go back only to 2015. This did not get him even halfway to 2001. He checked the rest of the Talenkos' file, hoping that there would be cell records going back to March of 2001, but did not find any. Still, there was only one person who would be able to confirm that with certainty. Nick dialed Agent Beck.

"I like where you are going with this," Beck said. "But unfortunately, no—we did not have any phone records for the Talenkos from March. That was before Trevor disappeared and before we began surveillance. But . . . you said their numbers were with AT&T?"

"Yes."

"Hmm. OK, then. There is actually something else we can try. AT&T runs a little data service for law enforcement. It's called *Hemisphere*."

"I've never heard of it."

"Well, that may be because your department cannot afford it."

Nick considered the 1980s-style wood paneling on the wall of his office. "You are probably right. What does it do?"

"Well, for starters, it has access to all call data since the mid '80s."

"Mid '80s?" Nick was taken aback. "*1980s?* We could track phones back then?"

"No, but AT&T simply never threw away any data, and eventually technology was invented that could analyze all that historical data. And now we have access to it, including roaming data so we can actually pinpoint locations and movement."

"Wow." Nick couldn't believe that Beck, who had already been his fairy godmother once when he got Nick access to the RCFL, had now pulled another rabbit out of the magic hat. "OK, great. What do you need from me to get the process rolling? A court order?"

"Nope. I can submit an administrative subpoena right from my office. No court order necessary. You should have the results in a day or two at the most."

Nick felt as if he had somehow stumbled into a fantastical parallel universe. Nothing in his job took just *a day*. Data requests took weeks. Lab results took months. "What's the catch?"

"No catch. The FBI pays a subscription fee, and AT&T delivers data and analysis."

"Just like that? Without a court order? Is that . . ." Nick searched for a word that would not offend Beck's handsome offer.

"—Constitutional? Probably not, but it's been in place since 2007. You can thank the war on drugs and the war on terrorism for this one. At the agency, we don't look this gift horse in the mouth."

"And . . . does the public know about this?"

"As little as possible. Look, I get it if you have reservations about using this, and I respect that. And you don't have to be involved. I can take it over from here and let you know if we find anything interesting. If we had this back in 2001, I would have used it then."

Nick was silent for a moment. This was his first run-in with a shady governmental surveillance program. He had qualms about it. But then his eyes fell on Abbi's case file on his desk. "No. Send it."

Tvv3nty-øn3

"Well, holy fuck" were the first words Roses typed when Claire logged into Tox Chat.

Claire had to smile. She had considered that talking to Roses could possibly be awkward after Claire's self-imposed radio silence for the last three months. After all, for most of the two-and-some years they had known each other, they regularly talked several times a week. Until Claire went cold turkey. But she had to. She needed to reset. At the end of last year, she was no longer the same person Roses had rescued from that support group for trauma survivors on Facebook. She had evolved. For the second time in those two-and-some years. First from a broken person trapped in her pain into a vengeful spirit with a hit list. And then she evolved again, into someone who was ready to be more . . . human. She no longer had the same anger. She no longer had the same objectives. She had to step away and figure out if she could handle this life without having to hide behind her hacker's superpowers. And over the last few months, she found out that she did not always need that power and control. And now, this time, it wasn't about her anymore. But still, talking with her old friend now, and watching their two green dots glowing side by side in the Tox Chat panel—*Kat* and *Roses*—she felt that old comfort and peace again.

"I missed you," Claire typed.

"I bet you did," Roses replied and added a smoochy emoji.

Even though she did miss Roses, contacting her was not a decision Claire made lightly. It took her two days. She read the

FBI files she got from Nick's computer cover to cover two times, trying to decide whether she should take the next step. Having this information in her possession was one thing. Choosing to act on it was a completely different matter. If she were to proceed, her life would change again. The way she looked at the world would change. Hackers looked at the world differently from the average person. When they looked at the world, they saw what was beneath the surface—the hardware, the software, and the flows of data that made the things on the surface work. They saw the digital scaffolding that was holding up the modern world. They looked for any weaknesses, vulnerabilities, and flaws. They looked for indirect approaches and hidden patterns that would allow them to get inside and take control. Their worldview was digital-first. Today, Claire had *some* digital in her world: social media, email—all the mundane stuff. But for the past few months she had stayed away from *the hard stuff*. There had been no SQL injections, no DDoS, no packet sniffing, no spoofing, no cracking, no logging, no scraping, no tapping, no smurfing, no pinging, no doxing. She had been clean for months. But that was all about to change. When Nick told her that Ben's death was the result of a sophisticated hack, Claire took it as a sign. Now, she *had* to get involved. And she was pretty sure Roses would want to get involved too, once she heard about the kidnapped children, child-trafficking rings, and phone hacks that could kill.

Roses agreed without hesitation. And now there they both were—Claire on her computer on the couch and Roses on hers, wherever in the world Roses was. Claire had missed *this*. Roses was Roses, and Claire was Kat, and everything was right with the world again.

They decided to start by looking for any traces of Ben online. As far as the proverbial haystacks went, this was a massive one. In the twenty-one years that passed between his disappearance and his death, the internet had evolved from a mere curiosity with bad websites, nerd chatrooms and illegal mp3 aggregators into a digital universe of trillions of images, web pages, social media posts, forums, chat rooms, and government databases. Looking for Ben in this vast universe was a daunting task, but there was an upside: the World Wide Web had since become embedded into every aspect of our existence. It was impossible to think that Ben would have managed to evade it completely.

The first order of business was to get several good, referenceable photos of Ben throughout the years. Of course, the only good photo they had at their disposal was from Ben's kidnapping case file, and in this photo, he was just a two-year-old little man with tiny shoulders, big round head, flattened nose, and open mouth staring into the camera with big brown eyes. They also had the plasticky-looking digital rendering of Ben at the time of his death from the forensic artist. This wasn't going to help much with what Roses and Claire needed. And they also had the photos from Ben's autopsy, but people never quite looked like themselves after they died—Claire had noticed this last week in Cape Girardeau. Luckily, Roses had access to some impressive government technology, and soon, she and Claire were in possession of five age-progression photos of Ben from a toddler to a preschooler, to an adolescent boy, to a young man. Comparing these new photos with the images they started with, Claire was impressed with how the age-progression algorithm managed to unmistakably capture Ben. AI was becoming scary-good these days.

With the photos at their disposal, they could now embark on the second phase—the facial-recognition search. The basic web search produced a handful of results: there was Ben's missing person profile on NamUs—the website of National Missing and Unidentified Persons System, and a couple of archived newspaper articles from the time of the disappearance. There was nothing else. No social media profiles, no company headshots, no school photos. Claire had expected as much. They had only scraped the surface of the web; it was time to dig deeper, beyond the reach of public web search engines like Google and Bing.

They started with the state DMVs to see if there were any IDs issued to Ben. Claire had already mentally resigned herself to having to spend many hours if not days working down the list of states, breaching their servers one at a time and scanning their media directories for facial recognition. But Roses had a better way. Unbeknownst to Claire, state, local, and federal law enforcement agencies participated in a data interchange called NLETS, which consolidated access to DMV and criminal systems. All Roses had to do was spoof a valid Originating Agency Identifier, and they were soon searching all the DMV systems of all fifty states and the District of Columbia from one convenient interface.

NLETS spat out a single result—an Ohio driver's license in the name of Tyler Wilcox with Ben's headshot in it.

"Wow, who is this?" Roses asked.

"Yeah," Claire responded. "He had a fake ID on him when he died."

"It's not a fake ID. This is a real ID from the Ohio state DMV. But it's issued to a false identity."

"?" Claire typed, not seeing the difference.

"A fake ID is made by a forger, who makes it look like the real thing," Roses typed out. "But this *is* the real thing, only with false information. Someone hacked the RealID system to switch out the photo and reissue this ID to Ben. That's some serious chops. What the hell was this kid into?"

Claire considered the significance of this new piece of information they had just learned about Ben. Was Ben a hacker, like her and Roses? And if not, then who hacked into a government database to get him this ID? Regardless of the answer, this was now another connection between Ben's life and hacking.

They next did an NLETS facial-recognition search of criminal databases, but it did not produce any hits. Ben had never been arrested. Under any identity.

With no helpful results from Clearnet or from the government databases, it was time to delve into the other side of the internet. Claire launched the Tor browser and joined Roses on the dark web. This was a long shot. The dark web thrived on anonymity and obscurity. It used different internet protocols than Clearnet sites did, so you couldn't just point Google at the dark web and get several million hits. You had to use specialized search engines like Ahmia, Torch, and Not Evil, and even among all of those, there were only a few thousand sites indexed on the dark web. But there were many, many thousands more. Maybe millions. No one knew for sure. That was the whole appeal of the dark web—the fact that without knowing the actual URL or stumbling on a link someone else posted, it was virtually impossible to find a site that did not want to be found. And the URLs themselves were not intuitive, not made up of real words like on Clearnet. Dark-web URLs were 56-character-long strings of random letters and numbers—impossible to infer the site's contents, and changeable on a whim, like burner phone numbers. This was great news for criminals and activists, and terrible news for investigators.

It had been a while since Claire had poked around the dark web. It hadn't changed much. It was still a rabbit hole of wikis, marketplaces, and message boards, linking to more wikis, marketplaces, and message boards. Claire clicked link after link, looking for anything promising. There were sites selling stolen credit card numbers, fake IDs, counterfeit US dollars, untraceable guns, money-laundering services, exotic pets, and every drug imaginable from cocaine, MDMA, and heroin to Viagra, Xanax, fentanyl and Oxy. After almost an hour of searching and clicking what seemed like hundreds of broken links, Claire typed a message she never in her life imagined she would type:

"How do we find the harder stuff?"

As impossible as it was to imagine, even in this den of criminality, some things seemed off-limits. No matter how deep she went, she had not come across any mentions of or links to child traffickers.

"Yeah . . . I don't know," Roses replied. "I've never really looked for this type of info before. But things are definitely looking a lot cleaner near the surface these days. We need to find a way to go deeper."

"What about child-porn sites?" Claire cringed. "Do you know any?"

"Umm . . . NO!!! *8-chan* used to have its share of filth, but it's pretty much all cartoon smut now. And the only real child-porn sites I've heard of were the ones taken offline years ago by the FBI and Interpol."

Claire did some mental math—Ben stopped being a minor five years ago. So, if he had been trafficked as a minor, any web evidence would have been from 2017 or prior. Would any sites like this still be around? Five years was like two decades in internet time.

"What about the Internet Archive?" she asked Roses. "Any chance they would have cached data from those busted sites?"

"No, the Internet Archive records get scrubbed when the site is taken down by the feds. But . . ." Roses stopped typing for a moment. "I do recall someone posting a dump of Boystown after it was taken down last year."

"What's a *dump*?"

"It's when someone takes the site backup files and posts them online in a new location after the feds shut down the original site. Sometimes it's just the images, or just the forums, or could be the entire website. Let me check a few pastebins to see if I can find it."

Claire knew about *pastebins*—these sites allowed anyone to post anonymous plain text notes, usually something illegal like links to black-market sites, doxed or stolen information, or entire hacking scripts up for grabs.

"Hmm. Looks like the Boystown dump is gone, but I found a few others. Here." Roses started screen sharing, and Claire watched the facial-recognition scanner program searching through a compressed archive file named *backpage.tar.gz*. The progress bar crawled slowly, but at 32% the status screen indicated there was one hit. Roses clicked it, and Claire held her breath as a web page rendered on the screen.

It was a personals ad, and the young man in the photo looked very young and definitely like Ben. Claire checked the date on the ad: November 11, 2014. Ben would have been fifteen. Looking at this page side by side with the age-progression photo, it was impossible to deny the likeness. The only difference was that in the personals ad, Ben's face looked thinner, and his hair was shorter, lighter, and messier. In the photo, Ben was wearing blue jeans and a simple white T-shirt, sitting on a bed in what looked like a hotel room. The breadcrumb links showed that the ad was listed in the Salt Lake City, Utah, classifieds under "men seeking men" section. The ad was short: "Pretty Boi looking for an older man to teach him." The ad identified Ben as "Billy, 18." Ben looked older than fifteen, but eighteen was definitely a stretch.

The phone number in the ad was an unfamiliar area code—*801*. Claire googled it and confirmed it was Salt Lake City. But it wasn't the same as the phone Ben had on him when he died. It must have belonged to Ben's pimp. And it was unlikely it would still be in service after nine years.

"Can we trace who had that number in 2014?" she asked.

"We can try," Roses said, "but it was probably a burner."

"What about the metadata on this pic?"

Claire watched as Roses checked the file properties on Ben's photo, but there was not much there besides the file dimensions and format—no device name, no location, no date, no other useful metadata. It had been scrubbed. Or it was taken with a basic camera—before smartphones began stamping GPS coordinates and other helpful information into every picture. In the background, the facial-recognition scanner stopped at 100%. There were no more results in the Backpage dump.

"I found one more we can try," Roses typed. She navigated through several directories and selected a new target file for facial recognition: *playpen.rar*.

They got a hit almost immediately, and when Roses opened it, it took Claire a moment to comprehend what she was looking at. And once she did, she recoiled in horror and involuntarily covered her mouth with her hand.

"Oh hell," message from Roses blipped in.

Claire forced herself to look back at the photo, focusing on the little boy's face. There was no doubt—the boy being molested was Ben. He looked to be about five or six years old.

Roses resized the viewer window and zoomed in, so that only the boy's face was in the window. Those were Ben's eyes.

"It's him," Claire typed. The status panel in the background kept raking in hits: *12 files ... 15 files ... 25*. Claire felt sick.

"This one is a web page," Roses typed.

Claire watched her open the file, ready to look away. It was a forum page on which a user named MrGiggles777 shared a link to a photo collection titled *Billy - 5*. The post was dated February 23, 2015.

"Do you think this is who took Ben?" Claire asked.

Roses was silent for a moment.

"It's hard to say," she finally replied. "Child porn gets passed around. These photos are from way before 2015. From 2004, if Ben was actually five. That's an eleven-year gap. This asshole probably reposted them from somewhere else."

But the simplest scenario was that this was him. This MrGiggles asshole took Ben, molested him, took the photos, and posted them. She felt her blood boil. Was this Victor Talenko himself? Or was it someone Victor sold Ben to?

Whoever he was, if this MrGiggles were here now, and if Claire had a gun, he would have a bullet in his head.

Roses checked the file properties on the photo—nothing again.

"Is there any more info on this user in the dump file?" Claire asked.

"No, the database is gone. This is just a static site export."

Now what? They got a taste of success. They had a city, a nine-year-old phone number, and a username from a website that was shut down years ago. The phone number was a long shot, but still worth following. What else? There had to be something else here. Or maybe *not* here? What indirect approaches could they use? What hidden patterns? And then it hit her.

"Many people reuse their usernames across websites," Claire typed. "We need to look for anyone else going by MrGiggles."

22

"We got lucky." Beck's deadpan baritone rumbled through the speaker of Nick's cell phone.

Nick had just pulled out of his driveway, heading to the station. It was hard to tell from Beck's voice if he was excited. "We did? Hemisphere traced the Talenkos' phone to Walsenburg?"

Beck chuckled. "Yes. And even better . . . we got them."

"You . . . got them?" Nick repeated, not comprehending. "You *got* the Talenkos?"

"Yes."

"How? Where? I thought you said they left the country."

"That's what we assumed. But they didn't. They changed their identities and moved to Indiana. The Fort Wayne field office picked them up last night."

"How did you find them?"

"Listen, I am happy to fill you in, but I am about to get on a plane to Indiana now. Do you want to tag along? We can swing by and pick you up in about . . . an hour or so." Nick heard the sound of jet engines in the background. "Do you know where the Centennial Executive Airport is? Hangar 4."

* * *

Flying out of a small airport was a new experience for Nick. A different experience. For starters, he did not have to park miles away in the economy lot and then take a bus to the terminal. Instead, he drove right up to the doors of Hangar 4 and parked in a totally free parking spot. *Free.* Then, as he walked in through the double glass doors, he found no lines of people, no grumpy TSA agents, and no unintelligible announcements on the overhead PA system. Instead, he found himself inside a hotel-like lobby with comfortable leather couches and a receptionist desk.

He did not have to wait long. The tinted-glass double doors at the other end of the lobby slid open, and Nick could suddenly hear and see the airfield behind them. A broad-shouldered man in a navy suit appeared in the doorway.

"Detective Severs?" The man approached. "Tim Beck." He stuck out his hand.

Special Agent Beck had a burly frame, a square head with neatly cropped gray hair, and a firm, calloused hand.

"You ready?" Beck asked, glancing at Nick's overnight duffel.

"Do I need to check in or anything?" Nick looked around for any sort of official, but the woman at the reception desk was fully absorbed with something on her computer screen.

"Nope," Beck said. "Just follow me."

The sun was still rising, and its early light was just beginning to etch out the crisp snowcapped peaks of the mountains in the west. Nick found being out on the airfield to be exhilarating. The brisk winter air smelled of jet fuel, and the sound of airplane engines promised adventure. They walked to a white, gleaming business jet waiting with the cabin door open. Inside, one of the pilots took Nick's bag, and Nick followed Beck into the cabin, which was outfitted with eight La-Z-Boy-looking seats. Nick settled into the one opposite Beck. The plush leather seat was nothing like the thin, firm, pleather-wrapped, non-reclining perches on a commercial flight. And, here Nick had two armrests he did not have to share with anyone. It was going to be very hard to go back to flying commercial after this. He wished Claire could experience this with him.

The pilot closed the door, and soon the pitch of the engines wound higher, and the plane touched off and began taxiing to the runway.

"Is this how you always travel?" Nick asked.

Beck rolled a laugh. "I wish! No—my director signed off on this since time is of the essence."

Nick nodded. "So—the Talenkos are really in custody?"

"Yep."

"How did you find them?"

"Hemisphere did. It can access the phone's historical location data. And it can also use an algorithm to identify when multiple phones follow the same movement patterns. This can indicate a person with multiple phones—for example, a burner and a regular phone. If we know who one number belongs to, we can then associate the other number to the same person. So, this is what happened with the Talenkos—two new numbers were activated and then traveled together with the phones already registered to Victor and Irina. And then, the old phones were turned off."

"So, you followed the new phones?"

"Exactly. When the Talenkos ditched their old phones and identities, the new phone numbers continued on with their new identities. And Hemisphere gave us their new names and address. They have been living under false names in Fort Wayne since 2004. The Fort Wayne FBI along with the Indianapolis office raided them at 3 a.m. this morning and now have them in custody." He thought about it and added: "Wish we had this technology back in 2001."

The engines roared louder, and the small plane sped confidently down the runway and then lifted into the sky. Effortlessly—without the prolonged, rumbling, labored acceleration of a commercial airliner hurtling toward the very last inch of the runway, overburdened with people and luggage.

The jet carved an ascending arc above Centennial and headed east, toward the rising sun. Nick thought about the

Talenkos waiting for them in Indiana. What sort of monsters were they? They had managed to evade detection for the last twenty years. How many children had they trafficked? Did they have information that would help him piece together what happened to Ben?

* * *

Fort Wayne in February was not a sunny place. As the plane descended, they left the vibrant blue heights and slipped into a thick gray cloud cover that turned into snow closer to the ground. As flurries streaked across the round window, Nick could make out the faint rectangles of buildings and the grid lines of streets beneath the wing. The city was blanketed in snow and gray daylight.

The Fort Wayne FBI had offices downtown on the corner of Main and Barr, on the tenth floor of a large glass-sided building with a bank name at the top. There were some shops and restaurants on the ground level and a parking garage around the back. This was a smaller regional office, Beck explained, with the main field office located in Indianapolis.

The local agent in charge was Steve Jensen, a ruddy Midwesterner with a mustache. On the TV screen in his office, Nick saw two video feeds from two separate interview rooms.

"Is this them?" he asked.

"Yes," Jensen nodded.

"Have they said anything so far?"

"Not much. During the arrest, Victor notified us that his wife has dementia. We have confirmed this with her physician. She became agitated during the arrest and had to be sedated. But even when the sedative wears off, I doubt she will be much help—the doctor said she is in advanced stages."

In the video feed, Victor looked stocky and round faced. He was sitting very still, as if frozen in time, staring at the surface of the table in front of him. Were it not for the rolling timer on the screen, Nick would have thought he was looking at a grainy freeze-frame. Irina was in the other feed. Her frame looked small and thin, and her head was resting on her outstretched arm on the table. Nick could not tell whether she was sleeping.

"Well, let's go talk with Victor, then," Beck said.

Victor looked up when they entered, and Nick saw not a monster but a tired, aged man. According to the FBI files, Victor was fifty-six, but sitting before them now, he looked older than that. With his sunken, bloodshot eyes, deeply carved wrinkles, and salt-and-pepper stubble, Nick would have placed him as mid-sixties.

"Where is my wife?" he asked. His voice was cracked and had just a shadow of an accent that was hard to place.

Beck pulled out a chair and sat down. Nick followed suit.

"I am Special Agent Beck, and this is Detective Severs. Your wife is safe in our custody."

"I need to see her. She can't be alone."

"Victor, I'll be honest with you," Beck said. "Right now, the best way for you to see Irina is to cooperate with our investigation."

Victor slumped over the table, his head hanging heavy and his broad shoulders suddenly looking bony and weak. He nodded his head, still looking down, and then straightened up in his chair.

"OK," he said.

"Do you know why you and Irina were arrested?"

Victor gave a slight nod. "Children."

"Tell me about your involvement with child trafficking."

Victor sighed. "What do you want to know?"

"Everything. From the beginning."

Victor took a slow breath and continued in his soft, slightly broken English. "Irina and I came from Belarus. Belarus Republic was part of Soviet Union, as you probably know. In the early '90s, when the Soviet Union fell apart, Belarus became independent. But this did not last. Soon, Russian government rigged elections and promoted their puppet dictator, Lukashenko. Things got worse. Politically and economically. I was twenty-five, and Irina was twenty-six. I worked for a university, and she was a bookkeeper. We wanted change. We wanted to leave Belarus, but it was almost impossible. Our government was corrupt. You had to know someone high up and have money for bribes. Irina's brother worked for a man who was . . . *connected*. We did not know what he did, but he seemed to know people high in government and even in Moscow. He said he could help us get visas and get us set up in America. We sold everything and scraped up enough money for his fee. And he came through."

"What was his name?" Beck asked.

"Azarev. Bogdan Azarev." Victor took a drink from a paper cup. "We arrived in New York in winter of '92. Azarev's men met us at the airport. They took our passports and brought us to an apartment in New Jersey. That's where we met Azarev's nephew Anatoli and found out what business he and his uncle ran in America. They trafficked people. They brought young girls from Europe into America and turned them into prostitutes. Azarev already ran trafficking operations in Europe and the Middle East, but he wanted to expand to America. With the Soviet Union falling, there was more trade between East and West, more people going back and forth, and it became easier to bring in people. Anatoli was in charge of Azarev's New York operations. But we—Irina and I—we were not prostituted. Because we were educated, he needed us to help run and expand his operations. We did not want to do this, but we did not have a choice. Anatoli and his men had our documents. They had guns. Anatoli said because we had met him and seen his face, he could not risk letting us go. So, if we did not do what he said, we would be killed. He was a scary man. A violent mobster. So, we did as he said. At first, he had us set up new girls. It was a hard job. They were so young, and most of them did not know what they got themselves into. They had no money. They spent all their money to pay the fee to come here. Anatoli had several apartments in the building. We put them up and took away their passports and told them they had to work off their lodging and food. Some understood and accepted this. Those who resisted were drugged and became addicts. We did not drug or beat the girls, but Anatoli's men did."

He looked at Beck and Nick. The gaze of his dark eyes was confident and sincere, but Nick knew some people were really good liars. How much of this would Nick be able to verify?

Victor continued. "We hated doing this, but we had no choice. We had nothing in this country. Nowhere else to go. After a year, he moved us up the chain. Irina managed the books, and I helped run operations. Food, doctors, clothes, rent, pimps—I managed it all. It was a closed operation. Irina and I wanted to get out, but we were constantly being watched. Eventually, I convinced Anatoli that he needed to expand beyond New Jersey, to places with less competition. I convinced him to let Irina and me apply for green cards so we could get jobs that would allow us to travel. It worked. He let us go to Phoenix with two of his guys. We started with six girls there, same operation as in New Jersey, but Irina and I got to live in our own house. It almost felt like we had normal lives. But then Anatoli visited us and gave us our new orders. His uncle started dealing a new product in Europe, and he wanted to do it in America, too. Anatoli said people would pay more money for it."

"Children?" Nick asked.

Victor nodded. "Anatoli said there was a strong demand. The younger, the better. We tried to protest, but he made it clear that we would be killed if we did not obey. And so, we had to do it. But we never stole children. We only took ones that parents did not want. We said we ran an adoption agency. It was Irina's idea. But it was a lie."

"How many children?" Beck asked.

"Seventeen, over the years."

"Which years?"

"1996 to 2001."

"Why did you stop in 2001?"

"We ran away."

Beck raised an eyebrow. "You expect me to believe you just left Anatoli's organization?"

Victor nodded. "We had been planning how to get away from Anatoli since we first got to America. All we had was each other. We could trust only each other. We had to do terrible things to survive. We had to get him to trust us enough to let us leave New Jersey. We also needed new identities to disappear. But it took a long time to build connections we could trust and get everything we needed. In 2001, we finally made it happen."

"And what happened to the children?" Beck asked.

Victor turned his gaze down.

"Where did they go?" Beck insisted.

"I can only guess. Anatoli liked to keep things compartmentalized. Different people had different parts. After Irina and I got a child, we paged a phone number, and someone would call us and tell us where to meet. This person we would meet was a courier. Usually a young woman. She would meet us somewhere discreet, and we would give her the child. We would never see the child again."

"And you don't know what happened to them?" Nick pressed.

"Some were sold."

"Where? To whom?"

"US, Canada, Middle East, Europe. I don't know who. People with lots of money."

"And others?"

"Prostituted through Anatoli's organization."

"Where?"

He shook his head. "Anywhere he had people. New York, Tulsa, Denver, Salt Lake. He did not tell us details. That's all I know. I am sorry."

"Did you ever take a child from Walsenburg, Colorado?" Nick asked.

Victor thought about it and nodded. "A little boy. In 2001."

"His name was Ben Harris. Do you know what happened to him?"

Victor shook his head. "He was picked up, like the others."

"What about Trevor Simeka from Tulsa, June of 2001?"

"He was our last one. I don't know where he ended up."

"Have you had any other contact with Anatoli or his people after you left Phoenix in 2001?"

"No."

Beck stood up. "OK, Victor. I'll have some paper brought in. I need you to write down everything you know—names, dates, addresses, phone numbers. Every single thing you can remember."

"I will. But it has been twenty years . . . if Anatoli's operation still even exists, much has probably changed."

"I understand. But I need you to do this, anyways. And keep in mind, if we can make any arrests or recover any of the missing children based on the information you provide, this could help your federal case."

"I understand, and I will help any way I can. But I don't care about my case." Victor's eyes pleaded. "I only care about Irina. She needs to be with me. To keep her in this reality."

Beck nodded. "Then my advice is the same as before. Try to remember as many details as you can." Beck exited the room, and Nick followed.

The information Nick got so far did not inspire much confidence. "Do you think we will actually get something useful out of him?" he asked.

"I am not holding my breath. After twenty years, this trail may have gone cold for good. But if this Azarev character is real, we should be able to find out more through our own channels."

23

There was a war coming. Anatoli did not yet know exactly when, but he knew it would be here soon. Very soon. Galitsyn had confirmed as much, and Galitsyn was never wrong. The preparations were already in motion. Russia was building up its troops at Ukraine's eastern border, and Belarus was to follow suit from the north.

Galitsyn was in Minsk again this week and wanted to meet. Maybe about the war, and maybe about business. Or not. One never knew what was on Galitsyn's mind. Not even when he was sitting right across the table. But he was a trusted connection. First to Uncle Bogdan, and now to Anatoli. Galitsyn knew about everyone and everything. He wasn't just in Lukashenko's inner circle—he had Kremlin connections, too. Perhaps he even whispered into Putin's ear on occasion. Anatoli suspected Galitsyn may have been a senior officer with the GRU—Russia's military intelligence branch, but that really did not matter. It wasn't a label that defined him—it was the connections and the information he possessed.

Driving to meet him now in the House of Government on Independence Square, Anatoli thought about the war. Not because he cared about Ukraine. He cared about Ukraine no more than he cared about Belarus, despite the fact that he was born in the latter and owned a house and a club in the former. What did that matter? He owned several houses in different countries. He had lived in several countries. Those were a matter of convenience and necessity dictated by his business and nothing more. He chose not to be limited by any single country's laws or opportunities. He was a citizen of the world. He found the idea of patriotism absurd, especially in Europe.

There were few things more ephemeral in Europe than national sovereignty. In his lifetime alone, several countries had ceased to exist in Europe, and several others had come into existence. One had to go back only a few decades—never mind centuries—to witness the power of time to redraw borders and allegiances. Invasions, revolutions, and re-settlings—no one was immune to those. Ukraine had been Polish, German, Turkish, Lithuanian, and Russian. Some more than once. The borders on the map today were only just the latest shape etched by the ever-changing political winds.

No, he did not care about Ukraine. But he cared about the war. War was an opportunity. Just like the breakup of the Soviet Union was an opportunity for Uncle Bogdan. And just like in 1991, there would be people who were prepared and those who were not. Anatoli would be prepared. When he was in America, he once watched from the boardwalk in Asbury Park in New Jersey as surfers bobbed in the water, waiting for just the right wave to swell, and when it did, they knew just the right moment to get up on their boards and ride the growing, thundering wall of water that churned and crushed everything in its path. Except them. This war was going to be Anatoli's moment. His wave.

Galitsyn met him in one of the small conference rooms on the ninth floor—with drab beige paint and curtains, same as much of this building. Anatoli wondered if Galitsyn dreaded coming here from the opulent chambers of the Kremlin, where the walls dripped with gold and malachite.

The old man was reading a newspaper. "Hello, Anatoli," he acknowledged without looking up. He folded the newspaper and plopped it down on the table and stood up to shake hands.

Anatoli shook his hand, glancing at the cover page—*Narodnaya Volya*—one of the opposition rags. Where did he get it? Lukashenko's police worked hard to take each copy out of circulation pretty much as soon as it came off the press.

Anatoli sat down. The table was a cheap, walnut-like veneer, peeling at the edges. Galitsyn looked good in his dark blue suit. He had aged well.

"You have something for me?" he asked, his gray eyes holding Anatoli steadily, as if under a microscope.

You old coot, Anatoli thought—*you are the one who called me!* He kept it cool. "I take it you have seen the news?"

Galitsyn opened the lid of his laptop and clicked a couple of times. *"Denver Post,"* he read out. "The man found near Highway 285 in Pine Lake, Colorado, has been identified as Ben Harris, aged twenty-three. Jefferson County coroner says cause of death is undetermined at this time."

He turned the laptop around, but Anatoli did not need to see the article. He kept his eyes on Galitsyn, waiting for him to ask.

Galitsyn smiled, which was maybe only the second time Anatoli had witnessed in all the decades he had known him.

"OK," he said. "Your flare for making a dramatic entrance did not go unnoticed in Moscow. You said he would be dead, and now he is. Who was this man?"

"It does not really matter. Let's just say he was an opportune target. Two birds with one stone, as they say."

Galitsyn nodded. "And you did this from here? With no one helping in America?"

"All remote. Like everything else after COVID," he added. A clever joke, he thought, but Galitsyn was all out of humor.

"And this technology is untraceable?"

"Completely."

Galitsyn tapped his fingers on the cheap veneer of the table. "How much do you want for it?"

It was Anatoli's turn to smile. "It's on the house," he said coolly.

Galitsyn raised his eyebrows. "Then *what* do you want for it?"

"Not a thing. Consider it a gift."

"A *gift*," Galitsyn said more so than asked, as if examining the meaning of this strange word.

"A tribute of goodwill to forge a long and fruitful business relationship." If one wanted to work with the Kremlin, one did not turn up to the deal empty-handed. One brought a tribute commensurate to the absolute power of that institution. This was the way. This is how it was during the Soviet decades, when bribery was rampant; this is how it was in ancient times, when one had to pay the ferryman to cross the river Styx. If one had to bribe one's way into the underworld, one would certainly have to do as much to do not-so-legal business with one of the world's superpowers.

"And what exactly would be the nature of this business relationship with the house of Azarev?" Galitsyn asked.

"Leverage," Anatoli replied.

"On whom?"

"A Dutch diplomat. A French judge. A British MP. A US intelligence officer—you choose."

"Kompromat?"

Ah—a nostalgic KGB word for compromising, career-terminating, marriage-ending, humiliating, I'd-rather-be-dead, I'll-do-anything blackmail. The dirt. Anatoli was selling access to information. This was the new way. In Uncle Bogdan's times, under the Soviet-run economy, tangible things were valued—contraband, drugs, hookers. It was those tangible products that had built the foundation of the Azarev empire. And when the internet came to be, it was Anatoli who led the Azarev enterprise into the new age. Uncle Bogdan almost cried when *Anatoli's* first porn websites started making money. But that was only the beginning of it all. For almost a decade now, they had been logging users, hacking webcams and microphones, and recording their clients in their most compromising moments.

Kompromat. And there was always someone willing to pay for kompromat. This was a whole new lucrative revenue stream from his existing business. The thought made his pulse quicken. Uncle Bogdan would have been proud. If Anatoli could make this deal with Moscow, new opportunities would take Azarev Enterprises to a whole new level.

He nodded. "Kompromat. Unlimited supply. More coming in every day."

"How good?"

"The worst. And I am not talking garden-variety hookers and porn. I am talking pedophilia and worse."

"*Worse?*"

Anatoli nodded.

"Do you have anything on Ukraine?"

Anatoli smiled again.

24

Victor finished writing his testimony around 7 p.m. The result was twenty-four handwritten pages, encompassing the last thirty years of the Talenkos' lives and criminal exploits. Beck made photocopies, and he and Nick read them over pizza and beer at the bar across the street from the FBI office.

The testimony was not a linear narrative but rather an aggregation of fragments in time, incidents, and conversations, as well as each abduction, with dates and notes in the margins, numbered paragraphs and arrows pointing up and down the pages. If nothing else, Victor was organized. There were names—first names, for the most part—cities, meeting places, money exchanges, child handoff details, vehicles, and a few partial pager and phone numbers.

Despite all the information included in these pages, Nick found nothing particularly illuminating or actionable as far as Ben's case was concerned. Beck was enthused to have additional details pertaining to several other missing cases, but given the age of this information, how solid was it? How much of it could actually be verified? It would take time to analyze all this, piece things together, and follow up. A couple of names stood out as promising leads: Bogdan Azarev and his nephew Anatoli Azarev. If the two actually ran a prostitution ring in New York, that should have been something that could be verified. Beck left a message for his bureau buddy in New York who covered organized crime, hoping this would connect to something. As for the rest of the names and numbers, these would take some time to match across the various state and federal databases. If these names were even real. There was work to be done, but Nick knew it was a long shot for any of this to actually lead to Ben's killers. If Victor's testimony was to be trusted, the Talenkos never met or knew anything about the buyers or traffickers who took delivery of the kids he and Irina procured.

By 11 p.m., Nick's head was buzzing, and he told Beck he was calling it a night. Everything seemed heavy here. Maybe it was the mile-deep drop in elevation between Pine Lake and Fort Wayne. Maybe it was the weight of Victor's life. In the hotel room, Nick took off his clothes and got into the shower. It was a nice room. A nice shower. In his line of work, Nick did not spend many nights in hotels. This wasn't like being at home. But it was nice. He closed his eyes and let the hot water roll over him. Just a block away, the Talenkos were finally spending their first night behind bars thirty years after they began their criminal track across the US. This was a success. A victory for law. But it was bittersweet. It came twenty years too late for Ben, and too late for the other children the Talenkos took. Victor and Irina had done such evil, and yet somehow, they were so very human at the same time. They were unforgivable. Those Belarusian mobsters were unforgivable. But what was even more unforgivable was that there was enough demand to keep these criminals in business. Right here, in the US, and around the world. Maybe he could find out what happened to Ben. Maybe even Trevor or Abbi. But these kids were just echoes from twenty, thirty years ago. What about all the ones that vanished after them? What about the ones disappearing right now? Normally, when Nick apprehended a criminal, he had the satisfaction of knowing that he had stopped them, at least temporarily, from committing more crimes, that he had protected the world from them. But not today. Yes, he and Beck got the Talenkos, but this was not going to stop anything.

He peeled back the tightly tucked sheets from the hotel bed and called Claire. It was good to hear her voice. Pine Lake was two hours behind Fort Wayne, and she sounded very much awake and maybe even a bit wired.

"So, did they do it?" she asked. "Did they take Ben?"

"Yes. And sixteen others. They literally drove around several states, stealing children."

"That's some scary shit."

"Yeah."

"Did they say what happened to Ben?"

"They handed him off to someone else in the organization. Like all the others. After that, Ben was either sold or put into a sex-trafficking ring."

"Hmm. Did you get any leads?"

"A few names and numbers to check out. Nothing spectacular."

She was silent for a moment, as if wanting to say or ask something.

"Hey, I saw you got the sword in the mail," she finally said.

"Oh, yeah," he recalled. "Did I leave it in the kitchen?"

"Uh-huh."

Nick switched his tired brain from thinking about Ben and the Talenkos. "It's such a fascinating piece. Do you know anything at all about it?"

"The story in the family was that my great-great-grandfather William brought it back to the States from the war in Europe."

"World War One?"

"I think so. But that's the extent of it. I don't know anything else about it. I can ask Uncle Alex."

"Yeah, that would be great. I may take it down to the station—maybe Ray or Jason know someone who can tell where it's from." Nick yawned. "Sorry."

"Tired?"

"Yeah."

"Are you coming home tomorrow?"

"Yep. First thing in the morning."

"OK, well, you better get some sleep, then. I love you."

"I love you, too. I will see you in the morning," he said.

He turned on the TV and started flipping through channels, but soon got tired of it and closed his eyes.

* * *

The FBI jet dropped Nick off at Centennial airport just after 9:30 in the morning. He drove home and found Claire in the kitchen, drinking coffee in front of her open laptop.

Seeing him come in, she got up and gave him a hug and a long kiss.

"Coffee?" was the first word she said to him.

"God, yes!" She knew him so well.

"How was Fort Wayne?" she asked, filling the brewing chamber of the Gaggia with freshly ground powder.

"No sun. Flat."

She smiled. "How was the flight?"

"Oh, honey. A private jet is the only way to travel. Whoever said flying is not what it used to be never tried flying from an executive airport. I don't think I can ever fly commercial again."

"Hmm." She smirked but did not laugh. Maybe he was too tired to be funny. She flipped the red toggle switch and let the Gaggia do its thing. She looked serious.

"Any more leads from the Talenkos?" she asked, setting his coffee on the table.

"Nothing new," he said and sat down. "Still have to run down those names and numbers Victor came up with. The Belarusian Mafia may be involved." He took a couple of big gulps of hot coffee like a parched man who had just crossed a desert. "I didn't even know there *was* a Belarusian Mafia. But nothing solid just yet."

"What are you going to do if this doesn't pan out?"

He set the mug down. "I don't know."

She nodded. "I may have something for you that could help."

He looked at her, not following. "Help with this case?"

She nodded again. "But I don't want you to get mad." She paused, watching him silently.

"Why would I—" Suddenly, it clicked. "Fuck, Claire! Tell me you did not hack my computer and take the case files?"

"I am sorry," she said, simply.

"How could you do this?!" His blood was rising. "These are official files. Any sign of tampering could screw up the whole case."

"I know. I should not have done that. But I really felt we could make a difference."

"We?"

"Yes—Roses and I."

He covered his face with his hands.

"But we really did not do anything illegal," she said. "Not yet, at least."

"Besides breaking into a police computer?"

She hung her head. "Well, that—yes. But nothing else."

He took a drink of his coffee, brooding. *How could he ever trust her? She was a hacker. And he was a fool.*

"So . . . do you want to see what we got?"

He sighed. As much as he wished he didn't . . . "Was it obtained legally?"

"I promise."

He nodded.

She turned her laptop around so he could see the screen. On the screen was a Backpage ad with a skinny young man in a white T-shirt. Nick leaned in. The young man looked familiar.

"Who is this?" he asked.

"Ben Harris in 2014, or thereabouts."

Nick looked at Claire and then back at the screen. "How can you tell? The ad says *Billy*."

"Because Roses and I did age progression of Ben's childhood photo and then we did a facial-recognition search on the dark web and found two results."

"How did you get into Backpage? It was taken down years ago."

"I know." She smiled. "Roses found a dump-file archive on the dark web."

Nick reread the ad. "And this was posted in Salt Lake City?"

"Yes. And that number is a Salt Lake City area code."

Nick stared at the photo. This *was* Ben. Same eyes. And this was evidence he had been trafficked for sex as a teenager. This was a dark turn for Ben's lifeline Nick had been trying to trace, but one he was pretty much expecting at this point. "Wait—" He looked at Claire. "You said you got *two* hits?"

She nodded. "But this one is much worse. Have you ever heard of the website called PlayPen?"

He shook his head.

"Until yesterday, neither had I. It was a website on the dark web created by a guy in Florida in 2014. The only purpose of the website was to share child pornography. By the time the FBI shut it down, it had over 150,000 users around the world."

Nick shook his head. "And . . . you found Ben there?"

She nodded, and her lips tightened, and a wrinkle formed on her forehead. Nick could tell she was holding back tears. He reached over and put his hand on hers. She clutched on to it and sniffled. "There was a whole bunch of sickening photos, Nick. And Ben is only five or six in them."

"And these photos were in that *dump file* as well?" Nick wanted to make sure he had a full understanding of where this new evidence was coming from.

She nodded. "But there is more. We got something else from the archived pages. The name of the account that posted those photos of Ben was MrGiggles777. Roses and I went through over fifty message boards on the dark web and found another post by an account with that name on a different site."

"What did he post?"

"A link to another child-pornography website."

Claire clicked a tab in her web browser, and Nick saw a light pink web page with an UPLOAD button in the middle of the screen. The logo above had a swirly lollipop, and the words *LoliTown Awaits*.

She looked at him. "This one is not taken down. It's a *live* site."

He froze. "This is live on the dark web? *We* are on the dark web right now?"

She nodded.

"Did you find Ben here?"

"We can't get in," she said. "The admins of this site require everyone who wants access to submit new, original child porn. Something the admins have not already seen anywhere else on the web."

Nick winced.

"I know, it's sick. But also clever in a way. The only people who would have access to original porn are pedophiles. The site admins are making sure only their own kind can get in."

"And they are also making sure the visitors incriminate themselves as a price of admission. Viewing child porn is one thing, but uploading it is distribution. That's a whole other level."

"I think this Mr. Giggles is the one who had Ben. Why else would he have photos from so long ago?"

Or maybe he was part of Azarev's organization? Nick stared at the pink page with the UPLOAD button, wondering who or what lurked behind it.

Claire squeezed his hand. "Are you still mad at me?"

Dammit. How could he be, after this? Claire did good, he had to agree to himself begrudgingly.

He rubbed her hand with his thumb. "You did really good," he said. "You *and* Roses really did great work. And . . . part of me really wants to support this hobby."

"And the *other* part?"

"The other part would very much like to know nothing about it."

"Why?"

"Claire, this is *highly* illegal material. I can't have my girlfriend involved in something like this."

"Nick—Roses and I did not break any laws. All the information I showed you was obtained legally—it's all right out there on the dark web. You just have to know where to look. I can send you the" —she stopped abruptly—"wait, is this because Roses and I got this from the dark web?"

He shrugged. "Well . . . yeah, kind of. It doesn't exactly have a shiny reputation."

"And you think the internet does? Yes, there is some evil on the dark web, just as there is on the internet *you* use every day. But the dark web also does a lot of good. If you live in an authoritarian country, it's the only safe place for people to communicate with one another without being spied on, or to access websites their government blocks on Clearnet, or safely share information with journalists."

She gave him a long look, but he kept silent. "I seriously don't see how you can have an issue with using this legally obtained information from the dark web, but then have absolutely no qualms about using questionably constitutional surveillance data from a big wireless provider that lets our government obtain anyone's location and phone data without a warrant."

Nick sighed. He hated being wrong, but she had him there. "Fuck. OK. You are right."

She squeezed his hand in both of hers. "Let me help you with this. You know I can. Just think of me as an independent consultant, or a research assistant."

He looked her over, contemplating what it would be like to interview her for a job, if he did not already know her. She definitely knew her stuff. She got results in just a couple of days with nothing but her computer. Results Nick probably would never have gotten.

"OK, fine," he said grumpily. "You can be my 'research assistant'"—he added air quotes around the last two words—"but on one condition."

"What?"

"You show me how to get on the dark web."

She winced. "Are you being serious?"

He nodded.

"Well . . . yeah . . .," she mumbled. "Of course."

Nick smiled. He had succeeded in dumbfounding his better half. "OK, you are hired. But it's not a real job, and you don't get paid." He stuck out his hand.

"That sounds perfect," she shook his hand.

"And you have to promise not to hack my computer anymore."

She smiled. "Deal."

"So, can you hack this?" He nodded to the pink web page on the screen.

"We are working on it. No obvious vulnerabilities so far, but we are not giving up yet."

Nick nodded. "Let me update Beck. Maybe he can help."

Tvv3nty-f!v3

Claire was a bit apprehensive about getting on a Zoom call with the FBI. She tried to get Roses to do it with her, but Roses declined. "Oh, hell no," were Roses' exact words. It wasn't that Claire was afraid. She wasn't. And besides, Nick had covered for her by telling Beck that she had done this research at his request. No, she wasn't afraid. But she *was* nervous. Because Beck was about to become only the third person in the whole world besides Roses and Nick to learn about her secret life online. And this wasn't a world she let just anybody in.

But on the Zoom call, she quickly felt at ease. Agent Beck had a calm demeanor and kind eyes. He listened attentively, without interrupting, and leaned in closer to the screen when she showed him the dumps of Playpen and Backpage, and then the posts of Mr. Giggles and the login page for LoliTown.

"Do you think your cyber team can find a way to bypass this login requirement and get us into this site?" Claire asked. "If we can get in, we may be able to identify who this Mr. Giggles is."

He leaned back in his chair and connected the fingertips of his hands together. "Well, first of all, Nick was right—this is great investigative work."

The way he said this—matter-of-factly, and without even a hint of flattery—sent a wave of warmth spreading through Claire's body. She nodded, wondering if she looked flushed.

"Secondly, *yes*—we can probably find a way into this site. I think it's best if we get together in person to compare notes and coordinate. I can fly out to Denver tomorrow. Can you two meet tomorrow afternoon?"

"Yeah," Nick said. "Of course. We can meet at the station"—he looked at Claire—"but you have to work, don't you?"

"I can have Tasha cover my shift."

"Are you sure?"

She nodded.

Nick turned to Beck. "OK, we are good for tomorrow."

Beck nodded. "OK. I will let you know my ETA once I get the flight figured out."

* * *

Claire had been to the Pine Lake police station on a few occasions before. She liked it—it had that quaint small-town charm. She liked the people Nick worked with, too. And the cowbell on the front door always sounded like Christmas. Seeing her walk in, Patty popped up behind the front counter.

"How are you, my dear?" she beamed at Claire. And then her face clouded. "Oh, I was so sorry to hear about your mother." She came around the counter to give Claire a hug.

"Thank you." Claire let Patty squeeze her. She looked around. "It's quiet here today."

"Yes, Ray is in meetings at the county, and Jason is at his mining job. But I don't mind—gives me some quiet time to get the monthly reports done."

"Where's Nick?" Claire asked, not seeing him in his office.

"He's setting up the meeting room. You can go on back."

Nick had commandeered the small conference room in the back of the station. It had a large table, a bookcase stuffed with three-ring binders and memorabilia, a large whiteboard on wheels by the window, and a flat-panel TV on the wall.

"What do you think?" Nick asked, stacking a couple of chairs out of the way to make the room feel a bit less cluttered.

"I think this will do fine," Claire said. She looked behind the TV. "Do you have a long HDMI cable so we can hook up the laptops?"

"Yeah," he said and rummaged through one of the cabinets at the base of the bookcase. "Here you go." He handed her a bundle of coiled-up wires.

She picked the longest one and plugged it into the side of the TV.

The cowbell jangled at the front, and even from the back of the building, she recognized Beck's distinctive radio-announcer baritone. He had a nice voice, and somehow, it carried throughout the building.

She and Nick went to the front to greet him, just in time to catch him flashing a warm smile at Patty: "I *love* those earrings."

"Oh, you are too sweet," Patty melted.

In person, Special Agent Beck had an imposing presence that Claire did not really fully appreciate over Zoom. His well-fitted suit did nothing to hide his hulking, broad build, which was topped with a square head with a square, cleanly shaven jawline and an old-school bruiser buzz cut somehow made to look distinguished in pure silver. It wasn't until Claire got closer to Beck that she saw his kind blue eyes and the wrinkles that appeared around them when he smiled.

"Claire, it's so nice to meet you in person."

She shook his big, warm, calloused hand.

"Severs. It's good to see you again." He greeted Nick with a clap on the back.

She and Nick took Beck to the conference room. Nick went to get a refill of coffee while Claire and Beck set up their laptops. As Claire opened her MacBook and logged in, she couldn't help noting from the corner of her eye that Beck typed in a hard-drive encryption password into his black Dell Latitude, and then entered what looked like Microsoft two-factor authentication code into the Authenticator app on his phone.

"So, where should we start?" Nick returned and closed the door behind him. "The timeline?"

"Sounds good to me," Beck replied.

Nick grabbed his laptop and the coffee and headed to the end of the table that had the whiteboard and the TV. Watching him take a sip, Claire considered whether she should tell him to cut back on caffeine. He really seemed to be drinking nothing but coffee these days.

"So, what do we know?" Nick picked up a dry-erase marker. "Ben was taken on March 9, 2001." He wrote Ben's name and the date on the left side of the board. He then drew an arrow to the right and wrote *Talenkos*.

"According to Victor, he and Irina had Ben for one or two days and handed him over to a courier in Denver." Nick drew an arrow from *Talenkos* and wrote *Courier—Denver, March 10-11, 2001*.

"Then the next time we have Ben surface online is what—Playpen or Backpage?" Nick asked, looking at Claire.

"Backpage," she said, checking her notes. "November 11, 2014."

Nick wrote this down, leaving a sizable gap after *Courier*. "And this was in Salt Lake City, right?"

"Yep," Claire responded.

Nick wrote *SLC* under the date. "And we had a phone number on that ad." He turned to Beck. "Have you had a chance to run it?"

Beck shook his head. "It was not an AT&T-affiliated number, so Hemisphere could not help. We'll have to get a court order to see if we can find out who it was assigned to during that period."

Nick nodded. "OK, and then we have the post on Playpen?"

"Yes. February 23, 2015." Claire confirmed in her notes.

Nick wrote down *MrGiggles777* above the information Claire provided and stepped back from the board, like a painter in mid-process. Claire wondered if this is what Nick used to look like when he was teaching. She liked watching his mind work.

"But these photos are not from 2015," he said. "The post said he was five, so that would make it 2004." He wrote *Photos taken—2004* and a big question mark above it.

"And then, Ben is killed on February 2, and we find his body the next day." Nick went to the right edge of the whiteboard and wrote down the final milestone in Ben's timeline.

They were all silent for a few moments, absorbed in the chronology. There were two big gaps on the whiteboard—ten years or so between those terrible photos and the Backpage ad. And then eight more years between the ad and Ben's death.

"What else? Anything missing here?" Nick asked.

"The Azarevs," Claire offered.

"Right," Nick said. He wrote *Bogdan Azarev—Belarus* at the top of the board and then drew an arrow pointing down and *Anatoli Azarev—NY* under it.

"I actually have an update on those two," Beck said, looking at his laptop. "Organized Crimes says Bogdan Azarev died in Belarus in 2017, and Anatoli went back there that same year and has not returned to the US. They suspect he has taken over the reins of his uncle's criminal enterprise, but they have not been actively tracking him since he left the US."

"Is that him?" Claire asked, looking at Beck's laptop screen.

"Yes." Beck turned the laptop around so she and Nick could see a glossy headshot of a middle-aged man in a blazer and no tie. "He runs a company called Azarev Enterprises registered in Belarus."

Claire studied the photo. Anatoli had a nice haircut and a rounded, cleanly shaven face with a square chin. He looked like a normal business executive, she thought. Polished and confident. She wasn't sure what she had expected, but it wasn't this face. Could this man have been running an international child-trafficking ring? "What does Azarev Enterprises do?" she asked, already googling the company name.

"Real estate development, mostly. He owns a couple of clubs and apartment buildings on the side. We have no evidence of illegal activity."

"Do you think he's gone legit?" Nick asked.

"I doubt it," Beck replied. "In my experience, guys at his level never do. They just get others to do the dirty work."

Nick looked back at the board. "So, we know Anatoli was connected to the Talenkos and the courier." He drew two downward arrows from Anatoli. "Hey!" He suddenly turned to them. "The RCFL tech said the malware on Ben's phone was likely based on military research from the Cold War. Belarus is a former Soviet republic. Maybe there is a connection there? Unless you think Ben did not stay with Azarev's organization? Do you think they sold him off to someone else?"

Beck grimaced. "I think they kept him. Remember what Victor said—Anatoli wanted to get into the business of trafficking children. To a sex trafficker, children are a much more exotic and valuable product than adults. You can charge more for them. And children retain that premium price until they come of age. That's ten or more years of very profitable trafficking. From the business perspective, it would make sense for Anatoli to hold on to such an asset. If he were to sell Ben, he would be giving up years of guaranteed income. I think everything we know so far points to the high probability that Ben was trafficked from Anatoli's organization after he was taken. Now, it's possible that Anatoli sold Ben once he came of age and became less valuable, but it's more likely that he kept him, since we know Anatoli also trafficked in adults."

"So, you think that Ben was trafficked his whole life, then?" Claire said. "Since he was taken as a child? Why didn't he escape?"

Beck nodded. "We've seen this before. It's hard to imagine, but by the time they become adults, this is all they know. If they were taken as children, they don't have IDs, don't have education, or any means of making it in the normal world.

Many are addicted to drugs, which reinforces their dependence on their handlers."

"And what happens when they get too old?"

"If they stop being profitable, their handlers cut them loose. Most become homeless. Most are addicts. Some try to turn tricks on their own or fall under the influence of a small-time pimp."

"So," Nick tapped the dry-erase marker in his hand. "If Anatoli's organization had Ben for most of his life, and this MrGiggles had access to Ben when he was five, it is probably not a stretch to assume that MrGiggles is not a random online pedophile but is in fact connected to Anatoli's trafficking ring."

Beck and Claire nodded in agreement.

"Now we just need to find him," Claire said. "If only we could get into LoliTown—"

"We did," Beck interjected.

"What?!" Claire spun in her chair toward Beck. "We have access?"

Beck nodded. "I just got the email from my cyber guys this morning. Want me to put it up on the TV?"

"Yes!" Claire said as Nick handed Beck the end of the HDMI cable.

When the picture appeared on the TV, Claire saw the familiar pink web page with a swirly lollipop logo and the words *LoliTown Awaits* at the top. But below, there was no longer the single UPLOAD button, but rather a typical-looking message board with rows of categories organized under two main headings: *Boys* and *Girls*. Under each heading were about a dozen categories. Claire scanned the category names: *Artistic; Themed; NannyCam; Adolescents (under 18); Kindergarten (3-6 yo); Toddlers (12-36 months)*. Next to each category name was the number of posts in that category and the date of the last post. All the categories on the screen had over a thousand posts. Many had over ten thousand.

"This is a very active board," Claire said.

"Yeah," Nick agreed, leaning closer to the screen. "And most of these categories had new posts added either today or yesterday."

"Can you scroll to the bottom of the page?" Claire asked.

Beck obliged.

"Whoa," Nick said.

There it was—like most message boards, LoliTown had the board statistics listed at the bottom: *Total posts: 2,039,281; Total members: 472,396*.

"This thing is massive!" Beck acknowledged. "PlayPen had *only* around 200,000 users."

"Wait," Claire said, suddenly realizing something. "You are not logged in as an admin? This shows you are logged in as a regular user. How . . . how did your team hack this?"

Beck shook his head. "We didn't. We had to go through the front door on this one."

"You . . . created an account?" Claire said the words, not understanding how this could have been the case.

"Yes."

"But . . . this site requires . . ."

Beck nodded slowly. "I know. We confiscate terabytes of this filth every year. I had my team find some more recent samples, and that's what we went with."

Nick and Claire exchanged a look.

"You are not saying the FBI uploaded child pornography to the web . . . are you?" Nick asked.

"Hey, I know it's not at all ideal. But it was the best option available. This site is hosted on a hidden private server on the dark web. With the caseload the Cyber Crimes team has today, it would have taken them weeks to get to this, and even then, there would be no guarantee they'd be able to hack this site. I know using such material as currency may seem inexcusable, but you must think of the big picture. When we take down a site like this, that's not all we do. We also ID the kids, we recover or rescue them, and we arrest traffickers and pedophiles. If I can use some of the confiscated material from our evidence files to get some of these kids out of their situation, I will make that trade any day."

Nick gave Beck a nod, but Claire could tell this was not sitting well with him. Claire herself had mixed feelings about this. On the one hand, uploading new child pornography seemed inexcusable. It would now be shared and passed around and become forever woven into the fabric of the internet, impossible to eradicate, haunting the victims with its very existence for the rest of their lives. But at the same time, this made all the sense in the world. To get to the missing children, they had to enter the underworld. And this was the price of entry. They had to feed these monsters. They had to become a little bit monsters themselves.

A navigation button at the top of the web page caught Claire's eye. "What's that—*Destinations?*"

Beck clicked on it. This new web page showed a world map with caption: *Do you fancy a trip to LoliTown? Use the map to explore available destinations.*

Beck hovered over the map and clicked on the US. The map of the United States popped up, and Beck clicked on Colorado. The map of Colorado appeared, with six pins on the map, each with a photo of a child's face. "Jesus," Beck grumbled under his breath. "They've set up a travel agency for pedophiles."

He clicked one of the pins—a little girl with pigtails. The pin expanded into a card titled *Cindy—6* with a brief description: *Gender: Female; Race: White; Location: Pueblo, Colorado.* A button below the description invited visitors to *Send a secure message to the host.*

Hosts? Claire thought. *Disgusting!*

Beck took a screen capture of the page and saved it to his computer. "I'll have my team back up all these listings. We can compare these against open cases."

"If we use that link to send a message, can we track the reply?" Nick asked.

COLD TRACE

Beck shook his head. "These guys are used to evading authorities. This is probably an encrypted messaging app integrated into their website."

"Can we use that Search box to check for MrGiggles?" Claire asked.

Beck clicked inside the search box at the top of the page and typed, pronouncing out loud: *MrGiggles777*. He clicked the magnifying-glass icon next to the box. The browser page went blank and then returned with a long list of results.

"Bingo," said Beck.

Nick stepped closer to the TV to read the search results. "This guy is chatty—most of these are forum discussions."

Beck scrolled farther down the page until there was a different type of search results in the list—*Marketplace*. Beck clicked the first one, and it took them to a page with a photo of a boy. The page was titled *Johnny—5* and was set up like an eBay product listing, with details indicating that this *collection* included four videos and twenty-nine photos. What followed in the description was a bulleted list of a half-dozen types of abuse depicted in the set. This set was rated 4.6 stars and had twenty-nine reviews. The price was fifty US dollars via cryptocurrency, and a convenient *Buy with Crypto* button was included.

Beck took a screenshot and went back to the search listings. There were five more *Marketplace* listings for MrGiggles.

"There, try the one that says *Billy*," Claire said.

Beck clicked it, and when the page loaded, Nick and Claire both said in unison:

"It's him."

Claire turned her laptop so Beck could see the age-progression photo of Ben.

Beck nodded gravely. This *collection* had four videos and twenty-three images. The price was the same—fifty dollars US in crypto.

"What do we do now?" Nick asked. "Should we buy it? Maybe digital forensics can get something off the files?"

Beck shook his head. "I'll have my team in Albuquerque do it. They have the right setup for such things. But I wouldn't hold my breath—these files are almost twenty years old."

"Can you click on the username?" Claire asked.

Beck complied, and the browser took them to the user profile page for MrGiggles777. It had a cartoony sad-clown avatar but no personal details—no age, no location, nothing.

"We still have no proof this MrGiggles was involved with Anatoli," Nick said. "He could have gotten these files from someone else."

"That's possible," Beck agreed. "This kind of material often gets reposted over and over. Whoever made these files in the first place may already be behind bars or dead. But the files just keep resurfacing like cancer."

Beck was about to click the Back button in his browser when Claire stopped him: "Wait, see the Activity section at the bottom? Can you click the *Destinations* link?"

Beck clicked the link.

A little girl's hazel eyes stared at them expressionlessly from the page. *Kimmy—5; female; black. Host: MrGiggles777.*

"He is a trafficker," Claire said.

Nick leaned closer to the TV. "Wait . . . that's in Grand Junction. That's only four hours away! *This fucker* is only four hours away. Message him. Message him and set up a sting. We can recover this girl and have him in custody tomorrow."

Beck raised his hands. "It's not that simple. If this was just one classified ad—sure. But this is a site with hundreds of trafficked children and almost a half million users. That's a big operation. We have to coordinate the takedown with field offices across the country and with international law enforcement."

"And how long will that take?" Nick asked, and Claire could tell he was heated about this, in his own steady, even-keel way. "Weeks? Months? We can help this girl *tomorrow*. She can be safe *tomorrow*, instead of continuing to be abused. What if she gets sold or moved? She could disappear forever. We *have* to get her now, while we can."

Nick looked to Claire for support, and she nodded enthusiastically. "We have to get her," she said. "And besides, this listing may be our only chance to catch Mr. Giggles. If we wait, and the listing goes down, we will have no way of contacting him."

They both stared down Beck, who leaned his broad frame back in the chair and exhaled a deep sigh.

"OK," he said and put the palms of his hands on the table. "Let me make some calls."

26

Nick ejected the magazine of his Springfield XD-M handgun and checked it. The heavy stick of polished steel held nineteen 9mm rounds. Stagger-stacked and ready, gleaming with their golden primer caps through the small, numbered holes at the back of the magazine. He put the magazine on the bed next to him and turned his attention to the pistol itself. The empty black frame felt like a toy without the weight of all those rounds. He raked back the slide, checking that the firing chamber was empty. Satisfied, he pressed the trigger and heard the reassuring empty click. He raked back the slide and pressed the trigger again. Click. He slipped the magazine back into the hollow grip and pushed it into place until he heard another click. The weapon was ready, and it felt like a weapon once more.

Nick liked this gun. He liked it better than the Glocks most cops preferred. He liked the balance the Springfield had, liked the way its grip fit between his thumb and index finger. Liked the way it fired at the range—with noticeably less muzzle flip than a Glock.

In his five years as a cop, he had never fired his weapon at anyone. He never wanted to until this morning.

"You planning to use that today?" Claire was looking at him in the bathroom mirror as she was putting in the tiny diamond stud earrings she wore to work.

"Come here," he said, slipping the Springfield into the holster. He picked up his laptop and opened it.

COLD TRACE

"Beck's team in Albuquerque is documenting and backing up material from LoliTown."

"Oh yeah?" she said, sitting down next to him. "As evidence?"

He nodded and typed in his password. "Beck sent me one of the videos Mr. Giggles is selling."

The screen unlocked, revealing a video player stopped on a freeze-frame showing a little boy sitting on the bed.

"That's Ben!" Claire said. "He's maybe three or four here." She looked at Nick. "Can I play this?"

"It's rough, Claire." Nick's voice cracked. "You sure you want to?"

She nodded and tapped Play.

A man's voice spoke off camera. *"How is it going there, Billy?"* The voice sounded clear and close, like in the old family videos in which the person filming is speaking to someone in the frame. The man was so close to the microphone, Nick heard his breathing. The voice was not unpleasant—soft and with a tone of parental gentleness, but without the exaggerated rising and falling inflections people often take on when talking to toddlers and pets.

The boy mumbled something, not taking his big, unblinking brown eyes from the camera. Claire leaned in and turned up the volume on Nick's laptop. The old audio hummed and crackled with the man's breathing.

"I want you to meet a new friend," the man's voice said. A man's torso moved into the frame—jeans and a dark T-shirt, but the camera could not see the man's face. The camera remained steady, probably mounted on a tripod.

"His name is Mr. Giggles." The man sat a clown doll in front of the boy.

Ben's gaze locked in on the clown.

"Do you like Mr. Giggles, Billy?"

"Yith," Ben said quietly, still watching the doll.

"Do you know what Mr. Giggles told me, Billy? He said he likes you, too. He wants to be your friend."

The boy nodded.

"Hey, you know what, Billy? Mr. Giggles is feeling a little hot. Can you help him take off his shirt?"

Claire stopped the video. She took a deep breath and looked at Nick.

"It's him," she exhaled. "This confirms that Mr. Giggles is not just some random pedophile—he had access to Ben after the Talenkos took him."

Nick nodded.

Claire looked back at the freeze-frame. "This video must have been made over twenty years ago. Who do you think he is? *What* is he? A pedophile? A pimp? A child-porn producer? All of the above?"

Nick shook his head. "I don't know." He had all those same questions ricocheting about in his brain. "But I intend to get this motherfucker today and find out."

She put her arms around him and kissed him. "Promise you'll be careful."

He brushed her hair away from her face and kissed her lips. "I will. I'll call you."

* * *

What started as a gray, overcast morning in Denver turned into flurries by the time they reached 8,500 feet of elevation at the ice-covered lake of Georgetown. Here, forty miles west of Denver, the outside temperature had already dropped fifteen degrees. But their two-vehicle convoy still had farther to go—farther west on I-70, climbing higher and higher. The lead vehicle—an unmarked black Suburban—carried Nick, Beck, and two FBI agents from the Denver office: Javier Torres, who was driving, and Randy Quinn, riding shotgun. The second vehicle was a white Econoline cargo van, carrying a squad of four operators of the FBI Hostage Rescue Team—HRT.

They passed the Loveland Pass ski area at the elevation of 10,800 feet, as the flurries turned into large, fluffy flakes. The chairlifts at Loveland were sparsely filled today, hauling bundled-up skiers to the whited-out peaks. Nick was thankful that this was a Wednesday. Had this been a Friday or a Saturday, both westbound lanes would have been packed with vehicles carrying skiers and boarders on their weekend pilgrimages to the snowy slopes of Keystone, Breckenridge, Copper Mountain, and Vail.

Today, traffic was moving at a good speed. When the Suburban entered the gaping mouth of the Eisenhower Tunnel and raced down its mile-and-a-half-long shaft deep below the Continental Divide, Nick considered that they were making good time. But the bright artificial lights and dry asphalt inside the tunnel proved to be a false promise. Upon exiting the tunnel on the other side, they were confronted with driving snow and red brake lights of vehicles slowing down to make the slippery, steep, and curvy descent toward Silverthorne.

Torres pumped the brakes to reduce speed, prompting Nick and Beck to grab the safety handles to not fly out of their middle-row seats.

"Shit," Nick said, looking at the snow sticking to and freezing on the Suburban's windows. He opened the Maps app on his phone and checked the traffic. The line of the highway was blue behind them and bright red all the way ahead to Vail.

"ETA?" Beck inquired.

"Right now, it's putting us there at 5:25."

"Fuck." This was the first time Nick had heard Beck curse.

They had planned to get into Grand Junction by 3 in the afternoon and have ample time to surveil, set up, and prep before the 9 p.m. meeting Beck had arranged with Mr. Giggles. But Grand Junction was still two hundred miles away, and there was nothing to guarantee the conditions would not deteriorate further. This was the chance one took driving in the mountains—nature called the shots here. Snow, ice, high winds, rockslides—one never knew what was around the next curve. Sometimes a slowdown. Sometimes a Road Closed sign. There was nothing Nick or anyone else could do at this point but to hope that the ETA on the traffic app would not slip even later.

Things got worse past Frisco. The long, curvy incline of the road proved to be too icy for many vehicles. On the wide shoulder, several semitrucks were pulled over, and their drivers, bundled in coats and overalls, now fought the blistering wind and snow to put chains on their eighteen-wheelers. This entire stretch of the highway incline, normally three lanes wide, had now been reduced to a single set of icy tire tracks, and in these tracks, a long, slow line of vehicles pressed forward, some barely at the limits of friction necessary to keep them moving uphill on the slick surface. Nick watched with concern as the rear wheels of the pickup in front of them would spin out every now and then, and its rear end would begin sliding sideways, but each time, the driver managed to keep the truck heading in the right direction. Nick checked the Suburban's speedometer—they were barely doing 15 miles per hour.

As the incline continued, the icy-white margins where the other lanes used to be had now become casualty fields, where some drivers had pulled over of their own free will, while others were deposited after a slippery spin, facing in any random direction except up the mountain. After their failed attempts to reach the top of the incline, they now sat on the sidelines, with their engines and windshield wipers running and their headlights on, watching the procession of traffic slowly moving past, and quickly becoming encased in sticky, fast-driving snow. Nick checked behind. The yellow headlights of the Econoline were still there, on the other side of the streaked, sloshy back windshield. The HRT guys were keeping up.

He tried not to watch the road ahead but found himself fixating on it nevertheless—especially once they cleared the top of the curve and started down another steep and icy decline. At any moment, he expected the long-bodied Suburban to lock up the wheels and slide off the road into the blizzard-filled abyss. Nick always preferred to be in the driver's seat, and having somebody else driving him under these conditions made him uneasy.

But he had to admit that Torres was doing a commendable job driving the six-thousand-pound vehicle through this blizzard. Nick reluctantly took a break from scanning and evaluating the road, only to find his mind become preoccupied with the clock. Time was passing excruciatingly slowly and yet with irreversible certainty. Each minute seemed like a loss and not a gain, and with each minute, the dot on Nick's phone moved only a fraction of a millimeter toward their destination. Mr. Giggles had instructed Beck to meet him at the Redlands Motel off US 6 just outside of Grand Junction. Would they get there before Mr. Giggles? Would the HRT team have enough time to prepare for the op? Would Mr. Giggles have Kimmy with him?

After Vail, the traffic moved faster, but 25 miles per hour was still not 70. Just after 5:30 p.m., they made a pit stop at a Conoco in New Castle. Grand Junction was still 70 miles away. The FBI guys got burgers and fries, and Nick was going to get just a coffee, but Beck talked him into eating. Nick considered that he had not had lunch and that this was going to be a long day, and so he agreed. He normally wasn't a fan of fast food, but today he needed calories, and the thin beef patty topped with bacon and melted cheese was the right tool for the job.

They refueled and ate quickly, and then got back on the highway. The snow was still not letting up, but the frozen icy crust on which they drove at the higher elevation had now turned to slush—they were on the western slopes of the Rockies now and were descending into warmer temperatures with every mile. Traffic was moving at around 50 miles per hour now, but still in single file, staying in the tracks of a snowplow truck somewhere up ahead. 50 was much better than 25, but now daylight was beginning to fade, and with the dark would come lower temperatures again and more ice. Nick kept his fingers crossed that there would be no accidents ahead.

They finally reached the outskirts of Grand Junction after dark, as the snow was falling in big, wet flakes. The Redlands Motel was an old-style motor lodge with two stories and individual unit entrances facing the parking lot—convenient, Nick thought, if someone wanted to avoid the hotel lobby cameras. Torres turned into the Phillips 66 gas station just east of the motel and parked in one of the spots facing it. From here, they had a sideways view of the front and east units and the attached parking. Nick spotted the Econoline in the strip mall next to the motel. The neon OPEN sign from one of the stores glinted from the wet metal skin of the van as it pulled deeper into the lot and disappeared in the dim alley behind the stores.

The handheld radio on the dash crackled with static. "Team Charlie in position. We have visual of the back and west side of the motel."

Randy Quinn picked up the radio and responded, "Confirmed." He then got up from the front seat and squeezed past Nick and Beck to get to the third row. From there, he reached into the cargo area and pulled out a bulletproof vest and handed it to Beck.

Nick checked his watch. It was now eight o'clock. "Do you think he will show?" he asked, watching the blizzard blow snow across the street separating the Suburban from the motel.

"No idea," Beck said. "We are here too late. We can't surveil the motel and the surrounding area. He may already be here. At this point, we can't risk spooking him. He is supposed to send me a secure message when he is ready. All we can do is wait." Beck placed his phone on the center console, in Nick's view.

Having already spent over nine hours in the Suburban today, another hour should have been a piece of cake. But the anticipation was excruciating. A blank click of the trigger behind Nick made him turn around, only to see Quinn in the back seat giving an M4 assault rifle a thorough check. Beck, too, pulled out his Glock and inspected the magazine, the slide, and the trigger. And that's when Beck's phone rang. He checked the number and furrowed his eyebrows as he answered.

"Yeah?"

The rest of the conversation was one-directional and brief, and the only other thing Beck said was "Damn" and then later "Understood." And then he hung up.

Nick gave him a questioning look.

Beck shook his head. "Bad news. My team just got booted from LoliTown."

"What? How?"

"No idea. They were in the process of scraping the listings from the site. And then the account got locked out."

"Can they create another account?"

Beck shook his head. "The website is now gone. Vanished."

"Gone? Do you think they took it down so they would not get busted?"

"It looks that way."

"How much data did your team get?" Nick asked.

"They scraped most of the listings, but there is not much we can do with this information outside the site. We may be able to match some of the listings against any missing-children records, but without access to the secure messaging on the site, there's no way to contact the sellers."

The thought that their lead on all those children had just slipped through their fingers made Nick queasy.

"I am worried that our little sting operation here may have been compromised," Beck said.

"What? Why? Do you think the people running the site can warn this asshole?"

"It's possible. Depending on how their site and the messaging app are integrated, it may not take much for them to figure out who we were in contact with."

"Fuck!" Nick whispered under his breath. Maybe he and Claire should have listened to Beck and waited for the FBI to organize their global sting. Maybe they should have been patient. Instead, they pressed Beck to risk it all for just one case, and now they may find themselves empty-handed.

They waited in silence as Nick ruminated about the possible outcomes from today, assuming the worst. He tried not to check his watch every minute, and when he finally checked it, the time was five minutes after nine. His heart sank. The fucker must have been warned. In all the time they'd been sitting here, only one vehicle had departed the motel—two women in a Honda SUV, and no new vehicles had arrived. It was over. In the darkness outside, the wind howled, whipping snow across the windshield, and now and then, whaling at the broad side of the Suburban with a gust.

Beck looked at his watch, sighed, and peeled open the Velcro strap of his vest. And then his phone buzzed.

He looked at it and retightened the Velcro on his vest. "It's him. We are on. Room 17."

In the back seat, Quinn blipped the radio, relaying the information to the HRT. Beck clipped a lapel mic to the vest and put on a Carhartt jacket over it. He zipped it up to hide his vest and then put in a small earpiece.

"Sound check Alpha," he said, fitting a worn-out baseball cap on his head.

"Reading you loud and clear, Alpha," the radio in Quinn's hand squawked.

Beck slipped the Glock inside his belt behind his back, gave the team inside the Suburban a nod, and got out of the vehicle.

"Approaching the motel," he said and started walking, keeping his head down in the gusty blowing snow.

Quinn moved up from the back row to Beck's seat and rested the handguard of his M4 carbine on the back of the passenger seat, watching the row of motel doors through the rifle's scope.

"Unit 17 is first floor, front of the motel," Quinn said into the radio.

In the driver's seat, Torres pulled back the slide of his Glock to load a round into the chamber. Outside, Beck crossed the street, walking calmly through the blizzard toward the snow-plastered cars in front of the motel.

"Almost at the door." Beck's voice crackled through the static of the wind.

Nick watched him approach the door. The blowing snow made it hard to see, but the audio quality was still good, and he heard Beck knock. There was a pause, and then the door cracked open, and a man appeared in the doorway. Nick could not make out his features, but he looked to be of medium build with light-colored hair.

"Hey! You Giggles?" Beck's voice changed, acquiring the smooth finish of a street hustler.

The man rolled a laugh. "In the flesh." A chill ran up Nick's spine—this was the voice from Ben's video! The man checked the parking lot. "Well, come on in."

Beck followed the man into the room, and the door closed behind him.

"Where did you travel from?" Nick heard the man ask.

"Why? You looking to be pen pals?" Beck responded suspiciously.

The man laughed again. "Hey, relax, friend. I am just making conversation. Thanks to COVID, it's been nothing but webcamming for two years. It's nice to see folks traveling again. There's just nothing quite like the real thing. Am I right?"

"You said it. Where is the girl?"

"She's nearby. But I will need the rest of the money first."

"No way. I already paid you half. I am not giving you a cent more until I know you actually have the product. Show me the girl, and then I'll pay you. Or I walk."

The radio went silent for a moment—perhaps the man considered his options. "She is in the next room," he finally said. "Come on." Nick heard a door opening.

"What's wrong with her?" Beck asked after a pause. "Is she sick?"

"—Hostage confirmed," the HRT squawked over the radio in a calm and clear half voice. "Charlie team advancing. Requesting EMT support."

"Copy that," Quinn responded, and Nick heard him dial 911 and request an ambulance.

"No—she's healthy," Giggles said. "Immaculate. I just gave her Benadryl to calm her down a bit. You know? You won't be disappointed."

"I am sure," Beck said.

"Now, let's see about that money," Giggles insisted.

Torres put the Suburban in Drive and let it casually roll out of the gas station parking lot, accelerating toward the motel just as Nick saw the four HRT guys in full gear advance in crouching formation from around the corner of the motel, heading toward unit 17.

"A deal is a deal," Beck said. "Give me a sec to get into my BitWallet. What happens once I pay you?"

"Well, you just go into that room with her, and I will stay here. You got my rules in the message. No rough stuff."

"And you'll be right here?" Beck asked.

"Yes, sir. I have to protect my girl," Giggles said just as Torres brought the Suburban to a stop in front of unit 17 and one of the HRT guys swung a battering ram into the door and it came flying wide open. Nick heard Beck's inhuman yell over the radio: "FBI! HANDS IN THE AIR! GET DOWN ON THE FLOOR!"

Quinn was somehow already out of the SUV and at the busted-open motel room door with his rifle raised. Nick got out, too, leaving his door ajar, and gripping his Springfield tightly in his hand. He walked into the room past the FBI agents cuffing the man lying face down on the grimy motel carpet. Nick opened the door to the adjacent unit 18 – a mirror reflection of the one he had just come from. There, a tiny figure was splayed out on the king-size bed. She had a red ballerina tutu, cream-colored leggings with gold sparkle, and a white, short-sleeved shirt. Nick did not expect this. She looked like a doll—dressed and groomed with care, left by someone on the white expanse of the king-size comforter. She was sleeping—he could see her tiny chest rising and falling. Nick sat on the bed next to her, and she sighed and turned toward him, still asleep. *Kimmy—5; female; black.* She was the child from LoliTown—Nick had no doubt. Same braided black hair. Same puffy little face. Just a different outfit.

Had she been to this motel before? This room? How many times? In the other room, Mr. Giggles was responding to questions, and the mere sound of his voice revolted Nick. He scooped up the tiny body, wrapping her in the comforter, and carried her outside, away from this room to a snow-covered bench under one of the windows. He sat there, holding the little girl wrapped in the blanket, and everything around them became still. The squawking of the police radios faded away. The snow was falling softly now. And in the distance, Nick heard the siren of an ambulance.

27

Duane Criddell was a forty-six-year-old real estate broker from Grand Junction, Colorado. He was also a pedophile and a child trafficker who went by the online handle MrGiggles777.

He did not resist the arrest. Lying face down on the motel room carpet with his hands cuffed behind his back, he complied calmly and readily, like a man who'd had a couple of decades to prepare for this possibility. When two burly HRT guys took him out of the room, still handcuffed, and helped him up into the Econoline's open back doors, Nick saw him give them a thank-you nod, with a polite half smile on his lips.

When the ambulance came, Nick took Kimmy's tiny limp body to the EMTs and let them take over. He hated to call her *Kimmy*—it was the name this monster gave her—but until they had ID'd her, this was all he had, and probably all she knew. The pair of EMTs—a guy and a gal who looked to be in their twenties took her vitals and concluded she was in stable condition but clearly lethargic, giving her responsiveness level *V* on the AVPU scale, meaning she was responsive to verbal prompts, even though her responses were little more than barely intelligible. The female EMT said this was consistent with a diphenhydramine drugging, which is what Benadryl was. She said they would take the girl to St. Mary's, where she could be monitored while she recovered. Torres went with them to meet with a child-services caseworker.

When Nick returned to the entrance of unit 17, the Econoline was just pulling away. He saw Quinn in the passenger seat. Beck was at the Suburban, taking off his tactical vest.

"Where are you taking him?" Nick asked.

"The weather is still shitty in the mountains. Quinn will take him to the Mesa County Detention Facility for the night, and we will move him to Denver tomorrow."

"Are we not going with them?"

"No, you and I have another stop to make."

"Where?"

"Duane's house. He told me we needed to go there."

"Where is it?"

"East from here, off state highway 330 just outside Grand Junction."

The snowfall had finally subsided, which was a good thing, because the way to Duane's house was a curvy mountain highway winding through a rocky canyon higher and higher above Grand Junction. They ascended one hairpin corner after another, until eventually the towering cliffs opened up, the road straightened out, and they found themselves on a high plateau. Up ahead, Nick saw house lights. This was a rural area, where properties were spread half a mile or more apart. Some were lavishly lit country estates with horse stables and multilevel manors. Others were shabby ranches with barbed-wire fences, tin-roofed outbuildings, and junk cars rusting in a field.

Duane's house was neither of these. When Beck slowed down and turned the Suburban down a snowy driveway, Nick saw a neat two-story farmhouse with a roofed porch, a sturdy-looking barn in the back, and a white three-rail fence separating the treed front yard from the highway. Beck parked at an angle, so that the headlights illuminated the front porch. The house was dark.

They exited the truck. The night sky was beginning to clear, and in the silver, shadowless light of reflected snow, Nick saw the fields behind the house and the snowy, jagged mountain range in the distance. This was an isolated area. Silent. Nick turned and looked around—there were no other house lights in sight.

Beck climbed the porch steps and jangled with the keys he took off Duane. It was so quiet here that Nick heard the latch turn. Beck pushed the door open and found the light switch.

Inside, the house was clean and updated—modern but with restraint. This was not what Nick expected. He expected a semi-trashed house with peeling wallpaper and furniture that Duane inherited from his grandmother. But instead, there were area rugs, quartz countertops, and dark stainless-steel appliances in the kitchen. Nick and Claire had been considering updating their kitchen, and he could tell the updates in Duane's house must have been done relatively recently and at no little expense.

Beck opened a door in the hallway—bathroom. He opened another one—"Bingo!"—stairs to the basement.

"Here we go," he said, turning on the stairwell lights and going down the creaky wooden stairs. Nick followed. The air down here smelled of household cleaner. Beck flipped another light switch at the bottom, and when the bright LED lights came on, Nick took a horrified step back. Under Duane's house was a meticulously set up daycare. The floor of the big open area was covered with large, bright red and blue rubber tiles, like the ones on shopping-mall playgrounds. In one corner of the room, a kid-height round table with chairs held neatly stacked drawing paper and a jar of crayons. A wall shelving unit displayed evenly spaced rows of clear plastic tubs with dolls, colorful building blocks, games, and toy cars. At the opposite corner was a full-size plastic playhouse with a mustard-yellow slide, a ladder, and a swing. The main wall was painted with a cartoonish mural depicting googly-eyed cars rolling through a hilly highway with leafy grass, ladybugs and flowers in the foreground and bright blue sky and pure white clouds near the drop-tile ceiling. The other three walls were each painted a different color—one light yellow, one light pink, and one powder blue. Next to the pink wall was a tripod with a camcorder.

"Jesus," Nick said.

"This is the most elaborate setup I've ever seen," Beck concurred.

"How . . ." Nick was lost for words. "How can a single, middle-aged man with no kids get all this built and not raise any questions?"

Beck shrugged. "It's not illegal to buy kids' stuff. And if anyone asks, he could say it's for his nieces and nephews or his grandkids staying with him."

The yellow and blue walls each had two doors. Nick opened the one closest to him—on the yellow wall. It was a bathroom—kids' sea themed, with mermaids, fish, and shells painted on the walls and submarines on the shower curtain. The next door was a small closet with a few kids' dresses and jackets on hangers and a plastic storage tub on the floor with photography lights and other camera equipment.

Do you like Mr. Giggles, Billy? Criddell's sugary voice from Ben's video echoed in Nick's head. He took another look at the basement. This did not look like the room in the video. But that was a long time ago. How many kids had Criddell had here? This place was making Nick feel queasy.

The doors on the blue wall had sliding deadbolts on the outside. The first one was unlatched. Beck pushed the door open and turned on the light. This was a little girl's bedroom with Pepto-pink walls, a white canopy bed full of stuffed toy animals, Barbie posters, and a fluffy faux-fur white rug. Through the open closet door, Nick saw a selection of short, colorful, and glittery things hanging on tiny hangers. This room was empty.

Nick put his hand on the handle of the second door and slid open the deadbolt. He pushed the door open—it opened heavily, with the weight of a solid-core door. When the door cracked open, he heard the sound of cartoons playing.

Soundproofed, he thought to himself, swinging the door open the rest of the way. Inside this room, the lights were on. This room was themed for a little boy, with blue walls, soft rubber mat flooring, and a red racecar bunk bed. He didn't see him at first, but as Nick absorbed the room, he saw a pair of eyes watching him from the pile of blankets in the murky corner of the bottom bunk.

Nick turned to Beck, unsure of what to say or do next, and Beck put his hand on Nick's shoulder to hold him back and stepped toward the bed.

"Hey, Johnny," he said, cautiously crouching down at the bunk bed, so his eyes were the same level as the boy's. "It's OK, buddy. Your *papa* sent us to get you. He is OK."

* * *

A few days ago, if someone had asked Nick to close his eyes and picture a pedophile in his mind, he likely would have envisioned a caricature-like cliché—an unattractive man with scrawny limbs, thick glasses with beady, shifty eyes, a greasy comb-over, stained sweatpants, and a wife-beater shirt.

Studying Duane Criddell under the bright lights of the FBI interview room, Nick had to admit that Duane Criddell did not look like a pedophile. His face was youthful for his age and attractively proportioned, and his light brown hair was full and nicely cut. He was of medium build and neither overweight nor scrawny. He dressed neatly: dark bootcut jeans with no holes and a faded red quarter-zip sweater. But what bothered Nick the most were his eyes—they were not shifty but rather calm and confident, willing to connect and hold the gaze. This made Nick uneasy. *Criddell was OK with being Criddell.* He spoke intelligently. He did not look like a predator. He did not look like an ugly, evil man. He looked like somebody's brother, or father. And this was the most terrifying thing, because Duane Criddell was indeed a monster.

"It's quite a collection of child pornography we found on your computer," Beck said. "And it's very well organized."

"Thank you," Criddell said earnestly.

"You take pride in it?"

"Certainly."

"You are aware, of course, that it is against the law to possess—never mind *to produce*—child pornography?"

Criddell smiled. "The way you say it makes it sound as if it is a choice. People can't choose who they are. Can't choose who or what they are attracted to. The law does not decide this. You know, *homosexuality* used to be against the law—still is, technically, in many states. Do you think this made people *choose* to be heterosexual instead? No. It is a primal urge. Some people want to fuck their iMac or their dog. I find nothing more comforting or desirable than the body of a little boy. This can't be beaten out of me or adjudicated away. Whether it's legal or not has no bearing. Don't tell me you've never broken or bent the law to get something you wanted. I am as much a part of this humanity as you are. You can smash the mirror if you don't like what you see, but it won't change what's in front of it. And I accept this, whether or not you do."

But it's not about what you *accept, you motherfucker,* Nick wanted to say. *Did* they *accept this? You hurting them. You touching them. It gets you excited, doesn't it? Hurting them excites you, and you record it so you can relive it again and again.*

Nick tried to keep his face like Beck's—in poker mode, cool and dispassionate. But he found himself clenching his fists under the table as he watched Duane's lips moving. He saw little Ben on this monster's bed—before all the scars and burns. Before Ben was dead. He felt the limp weight of Kimmy's little body in his arms. He saw the scared eyes of the little boy in Criddell's deadbolted basement room. What punishment could ever balance out this evil? All he wanted to do right now is reach across and smash Criddell's face into the table until there was only a bloody pulp left.

Criddell must have felt Nick's glare because he looked straight at him and smiled.

"When did you start trafficking for Anatoli Azarev?" Beck asked.

"In 99."

"How did you meet Anatoli?"

Criddell shook his head. "I didn't. In all these years, I have never met him. I've only heard the name."

"So, how did you come to work for him?"

Criddell reached over to the Styrofoam cup on the table and took a drink of water, his eyes crossing with Nick's again. He set the cup down. "I was twenty-three. A foolish young man just out of college. I was aware of my needs, but I had no idea how to be in this world. My first experience was with my friend's little sister. I was ten and she was five. Since then, I have learned exactly what I was. But living with that knowledge was not easy. I had no idea how my kind existed in this world. I wasn't interested in women, or even men, for that matter. What other options did I have? I could have cozied up to a single mother with a young child and spent the rest of my life sneaking in the shadows. That's what some men did, but I found even the thought of having to live with a woman revolting. I did not want to be entangled. So, I started paying for it . . . in seedy motels and massage parlors, where I was served dirty, abused children. But still, I became a regular. I was repulsed and addicted at the same time. The need was too great to control, but afterward I would feel remorse and pity for these children. One night, the fixer I dealt with in Denver pulled me aside and said the man he worked for was looking to expand. This fixer wanted to move on to teens. I could tell he did not like dealing with children. It showed. He was looking for someone to take over the operation."

"Why do you think he choose you?" Beck asked.

"I don't know. Maybe because he knew I would not be in it just for the money."

"So, you started in Denver?"

"Yes. Then I moved the operation from Denver to Grand Junction in 2002."

"Why?"

"Less police and federal authorities, and still on a major interstate."

"Where do you get the children?"

"From Anatoli's couriers. I get a message with time and place."

"How is the message transmitted?"

"Telegram app."

"Where do the children come from?"

"I've been told they are sold by their parents, but I don't know for sure."

"What happens then?"

"I take them in. I provide for them, and I teach them."

"Teach them what?"

"Everything." Criddell smiled disarmingly.

"Until what age?"

"Nine or ten. I don't deal in teens. They are not my clientele's cup of tea."

"So, what happens when they get too old?"

"They get transferred."

"How?"

"A courier takes them."

"Where?"

"Denver or Salt Lake City."

"What happens to them there?"

"I don't know."

"If you had to guess?"

"They are put to work with a different . . ."

"Pimp?"

"Manager," he said with a slight frown, and Nick could tell he clearly disliked that word.

"Do you remember Ben Harris?" Nick asked.

Criddell smiled. "Yes, of course. I remember them all. That's not the name I gave him, but I certainly saw *that* name along with his photo in the media at the time."

"What name did you give him?"

"I called him *Billy*."

"When did you see him last?"

"In February of 2008."

"What happened in 2008?"

"One of Anatoli's girls from Salt Lake City came and got him."

"A courier?"

Criddell nodded.

"Because he was getting too old?"

Criddell nodded again.

"Did you see him after 2008?"

Criddell shook his head. "No."

"How did you first meet Ben?"

"He was delivered to me in 2001."

"Who delivered him?"

"Vicky—one of Anatoli's girls in Denver."

"Did you get any other children delivered in 2001?"

"Yes—Tommy. He was six."

"Do you remember Tommy's real name?" Beck asked.

"I do," Criddell said and watched Beck silently.

Beck raised an eyebrow. "Are you going to tell me?"

"Let's come back to that in a bit," Criddell said as if he had a grand plan for his narrative.

Nick ground his jaw. He was ready to strangle the creep.

Beck let it slide. "So, what happened to Ben after he was delivered to you?"

"I managed and promoted him, as I did with Tommy. It wasn't hard. He was a cute boy."

"Did you rape him?" Nick asked.

Frown. "I had sex with him, yes. The perks of running this business." Criddell paused for a moment, as if reminiscing.

"Besides, it conditioned him for his future clients. Like any other profession, sex workers get better with practice."

"How did you *promote* Ben and Tommy?"

"Discreetly. It's all about the network. A pretty boy can fetch a very good price, if you position him to the right buyers."

"And did you . . . find the right buyers?"

Criddell's lips crooked into a slight scowl. "Let's just say, Billy had never worked truck stops while he was with me. Doctors, executives, judges. I've had cops, too."

Beck didn't bite. "And what about pornography?"

"Well, that's the real cherry, isn't it? You can sell it over and over, even after the boy gets too old. The good stuff sells well. And mine is good stuff. The themes, the settings, the lighting. Mine were top sellers. Because I knew exactly what those anonymous eyeballs wanted to see. Because I was just like them."

"On LoliTown?" Nick asked.

Criddell looked at him and smiled magnanimously. "When I started out, there *was* no LoliTown. We had tapes, then DVDs. But with websites, everything changed. Anatoli linked me to global distribution. Now, my videos stream all over the world."

Nick interrupted Criddell's ode of self-adoration: "Did you know that Ben died?"

"No. Poor boy. How?"

Nick glared back. "Does it really matter to you?"

"Yes, of course it matters. I did my best to protect these children. Even their mothers did not want them. I was the one to take care of them."

"He was killed," Nick said.

Criddell nodded. "And you think Anatoli had something to do with this?"

Beck merged back into the conversation: "How do you communicate with Anatoli?"

"Telegram."

"And the money? How does he collect it?"

Criddell looked amused. "It's all digital now. You should know. All crypto. All online. On LoliTown and the other sites. I have not had to bundle stacks of wrinkled twenties in over a decade."

"Who is running LoliTown?"

"Anatoli's syndicate. Impressive, isn't it?"

Beck did not say anything.

"I can help you take it down," Criddell offered, fixing his gaze on Beck.

"LoliTown?" Beck scoffed. "It's gone. Disappeared."

Criddell smiled. "Did you get booted? It's not gone. It just moved to evade you."

"What?"

"Anatoli's IT guys use AI to analyze website traffic. It can detect anything that looks like law enforcement activity. Then it kicks the user off and changes the URL. The legitimate users get a message with the new URL. I can get you the new link. And I can help you take it down." Criddell slipped into his enigmatic silence again, watching Beck.

"I am listening," said Beck.

"Not for free, of course. I want immunity."

"Duane, you've been trafficking children for over twenty years. Immunity is not going to happen."

"But think about it. LoliTown is one the biggest child pornography and trafficking rings on the web. Do you know how many registered users we have? Almost half a million." He smiled like a Cheshire cat. "Terabytes of material. And all those child listings. Three hundred and fifty-seven, last time I checked. All those little children all around the world. More than half of them are right here, in the States. Imagine bringing them home."

Beck watched Criddell intently. "You have to give me something, Duane, for me to take this offer seriously."

"Like what?"

"Something I don't already know."

"How about closing a missing person's case?"

"Who?"

"Tommy. I told you we would get back to him." Criddell smiled.

"OK? . . ."

"His real name was Trevor Simeka. He became sick in December of 2005 and passed away." Criddell paused and looked down at the table. "I can show you where his body is buried." He tilted his head slightly. "And if you take me up on my offer, maybe you can get to the other children. While they are still alive."

Beck leaned back in his chair, studying Criddell.

"Let's take a break," Beck said, getting up.

Nick followed him out. They walked in silence to the monitoring room a few doors down, where Beck headed straight for the K-Cup coffee machine and watched it, his arms folded and his hand rubbing his stubbled cheek unconsciously, as the machine burred and hissed, filling his Styrofoam cup. Nick approached a bank of computer monitors, two of which showed the room they were just in, from two different angles. In them, the solitary Criddell was maintaining composure, probably aware he was being watched.

"He is not what I expected," Nick said. "None of this is what I expected. His house, the kids' rooms, the way he talks about them. Like he . . . cares for these children."

Beck walked up, taking a cautious sip of hot coffee. "In a sick way, he does. He is what we call a *preferential* offender as opposed to a *situational* one. The preferentials tend to be more intelligent and organized. He sees himself as a mentor and a protector. And the sad part is, these kids bond to him. We see it all the time. He is the only parent-like figure in their lives. And the things he makes them do, they accept as the norm and as a fair price for his approval. It's not uncommon to have kids lie to protect their abuser, and to experience trauma from being removed from him. We have to tread carefully with them."

They watched Criddell in silence for a moment longer. Nick could tell Beck's mind was preoccupied.

"We . . . got him, right?" Nick asked. "You have everything you need for the federal prosecutor to make the case, right?"

Beck nodded, half-presently. "Oh, yes. The US Attorney's Office will have plenty to work with. Kidnapping, trafficking, possession of child pornography, production of and distribution . . . and then the actual assaults. We can match his voice to the voice in the recordings . . . he would not get out in his lifetime . . ." Beck's voice trailed off as if his mind was pursuing another train of thought.

Nick turned and stared at Beck point-blank. "Then tell me you are not actually considering the deal he is proposing?"

Beck's jaw tightened, and through the closely cropped gray hair, Nick saw a knotty vein swell in his temple.

28

On Friday, Nick resigned himself to spending the day at the station. With all the unplanned trips over the last couple of weeks, he had fallen behind on paperwork, and reckoning was overdue. He had reports to write and loose ends to tie up in Ben's case. He documented his second visit to Edie Harris and appended the signed confession she gave to the Huerfano County Sheriff's Office. He also documented his investigation of the Talenkos, their arrest in Fort Wayne, and Victor's statement connecting them to both Ben's disappearance and to Anatoli Azarev's organization. He then wrote a report on the research Claire had conducted that resulted in the arrest of Duane Criddell aka MrGiggles777 in Grand Junction. (He omitted Claire's method of gaining initial access to the case files.) Criddell's confession was important not only because it filled a large missing part of Ben's life, but because it also confirmed that Anatoli Azarev was more than just a distant echo from Victor's testimony about the events that took place twenty years ago. According to Criddell, Anatoli was still very much involved in the trafficking business, and this made him the leading person of interest in Ben's murder.

Nick glanced at the clock in the corner of his computer screen, as he had done more than once today. It was now 2:42 in the afternoon. He was expecting a call, and hoped he would get it today, so he could close out the week with some idea of a plan for going after Anatoli. He considered calling, but decided to give it more time and instead began typing up an email to

Huerfano County sheriff's officers to apprise them of the Talenko and Criddell statements so that they could fill in the remaining gaps in Ben's missing person case. At least that investigation was now complete.

3:27

Nicked picked up his phone and dialed.

Beck answered on the first ring. "Severs. You were on my list today."

"Yeah? You have good news?"

"We have ID'd both kids Criddell had. The girl is Latoya Cook, reported missing from Illinois two years ago, and the boy is Grady Pittman from Nebraska, missing for just over a year."

"That's great. How are they doing?"

"Good, considering what they've been through."

"Are you going to question the parents? Knowing Azarev's MO—."

"—Already being done. Child protective services will maintain custody in the meanwhile. Criddell also took our team to the location where he had buried Trevor. We exhumed the remains. There is not much more than bones left, but we will attempt a familial DNA match to confirm identity. Criddell says Trevor had died from flu complications. We likely won't be able to confirm it, but we will examine the remains for evidence of foul play."

So, Criddell kept his word. "What about Azarev and LoliTown?"

"Criddell got us back into the website, and our cyber team has identified that the website is hosted on a server based in Estonia. We are coordinating with Interpol to take it down."

"That's great news! What about Anatoli?"

"What about him?"

"How are we going to take him down?"

"We are not going after Anatoli."

"What?" Nick thought he had misheard. "Did you say you are not going after Anatoli?"

"We are not. Not now, at least."

"Why not?"

"The DC office said no. We don't have enough to take this further."

"What do you mean? We know his name, we know where he is, we have testimony that he was responsible for Ben's abduction, and trafficking, which makes him a solid person of interest in Ben's murder investigation. What else do we need?"

"Azarev Enterprises operates from Belarus, and Belarus is not going to cooperate with our investigation. The company has ties to the Belarusian government, and the Belarusian government is allied with Russia, which is in a particularly anti-Western mood right now, given their tensions with Ukraine."

"But Ben was an American citizen, kidnapped and killed on American soil. You are telling me just because his death was ordered from around the globe, there is nothing we can do?"

"I am sorry, Nick. Maybe we will get more actionable information when we take down LoliTown, but as it stands right now, we have nothing directly linking Anatoli to the website or to the phone malware. This makes for a very weak diplomatic conversation even under the best of political conditions."

"I bet if this was about terrorism or drugs, the government would be more than interested to have this diplomatic conversation."

He heard Beck sigh. "I am just being honest with you, Severs. I can't pursue Anatoli any further at this time."

Nick was silent.

"Our line of work can't play out like a Hollywood movie every time. We catch some bad guys, but others walk free, and maybe we catch them the next time. But you can't dwell on it. You've got to be able to appreciate the positives. Think about it—we caught Ben's abductors, you have his body, and you know how he died. Do you know how many missing persons cases I have where I would give anything to have just one of these things happen? Not to mention, think about LoliTown. We have already identified one hundred and twelve of the children being trafficked there. We are not just talking about taking down another porn site. We are talking about rescuing the actual kids who are being trafficked and abused by other Criddells or by their own family members. These kids are still alive, Nick. We can still save them."

Nick swallowed down a lump in his throat.

"You should feel good about this, Nick. You and Claire were instrumental in getting us to this point."

"Yeah . . . you are right." Nick cleared his throat. "So, Criddell . . . ? Does this mean you made a deal with him? Will he get off?"

"He will get a significantly reduced sentence, given his cooperation. But he will still have to register as a sex offender when he gets out."

"And you are OK with this?"

"No, Nick. Far from it. But on the scale of all evils, he is just one speck compared with LoliTown."

. . . And Ben is just one speck compared with all the children who would be rescued from LoliTown, Nick thought. This simple arithmetic was hard to argue with, but that did not mean Nick had to like it. He hung up with Beck and stared in a stupor at the screensaver on his monitor. His case, which had been rolling ahead at full steam just an hour ago, had suddenly screeched to a dead stop. He had a suspect he could not go after. Anatoli Azarev could have just as well been on the moon.

Maybe we catch them the next time, Beck said. When would that be? Abbi White's case on Nick's desk was still waiting for its day, forty years later. Nick couldn't let the same happen to Ben's case. He sat there for a while, thinking through any possible scenarios he could still play out against Anatoli. But nothing was panning out in his head. He needed a break. There were still a few to-dos left on his checklist for the day, but his call with Beck had depleted Nick's will to focus on work.

Everything seemed small and moot now. The station was dead quiet, as if attuned to the lowly state of his own morale. Patty had already left for the weekend and rolled the dispatch over to the county. Ray's truck was still in the parking lot, so he was probably still in his office, going down the rabbit holes of the internet, wherever they took him after the Civil War-period Sharps rifle he was researching earlier in the day.

The quietness of the office reminded Nick of his old teaching job. When he taught during the summer semester, this is how quiet the campus would get, especially late in the afternoon, when Nick was finishing up his office hours. There would be less than a half-dozen people in the whole building. Dead quiet. Those days seemed so far away. Like someone else's life. Why did he ever leave that job? There was predictability in it. Consistent results. Semester after semester. Kids would come and kids would go. He never had to make peace with letting a monster go free.

He took a deep breath and decided he was done with this day. He packed his bag, grabbed his car keys, and wished Ray a great weekend on his way out. Once in the driver's seat of the Tahoe, he called in a takeout order at Coloradough Pizza: one Red Rocks—BBQ chicken with bacon; one Garden of the Gods—veggies with feta; and an order of Rattlesnakes—baked jalapenos stuffed with cream cheese and wrapped in bacon. The first one was for him, the second for Claire, and the third for them to share.

At home, Claire opened a bottle of red, and Nick mixed himself a highball with Bulleit and ginger ale. They decided to eat outside, down by the firepit. Nick lit the fire, and soon, soothing waves of crackling heat washed over them, pushing away the cold evening air. The sun was already behind the mountain ridges, but its rays were still bright, coloring the feather-like wisps of high cirrus clouds overhead into flaming yellows, oranges, and pinks.

They ate pizza, and Nick caught up Claire on the news in the case.

"That's bullshit," she said, when he told her about the FBI not going after Anatoli.

"I know." Nick stared into the flames.

"So, what are you going to do now?"

He took a gulp of his highball. "All I can do at this point is try to build a stronger case. The more evidence I can dig up on Anatoli, the harder it will be for the FBI to say no. Maybe some new information will come to light when they take down those servers in Estonia. But I can't really rely on that. I need to find evidence actually tying Anatoli to the site. Or even better, evidence tying him to the malware on Ben's phone."

"I can ask Roses," Claire volunteered. "Hackers are communal animals. They tend to brag. Maybe someone heard something."

He thought about it, watching the dancing flames. "OK. Just please be careful."

* * *

As he lay in bed that night, Nick could not make his mind settle. Claire was already asleep in the crook of his arm, her naked body entwined with his. Her smooth skin felt hot against him. Her head was on his chest, and with every breath he inhaled the familiar aroma of her hair. And yet, his mind kept circling back to the case.

Through the bourbon haze in his head, the state of affairs looked even bleaker. Beck was right, of course—in their line of work, one had to focus on the positives. Because without them, all the negatives would crush you. And right now, they were threatening to crush Nick. The fear looming large over him now was that this was as far as he would ever get in this case. Anatoli Azarev seemed an unassailable entity over which Nick's law had no power. Anatoli could reach across half the world and kill someone in Nick's backyard, and yet Nick could do nothing about it. He could not drive his Tahoe over there. His badge, which gave him power and authority here, was completely useless there.

This could have been the bourbon talking, but Nick considered that he had not felt so helpless since he was thirteen, when his family moved to St. Joseph, and he had to start high school in a new town. This kid named Corey—a short, loudmouthed little a-hole in one of his classes, immediately zeroed in on Nick—the quiet, reserved new kid. He picked on Nick verbally through much of the class, and Nick did his best to tune him out, but at lunch Nick got to meet Corey's two friends—a tall, skinny kid everyone called Giraffe, and a husky kid called Robby. Apparently, Corey was the ringleader of this little gang. After lunch, the three of them accosted Nick in the hallway. Robby and Giraffe held Nick's arms to the wall while Corey spit a long loogie into his own hand and rubbed it over Nick's ears and cheeks, repeating, "*Wussy. Whatcha gonna do, wussy?*"

That night his parents knew something had happened. Nick did not want to tell them at first, because it seemed so shameful, and it made him want to cry just thinking about it. When he finally did tell, his father did the last thing Nick ever expected. This learned man with a professorial beard and wire-frame glasses put down the book he was reading, took Nick's scrawny, boyish hand into his, and folded Nick's fingers into a fist. He then held out his big, calloused palm and said, "Punch it."

The next day, when Nick heard Corey's "Hey, wussy" behind him at the lockers and felt Corey's slimy finger touch his ear, Nick turned around and slugged Corey in the face. Corey stumbled backward and fell on his ass, holding his hand to his nose. Blood began to trickle through Corey's fingers, and tears squirted from his eyes. Giraffe and Robby stood to the side, with their jaws agape. Later, Corey denied to the principal that Nick had punched him. Maybe even bullies had some twisted code of honor, or maybe it was just too embarrassing to admit and too damaging to his bad-boy reputation. It was easier to pretend it had never happened. Either way, he never touched Nick again, and never said another word to him, as if Nick and Corey no longer existed on the same plane.

Nick never backed down from a bully since then, but now, no matter how much he wanted it, and no matter how hard he squeezed his fingers into a fist, his arms just could not reach Anatoli. This man was evil incarnate. Powerful and untouchable. Would taking down LoliTown make any difference? Beck said it himself—new sites popped up as soon as the old ones were taken down. How many more souls was Anatoli going to entangle in his dark enterprise just because Nick could not stop him?

29

"Do we have a problem, Oleg?"

"It's nothing to worry about." Oleg opened his laptop and connected to the projector in the conference room. "The security algorithm detected a connection to one of our sites from a VPN server we've seen used by the FBI before."

"Which site?"

"LoliTown."

Anatoli felt the hairs at the base of his neck stand up, but his face did not show any reaction. *Why the FBI? Why now? Did it have something to do with Billy?* Maybe he should have just let Billy go. But then again, how could he? In 2013, Billy had been with a certain US state governor. And this governor was now a full US senator. Anatoli just couldn't risk it. What if Billy went to therapy or saw the senator's picture in the news? What if he suddenly remembered everything and went to the media? This information was worth a whole lot to Anatoli as blackmail and nothing at all if it came out as a public scandal. He could not risk it. It was just smart business to protect his investment.

"Is it possible they connected us to Billy's death?"

Oleg considered it. "Nah," he shook his head. "I doubt it. There is no way they could connect the phone malware to us, and as far as LoliTown is concerned, Billy was too old for it when we launched it. So, the FBI is probably just poking around. You know how the pigs are—always scanning, always digging. Just a coincidence."

Anatoli did not believe in coincidences. Especially not in the poorly timed ones. LoliTown was absolutely critical for his deal with Moscow.

"What's our exposure?" he asked. "What do we need to do?"

"Nothing. It's all taken care of. We expelled the user and moved the site as a precaution. The site is fully operational, and all legitimate users have access. However, there is one curious detail worth further investigation. I have an old buddy at Sandworm—the Russian GRU's hacking unit, and I asked him to check for any chatter or other indicators of FBI activity pertaining to LoliTown. He told me there is a hacker who has been making inquiries about LoliTown in the last few days. I don't have much information on them yet. But it could be connected. They could be working for the FBI."

"OK," Anatoli said. "Good work. I will have Max look into this. He will call you."

Oleg nodded.

"It's *critical* this site stays up." Anatoli made sure Oleg acknowledged this directive with another nod. "And we need to add some new users."

"Sure, I can run a pastebin campaign—drum up a few hundred new visitors."

"No." Anatoli shook his head. "I don't want just anybody. If I gave you names of specific people to bring to the site, do you think you can?"

"Of course. It can be as easy as doing a *hosts* file highjack to redirect their web traffic to LoliTown."

"And we can get proof?"

"Oh yeah—full logs: their IP addresses, site histories, time stamps. The visit durations may be a bit short, unless, of course, they like what they see." Oleg smirked.

"Good. I will have a few new names for you soon—see what you can do."

"You've got it."

Anatoli tapped on the table, considering. "There is one more thing," he said. "I need you to prepare to move all the critical parts of this operation to Minsk. We will be closing this office."

Oleg stared at Anatoli for a moment, to make certain Anatoli was being serious. Anatoli knew Oleg liked it here in Ukraine. He liked Kyiv. He liked the scene here—more European, more youthful. He liked OstTech and his team here. The smile melted from Oleg's lips. "When?"

"I don't know yet. Could be weeks, could be days."

"How much notice will I have?"

"Maybe days. Maybe hours. How will this affect our operations?"

Oleg exhaled quietly, gazed up into the empty corner of the ceiling for a moment, and then looked back at Anatoli. "Any legitimate operations, if you wish to keep them going, are all in the cloud—Microsoft, Salesforce, Workday. We can resume operations from anywhere—just hire new staff, if needed. As far as the *special* business interests are concerned, two of our websites are running from an anonymous server in the data center in Estonia, and the others are in Denmark, and my team can manage them from anywhere. And in terms of this office space, I would just need to do a security audit and a clean sweep, to make sure we don't leave anything behind if we have to leave in a hurry. I would also need to go back to Minsk to set up a few things so we can roll over our business to there. We will need some new hardware—easier to buy new than bring from here."

"Fine," Anatoli said. "Do it soon."

Th!rty

The day shift had two discharges and no intakes, and so the ward was at less than full capacity tonight. Claire finished her 1 a.m. rounds with bed 11 – a little boy named Adrian sleeping peacefully in the glow of the night-light. He was five—the same age as Ben in that video Criddell posted on LoliTown. That website, that menagerie of horrors, was a disease—no—just one symptom of the disease that was spreading through the world, poisoning minds, and harming kids. It normalized evil. The web made it so easy for it to spread and take root. Claire felt a little guilty about that fact. She loved the web. She loved having access to infinite information. But it was the same web that enabled this evil to reach such a scale.

Back at the nurses' station, her phone on the counter was blinking a blue light—new message. She unlocked the phone with some trepidation; it was unusual for her to get a text message at this hour of the night, even from Nick. But this was not a text. It was a Tox Chat message from Roses, which was unexpected, because they had not planned to talk till Friday, when Claire was off, and Friday was still two days away.

"Can you talk now?" the message said. It was time-stamped nine minutes ago.

Claire looked at her watch. "Sandy, I'm taking my break," she said to the older nurse, who was restocking the meds cart.

"OK, hon," Sandy responded without looking and went into the meds closet with her clipboard.

Claire typed as she walked to the break room: "What's up?"

"I have someone you need to talk to."

This was also highly unusual. Since their very first chat, it had always been just the two of them. Of course, Roses had other connections in the hacking underworld, but she was always the sole, safe intermediary for Claire. Never before had she brought someone else directly into contact with Claire.

"OK," Claire typed. "Right now?"

"Yes. Click this," Roses typed and then pasted an impossibly long URL that stared with *LeapChat* and continued with a seemingly endless mash-up of dictionary words: *https://www.leapchat.org/#FenceNegotiatorOftentimesMobilizeMugshotLaryngitisVelcroDyslexiaAwokeMugshotUtopiaRopelikeOnstageBroomShackIridescentGutlessSurferJawbreakerRopelikeAnesthesiaMutationUnflavoredHuddlingGnomish*

LeapChat? This was a new one for Claire. She clicked the link, and the Firefox browser window showed a popup asking her to pick a username. She typed in *Kat* and was taken to a blank chat window with two green bubbles already waiting—*Leo* and *Roses*. She went back to Tox Chat and messaged Roses: "Who is this Leo?"

"He has done work for the people running LoliTown."

Claire's blood boiled instantly. "He *works* for them?!"

"Yes. But give him a chance. Trust me."

This was a reach, but Roses had not let her down yet. Reining in her hatred and disgust, she switched back to the LeapChat window.

"OK, Leo," Roses typed. "Tell Kat what you told me."

* * *

The first-shift nurse got held up in traffic and was late, which delayed Claire's morning rounds. She texted Nick that she would not see him before he left for the station, and it was 8:10 in the morning when she finally left the hospital. But when she pulled in at home, she was surprised to see Nick's Tahoe still parked in the driveway. She double-checked her watch—8:37 a.m. She was even more surprised when she walked into the house and smelled bacon and heard music and something sizzling in a skillet.

Nick was in the kitchen, in front of the stove with a spatula in hand and a griddle and a large skillet going at the same time.

She quietly approached behind him. "What are you doing at home?" she said.

He jumped, startled, and shook the spatula at her. "You! Sneaky!" He laughed.

She pulled him in for a kiss. "Good morning."

"Yes, it is," he replied, smiling. "You are just in time. The hash browns need just a few more minutes, but the bacon and the pancakes are ready. Do you want juice or coffee?"

"Coffee," she said, not used to this kind of a spread after work. "Aren't you late?"

He packed a double shot of fresh grind into the Gaggia's brass portafilter and twisted it into the machine. "I got some good news this morning," he said, waiting for the Ready light to come on. "So, I called Ray and told him I'd be late."

"Oh, really? I have some news, too."

"Yeah? You want to go first?" he asked, clicking the On toggle now glowing amber. The Gaggia whirred to life, and Nick turned back to the stove to flip the hash browns.

"No, you go ahead." She sat down.

"OK." Nick turned off the skillet and moved it to a cold burner. "Beck called me this morning." He shut off the Gaggia and poured two sugars and a dash of half-and-half into Claire's cup. He stirred it and set it in front of her. "Last night, the FBI and Interpol took down LoliTown. They raided and arrested fifty-nine traffickers and rescued a hundred and twelve children across Europe and the US." He raised his coffee cup to Claire and smiled. "And none of this would have happened without you—my beautiful, smart, and amazing woman. Here is to you."

"Wow," Claire said, processing the significance of this news. She tapped her mug to Nick's. "A hundred and twelve kids?"

"Yep! And they think they can get more as they work through the data."

"I don't suppose Anatoli was one of the people they arrested?"

Nick shook his head. "They got two people who were running the site in Estonia, but no links to Anatoli. Not yet, at least."

Claire nodded and took a hot sip of coffee. Anatoli was smart, and he had been doing this for decades. He was probably many layers removed from the traffickers and the site admins.

Nick opened the cupboard and pulled out two plates. "What about *your* news?"

She took another sip of coffee. "I talked with the person who helped Ben."

Nick almost dropped the plates. "Whaaat?" He turned around, his smile half-melted.

"His name is Leo, and he works for an IT services company called OstTech based in Belarus. They have legitimate customers, but they also cater to more shady, adult-themed clients—porn, escorts, strip clubs. They set up websites, crypto commerce, streaming video channels—stuff like that. He said Ben was being trafficked in Salt Lake City. He said Ben did not have any documents, so Leo supplied him with a false identity, some cash, and a burner phone so he could walk away from his traffickers."

Nick abandoned the plates on the counter and sat down. "And he knew Ben how, exactly?"

"Leo first met him while setting up Ben's camming channel, back in 2020."

"Camming?"

"Using webcams for live streaming video sex chat. It became huge during the COVID lockdown."

"Uh-hum. And so, he just randomly decided to help Ben?"

"No, not exactly. Leo is part of an online group who search for missing children. He's been secretly scanning his clients' websites, using facial recognition and age-progression photos of missing children from around the world. That's how he ID'd Ben. He contacted Ben secretly and then used a courier service to get him the false ID and the burner phone."

"Why did he need a false ID?"

"He said Ben was not sure he could go back to his family. He had no memory of them. He wanted to check them out first."

Nick nodded, considering this new development. "And how did you meet this *Leo*?"

"Roses made a few inquiries in her hacker circles about anyone who might know anything about LoliTown or the malware involved in Ben's death. Leo contacted her through a friend of a friend."

"Does Leo know Anatoli?"

"Not personally, but he said Azarev Enterprises is one of OstTech's clients."

"And you think you can trust him? What if he works for Azarev . . ."

"He showed us the logs of his chats with Ben. I can send them to you. He also said he helped somebody else last fall—Phoebe McClain in England. I looked her up—she was kidnapped when she was three years old while on vacation with her parents in Belgium. And last October, twenty-five years old, she just walked into a police station in London. She said for all those years, she never knew she was somebody else. Until one day she was contacted by someone on the phone that only her pimp would text her on, and this person told her who she really was and asked her if she wanted to go home. He bought her a train ticket to London."

"Wow," Nick said.

"I know, right? And besides, what would Leo have to gain by talking to us? He is risking his life. If he is found out, who is to say Azarev's hackers won't come after him?"

"You are right. You should tell him not to risk it and to lie low. Besides, LoliTown is now history."

"But you know this won't be the end of it, right? These monsters that run this whole trafficking operation . . . they will just set up more LoliTowns. Maybe they already have."

He frowned. "I know."

"More sites will pop up. And the FBI will be playing whack-a-mole till the end of days. What if we could go further?"

"Further? Where?"

"To stop them, and all their operations. Once and for all."

"How?"

"Leo can be our man on the inside of OstTech. He can get us evidence linking Azarev to LoliTown or other trafficking activities."

Nick sighed. "And what if the FBI still say it's not enough to raise a diplomatic issue? He will have risked his life for nothing."

"We don't need the FBI."

"What do you mean? Who else would go after Anatoli?"

"The Red Hand."

Nick's raised eyebrows wrinkled his forehead. "Who the hell is the Red Hand?"

"It's a hacker's collective that takes down online criminal organizations. They are *white hat hackers*—ethical hackers."

"*Ethical?* As compared to what?"

"As compared to *black hat* hackers—ones that use hacking to commit crimes."

But they both break the law, Nick thought. "OK, and what would this *Red Hand* do, exactly?"

"Cyber warfare. Against OstTech *and* Azarev. They can lock him out of his own businesses, encrypt his data, release incriminating information to the media."

"And what will that accomplish?"

"Disrupt his operations. And compel Western governments to put pressure on Belarus to deal with him."

"They won't. He is a powerful man in Belarus. And his government won't listen to the West."

"You'd be surprised what power information can have. Especially the right information. If there are trade agreements at stake, or a risk of sanctions, he may turn out to be an easy sacrificial scapegoat for the Belarusian government."

"Be that as it may, how does this help Ben's case? It's not like we will get to put Anatoli in prison."

"Does it matter who puts him in prison and for what?"

"Yes. It does to me. Don't get involved in this, Claire."

Emotion flooded her. "But if *I* don't, who will? Who will do something about this? Clearly, not the FBI. State Department? The diplomats and the bureaucrats? The *big* people will handle this? And us little people—we just need to mind our little business? No, Nick. Little people got this one. Roses, and Leo, and I, and a bunch of other little *nobodies* will do something about this. You don't have to be a part of this, but we are not asking your permission. Don't you want this bastard to pay for what he did?"

He sat quietly, listening. She knew he did not like confrontations. But she couldn't just sit back and do nothing. She bitterly wanted justice. Justice for all those stolen kids who were sold and used and abused over and over again, until there was nothing left of them, and they were tossed to the side of the road like trash. She wanted vengeance. He was not going to talk her out of this.

He stood up and approached her. "I understand how you feel about this."

"But . . . ?" She fired back a defiant look.

"No *but*. I just understand how you feel." He pulled her into him and kissed her head.

Th!rty-øn3

Next morning, the story about the LoliTown takedown was all over the news. Claire read the BBC version that quoted a Europol official who thanked the FBI for its cooperation. The *Denver Post* version was syndicated from The Associated Press and quoted the FBI director in Washington, DC, commending the work of the Albuquerque field office. Albuquerque's *The Paper* quoted Special Agent Beck, who thanked the Pine Lake, Colorado, Police Department for its crucial role in the investigation. All the stories concurred that before it was taken down, the site had over 470,000 registered users. The ongoing investigation so far had resulted in 63 arrests and in 135 trafficked children being identified and rescued internationally. More arrests and rescues were expected as the investigation progressed.

In all the stories, there was no mention of a deal the FBI made with pedophile and child trafficker Duane Criddell. There was also no mention of Anatoli Azarev and his possible ties to the site and the trafficking ring. Claire was not surprised and was not particularly outraged. She had expected this, based on what Nick had told her. It did not matter that the newspapers did not know this. They would, in time. What mattered was that the right people knew this and were doing something about this. And that wherever he was, Anatoli Azarev was not having a good day, and had no idea there was more bad news coming his way soon.

She opened Tox Chat on her computer and clicked Roses' green bubble. "Hey."

"Hey," Roses replied. "Seen the news?"

"Yep. Nick gave me a heads-up yesterday. Does this change anything?"

"I don't think so. This was just one of Azarev's sites. The Red Hand is moving forward."

Claire knew from Roses that there were at least eight members of the Red Hand involved in this operation in some manner. But so far, Claire had not gotten to talk with any of them. The members of the Red Hand valued their anonymity, probably even more than the average hacker did. This was understandable, given that the Red Hand targeted organized-crime syndicates, and those types of organizations did not take lightly to threats. They had their own hackers, and they also had hit men. Anonymity was the only defense the members of the Red Hand had. Despite the ominous name, this group was not a Hollywood-style band of vigilante superheroes with a clubhouse and a secret handshake. They were complete strangers from around the world who knew one another only by their online handles and who came together to dole out justice and then parted ways till the next time. Roses mentioned the handles of only two of the Red Hands involved in this operation—Tristan and Marzana. Claire assumed Marzana to be of eastern European heritage after she looked up her name and found out it stood for the Slavic goddess of winter and death.

"Are they still doing recon?" Claire typed.

"Yes. They have penetrated OstTech and are now mapping out the network and key personnel."

Although it was the actual hacking attacks that always got all the glory in the news, Claire found the reconnaissance leading up to the attacks to be more exciting. Good attacks required good recon. This was clandestine, analytical work. Good hackers invested time to study their targets. It was like mapping out an unknown world starting from a blank page. Every organization was made up of people, places, and resources. People were typically the weakest link in its security. The company's website and its LinkedIn page were usually good places to source the lists of employee names and job titles. Once you had those, social media and the web provided additional information about their lives—pets, children, churches, parent organizations, alumni associations. People voluntarily put so much personal information out on the web. And if that wasn't enough, they also surrounded themselves with technology that could easily share even more information about them. They had phones and smartwatches that had access to their communications and location data, wherever they went. And they were hardly more secure at home. Here, their home-security cameras could provide detailed views inside and outside their residence, and smart speakers and TV remotes equipped with microphones could be used for eavesdropping. Some even had smart door locks and garage openers that could be remotely activated to disable their physical security. The point was, there was plenty of information that could be found out about someone in order to use them, without their knowledge, to gain access to their employer. Or gain leverage on them, if it came to that. And this was just the personnel part of recon. Claire knew that once the Red Hand gained access to even one system, they would begin scanning the company's network and mapping out other systems. When targeting large organizations, recon could take weeks or even months. And it had to be done without alerting their IT security teams or intrusion-detection systems.

"Have they found OstTech's client accounts?" Claire asked. "Anything on Azarev?"

"Not yet."

"Can't they use Leo for help?"

"No. You know they don't trust anyone they don't know."

Claire was not surprised, but she did not necessarily agree with this. She always saw strength in numbers. And she was sure Leo would have wanted to help. "Have you told Leo about the Red Hand?"

"No," Roses replied. No need for him to be aware of their operation. The less he knows, the better for his safety."

Claire thought that Leo could make up his own mind about what was best for him. However, if the Red Hand and Roses wanted him to be in the dark, she was not about to disregard their wishes. And if the Red Hand were not going to use him, maybe she'd see whether Nick or the FBI could.

32

A dusting of snow overnight transformed the world. Fresh snow made the first rays of the sun seem brighter, the blue of the sky more vibrant, and the morning air more invigorating. Nick backed the Tahoe out of his driveway, delighting in the crunch of tires over the pristine, dry snow. He rolled down his window and savored the primordial fresh while the Tahoe's heater pumped warmth into the cabin.

Instead of taking Third Street down to Summit to get to the station, as he normally did, today he made a snap decision and took a right before Highland Terrace onto the old unpaved forestry road denoted only with a small post with the numbers 551. This was the scenic detour. He switched the truck into four-wheel drive, and the Tahoe began to climb, swaying its heft dutifully as its tires rolled over loose rocks and washed-out ruts, managing to find the grip needed to propel the iron beast up the mountain. After about a mile, he reached a clearing at the curve in the road and pulled over.

He opened the slider on the heavy-duty metal coffee tumbler Claire got him for Christmas and took a sip of hot coffee. This was his spot. Like from an eagle's perch above the tops of snowcapped pines, from here, he could see for miles. To the west was the snowy wilderness of the Kenosha range, and to the southeast was the low-lying valley of Castle Rock, Franktown, and Larkspur. And farther south, at the base of the glimmering silhouette of Pikes Peak was Colorado Springs. Far below, on the snow-dusted plain, a long black ribbon of a coal train was moving slowly across the valley. Too far to hear. It was peaceful here, quiet.

"Creased ice and crystals of all hues," a long-forgotten quote popped into his mind as he took in the dazzle of the glittering snow all around him. *Thoreau*, he recalled with surprise, from the American lit class he taught all those years ago. He could remember the smell of dust and sun in that old classroom in Ophelia Hall.

The quote was from "A Winter Walk," an 1840s essay about an excursion into the serene winter wonderland. Thoreau was a transcendentalist. Nick liked the transcendentalists—they believed that innocence could be restored. They retreated into nature to contemplate their purpose in life and to transcend the corruptive influences of society. Nick wished more people were transcendentalists. There would probably be a lot less crime in this world.

But then again, these New England transcendentalists had never seen the ravages of the frontier winter. Here, in the rocky high plains, winter was not a wondrous occasion for contemplative constitutionals. For the settlers who managed to make it this far west, winter was death. Figurative and literal. Dormancy of wildlife and crops. Starvation of people and livestock. "The ghostly winter silence," as Jack London had later called it.

But now, blessed with the comforts of modern climate-controlled technology, Nick could once again find winter to be cozy and picturesque and an occasion for his own contemplation. Could innocence really be restored?

There was no denying the fact that returning to hacking had transformed Claire. She was more alive. Even after a long shift at the hospital, Claire felt lighter now, as if this new course of life recharged her each day rather than further draining her. She was more like . . . the Claire he first fell in love with. What was *Nick-the-cop* supposed to do with this? This was what brought

Claire happiness. Nick would have to learn to live with this, if he wanted to be with her. Did he?

This was a torturous question. After the last year, it was impossible to imagine his life without her. With someone else. Despite (or maybe *because*) of their troubled start, they were now closer than Nick had ever been with anyone else in his whole life. They were perfect for each other, and Claire's hacking past was the only point of unease for him. And still, even after he found out, he was the one who opened the door for her to come back into his life. Perhaps he let his heart and not his mind make that decision. And when they got back together, he never asked her to stop, and he never had to—she put away that part of herself of her own free will, and he never even thought of it again until just a few weeks ago.

Claire always said that intentions mattered, and so far, Nick had allowed that defense to deviate the needle of his moral compass. She had the right intentions when she hacked into his computer and stole the case files. Had she not done that, they would have never found LoliTown. Never arrested Duane Criddell. Never rescued Latoya and Grady, never mind the 135 other kids from LoliTown. But with this Red Hand thing, things were going much further, and intentions did not matter as far as law was concerned . . .

But then again, what was *law*? From a moral standpoint, law was a slippery concept at best. Law and morality were not always on the same side of the line. Not so long ago, slavery was legal in America. And so was domestic abuse. There have been laws in this country to keep people from drinking, women from voting, and the poor and minorities from reproducing. Was it not OK to break those unjust laws? Even Thoreau himself was once jailed for refusing to pay taxes because he did not want his tax money to support slavery and the war with Mexico.

Sure, those arcane laws were no longer laws, thankfully, and that was precisely the point. The body of law was always changing; at any given point in time, some laws were dying, some were evolving, and new ones were being born. This was the natural order of things. Law was reactive. It was always playing catch-up with new ideas and new threats. Ten years ago, the legal system did not have to worry about people's AI-driven cars running over pedestrians. Or about high-definition camera drones flying over people's backyards. Or about a criminal organization from a non-extradition country using a software virus to kill a young man with his own cell phone from across the world.

Nick stopped his train of rationalizations because he suddenly realized a cold fact that he probably knew all along in his heart. The question was not whether he could be with Claire. It was whether he could be with Claire and be a cop. What did it mean to be a cop? What was the primary measure of success? The *what*, the *how*, or the *why*—the *results*, the *methods*, or the *intentions*? All three? Whatever the magic mix, it was Nick's problem to figure out—not Claire's. Claire's business with Roses and the Red Hand was going to break laws. Maybe these would not be US laws, but that notion was of little comfort. Nick was wired differently. Aside from maybe minor shoplifting in his childhood and underage drinking in his youth, he really never felt a compulsion to knowingly break the law—he was a veritable Boy Scout.

But then again . . . didn't he punch that bully Corey to stop from being bullied? And didn't Beck post child porn on the web in order for the FBI to get access to LoliTown? And didn't Nick agree to use warrantless access to private phone data through Hemisphere to find the Talenkos? Evidently, following the rules got one only so far. Punching Corey was certainly against the school rules. But it was the only way forward. To stop a bully, Nick himself had to turn to violence. Maybe to stop evil hackers, one had to bring his own. If the Department of Defense, the FBI, the CIA, the NSA, and probably a bunch of other three-letter agencies could have hackers at their disposal, why couldn't Nick? He had exhausted the legal means of bringing this case to a resolution. Maybe the Red Hand and Roses and Claire could reach where the long arm of the law could not. Could Nick live with that?

* * *

When Nick finally pulled into the station's lot, he was surprised to find it almost full—there was Ray's Tahoe, Jason's pickup, Ruth's Ramcharger, and Patty's little Hyundai. Full house. Something was going on, and he hoped it wasn't bad news. He opened the front door with some trepidation, but then saw colorful balloons. He felt relief and instantly a new panic: *Whose birthday did he forget?*

"And here is the man himself!" Ray exclaimed and popped a confetti stick at Nick, and everyone broke out into spontaneous woots, hoots, and applause.

"What's all this?" Nick smiled, confused, and brushed confetti off his nose.

Ray picked up a framed certificate from the front counter and read out loud: "*From the US Department of Justice, Federal Bureau of Investigation, a special commendation to Detective Nick Severs of the Pine Lake Police Department in recognition of his outstanding assistance to the FBI in connection with its investigative efforts.*" Ray handed Nick the frame. "Signed by the director of the FBI himself."

Nick took the frame and examined the official seal of the FBI. "Huh," he said, not sure what else to say, and feeling a bit uncomfortable about being the center of attention.

Ray put his arm around Nick's shoulder, grinning from ear to ear under his silver mustache. "Now, what it does not say here is that our own Nick was instrumental in taking down an international child trafficking ring and in rescuing a hundred and thirty-five kids." Ray's strong cowboy arm gave him a vise-grip squeeze. "You are a helluva lawman, Severs!"

Patty clapped, formalizing this unofficial ceremony. Ruth's blue fuzz ball of hair floated toward Nick, and he saw her glistening eyes and lips pinched into a tiny squiggle. She looked like she was about to cry. Her thin arms reached for Nick's head, and she pulled him down to her face. "You are an angel," she whispered and planted a fragrant smooch on his cheek. "A guardian angel to those children."

"Thank you," Nick said, gently patting the old librarian's back and hearing Jason's boots thudding close.

"Nice job, man!" Jason planted a couple of hefty claps on Nick's shoulder.

"Thank you, guys—it was a team effort," Nick said, abashedly. "And, really, Claire deserves much of the credit."

"Well, tell her she is welcome to come work here." Ruth winked.

"Get your cake, everyone," Patty declared and put a paper plate with a thick slice of sprinkle-covered white cake and a plastic fork on the counter in front of Nick. "I'll wrap a piece for Claire," she whispered.

Nick smiled and looked over the colorful Pine Lake PD crew. It was a bit overwhelming to accept that all these people came to celebrate with him.

"OK," Jason said, stabbing a piece of cake onto his fork. "Tell us the whole story, from the beginning."

Nick thought back. "Well, I believe it all started with Millie's green chili breakfast burritos. Which I never got to eat."

* * *

After about an hour, the party crowd dispersed. Ruth had to get back to the library, and Jason also had somewhere else to be. Finally alone in his office, Nick drank his coffee, eyeing the FBI frame lying on his desk. At the front counter, Patty was on the phone with the county. Ray had retired to his own office, probably settling in for an early nap in his chair after the cake.

Helluva lawman. That was nice of Ray to say, but Nick did not feel that way. He did not feel much like a guardian angel, either. The glass-encased certificate was a hollow trophy. A reminder of a case not solved to his satisfaction. Right now, he did not want to look at it.

He opened his desk drawer and pulled out the Abbi White file. He checked the address listed on the incident report, stuck the file under his arm, and grabbed his car keys.

Logan Avenue was about ten minutes away from the station, on the southwestern edge of Pine Lake. To call it an avenue was generous, to say the least, as it was no more than a dirt road through the forest, dusted with snow to hide the stretches of bone-rattling washboard, and barely wide enough for two vehicles to pass.

Still, this was a pretty area—gentle rolling hills overgrown with pines. The driveways here were sparse, and the trees provided plenty of privacy. The few houses Nick drove past were simple one-story bungalows and single-wide homes with obvious additions made at some time throughout the decades. Some were set right by the road, while others farther back, in the trees. There were old camper vans and pickups parked in the yards, and a few chain-link-enclosed dog runs and big stacks of firewood covered with faded blue tarps. 2209 was an old mailbox nailed to a tree stump by the side of the road. The black paint was mostly flaked off, but the numbers were still visible, as if burned in like in a photo negative. A rutted, unpaved driveway curved into the thicket.

Nick parked the Tahoe just past the mailbox and stepped out. It was a cold day, and tall, dense pines blocking the sun made it even colder in the shade. He grabbed his coat from the back seat and slipped it on, and then got out the case file and pulled out the photographs.

It was quiet here, except for the dog barking in someone's yard not far away. Nick shuffled through the stack of photos until he found the right one and then took a few steps back and to the left to match the frame in the photo. The intersection looked about the same, except now there was snow on the ground. This is where the bus dropped off Abbi, according to the report. This was around 2:45 in the afternoon. The bus driver and the kids confirmed she exited the school bus and began walking up the driveway when the bus pulled away.

Nick looked up the driveway. The crooked shale path was in bad need of grading and clearing. It passed like a gully between the two sides of an embankment fringed with gnarled roots and drooping branches of the pines. A set of tire tracks in the snow meant someone had come or gone since this morning.

Standing at the mailbox, Nick confirmed that the house was not visible from the road. If Abbi started walking up the driveway, she would have disappeared from view where the driveway curved left.

Nick walked up the driveway. He stopped at the bend, under the pine branches looming overhead. He could not see the house from here. There was another bend in the driveway—maybe forty yards ahead, making a gentle right-handed switchback climbing farther up the hill. Nick looked back at the road. The mailbox was just barely visible. Another step up the driveway, and Nick would disappear out of sight for anyone watching from the road.

From the second bend, he could see the house. A shabby-looking cottage with chipped paint and grimy windows. He turned around and looked down the driveway. The straightaway between the two bends was not visible from the road or from the house. Somewhere along this stretch of the driveway, Abbi White vanished before ever making it home.

Or did she? Nick read the file, but if his experience with Edie Harris had taught him anything, it was to question everything.

The sound of a vehicle approached from up the road, and soon an old Chevy truck turned onto the driveway and slowly pulled up. Nick stepped to the side. The pickup rolled up even with Nick and stopped. The driver cranked down the window.

"Can I help you, Detective?" He was an old, sinewy man with sunken, stubbled cheeks and a worn trucker cap.

"Are you Gerald White?"

"Last time I checked," the man said without smiling.

Nick nodded. "Hi, I'm—"

"—I know who you are," the man said with a calm nod.

Slightly over a year into the job, Nick was still getting accustomed to people recognizing him when he had not the slightest idea who they were. Ray seemed to know every single resident of Pine Lake. Nick had a lot of catching up to do.

"What can I do for you?" Gerald White asked.

"I am looking into Abbi's case."

"After all this time?" Gerald kept his eye squarely on Nick. "Ray stopped thirty years ago."

Nick swallowed down the shame he saw in Ray's eyes when Ray mentioned this case. What could Nick say? "I am sorry," he said.

Gerald nodded again. "You want to come in?"

The house on the inside was much like it was on the outside—used and neglected. But it was warm, and it smelled like wood fire.

"You will have to excuse the mess," Gerald said, clearing a pile of hunting clothes from the kitchen table and pulling out a chair for Nick. "My wife passed seven years ago, and I am not much of a housekeeper. Coffee?"

"That would be great, thanks," Nick said.

Gerald walked into the living room, opened the iron door of the woodstove, and tossed in a split log. The living room did not have much furniture left—only a dingy, mustard-colored couch with springs showing through the cushions like ribs on an old cow, and a worn-out brown recliner into which Gerald piled the hunting gear from the kitchen table. The couch and the recliner faced the medium-sized cast-iron stove at the opposite wall. Judging by several pots hanging on the living room wall next to the woodstove, Nick guessed the gas range in the kitchen was not operational. But the old fridge apparently still was, as it emitted a continuous vibrating drone from the kitchen corner. A dozen or so photos were taped to its dinged and chipped door. Nick went closer to look. Some new and some old. Family Christmas portraits, kids' class and graduation photos.

"Do your kids live nearby?" Nick asked as Gerald returned to the kitchen to fill a camping coffee pot with water and grounds.

"No, they are kind of all over the place. John, my oldest, he retired from the air force and lives in Florida. He and his wife have grandbabies now. And Mary, my youngest, she is a teacher in Idaho."

In the mix of photos on the fridge, there was one of Abbi. A small class photo, like the one Nick saw in the case file, but more yellowed, cracked, and aged, like Gerald himself.

"You gonna ask me about that day?" Gerald said, heading back to the living room to put the pot on the stove.

"Yeah, I know you've told it many times, and I've read the old reports, but hearing it directly from you would be helpful." Nick got out his notepad and pen.

"It was 1979. Monday, September 10. I left for work at four in the morning."

"And where did you work?"

"C&R Cattle Ranch in Larkspur. They closed down in '92, but I know Ray confirmed with'em that I was there all day. You can ask him."

Nick nodded. "And where was your wife?"

"Diane was at home with our two youngest. John was seven, and he stayed home sick that day, and Mary was five. Diane was doing laundry. When she looked at the clock, she realized it was after three, and Abbi had not come home yet. So, she went outside to look for her but didn't find'er. She went to the neighbors to see whether the school bus came, and when she found out that it did, she went back home to call the school. Then she called the police. And the rest is in your files."

The coffeepot boiled in the living room, and Gerald got it and brought it into the kitchen. Nick watched his hand tremble as he poured coffee into a tin cup and handed it to Nick.

"Thank you." Nick blew into the steaming cup and took a cautious sip. "Was there anyone you suspected?"

Gerald shook his head. "No one especially, but probably suspected everyone, over the years. When you have no answers, you don't know who to trust."

"I have to ask you a very hard question. Could there have been an . . . accident at home?"

Gerald looked at the floor in silence for a moment. "You mean if Diane hurt our girl and covered it up?" He shook his head. "Never! She loved our kids more than life. That woman did not have a mean bone in her body. You should've saw her that day. I drove home 'sfast as I could after she called the ranch. She was hysterical. She knew something bad happened to our baby girl. She probably knew she would never see her again."

Nick nodded. "Sorry, but I had to ask."

Gerald took a drink of his coffee and stared into the stained, torn linoleum on the kitchen floor.

"Do you have anything of Abbi's that could have her DNA on it, like hair or baby teeth?" Nick knew this was a long shot, given how much time has passed, but it was a shot worth taking.

Gerald shook his head. "Ray asked the same about ten years ago. I am afraid there is nothing left after all this time. As Mary grew up, she used up most of her sister's things."

Nick nodded. "There is something else we could try. If you would be open to it, I can take your DNA sample, and we can use it to check against any unidentified persons files."

"You mean *dead* unidentified persons?"

Nick nodded.

"You can do that? Even without *her* DNA?"

"Yes, it's called familial DNA. Your and Abbi's DNA are similar enough for us to be able to identify any possible matches."

Gerald looked Nick in the eye. "Detective, I'll do whatever you think would help find her and put her to rest. I read the news about you. I know what you did for all those kids."

Nick nodded, wishing he did not have his own inflated fame to live up to. "I think it's worth a try. DNA technology has gotten a lot better."

Th!rty-thr33

Claire's fingertips hovered above the keyboard as she reread the string of code she had just typed into the black command-line interface on her laptop.

Over the last few days, while the Red Hand focused on OstTech and Azarev, she and Roses had other preparations to make. First, they had to find an identity broker on the dark web who could sell them the login credentials for an active employee of the Belarus Ministry of Energy. Claire was surprised to find that, despite this rather obscure request, the first identity broker they tried happened to have several available. And they were all guaranteed *unburned*—fully functional and collected without the knowledge of the victims using *phishing* attacks—spoofed emails from the corporate IT or HR departments directing unscrupulous employees to log in to some bogus corporate portal, where those login credentials were scraped, and the employees were forwarded back to a legitimate corporate website to avoid suspicion. Phishing was a simple ruse, but surprisingly still very effective.

Claire and Roses paid a fair price for the stolen credentials and used them to gain access to the ministry's network, where they located administrative access to Minsk-4 Power Plant and uploaded the BlackEnergy tool kit. BlackEnergy gave them control of the server so they could execute a script granting them access to the power grid's Supervisory Control and Data Acquisition system. It was this SCADA *shell*—Minsk-4's text-based command interface—that Claire now had open on her screen.

A message from Marzana dinged in their four-way LeapChat session: "Are you ready?"

Claire reread the command, which instructed the shutdown of the electrical substations KTP-1700, KTP-2317, KTP-2486, and Minsk-Paunochnaja. She added "-*f*" at the end of the command, a parameter instructing *forced* execution, which would override any alerts or requests for confirmation the system would otherwise generate in the power plant's control room.

Claire checked the time—it was 4:06 p.m. Denver time, which would make it 1:06 a.m. in Minsk—the perfect time for an attack to minimize civilian impact and to encounter the slowest incident response times.

"Ready," she typed.

"Go."

Claire pressed Enter, and the cursor on the screen stopped blinking for what seemed like the longest few seconds. Claire held her breath.

At last, the cursor blinked again and moved down to the new, blank command prompt. *Success!* Her command executed without any errors. Claire exhaled, feeling a bit shaky from the rush of adrenaline. Nothing changed in her world—not a single thing, but five thousand miles away, the whole northwestern quadrant of Minsk including the OstTech offices had just lost electrical power.

Her fingertips tingled as she typed. "Done."

This was only the beginning. Roses had the next act. Claire waited impatiently for Roses to provide an update. Finally, the dots next to her name showed her typing.

Roses' response dinged in the window: "Done."

Claire switched to the open browser window that had the Azarev Enterprises website pulled up. The home page showed a generic corporate glass building with generic, young, smiling corporate faces in the foreground. Claire clicked Refresh in the browser toolbar. The window turned blank, and after a few seconds returned an error message:

HTTP Error 503: The service is unavailable.

Claire smiled. *Code 503* was the calling card of a successful DDoS attack—*Distributed Denial of Service*. It meant that Roses had successfully raised a zombie bot army of hundreds of thousands of infected internet-connected devices—from personal computers to smart refrigerators and Wi-Fi-equipped cars. And she told them to go to www.azareventerprises.by, and to keep reloading that web page over and over, causing Azarev's web server to overload and become unable to service any new web-page requests—legitimate or not. *God bless the dark web!* Here, zombie bot armies were available for rent to anyone who needed to knock offline a government agency, a multinational corporation, or in this case, a criminal enterprise.

A DDoS attack on the Azarev website would set off all sorts of alarms and phones at the OstTech web security operations center, except at this particular moment, OstTech was in the dark ages, with no electrical power or internet connection. There was nothing they could do.

"Beginning exfil," Tristan messaged in LeapChat.

This is what all this was about—data exfiltration. This was the coup de grâce of the master plan composed and directed by the Red Hand. What Claire and Roses had done, figuratively, was drug the guard dog and create a distraction, clearing the way for the Red Hand to sneak inside and steal the mother lode of data.

Roses said there were nine members of the Red Hand involved, although only Tristan and Marzana came in direct contact with Claire. Nine world-class hackers may have sounded like a lot, but given the high number of targets and the tight timeframes, it was necessary. Over the last week, the members of the Red Hand had done the necessary groundwork so that today's operation could proceed as smoothly as it was.

They had gathered personal information on over two dozen individuals affiliated with Azarev's syndicate, starting with Anatoli himself down to his lawyers, accountants, and lieutenants. They also mapped out Azarev's maze of shell companies, subsidiaries, and suppliers, his multiple legitimate lines of business covering the gamut from real estate to logistics, as well as four other human-trafficking businesses in addition to LoliTown.

But their main target was business data residing in the internal information systems used by the syndicate—HR, sales, and accounting. It took time to infiltrate these and begin mapping out the data—accounts, transactions, and communications. The syndicate was a global operation, and much of its transactions and communications happened online rather than in person—web meetings, emails, chats, cryptowallets—everything was archived and retained; one just had to know where to look. If anything, there was too much data to sift through, and the Red Hand had to traverse with caution, identifying terabytes of data and mapping out anything of value without setting off the alarms.

"About 40% done," Tristan provided an update.

Great hackers were like great spies. They could enter the enemy's network without being detected and move about, mapping out targets and reading confidential data. But having access to read the data and being able to steal the whole damned archive were two completely different things. OstTech had data-loss-detection firewalls in place. The Red Hand could have spent many months cautiously siphoning out incriminating data on Azarev, one cocktail napkin at a time, under the watchful eye of OstTech's security measures, but this meant a constant risk of being discovered at any moment, and it also meant giving Azarev and OstTech more time to keep running their criminal affairs. Slow in this case was risky. And boring. Instead, the Red Hand preferred to do the job in one big heist. With the guard dog asleep, they could blow the doors off the vault and scoop up the mother lode. To get the data out quickly, they left Azarev's FTP server, which handled file transfers, unaffected by the DDoS attack. Forget stuffing files into duffel bags—today, the FTP server was going to be the cargo truck the Red Hand were going to back up to the vault, forklift all the data they wanted, and haul it right out of Azarev's network. The Red Hand were going to exfiltrate terabytes worth of data from Azarev Enterprises, with OstTech unaware and unable to do anything about it.

"80%."

This big-bang approach ensured maximum results, and it also lent itself to more publicity. Tomorrow morning, people would get on the web and wonder what happened to Azarev Enterprises. And this was just one factor that differentiated hacktivists from hackers. While *hacking* was all about gaining access and control, *hacktivism* had that added element of embarrassing the enemy. Publicly. It was about proving that your enemy was powerless against justice. Your justice. Taking down the Azarev site was just that—the embarrassment. An insult added to the injury.

"Exfil is complete. We're encrypting," Marzana updated.

And the injury was going to be great. The Red Hand's MO was complete disruption of their target's operations. They would not only publicly expose Azarev's crimes, but they would also do everything in their power to cripple his operations. That's why, after stealing Azarev's criminal business data, the Red Hand encrypted the drives on the syndicate's servers, to make them useless to anyone without the decryption keys. They also changed OstTech's administrative login credentials to prevent them from being able to restore Azarev's data from backup.

Claire could not help feeling a little proud of herself for being a part of this operation. She had never witnessed, never mind been a part of hacking on this level and on this scope. This group had the power to reach across oceans and continents with such precision and devastating effectiveness. This was all-out warfare, but yet there were no exploding artillery shells, no air-raid sirens, and no infantry charging forward from the trenches. Just the dead silence of data moving over the sub-Atlantic data cables.

"Done," Tristan said.

* * *

Nick lost track of time. After the visit with Gerald White, he drove to the county offices in Golden to submit the DNA sample for analysis at the Regional Crime Lab. He then returned to the station to go over the interviews from Abbi's investigation, and when he checked the time, it was already after six. He called Claire.

"Oh, jeez," she said. "Is it really 6:20? Sorry, time really got away from me today."

"Me too," he said. "Are you hungry? Want me to pick something up on the way home?"

"I'm starving," she said. "Do you want to go out? Maybe Mexican?"

"Yeah, that actually sounds really good." It had been a heck of a week, and he liked the idea of him and Claire sitting back and sipping their margaritas while someone else made dinner happen. "Cantina Azteca?" he asked. "I can meet you there."

Cantina Azteca was downtown—a block past Millie's, a straight shot from the station down Summit Street. Nick could have driven, but he decided to walk, giving him time to clear his head in the frosty air and leave work at the station.

When he got to the restaurant, Claire had already staked claim to the corner booth—her favorite vantage point for people watching. The place was only moderately busy and mostly with the locals, but the night was still young, and this being a Friday, the potential for entertainment was bound to increase.

He slid into the booth next to Claire, and she put her arm around his neck and kissed his ice-cold cheek.

"Hi," he said, smiling.

"Hi yourself, handsome," Claire winked just as the waitress brought chips, salsa, and two frosty shot glasses with golden liquid.

"Oh, what's this?" Nick raised his eyebrows. "Tequila? Are we celebrating?"

Claire smiled mysteriously. "Yes, we are."

She unlocked her phone and handed it to Nick. He took it, and his heart skipped when he saw the logo for Azarev Enterprises at the top of the screen. But the web page looked different from the way it did this morning. The logo had a red strike through it, and under it was a picture a blood-red handprint and the following text:

This website has been seized as part of an investigation and enforcement action by The Red Hand Collective. The investigation has uncovered a direct link between Azarev Enterprises and a criminal syndicate specializing in human trafficking and child pornography. A large number of incriminating records and communications have been seized and shared with the International Consortium of Investigative Journalists. The complete data set is also available to download from the links below.

Nick swallowed a lump in his throat and looked at Claire. Her eyes sparkled.

"Is this for real?" he asked.

She nodded. "It is. And since their data is now public, there is no reason why you can't use it to persuade the FBI to prosecute Anatoli. In the very least for child trafficking. And maybe, if you can convince Leo to testify, you could also find some evidence to connect him to Ben's death."

A tingle went up Nick's spine. "Holy shit," he muttered. Thoughts fired and bounced around in his brain like a broken ping-pong machine. "Holy shit, babe," he muttered again, unsure if he was happy or terrified. "Did you . . . did *you* do this?"

She shrugged one shoulder. "I helped."

Nick suddenly felt hot. His heart was racing at a fevered speed, and his hands tingled. He normally did not experience conflicting emotions, but right now he felt like he had just gone off a cliff at the bottom of which someone had left him the best present in his whole life. One part of him wanted to scream and the other to laugh.

The culprit was sitting next to him, measuring him with those beautiful mischievous eyes, her skin glowing softly in the dim light.

Nick looked at the phone again. Whatever mixed feelings still struggled to reconcile his head and his heart, the red strike through the Azarev logo looked infinitely satisfying. He put the phone face down on the table and took her hand.

"My God," he said. "You are amazing."

She smiled and picked up one of the shot glasses. "To the timely demise of Azarev Enterprises!"

Nick raised the other glass.

34

This was a nightmare scenario. Anatoli still was not exactly sure how everything fell so completely apart so quickly. Barely a week ago, Oleg was reassuring him that they had successfully deflected a possible FBI infiltration of LoliTown, and yet three days later, their web host was raided, their admins arrested, and the site was taken down. That was a big hit, but it shouldn't have been a critical one. This should have been no more than a temporary setback. The authorities would have found nothing connecting LoliTown to Anatoli, and Oleg had assured him he would have a clone of the site stood up from a backup on another host by the end of the week. But before that could happen, OstTech and Azarev Enterprises themselves were breached and doxed in the most damning way. It would take some undoing and rebuilding to get through this. The only upside was that Anatoli happened to be in Minsk when all this happened. Had it happened a few days later, he would have been in Germany, and possibly could have been detained.

He wasn't worried about fallout from the House of Government—even if there was to be an inquest, his connections in the Ministry of Internal Affairs and the Ministry of Commerce would help smooth things out, and the IT experts from OstTech would easily demonstrate that this whole affair was nothing more than a provocation perpetrated by the FBI (or maybe even the CIA) to undermine the human rights record of the Belarusian government at the cost of besmirching the reputation of a legitimate and successful Belarusian business.

Given the current political weather between the East and the West, this would not require much convincing.

However, with Moscow, things would require more damage control. Galitsyn would no doubt make it known that he did not appreciate the undue publicity, given the new arrangement. But before Anatoli could worry about that, he needed his business back online. Without it, there *was* no arrangement. Galitsyn was expecting the first batch of Ukrainian kompromat in three days. If Anatoli did not deliver, the future he had worked so hard to carve out for himself would be burned to a bed of ashes. Right now, this was a disaster all around. What did he miss? What did Oleg miss? He could have strangled Oleg, but he needed the bastard now more than ever.

"Can you at least get the website back?" He glared at Oleg. He needed to get those damned records off the company's front page.

Oleg stopped typing and looked up from his laptop. "We are, but it will take a day, maybe two."

His eyes were red and sunken, and his cheeks were peppered with stubble. This is where Anatoli found him—in the dark conference room of the OstTech office in Minsk, next to a pile of small paper cups from the office's espresso machine. He said he had been here for over twenty-four hours now, since right after the power outage began, and had stayed to sift through the wreckage when the power came back on. Anatoli believed him.

"Why so long?" Anatoli prodded.

"Because they didn't actually *hack* our site. They hacked the domain record and pointed our domain to their own name servers and then locked the domain with their own password. The site online now is not *our* site. It's theirs, but it shows under our domain. I have three of my guys working on it, but it will take time to get back our control of the domain record."

Those bastards. Anatoli knew enough about websites to appreciate this hack. You had to give it to them, this was quality work. Simple but effective. The name servers were responsible for taking people to the right website based on the domain name. Name servers translated the domain name into the site's IP address. Changing the name servers was simpler than hacking the actual website. It was like peeling off your neighbor's mailbox number and sticking it onto yours; now all their mail—or web traffic—was coming to you.

Those Red Hand bastards. These were the caliber of people Anatoli needed working *for him*. He watched Oleg typing feverishly, his pallid face lit only by the light of his laptop's screen. *This had to have been an inside job.* Oleg would surely deny this – none of *his* guys could have had anything to do with this. But this was all just too much and too fast. Someone must have helped the Red Hand. Someone at OstTech or maybe even at Azarev Enterprises. He would have Max look into this. Maybe even squeeze Oleg a bit. But these were all secondary priorities. The main goal right now was getting the data back.

Oleg stopped typing and buried his face in his hands. "Nothing," he said. "All the sites are down, and the video-production studio in Gdansk lost access to their entire asset library."

"So, how long to restore?"

"If they had hit only the Azarev Enterprises systems, we could have restored everything from OstTech in a day. But they hit OstTech, too. All of our internal systems are encrypted, and we are locked out of the cloud backups. Our only viable option right now is the Snowcube."

"What the hell is the Snowcube?"

"An offline backup appliance. It's like a suitcase with two petabytes of flash storage. Once a month, I back up everything from OstTech and Azarev to the Snowcube, and then it gets unplugged from the network. That's why they couldn't get to it, too—because it's offline."

"So, why the hell are we not restored yet?"

"Because it's all the way back in Kyiv in the OstTech safe room. It was supposed to get moved here with the next shipment. I'll have to go to Kyiv to get it."

Anatoli sighed. "No. You stay here and work on mitigation and getting our website back online. I will take a couple of guys and go pick it up."

Oleg nodded. "OK. Hey, did Max ever find that hacker who was poking around LoliTown before the FBI raid? You said he had a lead."

"He is still working on it. If he can get a phone number, we can just send them the brain bomb virus and get it over with. We have more important things to do."

"No, no. Don't do that." Oleg waved his hands. "We need to get leverage on this person."

"Why?"

"As a plan B. If they are connected to the Red Hand, they could get us the decryption key. If for some reason we can't get the Snowcube, the decryption key will be our only remaining option to get everything back."

35

On Saturday morning, the story about the Azarev breach had already made it into the news. First, *Eesti Ekspress* in Estonia picked it up, followed by Reuters in the UK and The Associated Press in the US. The initial reports were conservative, stating that the news outlets were investigating the claims made by the Red Hand hacking collective and verifying the authenticity of the data.

Nick went for a run in the woods. The news made him feel so much lighter about everything. True, this was not the instant gratification of putting Anatoli Azarev in handcuffs, but there was some undeniable satisfaction in watching the slow train wreck unfold, knowing Azarev was on that train.

After the run, he made coffee and called Beck. He updated him on the state of affairs without directly implicating Claire in the breach and suggested that an OstTech employee known as Leo could possibly be turned into an informant to tie Azarev to Ben's death. Beck said that this sounded promising and that he would review the information. But he tried to manage Nick's expectations, saying that even if they got enough evidence to indict Anatoli, they would likely not be able to do much else, given that the diplomatic relations between Belarus and the US had not improved since they last spoke, and if anything— deteriorated.

Nick thanked him, nonetheless, already expecting that. And then Nick asked him for a favor.

Beck was surprised by the request, and was initially apprehensive, but Nick reminded him in the nicest possible manner that Beck owed him. Without Nick, none of this would have been possible—not the multinational crackdown on the child trafficking and pornography ring, not the rescue of all those children, and not the arrests of all those pedophiles. Nick was not boasting, but simply pointing out the fact that when all this was objectively added up, one could not escape the conclusion that a favor was owed.

Beck said he would see what he could do.

* * *

The favor came through on Monday.

The federal detention center at FCI Englewood was located just off 285 and Kipling, on the outer fringes of Denver suburbia. Bounded on all sides with wide swaths of snowy fields, it looked like any other blocky, nondescript government building complex, until one got close enough to notice the guard tower and the perimeter of twenty-foot-tall chain-link fence topped with coils of razor wire. From here, the bluish snowcaps of the mountains looked just out of reach. There was a golf course nearby, and a residential subdivision. A school bus passed Nick on Quincy as he slowed down to turn into the parking lot. He wondered whether the people living around here knew what monsters were locked inside this facility.

He had to wait in a small interview room with no windows. It was so quiet here, the silence felt like soft pressure in Nick's ears. Finally, he heard a security door buzzer go off and then stop. Then another one, closer. He heard a key card beep at the door, and a young female corrections officer brought in Duane Criddell.

The CO measured Nick with a glance. "Do you want the prisoner in handcuffs?"

"No," Nick said.

"You got it." She expertly clicked open the cuffs and guided Criddell to the chair opposite Nick. "You need anything, you just holler." She swiped her card and exited the room. Nick heard the electronic locks clank shut.

Maybe it was just the harsh overhead lights in prison, but Criddell looked paler and older than the last time Nick saw him. His smart outfit had been exchanged for the Department of Corrections khakis and a white T-shirt. His light brown hair had grown out and lost the precision of its former cut.

But his eyes had not changed. Criddell's gaze was still calm and direct—not the lowered, cowering gaze of a seasoned convict. *Give it time,* Nick thought.

Criddell leaned back in the chair and crossed his legs. "I must admit, I was not expecting to ever see you again, Detective," he said with syrupy smoothness. "To what do I owe this pleasure?"

The sound of Criddell's voice hurled Nick back to the video of Ben. *Do you like Mr. Giggles, Billy?*

Nick forced his jaw to relax and unclenched his hand under the table. "Agent Beck arranged this consultation as part of your condition of cooperation with law enforcement," he said to the monster.

Criddell's lips melted into a smile. He liked being needed. "I believe I have been forthcoming with the authorities so far. Whatever you need, I am an open book. Now, what's on your mind?"

Nick cleared his throat. "How do I . . . find someone like yourself?"

"I beg your pardon?"

"Someone who abducts children."

Criddell's smile pursed, and he turned his nose slightly, as if from an unpleasant odor. "You mistake me for a predator. But I am not. I have never prowled neighborhoods looking for children to abduct and assault. Some men do. But not me. But . . . I have come across a couple of men like that."

"So, how do I find a man like that?"

Criddell was silent for a moment. "What was the gender of the child taken?"

"A girl."

"How old?"

"Eight."

"Where was she taken from?"

"From her driveway, after she was dropped off by the school bus."

"Any witnesses?"

Nick shook his head.

"Did you find the body?"

Nick shook his head again.

"And when was this?"

"1979."

"Can I see a photo?" Criddell looked at the file folder in front of Nick.

Nick was about to open the folder, but he caught Criddell's gaze and stopped himself. "No." There was no need for this monster to lay his eyes on Abbi.

Criddell sighed, lifted his eyes to the ceiling and studied the white grid of acoustic tiles. "Do you know why they call missing child alerts Amber Alerts?"

"No."

"They are named after Amber Hagerman. She was a nine-year-old kidnapped and murdered in 1996." Criddell paused.

"What's your point?"

Criddell's smile stretched out again. "My point is that twenty-six years later, they still have not caught the guy. And *they* had the body *and* a witness. And you hope to catch someone with neither after forty-three years?"

Nick breathed out in exasperation. "That's all you got? This won't get you any points with the FBI. You say you are different. You say you are not a predator. Did you really care for those children? Well, prove it. I doubt this child was taken to be adopted. Whoever took her *is* a predator. Help me find him. Tell me what to look for."

Criddell's smile reduced to a mere shadow, but his eyes remained locked on Nick. "Look for a family member or friend of the family."

Nick froze. "Why not a stranger?"

"A random stranger abducts targets of opportunity. He sees a child and acts on an impulse. But he does not get out of his car to grab the child. He does not want the child to scream and draw attention. Instead, he pulls up and talks to the child, makes them feel comfortable, and maybe gives them money in exchange for *showing* him where something is—something a child would know—maybe a pizza shop, or an ice cream parlor. The child gets into his car of their own will. But you see, all this takes time—talking with the child, making them feel at ease. Then he drives the child to the first private spot he can find just far enough away, and assaults them there, and whether he kills the child or lets them go, he will leave them there, because he had not planned this, and he panics. He wants out of this situation as quickly as possible." Duane paused dramatically. "But what *you* told me sounds like someone who had planned this—someone who knew when the girl would get off the bus and where he would need to wait for her. And the girl knew him, so she would feel comfortable getting into his car without needing convincing. So—look for a family member or a friend of the family. Someone who lives in a secluded location or has a cabin. He would have planned where to take her and where to get rid of her body so she would not be found."

Th!rty-$!x

On Monday, Roses wasn't online.

This was the week Claire started back on day shifts. She got to the hospital by 7 a.m. to find the ward at full capacity and spent the rest of the morning in a whirlwind, completing rounds, administering meds, talking with her little patients and their parents, and answering calls. So many calls. Day shifts were so much busier than the nights. It wasn't until almost noon that she was finally able to take a break, eat her sandwich, and spend a few minutes scrolling through the news feed. Over the weekend, she had become addicted to hitting Refresh on the news search for *Azarev Enterprises*. Each day, there was new coverage, as more and more outlets picked up the story. Today, as she skimmed through a couple of fresh headlines, she came across a BBC exposé on Anatoli's uncle Bogdan and his connections to Russia. She did not have time to read it on her break, but she bookmarked it for later. She decided to also share the link with Roses, but when she opened Tox Chat, she found that Roses was not there. For the first time in almost three years since Claire had known her, Roses' always-green Tox Chat bubble had gone gray.

Unusual as this was, Claire did not deem this cause for alarm. After all, everyone had to go offline at some point. Maybe Roses was in a place with no signal. By then, Claire's break was over, and she soon forgot about this peculiar occurrence as she got pulled back into the whirlwind, starting with an IV machine sounding out its *I'm empty* alert somewhere down the hall.

She got home at a quarter till eight in the evening, feeling both wired and exhausted at the same time. She showered while Nick warmed up dinner. They ate and caught up on each other's days, and then crashed on the couch to watch TV. Claire mechanically opened the news feed on her phone, and that's when she remembered about Roses. She opened Tox Chat. Roses was still not online. A worry settled in her chest. Did something happen? In this anonymous relationship she and Roses valued so much, Claire suddenly realized that she was powerless to do anything about this.

"Everything OK?" Nick asked her, and she realized she was staring at the black, timed-out screen of her phone.

"No. I don't know." She gave Nick a befuddled look. "Roses is offline. Roses is never offline."

He wrinkled his forehead. *"Never?"*

"Never, in all the years I have known her."

"Maybe she had a power outage?"

"She's been offline for at least seven hours now."

"Hmm. Do you know where she lives?"

She shook her head, feeling panic rising. "I don't even know what country she lives in. Nick, I don't know any of her family. I don't even know any personal details—not her real name, not her age or her nationality, not her height, the color of her hair or of her eyes. I've got nothing you'd need for a missing person report."

"What about the other hackers? The Red Hand? Do they know who she is?"

"I don't think so. But I'll ask." She checked the group chat with Tristan and Marzana, but they were both yellow—inactive. She was pretty sure they were both in Europe, so it would have been probably three or four in the morning where they were. Hackers were not a morning breed, but hopefully, in a few hours they would be up.

"I am sure she is fine," Nick reassured her with a smile. "Maybe she lost her phone or went camping."

"In February?"

"You said it yourself—you don't know where in the world she lives. Maybe she is in Australia." He smiled.

He was probably right. There had to be plenty of perfectly normal reasons someone—even Roses—would go offline for a day. Claire did her best to stop worrying. She watched TV with Nick for a while longer, and then they went to bed.

In the morning, Claire checked her phone as soon as she opened her eyes. Roses was still gray, Marzana yellow, but Tristan was green.

"Have you talked with Roses recently?" Claire typed.

"Umm. Not since Saturday. Why?"

"She's been offline since yesterday."

"Hmm."

"Did she say anything to you? Was she going somewhere?"

"No. Nothing."

Claire felt panic rising again. "Do you know anything about her? Where she lives? Her real name?"

"I think she is in the UK, but I am not certain. That's all I know. I'll ask Marzana when she gets on. She's the only other person I know who knows her."

Fuck, Claire cursed under her breath. Her brain raced through options until she suddenly realized a glimmer of hope. She found the bookmarked LeapChat URL she and Roses used to communicate with Leo. Leo was green.

"Hey Leo!" she typed and realized that she had not talked with him since before the FBI took down LoliTown and the Red Hand breached Azarev and OstTech. "How are you?" she added.

"Hi Kat," Leo typed. "I'm good, considering everything that's happened. I can't believe Red Hand did all this. Anatoli is so freaked out. Are you one of them?"

"I am not. But hey, have you talked with Roses recently?"

"Yeah—yesterday morning."

"You did?" Claire felt an instant warmth of relief. "Where is she? She is not online."

"She said she was coming to Ukraine. I think she is on the plane now."

"Ukraine? Why?"

"She asked me to look for evidence of Azarev being connected to the malware that was sent to Ben's phone. And I found something. In our document repository, there is a folder with scanned Soviet research papers from the '80s about sonic weapons. If OstTech created the app for Azarev, it would be in our code archive, which is on an offline storage appliance in our office in Kyiv. I told her I could get to the appliance but not crack its security. So, she said she would fly to Kyiv to do it. She is supposed to let me know when she lands so we can plan to meet."

Claire took a deep breath. *Roses was OK!* She wished Roses had told her that she was going to do this, but she probably wanted to keep Claire safe. This was a huge development. If Roses could secure evidence linking Azarev to Ben's death, it would let Nick finally make a solid case against Anatoli. As exciting as this was, Claire did feel a bit jealous that Leo was going to meet Roses, while Claire did not even know what she looked like.

* * *

Next morning, Claire woke up to find a message from Leo: "Roses did not make contact. Have you heard from her?"

She checked Tox Chat and LeapChat. "No," she replied. This was not normal. Something happened to Roses on the way to Ukraine or in Ukraine. Could Azarev have had something to do with this? The thought sent a chill down Claire's spine.

"What can we do?" Claire asked.

"She told me what hotel she was going to be staying at. I will go there. It's about a seven-hour drive from Minsk to Kyiv. I will leave in a couple of hours and should be there by midnight."

This was only a faint glimmer of hope. And a torturously long wait. "What can I do to help?"

"Where are you?"

"In the US."

"Oh. That's far. Is anyone from Red Hand closer? Maybe they can meet me and help?"

"Let me find out."

She sat in silence, hearing nothing but her heart hammering in her chest. Roses was gone. How could this have happened? And now Leo, too, was heading into the unknown, toward possible danger. Leo had already risked his life so many times to help people he did not even know. And what was Claire doing about it? What *could* she do from Pine Lake, Colorado? From her cushioned, safe, small-town American neighborhood?

37

"Diane White had a sister—Jane Emery," Nick said walking into Ray's office.

"Jane? Yeah, I remember Jane," Ray said. "She lived in Boulder with her family."

"You interviewed her at the time of Abbi's disappearance. But I did not see an interview of her husband, Dan."

Ray's brow furrowed. "Not initially. He was out of town on a business trip."

"But you did interview him later?"

"About a week later."

"Why?"

"We had no leads, and I was digging deeper anywhere I could."

"Did you find anything?"

"I found that Dan had a juvenile conviction."

"For what?"

"He molested one of his younger sister's girlfriends when he was twelve."

A chill ran up Nick's spine. "What did he say when you interviewed him?"

"He said he had nothing to do with Abbi's disappearance. And he felt very ashamed about his juvenile record. He begged me not tell anyone because he was afraid he would lose his basketball coaching position at his kids' school."

"And that's it? You let him go?"

Ray puffed out his cheeks and exhaled. "Severs, as much I wanted to solve this, I had nothing on him. He had no other infractions since he was a juvenile, and I had no evidence to tie him to the case. None."

"How good was his alibi?"

Ray shrugged. "Decent. He was a salesman for a tool company and frequently made overnight road trips throughout the region. His customers were mines, factories, and power plants. His wife and work confirmed he left for Alamosa the day before and he had hotel and gas station receipts. He was there for two nights."

Nick walked over to the large, framed map of the Front Range hanging on Ray's wall and located Alamosa at the southern edge of Colorado between Trinidad and Pagosa Springs.

"Do you think he could have had blocks of time we can't verify on this trip? A few hours here and there?"

"Oh, I'm sure. But he wasn't exactly the only one without an ironclad alibi. I did not completely rule him out, but I also had three registered sex offenders within a five-mile radius, and one of them did not have an ironclad alibi, either. Why? Why are you asking about Dan?"

"Because he owns fifty acres of mountain land south of Bailey."

"Dan? Not back then he didn't. I remember because I looked at his tax records. All of the family. There was no land. If there was, I would have checked it out."

"That's because it was in his father's name until 1992. When his father passed, the land was deeded to Dan. And according to the tax records, there is a cabin there."

"Well, I'll be . . ."

"Yeah." Nick studied the map. "Looks like Alamosa is a straight shot down 285 from Bailey. Maybe three hours or less. He could have done his sales calls on the first day, checked in at the hotel, and then driven back up to the property in Bailey the next day without anyone knowing."

Ray studied the map from behind his desk, smoothing his silver mustache in long, pensive strokes. "Want to drive out there and take a look around?"

"That's what Jason and I were thinking. Decide whether we want to request a search warrant."

"Well, hold on, then. I'll come with you two." Ray straightened up from his plush office chair and reached for his Stetson.

* * *

West of Bailey, they took County Road 64 up into the densely wooded ridges. The pines here were mostly firs—wide, tall, and bushy—not slender like the lodgepole pines in Pine Lake. The road carved languidly from side to side, following the snowy contours of the mountains as it climbed higher and deeper into the wilderness. Nick rode with Jason in his truck, watching out over the tall hood for their turnoff. They probably would have missed it if it weren't for the bank of five mailboxes—mismatched in sizes and shapes but sharing a single, long wooden rail. Jason slowed down, and that's when they saw the road sign—half-buried in the plowed embankment and plastered with snow, making it barely visible and utterly unreadable. Nick checked the GPS—this was Lost Creek Road. Jason turned, and the Dodge shifted down a gear as the climb became steeper. Judging by the tracks in front of them, this single track of packed and somewhat plowed snow was utilized sparingly by vehicles with aggressive, off-road tires. There wasn't much here besides snow, pines, and an occasional boulder rising from the snowdrift.

"Here, slow down," Nick said, comparing the terrain on the GPS with the plat map he printed from the county records. "It should be coming up."

There were no addresses here, and nothing marked on the GPS except for the green expanse on either side of the road.

"Is this it?" Jason asked after they cleared another turn in the road. There was no driveway visible, but there were two short wooden posts barely protruding from the snow, demarcating what must have been the entrance to the property. One post had a rectangular piece of white plastic nailed to it—probably at one time a Private Property or No Trespassing sign, although now completely faded.

Jason stopped the truck, and Nick scrupulously compared every notable feature on the tract map with the screen of the GPS.

"This is it," he finally confirmed.

They got out of the truck. Brisk mountain chill nipped at Nick's nostrils. Ray parked his Tahoe behind them, and Nick heard his boots crunch toward them.

"Doesn't look like anyone's been here for a while," Ray noted.

Nick had to agree. Instead of a driveway, there was a frozen wall almost two feet tall of plowed snow crumble. By the looks of it, no one had been here all winter, and possibly longer. And the driveway itself, if there even was one, was completely indiscernible under all this snow.

Nick scanned the tree line all the way across and to the top of the ridge. There was no sign of a cabin. Behind him, Jason rummaged through some gear at the back of his truck and returned with a mean-looking yardstick. He climbed onto the icy wall and pushed the yardstick into the snow on the other side. The stick broke through a thin crust of hardened snow and then plunged deep. Jason read out the verdict:

"Twenty-six inches. I wouldn't try driving through this, without knowing what's under this snow." He turned to Nick. "Want to try the drone?"

The propellers whirred into the sky, and on the large screen of Jason's phone, snow-covered pines slowly zoomed into the frame. Jason piloted higher and deeper into the property, away from the road. Soon, the buzz of the drone dissipated beyond the trees, and they were left to watch the scrolling tapestry of the woods in silence.

A curved line of the road appeared on the screen. Nick checked the plat map.

"That must be 64. Can you go more west? Southwest?"

Jason nodded, nudged the controller with his thumb, and the drone's frame panned to the left. The road disappeared from view, and the treetops once again filled the screen from edge to edge.

"Wait, what's that?" Nick pointed at the dark, angled dash among the green starburst outlines of the trees.

Jason flew closer and descended. There, under the cover of old firs, was the roofline of a small cabin, barely visible under the thick crust of snow.

"Can you go up a bit so I can see which direction this is?" Nick asked.

Jason increased the altitude until the thin curve of the road and the tiny shapes of their vehicles came into view. He stretched out his arm toward the woods.

"Ten o'clock," he said. "Maybe a little over half of a mile."

"I'm going to go check it out," Nick said.

"Not gonna be easy in this snow," Ray observed.

"Well, I am not waiting till spring," Nick said and went to get the snow boots and coat he had put in the back of Jason's truck.

The whirr of the returning drone approached, and Jason brought it in for a landing. "I'm coming, too," he said. He was already wearing his Carhartt overalls and winter hunting boots.

"Well, heck," Ray said, looking down at his square-toed Ariats.

"You don't have your snow boots in the truck?" Nick asked.

"Took them out the other day to dry. I wasn't planning to go for a hike today."

"Jason and I got this. You don't need to come."

"Well, I am sure as heck not going to wait here. I've waited for forty years." Ray got his winter parka from the truck and put it on.

Nick climbed up onto the ice wall and descended to the other side, sinking deeper with each step. By the time he reached the two posts, the snow was up above his knees. It was a dry, light powder on the surface with a hard crust underneath, through which Nick's boots broke with each step. He tried to discern the line of the driveway among the trees, pressing onward up the slope in slow, laborious steps.

"I should have brought my snowshoes for this one," Jason said, plowing through the snow behind Nick.

"You mean you actually own a pair?" Nick said, panting. It was a rhetorical question. He was not really surprised.

"Uh-hum," Jason responded.

"And they are *not* in your truck?" That part *was* surprising. Jason seemed to always have whatever piece of gear was needed in that truck of his, and he could probably weather out the apocalypse with just the contents of his beastly Dodge.

As the road behind them faded from view, the line of the driveway became harder to guess. The snowpack was not getting any easier, and each step was a strenuous undertaking. Nick was beginning to sweat. He stopped to unzip his coat. The bright Colorado sun baked from above. The tall firs rolled their heavy branches lazily in the breeze. Somewhere, a magpie cried.

Jason and Ray caught up. Feeling better with cold air inside his coat, Nick took another step and suddenly sank up to his chest in the snow.

"Fuck!" he exclaimed and heard the familiar wheezing start of Ray's laughter behind him.

"You OK there, Severs?" Ray said, clearing his throat. "Need help?"

Something cold trickled inside Nick's boot.

"I'd keep left, if I were you," he said grumpily. "I think I found a creek."

He labored to turn in the deep snow and grabbed Jason's hand to be pulled back onto the invisible higher ground.

They trudged like this to the top of the ridge, from where the cabin came into view. It was a small, one-story log structure with a porch and a firewood shed on the side. There was no smoke rising from the stovepipe, and there were no footprints in the snow around it. The porch steps were half-buried under the snow, and Nick had to feel his way up, holding on to the railing. Jason and Ray climbed up behind him.

"Nice little huntin' cabin," Ray said, knocking the snow off his boots on one of the posts. "Needs a little fixin'." He poked his finger into the dry-rotted wood at the corner of a window.

"Now what?" Jason peered inside the grimy window with his hands cupped around his face to block out the sunlight.

Nick looked at the weathered metal handle on the front door. He turned it, and the door squeaked open.

He turned to Ray. "Think we have enough for a search warrant?"

"Frank Warren is a judge here in Park County—he and I fish together. He'll sign the warrant, but I'm not sure there is much here to find." Ray glanced back at their deep tracks in the snow, disappearing in the trees. "Might as well take a look since we are here, before we make a trip out and back again."

Nick nodded. He was hoping for something along those lines. He knocked the snow off his boots and stepped inside.

He instinctively looked for a light switch, but there wasn't one. There was no electricity out here. Luckily, the daylight, amplified by the snow, provided adequate lighting. But it was a cold light. Nick could see his breath in here.

The interior of the cabin was sparse, consisting of only a small woodstove, a couch, and a rough-sawed lumber bunk bed. Nick turned on his flashlight and walked through the room, shining the light into the dim corners. There was not much to look at here. The bunk bed had just two bare mattresses—no pillows or blankets. There was a door on the back wall. Nick opened it—it was a closet with a couple of pillows and blankets folded neatly on the top shelf and some pots and pans on two other shelves. A dented old aluminum cooler was on the floor.

Nick closed the closet and then stared at the doorframe.

"What does this look like to you?" he asked Jason, who was standing nearby.

Jason stepped closer and examined a formation of four small screw holes on the door and two more aligned to them on the doorframe.

"Looks like someone had a deadbolt on this door at one time."

"Why would anyone want a deadbolt on the outside of a closet door?" Nick said, and suddenly felt uneasy.

He opened the door again and pulled up on one of the shelves. It nudged easily, and the pots rattled.

"Looks like the shelves come out," he noted and pulled the cooler out of the way. He crouched down and tilted his head, inspecting the space underneath with his flashlight. There was nothing unusual on the right side of the closet, but when the flashlight reached the other side, he froze.

"Chief," he said. "You'd better call your judge for that warrant."

Ray and Jason stooped down to look. There, just under the bottom shelf, illuminated in the bright spotlight, was the thick metal coil of a two-inch eyehook screwed deep into the back wall of the cabin. And in the wedge-like crook of the eyehook, where the end of the circle rod came back to the point where the circle began, in the pinch of that metal crevice, shining like a gold thread in the bright light, was a single strand of blond hair.

38

Nick texted Claire that he would be late. Very late. Ray had obtained the search warrant, and they took the hair as evidence. Then they waited for the forensics team to get there and set up and begin going through the cabin looking for prints, blood, or whatever other evidence could survive four decades. When Nick finally got home late that night, he was surprised to see that the house was completely dark. Claire should have been home, but when he opened the garage, her car was not there. Did he somehow forget that she was working tonight? With everything going on, that was possible. Or maybe somebody called in at the hospital, and she had to cover a shift at the last minute?

He dialed her number as he walked into the house. No answer. So, she must have been at work and her phone was put away. He turned on the lights in the kitchen and went back out to the Tahoe to get his wet snow boots and coat.

His phone rang—*Claire*. "Hey, hon," he said. "Where are you?"

"Umm, somewhere over the East Coast."

"What?!" The sound on her end was a bit fuzzy and distant, and he thought he had misheard her.

"Can you hear me? This Wi-Fi calling is flaky. Did you not see my note?"

"Note?" He dumped the wet bundle on the floor in the entryway. "No, I just got home."

"Oh." There was a moment of fuzzy silence. "I am on my way to Ukraine."

"What?! Ukraine? Why?"

"Roses is missing. She was going to Kyiv to meet with Leo. But she never showed up."

What the hell was Claire thinking! He couldn't believe she put herself in danger like this. His pulse thumped fast and hard in his temples. He suddenly felt hot. He crossed the living room to the back slider and went out on the deck, into the cold of the night. "That . . . that's terrible," he said, trying to not overreact. "Why was she meeting with Leo?"

"He thinks he can get proof that Azarev was behind the phone malware that killed Ben, but he needs help accessing it."

"OK. And why are *you* going?"

"I am going to meet with Leo and Marzana in Kyiv and see if we can find out what happened."

"Who is Marzana?"

"She is from the Red Hand. She is coming from Poland to meet us in Kyiv."

Nick's mind raced from thought to thought, trying to figure out the right things to say and do in situations like this. But he had never been in a situation like this.

"Hello? Are you still there?" Claire said.

She sounded so close and yet so far away. And she was getting farther with each second. "Yeah, sorry. I'm here. I just can't believe you . . . went to Ukraine just like that. Without us talking about it. It's not like running out for a gallon of milk." He took a deep gulp of cold air, trying to keep from boiling over.

She was silent for a moment. "I know. I'm sorry. I was just afraid you would try to talk me out of it. That we would get into a fight. I had my mind made up, and I did not want us to get into it. I know how you feel about this part of my life. And I couldn't just sit there for hours, waiting for you to come home so we could talk about it, when I could have been doing something to help Roses. Nick, it's only a thirteen-hour flight to Kyiv. Just thirteen hours, and I can be on the other side of the world, helping look for my friend. What choice would you make if you were in my shoes?"

Nick bit his tongue, feeling a bit defensive and wounded. But she *was* right. He would have tried to talk her out of it. They probably would have fought. And yes, he would have been just as determined if *he* were in her shoes. But what now? Dig in and argue about it? What good would that do?

"I just wish you would have waited," he finally said. "I would have gone with you."

"But you have your case to wrap up. I knew you couldn't leave today. Probably not even tomorrow. And I couldn't wait that long. Roses has already been gone for over forty-eight hours. You know every hour counts."

He breathed in the cold air and watched his breath evaporate into the night. "OK. What can I do to help?"

"Nothing, you just focus on your case. I will be gone for a couple of days at the most. I emailed you a LeapChat link. If you can't get hold of me on the phone, try it—Marzana is on it as well."

"OK," he said. "Claire?"

"Yeah?"

"Promise me something. Promise you won't go near that data Roses was going there for. Don't go anywhere near Azarev or OstTech. It's not worth it. You just look for Roses, and I will call Beck and have him work with Leo on the data. OK?"

He heard her soft breath on the other end. "I promise," she finally said.

"OK. Let me know when you land. I love you."

He hung up and walked into the kitchen. Sure enough—there was a notepad on the counter.

Flying to Kyiv to look for Roses. I'll call you. Don't be mad. I love you. P.S. Check your email. The note was signed with a shimmering lipstick imprint of her lips.

Kyiv. Nick opened the Maps app on his phone and typed it in. *So far away.* He zoomed into the map. *And so close to Belarus.*

When did this world become so uncomfortably small? Until a couple of weeks ago, Nick had never even used the words *Belarus* or *Kyiv* in a sentence, but now something that happened there, almost six thousand miles away, had a direct impact on his life. How was it that he was at home, and the woman he loved was flying there, alone, to the very frontlines of this cyberwar that his case brought into their lives? *His* case.

He dialed Beck. No answer. He left a message:

"Hey, Tim. This is Nick Severs. Just wondering whether you were able to make contact with Leo from OstTech? It sounds like he may be able to get new evidence pertaining to the phone malware, but he may need some help from your team. If you could call me back, that would be great. Thanks."

Nick hung up. He felt exhausted. He needed a shower. In their bedroom, a small shoebox was sitting open on Claire's side of the bed. He had seen it before. It was the shoebox Claire brought back from her mother's house. He looked inside—a stack of letters and a few mementos. A high school graduation tassel. A Northern Missouri State University student ID, like the one he used to have, but with the name and photo of Katie Daniels. He picked up the envelope from the top of the stack. It had worn, dog-eared corners and was addressed to Katie Daniels in Cape Girardeau, Missouri. The return address was a stamp from the United States Penitentiary, McCreary, Kentucky. Nick opened the envelope and pulled out a folded sheet of lined paper. The handwriting was rough – a mix of small and capital letters that struggled to stay aligned and orderly even in-between the lines.

> *"My dear Katie,*
> *Today is the 20th anniversary of my incarceration. I reflect on this occasion with the considerable benefit of time that has passed since the day I lost my freedom. You asked me if I would do anything differently had I known the consequences of my actions. It is an impossible question. I*

have missed so much since I have been locked up. My father died. You were born and grew up. I wish I had been around for these and so many other important parts of life. And yet, even if I could go back and take a different path, I do not believe that I would. The decisions I made in my youth were not made light-heartedly. I do not regret them, and I take full responsibility for my actions. Although there is so much I now know that I have missed, action is not a simple product of a pros and cons list. There will always be a thousand rational and valid reasons not to do something. But as long as there is even a single reason to do it that you really believe in, then that is all you need.

With love, your Uncle Alex."

Th!rty-n!n3

The Lufthansa flight took off from Denver International Airport at 9:20 p.m., and a little over thirteen hours later touched down in Kyiv's Boryspil International Airport at 7:30 p.m. local time the next day after a short layover in Frankfurt. She validated this intercontinental math in her head: nine time zones plus thirteen hours. Her brain was fuzzy, but the math worked. She was not used to such journeys. It left her with the same tired restlessness she got when switching from night shifts to days—the floaty feeling of time and circadian rhythms running counter to each other. A liminal state. Still, she was grateful the trip was only thirteen hours. She could not imagine how people managed this trip a hundred years ago, when crossing "the pond" took weeks. Like her great-great-grandfather William had done. More than once. It seemed like purgatory to her—day after day of nothing but one's own thoughts and the never-ending sea.

As it was, Claire could barely stand being in her head for just thirteen hours. Her thoughts turned endlessly from Roses to Nick and to what was awaiting her in Kyiv. She checked her Tox Chat and LeapChat using the plane's Wi-Fi probably a hundred times on this flight. Still—nothing. She pushed the terrible thoughts away, stubbornly, unrealistically refusing to assume the worst. Perhaps this was all just something silly—like Roses' phone and computer being stolen when she got to Kyiv. Maybe she was at her hotel right now, setting up a new computer, and Claire would get a message from her any second.

Claire also thought about Nick. She felt guilty. She should have talked to him before taking off like this. Why didn't she? The damned thirteen-hour flight gave her plenty of time to examine this question. The root of the problem seemed to be that she did not trust men. After what she'd been through, this was hardly surprising. For years, Uncle Alex was the only one whom she allowed to get close. And now Nick was in that circle. Nick saw her. He knew her and accepted her. He was so good to her. And what she was afraid of the most was that he would have proved to be someone she could not count on in this crisis. She was afraid she would find out that she was still alone. But she did not give him a chance. She should have.

After the plane landed, everything seemed to take excruciatingly long. They had to wait almost a half hour to deplane at the gate. Passport control took longer than that, and luggage and customs were not much faster. When Claire finally made it to the main floor of the airport, she was surprised to find it overwhelmed with departures. Long lines of people with luggage snaked around everywhere—at ticketing, luggage drop-off, and security. Over the noise of crying children and yelling adults, the airport officials shouted announcements at the masses in a language Claire did not understand.

When she finally managed to find her way through the crowds and exit into the fresh air outside, the evening had already set in. The air here smelled different than it did in Colorado. Even in winter, it smelled earthier, like rich farming soil. It was also colder here than in Denver. She put on her parka, zipped it up, and opened her Uber app to order a ride to the hotel. But the Uber app notified her that she was offline. For some reason, she did not have any signal here. She toggled the phone's airplane mode on and then off, hoping it would pick up a cell tower, but it didn't help. She restarted her phone, and while waiting for the operating system to load, realized that there was a taxi stand nearby with no waiting line and several cars parked at the curb. She shoved the phone in her pocket, and in just a couple of minutes she and her small suitcase were on their way toward downtown Kyiv, in the back of a shiny Mercedes minivan with an old-school yellow Taxi light on the roof.

Her driver was a young man dressed in business casual and sporting a nice haircut. He introduced himself as Dima in grammatically impeccable queen's English with a prominent Slavic accent. The airport was located in the woodland outskirts of Kyiv, and as Dima pulled the Mercedes onto the ramp for E40, Claire saw the lights of the city in the distance. She also saw that the airport-bound lanes of the highway were bright with the headlights of oncoming traffic. Their lane heading into the city was mostly empty.

"Is the airport always so busy?" she asked him.

"No. It's because of the tensions with Russia. Some people think there will be a war."

"A *war*?" Absorbed with the Azarev case, the Red Hand, and Roses, Claire hadn't really paid attention to the news recently. "Why?"

Dima shrugged. "It is the curse of Ukraine. It is the gateway between Europe and Russia. Throughout history, it has been invaded many times—by the Polish, the Lithuanians, the Tatars, the Ottomans, the Germans, the Russian tsars, and then the Soviets. Why should this century be any different?"

"What do the Russians want?"

"Well, that depends on whom you ask. Myself, I think Putin wants to rebuild the Soviet Union, and Ukraine is the crown jewel in his plan. It is rich in resources and agriculture, and it has access to the Black Sea. The only question is how far they will go this time. In 2014, they invaded the Crimean Peninsula and annexed it to Russia. For years, they have wanted to annex the Donbas and Luhansk regions in the east. Perhaps that is as far as they will go. This time." He looked at her in the rearview mirror. "If you don't mind me asking, what brings you to Kyiv at a time like this?"

"I am looking for a friend," she said and considered how crazy that sounded when she said it out loud, given that she had never met Roses in person and had no idea what she looked like. She checked her phone. She still had no bars here—hopefully in the city it would be better.

The dense woods on the side of the highway gave way to industrial and commercial buildings. Kyiv was a large city like any other. After a while, the trees and the buildings in her window disappeared as the van crossed onto a modern six-lane bridge over a vast, ice-covered river. In the dusk, the white of the river seemed to glow, and the downtown lights glimmered on the other shore. Soon, the tires rumbled over cobbled streets. This city was a mix of old and new. Claire saw restaurants, banks, and shops here, with bright lights, display windows, and colorful signs.

Dima stopped the car in front of a tall art deco glass tower wedged between two baroque-style facades of the neighboring buildings.

"This is you," he said. "Hotel Eleven Mirrors."

He left the car running and went to the back to get Claire's bag as she got out onto the snowy cobblestones. It seemed the air was even frostier here, maybe because of the proximity of the river. She saw her breath in the air as she took the handle of her small suitcase and was about to roll it up to the front door of the hotel when someone latched on to her arm. Startled, she looked over and saw a young woman with piercing green eyes and locks of black hair sticking out from under a red knit hat.

"You need to come with me, Claire," she said, pulling her along down the sidewalk, away from the hotel. "Don't look at the hotel. My car is right there."

"Wait . . . why? Who are you?" Claire dug in like a child determined not to go a step farther.

"I am Marzana. Your man sent a message."

40

That night, Nick did not sleep well. This was in part because Claire was not there. Although he had become used to sleeping without her when she worked nights, this was different. He was worried about her. As he tossed and turned and flipped his pillow for the hundredth time, a million terrible scenarios ran through his mind, but he chased each one away. *She would be fine.* Even without him there. She was tough and smart. And she had Leo and Marzana there. But . . . she was going to a completely strange country, and meeting people she had never met before, in connection with other, very dangerous people.

If he forced himself to think of anything else, his thoughts turned to the Abbi White case. There was something about that cabin—he could feel it. It was as if there was a presence there, waiting. Ray said he would request cadaver dogs but was not sure whether they could do anything, with the snow being so deep.

Somewhere in the midst of thinking about all this, Nick managed to drift asleep a few times, in fragments, only to wake up time and again, and have to repeat the cycle all over.

His alarm went off when he was finally in a deep sleep. He got himself out of bed, feeling utterly exhausted, and stumbled into the kitchen, where he made himself a double espresso and drank it at the kitchen table, watching the sky begin to lighten in the window. He showered, got dressed, and made another double espresso.

When Nick got to the station, Ray was already in his office, rummaging through papers.

"What are you doing?" Nick asked.

"I'm going to bring in Dan Emery for questioning."

"You don't want to wait until DNA on the hair comes back?"

"Severs, I've waited forty years for this. I am not waiting any longer. I want to see what the son of a bitch says with the threat of a DNA match coming back."

This was a smart play. After all, the lab may not get *any* DNA from a single hair that old. But Emery did not need to know that. If he was guilty and believed a match was imminent, a smart man would cooperate and confess in hopes for a reduced sentence.

Nick's phone rang—*Beck*.

"Severs—I have some news about this OstTech company."

Nick walked to his office and closed the door. "Yeah? What?"

"I did a search on JWICS—it's the intelligence-sharing system we have with the NSA, CIA, and a few other agencies. And I found an NSA bulletin on them."

"On *OstTech*? Why?"

"Looks like the NSA has been watching them for a while. These people are bad news. They have ties to the hacking groups inside the GRU—Russia's military intelligence. Which means they have ties to the Kremlin."

"The Kremlin? They run sex sites for Azarev. What would the Kremlin want to do with them?"

"Well, based on the early analysis of some of the data from the recent breach by Red Hand, OstTech went out of its way to uncover the real identities of the site users. The NSA believes they were doing this to collect blackmail material on high-profile individuals around the world."

Nick closed his eyes. It all suddenly made sense. OstTech's shadowy connection to Azarev, the weaponized malware. *Maybe that's why they killed Ben? Maybe he knew something?*

"Have you talked to Leo yet? Maybe he can help connect some of the dots?"

"Yeah, about this Leo guy . . . He is dead."

"What?! How?"

"Looks like he was killed. I saw the NSA report. The police in Minsk were called out for a disturbance and found him dead in his apartment building with a gunshot wound to his face."

"Oh my God." Nick felt his blood rising. *Claire!* "Did you say this was in Minsk?"

"Yeah."

Nick felt some minor relief—Claire was not going anywhere near Minsk. "Are you sure the NSA have the right guy?"

"Yeah. The police confirmed he worked at OstTech. Looks like his real name was Nikolai Smolnikov, but he went by Leo. When did you talk to him?"

"I didn't. Claire did. Just yesterday."

"Yesterday?"

"Yeah. She is actually flying to Kyiv now. She was supposed to meet up with Leo there to look for a friend of hers."

"Nick, that's impossible. Leo was killed on February 1."

"What? No. That has to be a mistake."

"No mistake. I saw the police report obtained by the NSA."

"But . . . Claire has been talking with him for a week now. And Roses was talking to him, too, before she . . . *FUCK!!!* I'll have to call you back—"

Nick hung up without waiting for Beck's reply and hurriedly dialed Claire. No answer. He texted her: *Leo dead since Feb 1. Don't meet anybody. It's a trap. Call me.*

He hit Send and watched the spinning circle under the message as it was being sent. But then the circle changed to a red *X* error: *Unable to send. Number not in service.*

"Oh, what the fuck?! *FUCK!*" Nick slammed his fist into his desk. There *had* to be some way of alerting Claire! *EMAIL! Claire said she sent him an email with some link!* He opened his email, and there it was—the message from Claire. There were two links in the email, and they both looked unlike any link Nick had ever seen before. They both began with *leapchat.org* and were followed with a very long chain of random words such as "Powerboat," "Giraffe," "Azure," etc. The first link was labeled *Kat, Roses, and Leo*. The second one was labeled *Kat, Tristan, Marzana*.

Nick hesitated a moment and clicked the second link. His web browser opened and asked him to create a username. He thought about it and typed in *Nick*. The browser page revealed a blank chat window. Nick was the only name in the chat, with a green bubble next to him. He waited for a few moments, not sure of how this worked. Finally, he exhaled and retyped his failed text message:

Leo was killed Feb 1. Don't meet anybody. It's a trap. Azarev's sites are collecting blackmail for the Kremlin. Call me.

He hit Submit. His message appeared in the chat, but nothing else changed. He waited, watching the screen. Five minutes passed, and no one showed up.

He tried calling and texting Claire's phone again, but it was as if her number had never existed.

"Severs?" Ray knocked and cracked open the door to Nick's office. "Hey, I'm about to head to Boulder to pick up Dan Emery. Want to come along?" He had his coat on and his hat in his hand. His eyes registered Nick's face. "Hey, what's wrong?"

Nick shook his head. "It's Claire. She needs my help. I can't explain everything right now, but I will later. I need to go. I'm sorry."

Ray nodded. "Of course. Go! Don't worry about this—if I need, I will get Jason to help. Let me know if I can do anything. Go."

Nick grabbed his keys and dialed Beck on his way to the Tahoe. Beck answered on the first ring.

"If Leo was killed on February 1, that was one day before Ben was killed. Azarev must have found out that Leo was helping trafficked children return home, so he had him killed. And then he killed Ben to tie up the loose ends."

"That's possible," Beck conceded.

"Tim, listen. This is all connected. Claire's friend Roses had been talking to someone pretending to be Leo for weeks. Ever since we started poking around LoliTown. Roses is the one that brought in the Red Hand to take down Azarev. And then Roses just disappeared two days ago. Maybe because Azarev wanted retaliation or maybe because he wants to get close to the Red Hand. And then this fake Leo started talking to Claire, and she just flew to Kyiv because he said he would help her look for Roses, and now I can't reach her by phone or computer."

"Oh, God," Beck graveled into the phone.

"Yeah."

"What are you going to do?"

"I am going to get on the next plane to Kyiv."

Førty-øn3

"Nick? On LeapChat? *My* Nick?"

Marzana threw Claire's suitcase in the back of her old two-door hatchback, got in the driver's seat, turned on the engine, and cranked up the heat. She stared deadpan at Claire. "I don't know. How many Nicks do you know? Either way, his information checked out. Tristan confirmed it with police records. Leo has been dead for over three weeks now."

She handed Claire a straightened paper clip.

"What's this?" Claire asked.

"Turn off your phone and take out the SIM card."

Claire popped the slim bumper case off her phone and used the tip of the paper clip to eject the tiny tray holding the SIM card. She took the card out and put it in her jeans pocket. Appeased, Marzana pulled out of the parking spot and took a turn off the main street and then another, taking them away from the bright lights of downtown Kyiv.

Claire slipped the black inert slab of her phone back into her bag. "I didn't get any messages from him. I've had no service at all since I landed."

"Maybe Azarev's people hacked your phone. We can look at it later. But you shouldn't be using your own phone right now, anyways."

"I need to let Nick know I am OK."

"Here." Marzana reached into her coat pocket and pulled out a phone. "You can use this one. It's a local burner I picked up earlier today. So far it seems to be working." She unlocked the phone with her thumbprint and handed it to Claire.

Claire took the phone. The browser app was already open to LeapChat. She read Nick's message. His bubble was yellow. She couldn't reply as herself in this browser window because Marzana was logged in here, so she copied the URL and pasted it into a new tab and hit Enter. When the username prompt came up, she typed in *Kat*, and then:

I am OK. My phone is not working. With Marzana now. I will call as soon as I can.

She hit Send and turned off the phone's screen. They were driving across a bridge again—a different one—this time, the bright glow of the city was behind them.

She looked at Marzana, whose features were illuminated every now and then by the headlights of the oncoming cars. She looked to be in her mid-twenties. Now that she was not wearing her beanie, Claire could see the shiny raven-black hair shaved short on the sides—Skrillex style—and swooping across her forehead like a black wing. She had a nose ring and a tattoo of three stars behind her ear.

"Where are we going?" Claire asked.

"We need to get out of Kyiv. Azarev's people will be looking for us there. And we can't fly out—all the planes are now grounded. I know some people in Bila Tserkva down south. They can help."

Her English was good—just as the taxi driver's, but the accent was different. People from these parts could probably tell a Polish accent from a Ukrainian one the same way people in the States could distinguish between the accents from Alabama and Minnesota. Here, Claire's untrained ear could detect only that they were different.

"You called me Claire back there, in the street. How did you know my real name?"

"Sorry. We had to use the passenger manifest to ID you, so I would know what you looked like. Anonymity is pretty much impossible once you venture offline." She looked at Claire and smiled.

They were on the outskirts of Kyiv now, and patches of dark woods raced past the car's window. Claire wondered if Roses was somewhere out there in this dark Ukrainian night.

"If Leo has been dead this whole time, Roses and I have been talking with somebody from Azarev's syndicate." All the innocent possibilities had now evaporated, and Claire was left with a heavy feeling. "They have her, don't they?" And then, the unimaginable. "Do you think she is still alive?"

Marzana kept her eyes on the dark highway, but Claire thought she saw her eyelash quiver. "There is a chance."

Claire shrank into her seat. *A chance.* This was all Claire's fault. She was the one who got Roses mixed up in all this. Mixed up with people who killed anyone who crossed them, as they killed Ben and Leo. But Roses . . . wouldn't Roses be useful to them? Useful how? Maybe to decrypt their data. Maybe to get to the Red Hand team—to Tristan, Marzana, the others. *Or Claire herself?!* Why her—Claire did not know much. But Azarev's people did not know that. They were just doing their own investigation—identifying the cast of characters responsible for the attack. Claire's heart sank—what did she tell this person she thought was Leo? Did she disclose something about herself? Nick? The FBI? What other lies did he tell *her*?

"Wait," she suddenly realized. "We don't even know if Roses ever came to Ukraine. That's just what Leo told me."

"She did." Marzana nodded without taking her eyes off the road.

"How do you know?"

"I verified the flight manifest."

"You mean . . . you know Roses' real name?!"

Marzana nodded again.

"Are you not going to tell me?"

Marzana looked at Claire for a moment and then refocused on the road, not saying anything.

"You don't *trust* me?" Claire riled up. "I just flew across half the world to look for her."

"Alice Redding," Marzana uttered.

"Where is she from?"

"She's an American expat living in London, last I knew."

"How long have you known her?"

Marzana thought about it. "Nine or ten years, I think."

"How did you meet her?"

"At a Black Hat conference in London." Claire saw her smile softly. "She hacked the hotel Wi-Fi to invite all the guests to the happy hour of the Interpol conference taking place at the same time."

"Wait a second. You *met* her in person? So, you actually know what she looks like?"

"Yeah . . . at least what she looked like back then. She's about your height, with blue eyes, red hair, and a rose tattoo on her thigh."

"Thigh . . . ?" Claire took a second to get the meaning. "Oh! . . . You guys . . . ?"

Marzana smirked. "Just during the conference. We both wanted to keep it uncomplicated."

"And you have not seen each other since?"

Marzana shook her head. "But we have worked together on a few projects over the years."

"The Red Hand?"

"And a few others."

Claire nodded. "OK, so, you know that she landed in Kyiv. Do you know where she went afterwards?"

Marzana shook her head. "I have not had time to dig any deeper. But my friends should be able to help."

Outside Claire's window, the dark forests gave way to snow-covered fields. The moon was rising, and she watched its light shimmering ghostly off the snow like off water. This moment felt surreal. Only yesterday, she was at home in Pine Lake. And now she was being driven deep into the dark, frozen Ukrainian countryside by a Polish hacker.

42

In the parking garage of the Denver International Airport, Nick found a spot on level five—the closest to departures. A good omen, Nick hoped. When his phone dinged with an incoming message, he unlocked it, praying that this was Claire, but instead found an alert from American Airlines that his flight to Kyiv was canceled. He hurriedly opened his American Airlines app and searched for another flight to Kyiv but found none. This was odd. Undeterred, he opened the web browser and went to Priceline to find another airline with a flight to Kyiv today. The Priceline page thought about his request for a few seconds and came back with a note that there were no flights to Kyiv due to a travel advisory. Nick clicked the travel advisory and read it, and then, in disbelief, opened CNN news.

Oh. My. God.

He felt as if ice broke under his feet and he fell through, and freezing water took his breath.

Russia invaded Ukraine.

He dialed Beck.

"Yeah, I am seeing it," Beck said.

"Can you get me on a plane to Ukraine?"

"Nick, there aren't any. No airline will go anywhere near Ukraine right now. Not after the Malaysia Airlines flight was shot down there in 2014."

"What about non-commercial? You said you have contacts in the NSA."

"I don't know, Nick."

"*C'mon, Tim! It's Claire!* If Russia is at war with Ukraine, you know we've got to be flying busloads of defense and intelligence personnel over there right now. *I've got to get there,* Tim."

"OK. Let me see what I can do."

Førty-thr33

Marzana drove on an access road along railroad tracks. The small hatchback bounced and body-rolled over the potholes and the ruts, its headlights slashing at the darkness, carving out slivers of the surroundings. This was a warehouse district, and a shabby one at that. The buildings were in mixed condition—some were well maintained and protected behind concrete walls and iron gates. But many were dilapidated, sitting behind chain-link fences with busted gates, their windows broken, and their corrugated metal skins torn and peeled back as if by some monstrous can opener, exposing their metal skeletons and the dark voids within. Claire wondered what sort of friends Marzana had in a place such as this.

They parked in the loading yard of a two-story industrial building with a rusty blue door and no windows on the first floor. The second floor had windows, and Claire saw dim light coming through the thin veil of curtains.

Marzana shut off the engine and turned to Claire. "So, I have to warn you. My friend Alena . . . she was part of the Red Hand operation. And . . . she is a witch."

"A *witch*?" Claire gave her a bewildered stare. This was the last thing she expected to hear right now. Sure, she had seen Craft back in middle school and wanted to be the goth teenager in dark eyeliner burning candles and scaring her friends with tarot cards at a sleepover. But c'mon . . . Now? "I thought your friends were . . . hackers?"

"They are. They just come to it from a different angle. Holistic."

"*Holistic* hacking?"

"Yeah. Think about it—magic is all about moving and controlling the energy that surrounds us. And what is the internet if not a massive cloud of energy—a bunch of electronic signals pulsing back and forth from one point in space to another. Tiny particles flowing through metal wires, or bursts of light down the fiber-optic cable. Five billion people use the internet. That's more than half of the entire human civilization. That's billions of eyeballs and hands jacked into a digital astral plane. Typing, scrolling, and clicking. Ones and zeros, light and dark. They make this energy happen. Nothing else in the world has so much human energy plugged into it 24/7—hopes, dreams, desires, anger, and hatred. Without people keeping it alive, the internet would not exist, would not flow. But there is also a feedback loop. The internet can make people happy, sad, obsessed, depressed. It can drive them to insanity, murder, or suicide. That energy works both ways. When we hack, we don't just hack the hardware. We can also hack the people that use it."

"And . . . *you* believe this, too?"

"I think there is something to it, yes."

Claire considered her bearings in this new reality. "So . . . is she a Wiccan?"

Marzana smiled. "No. Wicca is for suburban mommies. Alena does not need organized religion. She is the real deal. Here in the old world, we have old roots. They are always with us. Regardless of what the modern world looks like. One thing I can tell you for sure is Alena sees deep inside your soul. But . . . if you don't believe in all this, that's fine—all you need to know is she is a great hacker, and she can help us look for Roses."

Claire had no personal problem with witches. And she figured she had no authority in spiritual matters to tell anyone they were wrong. Until now, witches did not occupy much of her daily awareness, and her idea of them was probably the same as it was for most Americans—a confused paradox of scary, ugly, and sexy all at the same time, similar to the general public's sentiment on vampires. If Claire was destined to cross paths with a real-life witch today, a *hacker* witch seemed like a timely happenstance. She nodded to Marzana.

They exited the car and walked a few crunchy steps in the snow to the rusty blue door. The night was frosty and clear, and the sky above was pitch-black and full of stars. There was music playing in the building. Marzana banged on the door with her fist.

The door was opened by a scrawny teenage boy in oversized sweatpants, T-shirt, and a lopsided mop haircut. Claire heard a rap song she did not recognize booming somewhere inside the building. They followed the boy through the rubble of broken wooden pallets, smashed cardboard boxes, and knocked-over shelving units, and then up some metal stairs to the second level, where the music was coming from.

Despite the peeling paint on the walls, the second floor was a veritable upscale loft when compared with the lower level. For starters, it had furniture—a ripped plush couch, several mattresses and sleeping bags on the floor, and two large makeshift tables constructed from metal file cabinets topped with entry doors that had been taken off their hinges and laid flat, with handles still attached. On these tables towered several sticker-plastered computers and monitors. The space was decorated with what looked like bedsheets covering the windows, string lights, and a large TV playing the news on the wall. A couple of upturned crates in front of the couch held some magazines, a cereal bowl full of cigarette butts, and a beat-up boom box with a blue LED ring light around the speaker, emanating the rap they heard from the outside. Now that she was closer, Claire realized the song was not in English.

She counted seven people in the room—two huddled at a computer; one on a mattress, watching something on her phone; and a group of three smoking by a doorless doorway that led to another room. But Claire guessed the main person in the room was on the couch—the young woman with black cornrow braids, metal rings in her eyebrows and nose, black army boots propped up on the crate, and a notebook computer with a large anarchist's star sticker in her lap. Her big dark eyes checked the visitors over the brim of her laptop screen.

"Khto vona?" she asked without turning her head.

"This is Kat," Marzana replied in English. "She is Roses' friend. She helped hack Azarev."

The witch lifted her gaze to Claire, and Claire felt a shiver in her body. This girl could not have been older than twenty-five, but staring into her gaze was like staring into the dark kernel of the universe itself.

The witch returned her attention to her screen. "She's no hacker," she said in broken Slavic English. "She's a script kiddie."

Claire grinned. *Script kiddies* was what the *real* hackers called the wannabes. Script kiddies didn't know the tech intuitively. Script kiddies did not write their own code. They used code—*scripts*—written by the pros and made commercially available complete with help files and video tutorials. Compared to Roses, Marzana, Tristan, and this Ukrainian badass witch, Claire *was* a lame script kiddie.

"Fair enough," Claire said. "I haven't been hacking since I was two, and if you want a pissing contest, you win. I did not come here for that. I came all this way to look for my friend, and I was told you could help. If you can't, I'll be on my way."

The witch looked up again and smirked. *"American?* Slow your roll, Barbie girl. You are far away from Kansas. How did you get to Bila Tserkva?"

"I flew to Kyiv."

Alena's big black eyes moved to the TV on the wall. The news program showed firefighter crews putting out a burning, partially collapsed building in the city street, with red, yellow, and blue emergency lights flashing reflections off the wet pavement and the surrounding buildings. "*This* is Kyiv. Kyiv is being bombed now. We are at war. The airport is closed. You are not going home any time soon."

Claire stared at the TV, struggling to reconcile the image on the screen with the streets where she was just hours ago. "They are bombing *Kyiv*? I thought the Russians just wanted Donetsk and Luhansk?"

On the TV, a fiery streak in the dark sky was being tracked in a shaky, zoomed camera frame until it struck a high-rise apartment building and exploded into a fireball. The camera zoomed out to show the street, where people ran and took cover from the falling debris.

"I think it's pretty clear what they want," Alena said. "Yesterday, these people were going to coffee shops and grocery stores, going to work, and taking their kids to school. Today, they are pulling their loved ones out of the rubble that used to be their homes. Yesterday, we could have helped you look for your friend. Today, we can't."

Claire turned back to Alena. "Why can't you?"

"We are at war. On TV, you see Russian rockets and tanks, but you don't see their hackers targeting our power grids, communications nodes, and government websites. Yesterday, we were just hackers. Today, we have to be Ukraine's resistance."

On the TV, first responders were pulling a mangled body out of rubble. This horror was unspeakable, but Claire wasn't going to give up on Roses. "What if I told you that Azarev uses OstTech to collect blackmail information on the Kremlin's adversaries? What if they have something on the Ukrainian president? Your prime ministers?" This was only a guess. A logical guess. And the last play Claire had left.

Alena's eyes zoomed to Marzana. *"Kompromat?"*

Marzana nodded. "You know how the Russians operate."

Smart girl, Claire thought. She followed Claire's lead without skipping a beat.

"If you are at war with Russia, you will need all the Western help you can get," Claire said. "Can you really afford to have these people operating unchecked? Can you afford the risk of them leaking information that will make your Western neighbors question who the good guys are? We can work together to find them. Maybe they have Roses and maybe not, but either way, you will learn more about your enemy and how to fight them."

Alena shut the lid of her anarchist laptop and stood up. She was skinny and tall. Taller than Claire. And even taller in her combat boots. She approached and looked Claire in the eyes, fixing there for a moment, her head tilted slightly, as if trying to discern something in the reflection.

"Give me your hand," she demanded, and held out her own, palm up. Her long fingers had henna-like tattoos extending to her wrists and disappearing under the long sleeves of her baggy sweatshirt.

Claire hesitantly placed her hand into Alena's, who covered it with her other hand. The witch's hands felt rough but warm. The piercings in her face gleamed in the electronic light of the room, and when Alena leaned closer, Claire felt as if the witch was burrowing deeper into Claire's head.

"Ti buv tut ranishe," Alena whispered hoarsely.

"What?" Claire whispered. She wanted to pull her hand back, but found herself suddenly unable to do so, and unable to break the magnetic traction of Alena's black eyes. In the back of her mind, she felt like a rabbit charmed by the snake. In the back of her chest, she felt her heart racing like a caught rabbit's.

"She says you've been here before," Marzana translated.

"No," Claire shook her head.

"Krov tvoya znaye," the witch whispered.

"She says your blood knows—"

"—Your blood knows this land," Alena said in her broken English as she let go of Claire's hand. "The blood of your ancestors has been spilled here, *sokil*."

"*Sokil?* What does that mean?"

"A falcon," Marzana said.

"Your spirit guide," Alena said. "You should trust it more." She touched Claire's cheek, and Claire suddenly felt peculiar—lightheaded, and weightless and filled to the brim all at once. Tears welled up in her eyes.

"OK," Alena said, withdrawing her hand. "Show me what you have on Azarev."

"What the hell was all that all about?" Claire whispered to Marzana, wiping the corners of her eyes with her sleeve.

Marzana smiled, pulling out her laptop and setting it up on the table. "That was Alena. You should feel lucky—she does not read just anyone."

This whole *reading* thing caught Claire off guard. There was something there that Alena reached in and touched, but Claire did not know what to call it. And she did not have time for that now.

"We have rootkit access to over a hundred cell phones across Azarev's organization," Marzana said. "We need to parse through their location data over the last four days, focusing on any that have been in the vicinity of Kyiv, where they could have crossed paths with Roses."

"OK," Alena said. "Let's divvy up the list and get to work." She turned to the group working at the other table. "Hey, Marko, we need your help."

44

As the Tahoe barreled down the dark, empty stretch of Colorado 470, Nick considered that although he was not a religious man, right now he would gladly pray to any god or goddess who could guarantee that he made it to the Centennial Executive Airport on time.

Beck pulled some major strings and got Nick on the FBI flight to DC, and then onto a State Department plane leaving for Poland from the Langley–Eustis Air Force Base tomorrow morning. The rest of Nick's itinerary was still *fluid*—as Beck put it. If everything worked out, the State Department office in Poland would assist Nick with crossing into Ukraine.

Nick tried to keep a cool head. Claire's phone line was still dead. She sent him a message through LeapChat that she was OK and that she was with Marzana, but that was many hours ago, before the war started, and Nick had not heard from her since then. At this point, his plan was simple: first, get to Ukraine, and second, find Claire. The rest he would figure out once those two things happened.

He spent the last couple of hours scouring travel sites for any possible ways of getting into Ukraine. As Beck said, all commercial flights to Ukraine had been canceled indefinitely, which left only one option—flying into one of the friendly bordering countries such as Moldova, Romania, or Poland, and then crossing into Ukraine by land. But the airlines were already overwhelmed with travel disruptions in the region, and the earliest flight Nick could get anywhere close to Ukraine was to

Bratislava, Slovakia, next Monday, which would get him there late on Tuesday, after two layovers and still nine hundred miles away from Kyiv. Nick gritted his teeth as he bought this ticket before someone else snagged it. What would he do, having to wait to leave for four days? He would go crazy.

In between searching the travel websites, he obsessively refreshed the news feeds on every news outlet he could think of. The war seemed to be unfolding in slow motion, as the same news reports kept replaying from several hours ago. Now there were indications that Belarus was assisting Russia with its advance from the north, and that Kyiv would be in their direct path. The news made him even more edgy and impatient. Would he get to Kyiv before the fighting and the Russians? Ukraine seemed so impossibly far. How was it possible that we had supercomputers in our smartphones and rockets taking billionaires on joyrides to space, but we still had to travel across the Atlantic the same way our grandparents did?

And that's when Beck called.

When Nick pulled into a parking spot at Hangar 4, the clock on his dash said 9:47 p.m. If everything went according to plan, he would be in Poland by this time tomorrow. If he was lucky, he might even be in Ukraine, making his way to Kyiv. To Claire.

45

Anatoli hated Kyiv. He hated the whole of Ukraine, for that matter. And all Ukrainians. But he would never admit that to anyone. Admitting it would serve no purpose. It would not change his feelings in any way and would only alienate a large portion of his customers.

Yet here he was, back in Ukraine. There was history here. In November of 1943, Anatoli's grandfather crossed the Dnieper River with General Vatutin's First Ukrainian Front Army as part of a major Soviet offensive to liberate the west bank of the river from German occupation. In this offensive, the Germans lost 250,000 soldiers. The Soviets lost 850,000 and liberated Kyiv and the rest of the west bank. *Such is the price of freedom,* as they say. Anatoli's grandfather survived the offensive and was promoted to Vatutin's staff. He went on to push the Germans farther and farther out of Ukraine until he was killed on February 28, 1944. Not by the Germans. And not even in a battle. Vatutin and several of his staff were ambushed near Rivne, a city they had liberated, by the Ukrainian Insurgent Army—a gang of ungrateful, ultranationalist guerrillas. Anatoli's grandfather died in that ambush. Vatutin died from his injuries several weeks later.

This was the history Anatoli learned from his family. *These people* were the reason his grandfather was only a faded photograph in Anatoli's life. Forever twenty-three years young. What was the lesson here? Anatoli did not know. But that photograph was what he saw any time he looked into any of their eyes.

Max was driving. Anatoli trusted Max. Bukashev was in the front passenger seat. Max trusted Bukashev. Max and Bukashev had served together—first in the first Chechen war—just kids then. Then with the Wagner Group. Max had been with Anatoli for fifteen years now. Anatoli hired him from Wagner. Max was loyal and would follow Anatoli to the ends of the earth. Bukashev had stayed with Wagner as a mercenary for almost ten more years after Max left. Max vouched for him. Bukashev had skill and experience. But Anatoli knew mercenaries had no loyalty.

It took them almost nine hours to get from Minsk to Kyiv. The border was a mess—troops on both sides. Lines of cars and people trying to get in or out. Everybody was jumpy. By the time they got to OstTech's Kyiv offices, it was already after dark. The Snowcube was exactly where Oleg said it would be. It was the size of a medium suitcase, and its thick plastic shell made it look like it could survive being dropped from an airplane.

Anatoli decided not to drive back the same night, despite Max's insistence. Instead, he had Max take them to the Intercontinental Hotel, where they had steak dinner and drinks, after which Anatoli went up to his room and passed out on his bed.

In the morning, when he sat down to eat breakfast in his room, he turned the TV to news and cursed out loud.

Fucking Galitsyn!

In the early hours, Russians had crossed into Ukraine. *A fucking warning would have been nice!* There was a major offensive east of Dnieper and another one in the north from Belarus. As Anatoli buttered his croissant, he considered this new development. Their route north back to Minsk was now cut off. To the west, border crossings to Poland were overwhelmed with people fleeing Ukraine, and Anatoli could not risk Ukrainian *or* Polish border troops scrutinizing the contents of the Snowcube, especially since all three of them were traveling on Belarusian passports. Their only remaining option was to go south—to Odesa. From there, they could take the Snowcube out of the country on Anatoli's boat and take it to Minsk by way of Romania or even Bulgaria.

There was, of course, another option—to go east. For the briefest moment, Anatoli considered reaching out to Galitsyn and going back to Belarus through Russia, but he instantly dismissed it as not viable, even as the last resort. He absolutely could not trust Galitsyn or anyone in the Kremlin to get close to all this data. His future depended on his being able to sell it to Russia piece by piece—not taking it to them for free in one convenient box.

A loud boom outside took him out of his contemplations. The china and the silverware on his tray rattled. He went to the window and pulled open the sheer curtains. A building two blocks down the street had smoke rising from the gaping, crumbling opening where the facade of windows and balconies used to be. About half a mile away, another explosion sparked. Anatoli saw the flash but did not hear it behind the thick hotel windows. He scanned the skies but did not see any planes. Must have been a missile or a drone.

From his high-floor window, Anatoli saw emergency vehicles making their way toward the first building, where rubble and dust were still settling in the street. War always made fertile ground for profit. Someone was making and selling these weapons. Profit. One day, there would be reconstruction here. Rebuilding. Profit, again. Thank God for capitalism, he thought. Capitalism knew how to turn war into profit and progress. Socialism never figured it out. *That's why the allmighty Soviet Union fizzled out after only seventy years.* Capitalism, on the other hand, was doing just fine. *In* war and *after* the war. After the war, capitalism knew how to not hold a grudge. As long as there was an opportunity for profit, everyone would get along just fine. Mercedes, BMW, Mitsubishi—all had built war machines that killed thousands if not millions in World War II. And they used thousands and thousands of POWs as slave labor. But less than ten years after the war, America and Europe lined up to buy their machines. Bayer made chemical weapons in World War I, and poison gas for the Nazi concentration camps in World War II, but soon after the war, every household in the West was buying its patented Aspirin. Holding grudges was bad for business. *No hard feelings,* as they say. Sentimentality was bad for business.

His phone buzzed—Max was calling him, doubtlessly wanting to get going and to get out of here as quickly as possible. He was right, of course, but Anatoli did not pick up. He texted Max that he would meet him in the lobby, and finished his coffee, watching in the window as the building that was struck half a mile away turned ablaze, and sooty smoke streamed thick into the morning sky. Kyiv was burning. Anatoli felt a rush. He wasn't afraid. In fact, the proximity of danger right now excited him. He had lived insulated from real danger for so long. Not the danger of being caught by the authorities—worse. The danger that came with putting his life on the line. The last time he felt it was in 1987, sitting in the passenger seat next to Uncle Bogdan as they drove through the night, smuggling a van full of girls through Poland. Someone had tipped off the Jankowski gang, and Uncle Bogdan told him that if they were caught, they would all be killed. But they went on this run anyway, to secure his uncle's expansion into Germany.

There were moments in life when one had to prove his commitment to his goals by staking everything he had. Anatoli had now arrived at such a moment. Without the websites and the kompromat, what did he have left? The sex-trade operations in Europe and America? But those were his uncle's dream—not Anatoli's. Anatoli had worked too hard for the last two decades to get to this point. Without this box of data, which he now needed to extract from Ukraine, there would be no Galitsyn, no

Kremlin, no future. And future was being made right before his eyes, on the other side of this window. All he needed to do was put some skin in the game.

46

The gray twin-engine jet of the State Department tilted its wing, and Nick saw the city. The setting sun was hanging low over the horizon, and in its final rays, the river and the rooftops glimmered under the wing.

Nick surveyed the landscape. There were some low mountains with strips of snow south of the city, but most of the surrounding area was fields and forests colored in the camouflage varieties of medium browns with patches of dark green.

The pitch of the engines changed, and the plane leveled out for the final approach. As if on cue, Russ, the robust young man in the seat next to him, awakened and straightened up. Russ looked to be in his late twenties and had the appearance of a marine stuffed into a fitted business suit. Before they took off, Russ introduced himself simply as *working for the government*, without specifying which agency. He slept most of the way here like someone flying on a vacation rather than to a war zone. He looked fresh and rested. Nick had not caught a wink.

"Do you know anything about this place?" Nick asked him.

Russ squinted at the dusky landscape outside the window. "Rzeszow? It's one of the bigger cities in eastern Poland, which is not saying much. It used to be a Soviet base during the Cold War. Now it's a staging site for the allied military aid. It's one of the closest NATO landing sites to Ukraine. The border is about sixty miles . . . *that* way." He pointed in the direction opposite of the setting sun.

Nick leaned closer to the window and peered into the darkening eastern horizon. That's where Claire was. Where he needed to be. His phone buzzed in his pocket—he had kept it on during the flight, and the buzz told him that it had just picked up a local cell tower. He eagerly opened the browser and refreshed the LeapChat page. He hadn't heard from Claire since she let him know she and Marzana were safe. Now, as the browser's Refresh circle turned around and around, he anxiously awaited an update. The wheels touched the ground, and the plane hurtled down the runway, the reversed thrust of its engines screaming to slow it down.

LeapChat was still trying to refresh, so Nick checked his text messages. He had one from Ray. *Emery confessed. Took Abbi.* Nick reread the message and breathed a sigh of relief. They had just cracked a forty-year-old cold case. A huge victory on any other day, but it felt small today, considering everything else Nick was up against right now. Still, he would take this small victory just the same. He cursed the old cowboy for being a man of few words. There were so many questions Nick wanted answered. A confession was great, but a solid case needed evidence. Did Emery give up the location of the body? Did the CSI recover any evidence from the cabin? Was the hair from the cabin a match to Abbi? None of this was in Ray's text. Nick had an impulse to text all these questions back to Ray but didn't. All that would have to wait till Nick got back. He closed the text message and checked the LeapChat page—it was still trying to load. He hit Refresh again, and this time Claire's message popped up: *We are in Bila Tserkva.* And then another one: *Call you soon.*

He checked his call log. It was empty. He opened the Maps app and searched for *Bila Tserkva*. It was a city south of Kyiv and, according to the app, nine hours and twenty minutes away from Rzeszow. On the map, Bila Tserkva still seemed too close to Kyiv. How safe was Claire there? How safe was she anywhere in Ukraine in this moment? As the plane taxied past rows of camouflage-colored military vehicles and crates of cargo, Nick got the distinct feeling that this conflict would not resolve quickly.

When he stepped off the airplane onto the wet tarmac, the air was cold and damp. He could see his own breath, so the temperature must have been close to freezing. A man approached him—an older man wearing a nice wool coat and a knit hat.

"Detective Severs?" The man took off his glove to shake Nick's hand. "I'm Martin Woelk with the State Department."

Nick shook Woelk's hand.

"I understand your wife was visiting a friend in Kyiv when the bombardment started?"

Nick was about to correct him that Claire was his girlfriend, but decided it was best to keep things simple and play along with whatever story Beck had told his government buddy to get Nick here. He nodded.

"Do you know where she is now?" Woelk asked.

"She said they left Kyiv and are now in"—he had to look at his phone to say the name right—"*Bila Tserkva?*" He said the name as a question, unsure of his pronunciation.

Woelk nodded. "*White Church*. It's about sixty miles south of Kyiv. She should be safe there right now, but who knows for how long. The Belarusian Army is pushing south toward Kyiv. Fighting may spill over into the neighboring cities."

"So, how do we get her out of there? Do you have people there?"

"I'll be honest with you—we don't have a lot of options. Ironically, if she were still in Kyiv, our people there could have helped. But where she is now, we don't have any resources. And there is also no reliable transportation right now. Flights are grounded. Trains are disrupted and overfilled with refugees. Does she have access to a car?"

"I don't know. I can ask her."

A convoy of several canvas-covered military trucks heavily rumbled past, spewing blue diesel smoke and shaking the concrete under Nick's feet.

"Where are *these* going?" Nick asked. "Can I hitch a ride there with one of the supply convoys?"

Woelk shook his head. "We don't send convoys over the border because they are easy targets for Russian planes and missiles. Most of the supplies get unloaded at the border and transferred to Ukrainian vehicles. It's unlikely you fill find one headed to Bila Tserkva."

"OK, then can you get me a car? I could be there in nine hours."

"That's nine hours under normal conditions. Not right now. Russian missile strikes are spreading farther west. There are bridges out, highways closed. And the conditions will get only worse as you get closer to Kyiv."

"Look, I get it, it will be hard, but I *am* going east," tired Nick snapped. "I can't just sit and wait for her to make it out on her own. I'll go buy my own damn car if you can't get me one."

"Nick, listen." Woelk put his hand on Nick's arm. "Our best option is that she does not stay in Bila Tserkva. Things can escalate in that region very quickly. If she has access to a car, she needs to start moving west or southwest, to get into a safer area. There may still be missile strikes, but at least there will not be any ground fighting. And while she is doing that, we will drive toward her and meet her halfway."

"We?" Nick was taken aback. "Martin, that's kind, but I can't ask you to do this."

"You don't need to ask. Besides, without me, you won't get across the border. I know you are a lawman in Colorado, but your badge won't get you far in these parts."

Førty-$3v3n

"Play it again," Claire said. They had been compiling location data for hours, and her eyes were blurry with the endless lines of code now burned into her tired retinas.

On the large TV screen on the wall of Alena's compound, a map of eastern Europe was superimposed with dozens and dozens of little glowing red dots. These were all the phones they had been able to track for Azarev's people. Marko, a hacker with a round face and glasses, was at one of the computers connected to the TV.

"OK, this is four days ago," Marko said, and the dots reset to their starting positions. There was a large concentration in Minsk, three in Kyiv, and a few others peppered throughout Poland, Romania, Slovakia, and Estonia.

"Ready?" Marko asked.

Claire nodded. Marko hit a key, and the time-lapse started. The dots moved about like insects in a hive—in small loops and vectors, crawling about the map. Then, three dots moved up from Kyiv, heading toward Minsk.

"This was three days ago," Marko said.

The dots remained concentrated around Minsk for some time, until two dots left Minsk and began moving down toward Kyiv.

"This was yesterday," Marko said. The two dots made it to Kyiv, moved about the city, and then traveled out of Kyiv together toward Bila Tserkva and then farther south.

"This was earlier this morning, after the bombardment of Kyiv began."

The dots came from Kyiv down the same highway Claire and Marzana had driven just hours before. *Was Roses with them?* The dots continued south through Ukraine to the very bottom and stopped near the edge of the blue portion of the map.

"And this is right now?" Claire asked.

"Yes."

"What is this? The ocean?"

"The Black Sea. They are a few miles outside of Odesa."

"Do we know who they are?"

"Yes," Marko said. "Max Clementis, head of corporate security, and Vladimir Bukashev, also from corporate security."

Claire moved closer to the TV and studied the two dots on the map. They moved ever so slightly, quivering like cells of a virus under the microscope.

"It has to be them," she said. "They came down to Kyiv when Roses arrived and grabbed her, but then the war started, and they could not take her back up to Minsk. But why would they go to Odesa? What's there?"

"It's a major seaport," Alena said. "So, they could smuggle her out of Ukraine to pretty much anywhere. Eastern Europe, Middle East, or even Russia."

"Azarev Enterprises actually owns the house they are at," Marko added. "Let me pull it up. Here is the real estate listing from 2018, before they bought it."

Claire could not read the Slavic text, but the photos spoke for themselves—it was a luxury coastline villa in Mediterranean style perched on a cliff above the sea.

"Doesn't look like an office building. Must have been a tax write-off for Anatoli," Alena said.

"And it's right next to the Russian-annexed Crimea," Marko added.

Alena nodded. "Close to his Kremlin overlords."

"According to the tax records, Azarev Enterprises also owns two warehouses and a fishing boat in the Odesa port."

"How long would it take us to get there?" Claire asked.

"Normally, around five hours by car. But now with the war . . . could be double that."

"Fuck!" Claire felt like hitting something. The dots flickered on the screen, teasing her. She looked at Marzana. "We have to try. They may have her."

"And say you do get there, then what?" Alena said. "What will you do against two, probably armed, gangsters? And there could be more than two—these are just the two we are tracking. I may know someone closer. Let me make a call."

Alena walked back to the couch with her phone. Marzana lit a cigarette and offered Claire the pack. Claire shook her head instinctively, but then changed her mind and reached out and took one. It had been years since she smoked. The chirp of the lighter, the sizzle of the wrapper burning in the flame. Such familiar, long-forgotten sounds. She inhaled, and the hot smoke filled her lungs. The nicotine rush. Suddenly, she was eighteen again, back home after leaving the college. Angry, scared, alone, and broken. She smoked cigarettes on the roof of the house, reading Uncle Alex's prison letters and watching the long cargo barges creeping up the Mississippi. That was the last year she was Katie Daniels. She took another hit and put out the cigarette without finishing it.

Alena came back. "My brother Kiryl is a commander of a resistance brigade. They are near Kherson, about two hours away from Odesa. He said he will take several guys to check this out."

"Really? They will?" Claire felt lightheaded with relief. "That's great. Tell them thank you."

"No need. When I told him these two gather intel for the Russians, he *wanted* to go. I've already sent him the address. He will update us when they get close."

Claire checked her phone—it was almost two in the afternoon. She suddenly felt tired.

Did Alena sense this? Because she suddenly turned to Claire and said: "Are you hungry? There are some noodle cups in the kitchen. And bottled water."

Claire couldn't remember the last time she ate—it was probably the Lufthansa cookies and coffee somewhere over western Europe many hours ago. She went through the doorless doorway at the back of the room and found the break room with a kitchenette. There was a Costco-sized pack of noodle cups on the counter. It was a brand she had never heard of and with an unfamiliar picture on the lid, but somehow, it was the exact same shape and size as the dollar ones in the stores back in the States. She filled it with water to the line and stuck it in the microwave. She guessed three minutes were three minutes on any side of the world.

While the noodles were cooking, she went into the restroom located next to the kitchen. The restroom had three stalls, four walls with missing tiles, and one sink with an old, delaminating mirror. This was not exactly the boutique hotel she had booked in Kyiv. If this warehouse had been listed on Airbnb, the host probably would have described it as "Industrial Shabby Chic." To Alena's credit, the place was clean despite its dilapidated condition and the half-dozen young hackers in the other room. There were no piles of pizza boxes and empty beer bottles in the kitchen, and the bathroom looked and smelled better than those in any of the college bars Claire had been to. Whatever matriarchal hacker commune Alena was running, they kept a tidy ship.

Claire looked in the mirror and hardly recognized herself in the stained, distorted reflection. Her hair was a mess, she had dark circles under her eyes, and she felt grimy from the travel. She washed her face with lukewarm water, fixed her hair, and returned to the kitchen with the beep of the microwave. She took her noodles and a bottle of water and slid into a diner-style booth. As she ate the comfortingly warm noodles, she considered the state of affairs. Being trapped in a war zone was not exactly part of her plan, but the hope of finding Roses kept her spirits up. She thought about Nick. She missed him. She missed talking with him. It had been only two days since she saw him, but with everything that had happened, it felt like so much longer than that. She wished she could be home with him right now. *Her* home, her town, her country. She wished she was sitting with him by the firepit he built, having a drink, and telling him all of her crazy adventures. But he was half the world away right now. Her whole world was half the world away.

Warm food made her feel even more tired. She stretched out on the vinyl cushion of the bench. If she were in her own bed right now, she could have pressed her back into Nick and felt the weight of his arm wrapped around her. She wondered what he was doing right now in Pine Lake. She closed her eyes, trying to do the math to figure out what time it was back home, but immediately fell asleep.

* * *

Someone shook her. "Wake up—they are on the move."

Claire opened her eyes to see Marzana standing over her.

"Who?" Claire asked, still trying to figure out where she was.

"Azarev's men. Come on."

Claire jumped to her feet. In the main room, Alena, Marko, and the rest of the hacker gang were in front of the TV. Alena had a cell phone in her hand and earbuds in.

Claire looked at the screen. The two red dots were no longer at the beach house but were now moving—overlapping and nudging in short spurts down some road on the map.

"Where are they going?" Claire asked.

"We don't know yet," Marko replied.

Claire checked her phone: 5:12 p.m. "Where is Alena's brother?" she asked.

Alena pulled out one of the earbuds. "Kiryl and his team are still about ten minutes away." She pointed to the top right corner of the map, where a green dot was nudging along a highway.

"Tell them to hurry," Claire said, trying to decide whether the green dot was getting any closer to the red ones.

"I have," Alena said.

"I have the video feed from one of the phones," Marko said. "Let me cast it."

"You hacked their phone cameras?" Claire asked.

"Yeah," Marko grinned. "And mics. All thanks to the root access you provided. And I disabled the camera indicator light, so they can't tell we are eavesdropping."

A small video player popped up over the map on the screen. Marko moved it so it would not cover up the dots. The video feed was from an odd angle—looking up at the ceiling of a vehicle. The phone must have been lying in the center console. Claire saw a partial frame of the driver—he had a cleanly shaven jawline. There was another man in the passenger seat, but only his arm was visible.

"Anything from the other phone?"

"No, it's dark—must be in the pocket."

"You said you have audio?"

"Yeah, let me turn it up."

Marko picked up the remote control and aimed it at the TV. They heard white noise with occasional pops and clicks. A man's voice said something, but it sounded muffled.

"What did he say?" Claire asked.

"I don't know," Alena said. "It didn't sound Ukrainian. Maybe Belarusian or Russian."

Was Roses in this car? In the back seat? Claire wished the green dot would move faster. The man's voice said something again, and the driver nodded.

"Something about a boat," Marko said.

"Shit!" Claire felt panic. "They are going to the port?"

"No," Marko said. "The Odesa port is in the opposite direction. But . . ." He typed something and studied the monitor of his computer. "There is a marina in the area. Here." Marko added a pin to the map.

"Fuck!" Claire exclaimed. The red dots were definitely moving in the direction of the pin. "They are going to take Roses out of the country."

On the map, the chase was progressing at an excruciatingly slow pace, and the green dot seemed no closer to the red ones than five minutes ago. In the video feed, the driver turned the steering wheel. The red dots angled to their right and proceeded down the access road to the marina.

"I just sent the new location to my brother," Alena said. "They are eight minutes out."

The red dots stopped near the blue edge just under the pin. Marko zoomed in, and Claire saw the parallel rake lines of boat slips in the water.

In the video feed, the driver picked up his phone, and the video went black. Claire and the team now had no eyes. There was a sound of a car door being shut. Then another and one more. *Three people?* There was a rustle, as if something was being slid, heavy breathing, and then another car door shutting. *Maybe the trunk or the tailgate?* There was more heavy breathing and sounds of steps on the gravel and then on something more solid like a boardwalk.

"They are on the dock." Marko zoomed in more, and they watched the red dots move down the long plank of the dock and then turn down one of the boat slips.

The green dot was now close to the marina access road.

"Kiryl is sending me his body cam uplink." Alena said. "Marko, can you patch this through?"

Another video feed appeared on the TV. The vantage point was inside a vehicle—the second row of seats in an SUV. Claire could see three other men in the vehicle besides Kiryl. The security gate of the marina appeared in the beams of the headlights. The vehicle stopped.

"Let me turn up the audio," Alena said, and they heard the men in the SUV exchange words in Ukrainian.

"He said they will proceed on foot from here," Marzana translated. "Because they don't have time to mess with the security gate."

Kiryl and his men got out and walked to the back of the SUV. Claire saw that they were wearing dark tactical vests and sidearms. Under the open liftgate of the SUV's cargo hold, they put on face masks and helmets. As they snapped in the magazines into their assault rifles and pulled back the charging handles to chamber the first round, Claire suddenly felt trepidation. She did not expect this. She wasn't sure exactly what she was expecting, but it wasn't this. Alena's brother and his buddies were not a bunch of country boys in a pickup truck armed with tire irons and baseball bats. The sound of the first round being chambered drove home the realization that her search for Roses had just entered a new and unfamiliar phase. Claire, Roses, and Marzana were accustomed to more indirect measures to attack their targets—using information and technology—not bullets. This escalation made Claire uneasy.

Kiryl's team went around the security gate and proceeded down the treed access road to the opening—a large, paved lot with a row of boats on racks and trailers parked at the back. The dusk was fading, and Kiryl's body cam switched to night vision. There was a single SUV parked in the lot near the entrance to the dock and the boat ramps. Beyond the elevated line of the dock, Claire saw the silhouettes of the boats in the slips. Many boats.

Alena said something into her phone in Ukrainian. Claire looked at Marzana.

"She told them it's the fourth slip on the right," Marzana said. Claire checked the map—the red dots were still in the same spot in the fourth slip on the right. And the green dot was creeping closer, now coming up on the third slip. In the body-cam feed, the man in front of Kiryl took a position behind the stern of another boat with his gun trained at slip 4. He signaled, and Kiryl moved forward and past him, and when he took his new position, the boat in slip 4 came into view at the end of Kiryl's gun sights. The boat's interior lights were on.

"It's a fucking yacht," Marko said.

That it was—a large white-and-chrome powerboat impossible to mistake for a fishing vessel even at night. The smooth, white side rose high next to the boards of the slip and swooped down toward the extended lower deck at the back. Claire did not see anyone topside. One of Kiryl's men advanced, grabbed the side rail at the back of the boat, and softly slipped aboard. Another one followed. Then Kiryl.

The lower deck at the stern was a spacious sundeck with loungers and a pair of sliding glass doors leading to what looked like a dining room with a table and chairs and a bar with a mirrored back wall. There was no one in the room. As Kiryl slid open one of the doors, Claire saw all four of the commandos appear as ghostly masked reflections in the mirror behind the bottles. In the interior lights, Kiryl's body cam switched from night vision and was now showing the detail in full color.

The team moved silently, with only Kiryl's measured breathing coming through the audio. But suddenly another sound cut in—a low, muffled drone, like the rattle of a distant generator.

Kiryl whispered something, and Marzana translated: "They started the engines."

From the dining room, two hallways curved toward the front of the boat—one on either side of the bar. Kiryl signaled two of his men to take the hallway on the left while he and another commando proceeded down the right one. For a few long seconds, they moved in silence, with only the hum of the engines accompanying the cautious advancement of the barrel of Kiryl's rifle down the narrow corridor that curved like an endless blind corner.

A loud thud somewhere off the camera made Claire jump. She heard men shouting *Na zemlu! Na zemlu!* and then a man appeared from around the corner, running straight toward Kiryl. Before Claire had time to gasp, Kiryl turned his gun, and the man's surprised face slammed right into the butt of Kiryl's rifle. The man flew backward and crashed to the floor. Kiryl picked up the handgun Claire did not even notice the man had, and Kiryl's partner rolled the man over and zip-tied his hands.

The room from which the man had run looked like a study with leather armchairs, a desk, and a bookcase wall. There were two men lying face down on a Persian rug in the middle of the room, with one of Kiryl's men zip-tying their wrists and ankles while another stood near with his rifle pointed at them. Kiryl's partner pushed the man from the corridor, stumbling, into the room and directed him to lie on the floor next to the other two. Kiryl asked something in a raised voice, but the men on the floor remained silent.

Claire scanned the room in the frame for any sign of Roses. "Have him ask about the girl."

Alena nodded and spoke into the phone.

"De divchyna?" Kiryl said and shoved at one of the men on the ground with his boot. "Don't want to speak Ukrainski? I won't talk to you in Russki. Where is the girl?" he repeated with a heavy accent.

"What girl?" one of the men on the floor mumbled.

Kiryl said something to his men, and two of them left the room.

"He sent his men to search the rest of the boat," Alena said to Claire. "Wow." She suddenly straightened up. "What the fuck is that?" She said something to Kiryl in Ukrainian.

Kiryl walked up to the desk on which sat a container the size of a medium suitcase. It looked rugged—with overmolded corners and built-in handles. Kiryl knocked on its side. It sounded solid.

"What is that?" Marzana asked.

"That's a fucking Snowcube," Alena breathed out.

Marko whistled. "It's a hardened offline storage device for data transfer," he explained to Claire. "This thing looks like it could survive a missile strike."

"That is more or less the idea," Alena replied. "The question is what's on it."

Kiryl's men returned and shook their heads. Alena looked at Claire. "There is no one else on board. Sorry."

Claire's heart sank, but she forced herself to keep hope alive.

Kiryl's men lifted their captives up to their knees. The first one was the one Kiryl had hit in the corridor—he had a bloody cut on his face and a swollen eye. He looked up at his captors defiantly and spat a bloody wad onto the commando's boots. For that he got a kick in the stomach with the same boot. Another commando grabbed him by the shirt collar and straightened him back up into the kneeling position.

The second man was raised to his knees. He did not try anything. He just measured his captors with a steady gaze and his jaw set. His closely cropped hair made him look like a convict. His cold gaze gave Claire the chills. He looked hardened. Like a man who was used to violence. Used to doling it out.

The third man looked quite a bit older than the other two—well into his fifties. He had neatly cut salt-and-pepper hair and a rounded, cleanly shaven face with a square chin.

Claire froze.

"That's Anatoli Azarev," she said hoarsely and had to clear her throat. "That's Anatoli."

"Are you sure?" Alena said.

"Holy shit! She's right," Marko exclaimed and pulled up a corporate photo of Azarev on the TV screen next to the live stream from Kiryl's body cam.

Alena said something in Ukrainian to Kiryl.

"It must be the kompromat data on that device," Marzana said.

Was Azarev not here for Roses?! Was he here for this? "Ask them where Roses is," Claire said. "Please. Ask them where the English girl is."

Alena relayed into her phone. Claire watched as Kiryl swung the rifle out of the way, got his handgun out of the holster, and raked back the slide to chamber the round. He stepped up to the man with the smashed face.

"De divchyna anhliyska?" Kiryl graveled at the man. "Where is the English girl?"

The man looked at Kiryl with hatred and spit on the floor again.

"AAH!" The sound of the gunshot made Claire recoil. She covered her mouth with her hand. The bullet entered the man's face at close range and blew the back of his head out in a gory plume of blood, tissue, and bone. Marzana gasped. Marko covered his eyes. Alena did not flinch. The body on the screen slumped over and toppled to the floor. Claire felt sick. How did it come to this? This is not what she wanted. She felt completely not in control of this situation. She was about to ask *Why?!* but then Azarev spoke.

"I can take you to her. This English girl. But you have to let me and that case walk away." His voice was smooth, and his English was near-perfect. Better than anything Claire had heard in this part of the world. It was almost more New York than Slavic.

"Where is she?" Kiryl walked up to Azarev with his pistol still in his hand.

"Let me make a call. We can do an exchange. Me and my friend here and the case for the girl. She is not far."

Kiryl put the gun to the head of the man next to Azarev. The man glared at Kiryl.

"Where is she?" Kiryl repeated.

"Let me make a call," Azarev said with a small nod.

Kiryl pulled the trigger. Claire closed her eyes barely in time, but the sound still reverberated through her body. When she opened her eyes, the second man's body was on the floor, sprawled backward on the Persian rug. Azarev was the only one remaining on his knees.

"Where is the girl?" Kiryl repeated.

"We can make this work," Azarev reassured, keeping amazingly calm under the circumstances. "Me and the case for the girl. It's a good trade," he added with polished earnestness.

Kiryl stepped back and said something in Ukrainian in half voice.

"Let him make the call," Claire said to Alena. "For God's sake. Just let him make the call."

Alena said something to Kiryl on the phone. Marzana put her hand on Claire's shoulder.

Kiryl stepped back in front of Azarev. "Last chance, Anatoli."

Azarev raised his eyes at Kiryl and then looked directly into Kiryl's body cam, as if recognizing that there was someone else on the other end, pulling the strings. He smiled slightly, looking directly into Claire's eyes.

"A phone call. Or you will never see her aga—."

The gunshot ended his sentence before he did.

Claire screamed. "Aah! Why?! No! No, no!!!" She covered her face and shook her head, flooded with horror and outrage. "How could you do this?" She screamed at Alena. "You could have at least let him make the call."

"He was lying." Alena watched Claire calmly.

"You don't know that!"

"I do. But even if he wasn't, this man was an enemy agent. He was working against us on our own soil. Letting him stay alive would have meant a chance that he might escape. A chance that he might use that data. That's a chance we can't afford to take right now."

"You chose *that box* over Roses?"

"Yes. If it contains data that our enemy could weaponize. Our first priority is to take it away from them."

"But . . . you could have just brought him here. We could have made him talk."

"I am sorry about your friend. But we don't have the luxury of worrying about one missing British girl. We did what we promised. Kiryl and his men don't have time to drive prisoners around—they are needed back at the front line. And we here have our battles to fight, too." Her black eyes burned into Claire. "Peacetime rules do not apply now. Our people are dying at the hands of invaders. And the only thing we need to be worrying about now is how to turn our land into their graveyard."

In the live stream on the TV, Kiryl's men stepped over Anatoli's body, grabbed the Snowcube by the handles, and carried it out of the room. Alena turned off the video feed. On the map, the green dot began moving away from the two red ones.

Marzana pulled Claire close. "We'll find her. We'll keep looking as long as it takes."

Claire felt numb. The phone vibrated in her pocket. She unlocked it and stared at the message, trying to wrap her head around it.

"Everything OK?" Marzana asked.

"Yeah . . . It's Nick . . . He says he just landed in Poland."

48

Woelk's car was a European-sized SUV. A French Peugeot, as Nick identified from the chrome badge depicting a lion standing on its hind legs. The Peugeot was small. Riding in the passenger seat, Nick was almost rubbing shoulders with Woelk. It was definitely not a hulking mountain of iron on four wheels like the American Chevy Tahoe or the Ford Expedition. Not only was this SUV small, but it also came with a manual transmission—something Nick had not seen for quite some time now in late-model vehicles in the US. The last time Nick drove *a stick* was when he was sixteen—and that also happened to be the *first* time he drove a stick. His father had insisted Nick learn the *proper* way to drive first, before taking on *an automatic*. Ironically, the only stick-drive vehicle they could find in the family was an old 1970s Ford truck on his grandfather's farm. Nick's father spent several weekends getting that rusted wreck to run before Nick was finally subjected to the lesson. He still remembered the cold sweat and the utter terror that felt like a scream stuck his throat as he climbed behind that big, skinny steering wheel. He did his best to see where he was going over the big hood while his brain did its worst to coordinate his arms and legs to the right combination of the clutch, the brake, the accelerator, and the gearshift. After a half dozen of jerky, white-knuckled laps around the inner periphery of the farm, his father directed him onto the open road, where Nick mastered the slipshod steering and the catatonic clutch just enough to goad the backfiring bucket of bolts up the incline to one of the asphalt summits of Nebo Hills Road and then about a mile farther, at which point the resurrected metal beast sputtered and died in a cloud of white steam, surrounded with a pastoral landscape of grassy fields, cattle, and groves, and five miles short of Missouri City. This turned out to be the old Ford's final death and also the conclusion of Nick's education in the art of manual transmission.

Woelk made it look effortless.

The little Peugeot's engine purred reliably down the road, and its heater pushed out a steady flow of heat. They cleared the border checkpoint at just around sunrise and continued eastbound on M10, which soon turned into a two-lane country road cutting through the rolling winter plains of rural Ukraine. Forests of bare birches and dark green pines made up most of the scenery here, broken up with an occasional village—a few hut-like bungalows on the side of the road with front-yard fences that went all the way up to the shoulder. Then more forests.

Nick worried about Claire. Something happened on this trip. When they talked on the phone just before he and Woelk left Rzeszow, she told him that she was safe and that the lead she had on Roses had turned out to be a dead end. But he could tell that there was something else. She was not OK. Something she had seen or experienced affected her deeply. With some of the footage of the war he had seen in the news, he imagined she had probably seen worse, being so much closer. He wasn't going to pry. Not over the phone. Not now. There would be time to talk later. Right now, he had to focus on getting her safely out of Ukraine. Luckily, her friend Marzana had a car and was willing to drive Claire west, to meet Nick and Woelk halfway.

In Lviv, Woelk took the exit for N02. As the highway curved around Lviv, Nick scanned the skyline for signs of war. So far, this big city in western Ukraine appeared to have been spared, unlike Kyiv or Kharkiv to the east, which had already been bombarded for two days. How surreal those news photos and videos were—modern cities with high-rises, store windows, and restaurant patios, and warplanes in the skies and missiles striking apartment buildings, and people's living rooms and kitchens, half-destroyed, suspended on crumbling concrete cornices several stories above the street, and rubble and people's possessions strewn down below. How could this be? The sanctity of people's homes crushed and turned inside out. All those carefully constructed lives, routines, and plans wiped away in a single day.

If this could happen here, could it happen in Denver? In Kansas City?

There had always been wars, as long there was humankind, so why did this one seem so shocking? Perhaps because it showed that such indiscriminate barbarity could come so easily from one of the world's most developed nations. Thousands of years of culture and progress did not change a thing. It did not matter that Russia had given the world some of the brightest artists, writers, and scientists. It did not matter that Russia itself had been invaded countless times through the centuries and had sacrificed millions of its people in World War II to help rid the world of Nazism. Countries had no memory. Countries had no moral codes. There were only people, and people had greed. And people drew their own lines they were willing to cross.

N02 took them deeper east. The forests had thinned out here, replaced with long stretches of barren winter steppe. The sun was now higher in the sky. There was quite a bit of traffic coming in the opposite direction—west—and almost no other cars traveling east. Nick checked his phone—again. Since they left, he had been keeping track of their progress and updating the trip calculations using the Maps app. The farther they got from Lviv, the weaker his phone's signal became, occasionally dipping to one bar or no bars at all. Still, every time he got a signal, Nick checked for progress updates from Claire. She and Marzana had left White Church a little over two hours ago, driving west, and if nothing slowed them down, they would meet somewhere near the small dot on the map labeled Holoskiv.

Outside of Ternopil, the highway widened, and industrial and commercial buildings began to appear, followed by billboard advertisements and gas stations. Woelk slowed down when a large gas station came into view. It had an attached supermarket and a restaurant.

"Better top off," Woelk said. "Never know what we'll run into up ahead."

They pulled up to the pump, and Nick got out to stretch his legs while Woelk refueled. Many of the cars at the station had bags, boxes, and suitcases stacked up high behind the windows. Nick guessed most of them were headed west.

At the diesel pumps, two semitrucks roared to life, drawing Nick's attention. They rumbled heavily with their engines and spewed sooty smoke from their exhaust stacks as they slowly crawled out into the open, each pulling a long flatbed trailer, each loaded with two tank-like camouflaged military vehicles. These machines looked bulkier than regular tanks and had shorter, smaller-caliber cannons. The semis pulled up to the intersection and signaled to turn left—east, the same way as Nick and Woelk were headed.

"What are those?" Nick asked.

Woelk glanced up from the pump. "Bradley Fighting Vehicles. Basically, armored personnel carriers with a 25mm chaingun."

The angular slabs of armor on the Bradleys looked new, clean, and freshly painted. "Part of the US aid?" Nick asked.

"Yep."

The semis got a break in the traffic and slowly crept through the intersection, grumbling with their engines, puffing their exhaust stacks, and scraping their gears. The Bradleys must have been heavy. Woelk finished pumping gas, and said he wanted to get some coffee. Nick checked the distance to Holoskiv on his phone—twenty-six minutes away. He followed Woelk reluctantly into the supermarket, wishing they were already back on the road, speeding toward Claire.

This was a nice, modern gas-station café, like a Maverik's or a QuikTrip back in the States, with rows of coffee carafes with colorful labels. Nick pulled a medium paper cup from the dispenser and walked down the coffee aisle, unable to read any of the labels and relying on the label pictures to help make an informed decision. He made it halfway down the aisle when one of the labels stopped him. It was done in the color-block stencil style, like the famous Obama Hope campaign poster, but depicted a mustached man with a revolver in one hand and a saber in the other. The saber looked just like the one from Claire's family—without the handguard. The text under the image consisted of only one word—*MAXHO*. Nick took a picture of the label with his phone and then stuck his cup under the *MAXHO* carafe and poured himself what looked like dark roast.

Back in the car, Nick showed Woelk the picture on his phone. "Do you know who this is?"

Woelk started the car and glanced at Nick's phone. "Yeah. That's Nestor Makhno. He was the leader of the Ukrainian Anarchist Army that fought the Soviets after the Bolshevik Revolution. He's become sort of an icon of resistance since the Russians took over Crimea eight years ago." Woelk steered the Peugeot across the intersection and back onto the highway, heading east.

"He fought the Soviets? Why?"

"Well, back around 1920, there was a civil war in Russia. The Soviets were fighting various factions, trying to regain control of all the former lands of the Russian Empire. Ukraine used to be part of that empire but wanted independence. And Makhno led one of the resistance armies."

The highway turned rural again, with more forests, farm fields, and villages slipping by.

Nick studied the picture. Claire said her great-great-grandfather had fought in World War I. That was around the same time period. With so much weaponry strewn throughout Europe at that time, it was possible the saber came from this region.

His phone rang. It was Claire.

"Hi," he said. "Where are you?"

"We just passed Holoskiv." The connection was poor—clipping in and out. "Where are *you*?"

"We had to stop for gas. Looks like we are about ten minutes from Holoskiv. So, that means less than that to you! What do you see? What's around you?"

"Ummm. Trees." She laughed. She sounded tired, but it was good to hear her laughter.

"Same here, trees." Nick smiled. "What car are you in?"

"A light blue hatchback," she said. "Sorry—Marzana says it's a *Lada*."

"A light blue Lada," Nick repeated, looking at Woelk, and Woelk nodded in acknowledgment. *Good*—because Nick had no idea what a Lada looked like. He scanned the oncoming traffic in anticipation.

"What car are *you* in?" she asked.

"A small white SUV, a *Peugeot*." Nick said. "What do you see now?"

"Still trees. Wait. I see something up ahead. Looks like two semis carrying tanks."

The Bradleys! The semis got a head start on Nick and Woelk at the gas station, but they were slow, and the Peugeot was probably close to catching up to them, maybe just around that curve in the road up ahead. Nick leaned forward in anticipation, studying every vehicle that emerged from around the curve, and expecting to see a light blue Lada at any moment.

And that's when a fiery streak dashed like a meteor across the sky in front of them, and another one followed. Before Nick had a chance to consider what this was, a double explosion rumbled, and a massive fireball rose above the treetops.

"*CLAIRE!!!*" Nick screamed into the phone as Woelk slammed on the brakes and veered the car onto the shoulder and stopped.

"*CLAIRE!!!*" But the line was dead. There were no more cars coming from around the curve.

"*GO!!!*" Nick yelled at Woelk. "We have to go."

But Woelk pressed his hand into Nick's chest. "Nick, wait just a minute. There could be another strike."

But Nick had already snapped off his seat belt and shoved the car door open. He ran toward the edge of the trees as fast as the heels of his boots could kick back the asphalt, with his heart pounding out of his chest and his lungs gasping to find a rhythm. The fireball beyond the trees had turned into a tower of thick black smoke churning, twisting, and billowing into the sky as if fed by a hundred coal furnaces. But Nick's sole focus was on the apex of that curve, slowly opening as he ran closer, and the only thought pulsing through his mind was a simple mantra to which he held on with all his stubbornness—that the world on the other side of those trees had not changed. That the trees on the other side were the same trees, that the snow was the same, the asphalt was the same, *and the light blue Lada* . . .

But when Nick finally cleared the edge of the woods, on the other side he saw hell. The landscape here had been transmogrified into a plain of burning, twisted wreckage, broken concrete, splintered trees, and black, upturned earth where snow used to be. Smoke drifted through the air like dark fog. As Nick ran past the burning overturned trailer of one of the semis, he felt the hot breath of the fire on his face. A Bradley vehicle had been thrown clear and was now on its side in the trees, with its turret missing. Another Bradley was burning in the median between the lanes, with smoke and flames pouring out from where its turret used to be, and its rear access hatch hanging off by a single hinge. The semi's cab was crumpled and also completely engulfed in a raging, roaring fire. *Their fuel tanks were full*, Nick thought, making his way between the burning vehicles. The heat was intense, and the smoke smelled of burned rubber and hair, and of something chemical, making his eyes burn.

Through patches of smoke, he saw a body in the road. Nick ran to it to find a young man in a camouflage jacket, jeans, and black high-top Nikes. His limbs were thrown in crooked, broken lines, and his torso and neck were ripped open with a horrific wound. He wasn't breathing. Nearby, a crater marked the spot where the leading semi had been. The asphalt there was gone, and the semi itself, along with the Bradleys it was carrying, was now a single, mangled mass of metal burning on the side of the highway in a vortex of fire.

Through the smoke and his watering eyes, Nick spotted a silver passenger sedan in the opposite lane—crumpled and pushed into the guardrail, with glass scattered all around. He could see the driver slumped over the steering wheel. But Nick's attention was already on something else—the passenger car farther ahead in the median. It was flipped upside down onto its smashed roof. The car was blue. Nick lurched toward it, his boots slipping on the debris and his lungs burning. He reached it and dropped down on his knees on the shattered glass next to the window.

It wasn't Claire!

The driver was an older man—dead or unconscious, hanging by the seat belt with his face covered in blood. The passenger was an older woman, also upside down, who appeared to be stunned but not otherwise harmed.

Woelk ran up behind him. "I called the emergency services," he said, out of breath. "They are sending ambulances. Shouldn't be long." He stooped down to check the woman's pulse.

Nick jumped back to his feet and rescanned the carnage around him, looking for any other damaged vehicles. There were none. Everything was silent except for the fire roaring and popping as it devoured men and machines. The traffic in the westbound lane had stopped a safe distance away, and Nick could see people getting out of their cars, but with the smoke eating at his eyes, he could not make out the details.

And then he heard his name. A shout from a distance.

"*Niiiiick!!!*"

Claire was running to him—a single familiar shape that tore away from all the stopped cars and people and was now crossing over the snow and the upturned earth toward him.

He ran to her, and they crashed into each other's arms, and as he kissed her through the tears, holding her tight and feeling her familiar body in his arms, he realized just how close he came to losing her forever. Here, half the world away from home, in the middle of a war-torn foreign land, he swore to himself that he would never lose her again.

Førty-n!n3

The Lufthansa Airbus 320 pushed off from the gate at 6:05 a.m. As the plane began to roll down the taxiway, Claire watched the terminal of the John Paul II International Airport in Kraków fade into the gray winter sky. Soon, she and Nick would land for a layover in Munich, and then fly west until they reached the foothills of the Rocky Mountains in Denver. Soon, this wild whirlwind of people and events that carried her, like a jet stream, halfway around the world would be over. For her.

She thought about Marzana, in her puffy winter jacket, standing by her light blue Lada at the edge of that part of the highway where missiles had torn apart vehicles, people, and earth. Marzana chose to stay behind in Ukraine, to return to Alena and her hackers to help them fight. As she and Claire hugged goodbye, perhaps seeing each other in person for the last time, Marzana promised she and Claire would keep looking for Roses until they found her. This was going to be Claire's mission once she got back home. Roses had a real name now, and that made things feel much more hopeful.

It seemed unreal that after all that happened, Claire was going home now, back to Colorado, where she had her job and her house waiting for her. How could things go back so easily to the way they were before all this? They couldn't. Nothing was the same. So much had changed simply because she opened her laptop and reached out to Roses. Cause and effect. And now she had lost Roses. And almost lost Nick. And saw three men executed before her eyes. Driving from Bila Tserkva with

Marzana, Claire had replayed the events over and over in her head, trying to find a version in which where she was not responsible for the events of the last few days. She couldn't.

Long ago, she asked Uncle Alex how he knew whether he was doing the right thing when he was setting off all those bombs. He said it was easy—all he had to do was ask himself if the right people would suffer as a result of his actions, and if the right people would benefit. That seemed easy in theory. She had never before caused another person's death. When that happened to Uncle Alex, he quit. But she could not. At least not until after she found Roses. Azarev and his men deserved what came to them, didn't they? And the world was better without them. But she didn't feel good about that. Even though she was not the one who pulled the trigger, she felt as if she lost something. Some part of her innocence she did not know she had but which now was gone forever from her life.

But not *all* things had turned to worse. Somehow, she and Nick had gotten closer through this ordeal. She needed to be honest with Nick from now on. They both needed to learn to be better at communicating, listening, and being partners. And she had to make the first move, because she still had not told him about Azarev. She did not know how. She even briefly considered not telling him at all, because she was afraid of how he would react. But this had to stop. She loved him, and she *wanted* to be able to confide in him, and so they couldn't continue to maintain this artificial line that divided her world from his. She knew he was not exactly comfortable with this part of her life, but she couldn't continue worrying about where the line was each time, about where to start telling him and where to stop.

The plane turned and stopped, perched at the start of the runway. Above the treetops, the horizon was beginning to glow. A bird of prey swooped across the sky toward the trees. *A falcon?*

"Azarev is dead," she said and looked at Nick.

"Whaaat?" Nick turned his head. "He *is*? How?"

"Does it matter?"

Nick bit his lip, probably deciding if he really wanted to know. "Are you sure?"

She nodded. "I watched it happen."

They were standing still, but the growl of the plane's engines elevated to a crescendo. Nick reached over and found her hand. Their fingers interlocked.

"Tell me," he said, looking at her tenderly. "Everything."

The brakes let go, and the metal bird launched forward, accelerating like a projectile. The runway rumbled and vibrated under the floor panels, getting louder and louder, until it suddenly released, and they rose into the sky just as the first rays of the sun broke through the horizon.

Epilog

They landed in Denver around 2:30 in the afternoon. Nick could have stopped by the station or at least called Ray, but he did not want to. Instead, he and Claire went home, got a pizza from Coloradough, opened a bottle of Malbec, and lit the firepit in the backyard.

They talked a lot on the plane. About Azarev, and about Roses, and the war. Nick told her about the break in the Abbi White case. And Claire told him about the witch she met in Ukraine. There was a new level of closeness between them, a new camaraderie people gained only after a shared experience. Ben's case was that experience for them. Although they had worked on it separately at times, they were together now, at the end. At the closure. The closure Nick was certain he would never have without Claire.

Sitting with her now in their backyard, listening to the music of the pine needles and bark popping in the fire, he considered how lucky he was.

When he went to the station the next morning, he saw an old, rusted-out Chevy pickup truck in the parking lot. It looked familiar, but after everything he had been through over the last few days, it took Nick a minute to place it. It was Gerald White's.

Patty was on the phone at the front desk, but she grinned and waved at Nick eagerly when he walked in. He smiled and waved back. Gerald and Ray were standing in Ray's office. Seeing Nick, Gerald turned and walked toward him. Nick put out his hand to shake, but the old man instead pulled Nick in and hugged him, holding him tightly. Nick did not expect that, but he had long come to accept that people showed their emotions in different ways. So, he just stood there, still in his coat, letting himself be bear-hugged, and gently patting the old man's bony back.

Gerald finally pulled away and held Nick at arm's length. "Thank you," he said, with tears rolling down his cheeks. Looking at the old man's wrinkly face, Nick could not tell whether Gerald was crying or laughing.

"We found Abbi," Ray said, approaching.

Nick's heart sank. "I am so sorry." He squeezed Gerald's skinny arm. "Where?"

"In California," Gerald beamed.

"What . . . ?" Nick looked at Ray, utterly confused.

"Abbi is alive," Ray said, his own face laughing with a million wrinkles. "Emery abducted her from the driveway. He offered her a ride to the house but instead he drugged her and kept her in his cabin for two days. But he said he couldn't kill her. So, he drove her across the Utah state line and abandoned her at a truck stop. A family from California found her walking along the highway. She did not speak a word for several months after they found her, and she did not remember a thing about her past. They took her in and raised her, and she's lived in California ever since. She knew she was adopted, so last year she submitted her DNA to one of those heredity sites, and when you ran Gerald's DNA through GEDmatch, we got a hit! She landed at Denver International about an hour ago. In fact . . . this is probably her."

Nick turned around just as the cowbell on the door behind him rang.

ALSO AVAILABLE

A gripping spy thriller based on incredible true events.

After the 1917 revolution, Russia is teetering on the brink of civil war. When the Soviet head of state Lenin is shot by an assassin, agent Anna Sokolova is tasked with hunting down British spy Sidney Reilly who set in motion an audacious plot to alter the course of Russian history. Book one of Anna Sokolova series.

A bitter, bloody tour de force
"Wrenchingly emotive, deftly written and tremendously powerful."
– Book Viral Reviews

★★★★★ *Highly Recommended!*
"Commissar deserves a place alongside the best in early 20th c. Russian historical fiction." – Chanticleer Reviews

"A taut mystery and espionage story." – Seattle Book Review

Finalist – 2022 Hemingway International Book Awards

Made in the USA
Columbia, SC
14 June 2024